W.H.G Kingston

From Powder Monkey to Admiral

outlook

W.H.G Kingston

From Powder Monkey to Admiral

1st Edition | ISBN: 978-3-75236-873-4

Place of Publication: Frankfurt am Main, Germany

Year of Publication: 2020

Outlook Verlag GmbH, Germany.

Reproduction of the original.

W.H.G. Kingston

"From Powder Monkey to Admiral"

Introduction.

A book for boys by W.H.G. Kingston needs no introduction. Yet a few things may be said about the origin and the purpose of this story.

When the *Boys' Own Paper* was first started, Mr Kingston, who showed deep interest in the project, undertook to write a story of the sea, during the wars, under the title of "From Powder-monkey to Admiral."

Talking the matter over, it was objected that such a story might offend peaceable folk, because it must deal too much with blood and gunpowder. Mr Kingston, although famed as a narrator of sea-fights, was a lover of peace, and he said that his story would not encourage the war spirit. Those who cared chiefly to read about battles might turn to the pages of "British Naval History." He chose the period of the great war for his story, because it was a time of stirring events and adventures. The main part of the narrative belongs to the early years of life, in which boys would feel most interest and sympathy. And throughout the tale, not "glory" but "duty" is the object set before the youthful reader.

It was further objected that the title of the story set before boys an impossible object of ambition. The French have a saying, that "every soldier carries in his knapsack a marshal's baton," meaning that the way is open for rising to the very highest rank in their army. But who ever heard of a sailor lad rising to be an Admiral in the British Navy?

Let us see how history answers this question. There was a great sea captain of other days, whose fame is not eclipsed by the glorious reputations of later wars, Admiral Benbow. In the reign of Queen Anne, before the great Duke of Marlborough had begun his victorious career, Benbow had broken the power of France on the sea. Rank and routine were powerful in those days, as now; but when a time of peril comes, the best man is wanted, and Benbow was promoted out of turn, by royal command, to the rank of Vice-Admiral, and went after the fleet of Admiral Ducasse to the West Indies. In the little church of Saint Andrew's, Kingston, Jamaica, his body lies, and the memorial stone speaks of him as "a true pattern of English courage, who lost his life in defence of queen and country."

Like his illustrious French contemporary Jean Bart, John Benbow was of humble origin. He entered the merchant service when a boy. He was unknown till he had reached the age of thirty, when he had risen to the command of a merchant vessel. Attacked by a powerful Salee rover, he gallantly repulsed these Moorish pirates, and took his ship safe into Cadiz. The heads of thirteen of the pirates he preserved, and delivered them to the magistrates of the town, in presence of the custom-house officers. The tidings of this strange incident reached Madrid, and the King of Spain, Charles the Second, sent for the English captain, received him with great honour, and wrote a letter on his behalf to our King James the Second, who on his return to England gave him a ship. This was his introduction to the British Navy, in which he served with distinction in the reigns of William the Third and Queen Anne. But his obscure origin is the point here under notice, and the following traditional anecdote is preserved in Shropshire:—When a boy he was left in charge of the house by his mother, who went out marketing. The desire to go to sea, long cherished, was irresistible. He stole forth, locking the cottage door after him, and hung the key on a hook in a tree in the garden. Many years passed before he returned to the old place. Though now out of his reach, for the tree had grown faster than he, the key still hung on the hook. He left it there; and there it remained when he came back as Rear-Admiral of the *White*. He then pointed it out to his friends, and told the story. Once more his country required his services, but his fame and the echo of his victories alone came over the wave. The good town of Shrewsbury is proud to claim him as a son, and remembers the key, hung by the banks of the Severn, near Benbow House. Whatever basis of truth the story may have, its being told and believed attests the fact of the humble birth and origin of Admiral Benbow.

Another sailor boy, Hopson, in the early part of last century, rose to be Admiral in the British Navy. Born at Bonchurch in the Isle of Wight, of humblest parentage, he was left an orphan, and apprenticed by the parish to a tailor. While sitting one day alone on the shop-board, he was struck by the sight of the squadron coming round Dunnose. Instantly quitting his work, he ran to the shore, jumped into a boat, and rowed for the Admiral's ship. Taken on board, he entered as a volunteer.

Next morning the English fleet fell in with a French squadron, and a warm action ensued. Young Hopson obeyed every order with the utmost alacrity; but after two or three hours' fighting he became impatient, and asked what they were fighting for. The sailors explained to him that they must fire away, and the fight go on, till the white rag at the enemy's mast-head was struck. Getting this information, his resolution was formed, and he exclaimed, "Oh, if that's all, I'll see what I can do."

The two ships, with the flags of the commanders on each side, were now engaged at close quarters, yard-arm and yard-arm, and completely enveloped in smoke. This proved favourable to the purpose of the brave youth, who mounted the shrouds through the smoke unobserved, gained the French Admiral's main-yard, ascended with agility to the main-topgallant mast-head, and carried off the French flag. It was soon seen that the enemy's colours had disappeared, and the British sailors, thinking they had been hauled down, raised a shout of "Victory, victory!" The French were thrown into confusion by this, and first slackened fire, and then ran from their guns. At this juncture the ship was boarded by the English and taken. Hopson had by this time descended the shrouds with the French flag wrapped round his arm, which he triumphantly displayed.

The sailors received the prize with astonishment and cheers of approval. The Admiral being told of the exploit, sent for Hopson and thus addressed him, "My lad, I believe you to be a brave youth. From this day I order you to walk the quarter-deck, and if your future conduct is equally meritorious, you shall have my patronage and protection." Hopson made every effort to maintain the good opinion of his patron, and by his conduct and attention to duty gained the respect of the officers of the ship. He afterwards went rapidly through the different ranks of the service, till at length he attained that of Admiral.

We might give not a few instances of more recent date, but the families and friends of those "who have risen" do not always feel the same honest pride as the great men themselves in the story of their life. While it is true that no sailor boy may now hope to become "Admiral of the Fleet," yet there is room for advancement, in peace as in war, to what is better than mere rank or title or wealth,—a position of honour and usefulness. Good character and good conduct, pluck and patience, steadiness and application, will win their way, whether on sea or land, and in every calling.

The inventions of modern science and art are producing a great change in all that pertains to life at sea. The revolution is more apparent in war than in peace. There is, and always will be, a large proportion of merchant ships under sail, even in nations like our own where steam is in most general use. In war, a wooden ship without steam and without armour would be a mere floating coffin. The fighting *Temeraire*, and the saucy *Arethusa*, and Nelson's *Victory* itself, would be nothing but targets for deadly fire from active and irresistible foes. The odds would be about the same as the odds of javelins and crossbows against modern fire-arms. Steam alone had made a revolution in naval warfare; but when we add to this the armour-plating of vessels, and the terrible artillery of modern times, "the wooden walls of old England" are only fit to be used as store-ships or hospitals for a few years, and then sent to the ship-yards to be broken up for firewood. But though material conditions have changed, the moral forces are the same as ever, and courage, daring, skill, and endurance are the same in ships of oak or of iron:—

"Yes, the days of our wooden walls are ended,
And the days of our iron ones begun;
But who cares by what our land's defended,
While the hearts that fought and fight are one?
'Twas not the oak that fought each battle,
'Twas not the wood that victory won;
'Twas the hands that made our broadsides rattle,
'Twas the hearts of oak that served each gun."

These are words from one of the "Songs for Sailors," by W.C. Bennett, who has written better naval poems for popular use than any one since the days of Dibdin. The same idea concludes a rattling ballad on old Admiral Benbow:—

"Well, our walls of oak have become just a joke
And in tea-kettles we're to fight;
It seems a queer dream, all this iron and steam,
But I daresay, my lads, it's right.
But whether we float in ship or in boat,
In iron or oak, we know
For old England's right we've hearts that will fight,
As of old did the brave Benbow."

But, after all, even in war, fighting is only a small part of the sum of any sailor's life, and the British flag floats over ships on every sea, whether under sail or steam, in the peaceful pursuits of commerce. The same qualities of heart and mind will have their play, which Mr Kingston has described in his stirring story,—a story which will be read with profit by the young, and with pleasure by both young and old.

Dr Macaulay, Founder of "Boy's Own Paper."

Chapter One.

Preparing to start.

No steamboats ploughed the ocean, nor were railroads thought of, when our young friends Jack, Tom, and Bill lived. They first met each other on board the *Foxhound* frigate, on the deck of which ship a score of other lads and some fifty or sixty men were mustered, who had just come up the side from the *Viper* tender; she having been on a cruise to collect such stray hands as could be found; and a curious lot they were to look at.

Among them were long-shore fellows in swallow-tails and round hats, fishermen in jerseys and fur-skin caps, smugglers in big boots and flushing coats; and not a few whose whitey-brown faces, and close-cropped hair, made it no difficult matter to guess that their last residence was within the walls of a gaol. There were seamen also, pressed most of them, just come in from a long voyage, many months or perhaps years having passed since they left their native land; that they did not look especially amiable was not to be wondered at, since they had been prevented from going, as they had intended, to visit their friends, or maybe, in the case of the careless ones, from enjoying a long-expected spree on shore. They were all now waiting to be inspected by the first lieutenant, before their names were entered on the ship's books.

The rest of the crew were going about their various duties. Most of them were old hands, who had served a year or more on board the gallant frigate. During that time she had fought two fierce actions, which, though she had come off victorious, had greatly thinned her ship's company, and the captain was therefore anxious to make up the complement as fast as possible by every means in his power.

The seamen took but little notice of the new hands, though some of them had been much of the same description themselves, but were not very fond of acknowledging this, or of talking of their previous histories; they had, however, got worked into shape by degrees: and the newcomers, even those with the "long togs," by the time they had gone through the same process would not be distinguished from the older hands, except, maybe, when they came to splice an eye, or turn in a grummet, when their clumsy work would show what they were; few of them either were likely ever to be the outermost on the yard-arms when sail had suddenly to be shortened on a dark night, while it was blowing great guns and small arms.

The frigate lay at Spithead. She had been waiting for these hands to put to sea. Lighters were alongside, and whips were never-ceasingly hoisting in casks of rum, with bales and cases of all sorts, which it seemed impossible could ever be stowed away. From the first lieutenant to the youngest midshipman, all were bawling at the top of their voices, issuing and repeating orders; but there were two persons who out-roared all the rest, the boatswain and the boatswain's mate. They were proud of those voices of theirs. Let the hardest gale be blowing, with the wind howling and whistling through the rigging, the canvas flapping like claps of thunder, and the seas roaring and dashing against the bows, they could make themselves heard above the loudest sounds of the storm.

At present the boatswain bawled, or rather roared, because he was so accustomed to roar that he could speak in no gentler voice while carrying on duty on deck; and the boatswain's mate imitated him.

The first lieutenant had a good voice of his own, though it was not so rough as that of his inferiors. He made it come out with a quick, sharp sound, which could be heard from the poop to the forecastle, even with the wind ahead.

Jack, Tom, and Bill looked at each other, wondering what was next going to happen. They were all three of about the same age, and much of a height, and somehow, as I have said, they found themselves standing close together.

They were too much astonished, not to say frightened, to talk just then, though they all three had tongues in their heads, so they listened to the conversation going on around them.

"Why, mate, where do you come from?" asked a long-shore chap of one of the whitey-brown-faced gentlemen.

"Oh, I've jist dropped from the clouds; don't know where else I've come from," was the answer.

"I suppose you got your hair cropped off as you came down?" was the next query.

"Yes! it was the wind did it as I came scuttling down," answered the other, who was evidently never at a loss what to say. "And now, mate, just tell me how did you get on board this craft?" he inquired.

"I swam off, of course, seized with a fit of patriotism, and determined to fight for the honour and glory of old England," was the answer.

It cannot, however, be said that this is a fair specimen of the conversation; indeed, it would benefit no one were what was said to be repeated.

Jack, Tom, and Bill felt very much as a person might be supposed to do who had dropped from the moon. Everything around them was so strange and bewildering, for not one of them had ever before been on board a ship, and Bill had never even seen one. Having not been much accustomed to the appearance of trees, he had some idea that the masts grew out of the deck, that the yards were branches, and the blocks curious leaves; not that amid the fearful uproar, and what seemed to him the wildest confusion, he could think of anything clearly.

Bill Rayner had certainly not been born with a silver spoon in his mouth. His father he had never known. His mother lived in a garret and died in a garret, although not before, happily for him, he was able to do something for himself, and, still more happily, not before she had impressed right principles on his mind. As the poor woman lay on her deathbed, taking her boy's hands and looking earnestly into his eyes, she said, "Be honest, Bill, in the sight of God. Never forget that He sees you, and do your best to please Him. No fear about the rest. I am not much of a scholar, but I know that's right. If others try to persuade you to do what's wrong, don't listen to them. Promise me, Bill, that you will do as I tell you."

"I promise, mother, that I will," answered Bill; and, small lad as he was, meant what he said.

Poor as she was, being a woman of some education, his mother had taught him to read and write and cipher—not that he was a great adept at any of those arts, but he possessed the groundwork, which was an important matter; and he did his best to keep up his knowledge by reading sign-boards, looking into book-sellers' windows, and studying any stray leaves he could obtain.

Bill's mother was buried in a rough shell by the parish, and Bill went out into the world to seek his fortune. He took to curious ways,— hunting in dust-heaps for anything worth having; running errands when he could get any one to send him; holding horses for gentlemen, but that was not often; doing duty as a link-boy at houses when grand parties were going forward or during foggy weather; for Bill, though he often went supperless to his nest, either under a market-cart, or in a cask by the river side, or in some other out-of-the-way place, generally managed to have a little capital with which to buy a link; but the said capital did not grow much, for bad times coming swallowed it all up.

Bill, as are many other London boys, was exposed to temptations of all sorts; often when almost starving, without a roof to sleep under, or a friend to whom he could appeal for help, his shoes worn out, his clothing too scanty to keep him warm; but, ever recollecting his mother's last words, he resisted them all. One day, having wandered farther east than he had ever been before, he found himself in the presence of a press-gang, who were carrying off a party of men and boys to the river's edge. One of the man-of-war's men seized upon him, and Bill, thinking that matters could not be much worse with him than they were at present, willingly accompanied the party, though he had very little notion where they were going. Reaching a boat, they were made to tumble in, some resisting and endeavouring to get away; but a gentle prick from the point of a cutlass, or a clout on the head, made them more reasonable, and most of them sat down resigned to their fate. One of them, however, a stout fellow, when the boat had got some distance from the shore, striking out right and left at the men nearest him, sprang overboard, and before the boat could be pulled round had already got back nearly half-way to the landing-place.

One or two of the press-gang, who had muskets, fired, but they were not good shots. The man looking back as he saw them lifting their weapons, by suddenly diving escaped the first volley, and by the time they had again loaded he had gained such a distance that the shot spattered into the water on either side of him. They were afraid of firing again for fear of hitting some of the people on shore, besides which, darkness coming on, the gloom concealed him from view.

They knew, however, that he must have landed in safety from the cheers which came from off the quay, uttered by the crowd who had followed the press-gang, hooting them as they embarked with their captives.

Bill began to think that he could not be going to a very pleasant place, since, in spite of the risk he ran, the man had been so eager to escape; but being himself unable to swim, he could not follow his example, even had he wished it. He judged it wiser, therefore, to stay still, and see what would next happen. The boat pulled down the river for some way, till she got alongside a large cutter, up the side of which

Bill and his companions were made to climb.

From what he heard, he found that she was a man-of-war tender, her business being to collect men, by hook or by crook, for the Royal Navy.

As she was now full—indeed, so crowded that no more men could be stowed on board—she got under way with the first of the ebb, and dropped down the stream, bound for Spithead.

As Bill, with most of the pressed men, was kept below during this his first trip to sea, he gained but little nautical experience. He was, however, very sick, while he arrived at the conclusion that the tender's hold, the dark prison in which he found himself, was a most horrible place.

Several of his more heartless companions jeered at him in his misery; and, indeed, poor Bill, thin and pale, shoeless and hatless, clad in patched garments, looked a truly miserable object.

As the wind was fair, the voyage did not last long, and glad enough he was when the cutter got alongside the big frigate, and he with the rest being ordered on board, he could breathe the fresh air which blew across her decks.

Tom Fletcher, who stood next to Bill, had considerably the advantage of him in outward appearance. Tom was dressed in somewhat nautical fashion, though any sailor would have seen with half an eye that his costume had been got up by a shore-going tailor.

Tom had a good-natured but not very sensible-looking countenance. He was strongly built, was in good health, and had the making of a sailor in him, though this was the first time that he had even been on board a ship.

He had a short time before come off with a party of men returning on the expiration of their leave. Telling them that he wished to go to sea, he had been allowed to enter the boat. From the questions some of them had put to him, and the answers he gave, they suspected that he was a runaway, and such in fact was the case. Tom was the son of a solicitor in a country town, who had several other boys, he being the fourth, in the family.

He had for some time taken to reading the voyages of Drake, Cavendish, and Dampier, and the adventures of celebrated pirates, such as those of Captains Kidd, Lowther, Davis, Teach, as also the lives of some of England's naval commanders, Sir Cloudesley Shovell,

Benbow, and Admirals Hawke, Keppel, Rodney, and others, whose gallant actions he fully intended some day to imitate.

He had made vain endeavours to induce his father to let him go to sea, but Mr Fletcher, knowing that he was utterly ignorant of a sea life, set his wish down as a mere fancy which it would be folly to indulge.

Tom, instead of trying to show that he really was in earnest, took French leave one fine morning, and found his way to Portsmouth, without being traced. Had he waited, he would probably have been sent to sea as a midshipman, and placed on the quarter-deck. He now entered as a ship-boy before the mast.

Tom, as he had made his bed, had to lie on it, as is the case with many other persons. Even now, had he written home, he might have had his position changed, but he thought himself very clever, and had no intention of letting his father know where he had gone. The last of the trio was far more accustomed to salt water than was either of his companions. Jack Peek was the son of a West country fisherman. He had come to sea because he saw that there was little chance of getting bread to put into his mouth if he remained on shore.

Jack's father had lost his boats and nets the previous winter, and had shortly afterwards been pressed on board a man-of-war.

Jack had done his best to support himself without being a burden to his mother, who sold fish in the neighbouring town and country round, and could do very well for herself; so when he proposed going on board a man-of-war, she, having mended his shirts, bought him a new pair of shoes, and gave him her blessing. Accordingly, doing up his spare clothes in a bundle, which he carried at the end of a stick, he trudged off with a stout heart, resolved to serve His Majesty and fight the battles of Old England.

Jack went on board the first man-of-war tender picking up hands he could find, and had been transferred that day to the *Foxhound*.

He told Tom and Bill thus much of his history. The former, however, was not very ready to be communicative as to his; while Bill's patched garments said as much about him as he was just then willing to narrate. A boy who had spent all his life in the streets of London was not likely to say more to strangers than was necessary.

In the meantime the fresh hands had been called up before the first lieutenant, Mr Saltwell, and their names entered by the purser in the ship's books, after the ordinary questions had been put to them to ascertain for what rating they were qualified.

Some few, including the smugglers, were entered as able seamen; others as ordinary seamen; and the larger number, who were unfit to go aloft, or indeed not likely to be of much use in any way for a long time to come, were rated as landsmen, and would have to do all the dirty work about the ship.

The boys were next called up, and each of them gave an account of himself.

Tom dreaded lest he should be asked any questions which he would be puzzled to answer.

The first lieutenant glanced at all three, and in spite of his old dress, entered Bill first, Jack next, and Tom, greatly to his surprise, the last. In those days no questions were asked where men or boys came from. At the present time, a boy who should thus appear on board a man-of-war would find himself in the wrong box, and be quickly sent on shore again, and home to his friends. None are allowed to enter the Navy until they have gone through a regular course of instruction in a training ship, and none are received on board her unless they can read and write well, and have a formally signed certificate that they have obtained permission from their parents or guardians.

Chapter Two.

Heaving up the anchor.

As soon as the boys' names were entered, they were sent forward, under charge of the ship's corporal, to obtain suits of sailor's clothing from the purser's steward, which clothing was charged to their respective accounts.

The ship's corporal made them wash themselves before putting on their fresh gear; and when they appeared in it, with their hair nicely combed out, it was soon seen which of the three was likely to prove the smartest sea boy.

Bill, who had never had such neat clothing on before, felt himself a different being. Tom strutted about and tried to look big. Jack was not much changed, except that he had a round hat instead of a cap, clean clothes, and lighter shoes than the thick ones in which he had come on board.

As neither Tom nor Bill knew the stem from the stern of the ship, and even Jack felt very strange, they were handed over to the charge of Dick Brice, the biggest ship's boy, with orders to him to instruct them in their respective duties.

Dick had great faith in a rope's-end, having found it efficacious in his own case. He was fond of using it pretty frequently to enforce his instructions. Jack and Bill supposed that it was part of the regular discipline of the ship; but Tom had not bargained for such treatment, and informing Dick that he would not stand it, in consequence got a double allowance.

He dared not venture to complain to his superiors, for he saw the boatswain and the boatswain's mate using their colts with similar freedom, and so he had just to grin and bear it.

At night, when the hammocks were piped down, the three went to theirs in the forepart of the ship. Bill thought he had never slept in a more comfortable bed in his life. Jack did not think much about the matter; but Tom, who had always been accustomed to a well-made bed at home, grumbled dreadfully when he tried to get into his, and tumbled out three or four times on the opposite side before he succeeded.

Had it not been for Dick Brice, who slung their hammocks for them, they would have had to sleep on the bare deck.

The next morning the gruff voice of the boatswain's mate summoned all hands to turn out, and on going on deck they saw "Blue Peter" flying at the fore, while shortly afterwards the Jews and all other visitors were made to go down the side into the boats waiting for them. The captain came on board, the sails were loosed, and while the fife was setting up a merry tune, the seamen tramped round at the capstan bars, and the anchor was hove up.

The wind being from the eastward, in the course of a few minutes the gallant frigate, under all sail, was gliding down through the smooth waters of the Solent Sea towards the Needles.

Tom and Bill had something fresh to wonder at every minute. It dawned upon them by degrees that the forepart of the ship went first, and that the wheel, at which two hands were always stationed, had something to do with guiding her, and that the sails played an important part in driving her on.

Jack had a great advantage over them, as he knew all this, and many other things besides, and being a good-natured fellow, was always ready to impart his knowledge to them.

By the time they had been three or four weeks at sea, they had learned a great deal more, and were able to go aloft.

Bill had caught up to Jack, and had left Tom far behind. The same talent which had induced him to mend his ragged clothes, made him do, with rapidity and neatness, everything else he undertook, while he showed a peculiar knack of being quick at understanding and executing the orders he received.

Tom felt rather jealous that he should be surpassed by one he had at first looked down on as little better than a beggar boy.

It never entered into Jack's head to trouble himself about the matter, and if Bill was his superior, that was no business of his.

There were a good many other people on board, who looked down on all three of them, considering that they were the youngest boys, and were at everybody's beck and call.

As soon as the frigate got to sea the crew were exercised at their guns, and Jack, Tom, and Bill had to perform the duty of powder-monkeys. This consisted in bringing up the powder from the magazine in small tubs, on which they had to sit in a row on deck, to prevent the sparks getting in while the men were working the guns, and to hand out the powder as it was required.

"I don't see any fun in firing away when there is no enemy in sight," observed Tom, as he sat on his tub at a little distance from Bill.

"There may not be much fun in it, but it's very necessary," answered Bill. "If the men were not to practise at the guns, how could they fire away properly when we get alongside an enemy? See! some of the fresh hands don't seem to know much what they are about, or the lieutenant would not be growling at them in the way he is doing. I am keeping my eye on the old hands to learn how they manage, and before long, I think, if I was big enough, I could stand to my gun as well as they do."

Tom, who had not before thought of observing the crews of the guns, took the hint, and watched how each man was engaged.

By being constantly exercised, the crew in a few weeks were well able to work their guns; but hitherto they had fallen in with no enemy against whom to exhibit their prowess.

A bright look-out was kept from the mast-head from sunrise to sunset for a strange sail, and it was not probable that they would have to go long without falling in with one, for England had at that time pretty nearly all the world in arms against her. She had managed to quarrel with the Dutch, and was at war with the French and Spaniards, while she had lately been engaged in a vain attempt to overcome the American colonies, which had thrown off their allegiance to the British Crown.

Happily for the country, her navy was staunch, and many of the most gallant admirals whose names have been handed down to fame commanded her fleets; the captains, officers, and crews, down to the youngest ship-boys, tried to imitate their example, and enabled her in the unequal struggle to come off victorious.

The *Foxhound* had for some days been cruising in the Bay of Biscay, and was one morning about the latitude of Ferrol. The watch was employed in washing down decks, the men and boys paddling about with their trousers tucked up to their knees, some with buckets of water, which they were heaving about in every direction, now and then giving a shipmate, when the first lieutenant's eye was off them, the benefit of a shower-bath: others were wielding huge swabs, slashing them down right and left, with loud thuds, and ill would it have fared with any incautious landsman who might have got within their reach. The men were laughing and joking with each other, and the occupation seemed to afford amusement to all employed.

Suddenly there came a shout from the look-out at the masthead of "Five sail in sight."

"Where away?" asked Lieutenant Saltwell, who was on deck superintending the operations going forward.

"Dead to leeward, sir," was the answer.

The wind was at the time blowing from the north-west, and the frigate was standing close hauled, on the starboard tack, to the westward.

The mate of the watch instantly went aloft, with his spy-glass hung at his back, to take a look at the strangers, while a midshipman was sent to inform Captain Waring, who, before many minutes had elapsed, made his appearance, having hurriedly slipped into his clothes.

On receiving the report of the young officer, who had returned on deck, he immediately ordered the helm to be put up, and the ship to be kept away in the direction of the strangers.

In a short time it was seen that most of them were large ships; one of them very considerably larger than the *Foxhound*.

The business of washing down the decks had been quickly concluded, and the crew were sent to their breakfasts.

Many remarks of various sorts were made by the men. Some thought that the captain would never dream of engaging so superior a force; while others, who knew him well, declared that whatever the odds, he would fight.

As yet no order had been received to beat to quarters, and many were of opinion that the captain would only stand on near enough to ascertain the character of the strangers, and then, should they prove enemies, make all sail away from them.

Still the frigate stood on, and Bill, who was near one of the officers who had a glass in his hand, heard him observe that one was a line-of-battle ship, two at least were frigates, while another was a corvette, and the fifth a large brig-of-war.

These were formidable odds, but still their plucky captain showed no inclination to escape from them, but, on the contrary, seemed as if he had made up his mind to bring them to action.

The question was ere long decided. The drum beat to quarters, the men went to their guns, powder and shot were handed up from below, giving ample occupation to the powder-monkeys, and the ship was headed towards the nearest of the strangers. She was still some distance off when the crew were summoned aft to hear what the captain had to say to them.

"My lads!" he said, "some of you have fought under me before now, and though the odds were against us, we licked the enemy. We have got somewhat greater odds, perhaps, at present, but I want to take two or three of those ships; they are not quite as powerful as they look, and if you will work your guns as I know you can work them, we'll do it before many hours have passed. We have a fine breeze to help us, and will tackle one after the other. You'll support me, I know."

Three loud cheers were given as a response to this appeal, and the men went back to their guns, where they stood stripped to their waists, with handkerchiefs bound round their heads.

Notwithstanding the formidable array of the enemy, the frigate kept bearing down under plain sail towards them.

Our heroes, sitting on their tubs, could see but very little of what was going forward, though now and then they got a glimpse of the enemy through the ports; but they heard the remarks made by the men in their neighbourhood, who were allowed to talk till the time for action had arrived.

"Our skipper knows what he's about, but that chap ahead of the rest is a monster, and looks big enough to tackle us without the help of the others," observed one of the crew of the gun nearest to which Tom was seated.

"What's the odds if she carries twice as many teeth as we have! we'll work ours twice as fast, and beat her before the frigates can come up to grin at us," answered Ned Green, the captain of the gun.

Tom did not quite like the remarks he heard. There was going to be a sharp fight, of that there could be no doubt, and round shot would soon be coming in through the sides, and taking off men's heads and legs and arms. It struck him that he would have been safer at school. He thought of his father and mother, and brothers and sisters, who, if he was killed, would never know what had become of him; not that Tom was a coward, but it was somewhat trying to the courage even of older hands, thus standing on slowly towards the enemy. When the fighting had once begun, Tom was likely to prove as brave as anybody else; at all events, he would have no time for thinking, and it is that which tries most people.

The captain and most of the officers were on the quarter-deck, keeping their glasses on the enemy.

"The leading ship under French colours appears to me to carry sixty-four guns," observed the first lieutenant to the captain; "and the next, also a Frenchmen, looks like a thirty-six gun frigate. The brig is American, and so is one of the sloops. The sternmost is French, and is a biggish ship."

"Whatever they are, we'll fight them, and, I hope, take one or two at least," answered the captain.

He looked at his watch. It was just ten o'clock. The next moment the headmost ship opened her fire, and the shot came whizzing between the ship's masts.

Captain Waring watched them as they flew through the air.

"I thought so," he observed. "There were not more than fifteen; she's a store-ship, and will be our prize before the day is over. Fire, my lads!"

he shouted; and the eager crew poured a broadside into the enemy, rapidly running in their guns, and reloading them to be ready for the next opponent.

The *Foxhound* was standing along the enemy's line to windward, and as she came abreast of each ship she fired with well-directed aim; and though all the enemy's ships in succession discharged their guns at her, not a shot struck her hull, though their object evidently was to cripple her, so that they might surround her and have her at their mercy.

Tom, who had read about sea-fights, and had expected to have the shot come rushing across the deck, felt much more comfortable on discovering this, and began to look upon the Frenchmen as very bad gunners.

The *Foxhound's* guns were all this time thundering away as fast as the crews could run them in and load them, the men warming to their work as they saw the damage they were inflicting on the enemy.

Having passed the enemy's line to windward, Captain Waring ordered the ship to be put about, and bore down on the sternmost French ship, which, with one of smaller size carrying the American pennant, was in a short time so severely treated that they both bore up out of the line. The *Foxhound*, however, followed, and the other French ships and the American brig coming to the assistance of their consorts, the *Foxhound* had them on both sides of her.

This was just what her now thoroughly excited crew desired most, as they could discharge their two broadsides at the same time; and right gallantly did she fight her way through her numerous foes till she got up with the American ship, which had been endeavouring to escape before the wind, and now, to avoid the broadside which the English ship was about to pour into her, she hauled down her colours.

On seeing this, the frigate's crew gave three hearty cheers; and as soon as they had ceased, the captain's voice was heard ordering two boats away under the command of the third lieutenant, who was directed to take charge of the prize, and to send her crew on board the ship.

Not a moment was to be lost, as the rest of the enemy, under all sail, were endeavouring to make their escape.

The boats of the prize, which proved to be the *Alexander*, carrying twenty-four guns and upwards of a hundred men, were then lowered, and employed in conveying her crew to the ship.

The American captain and officers were inclined to grumble at first.

"Very sorry, gentlemen, to incommode you," said the English lieutenant, as he hurried them down the side; "but necessity has no law; my orders are to send you all on board the frigate, as the captain is in a hurry to go in chase of your friends, of which we hope to have one or two more in our possession before long."

The lieutenant altered his tone when the Americans began to grumble. "You must go at once, or take the consequences," he exclaimed; and the prisoners saw that it would be wise to obey.

They were received very politely on board the ship, Captain Waring offering to accept their parole if they were ready to give it, and promise not to attempt to interfere with the discipline and regulations of the ship.

As soon as the prisoners were transferred to the *Foxhound*, she made all sail in chase of the large ship, which Captain Waring now heard was the sixty-four gun ship *Mènager*, laden with gunpowder, but now mounting on her maindeck twenty-six long twelve-pounders, and on her quarter-deck four long six-pounders, with a crew of two hundred and twenty men.

Her force was considerably greater than that of the English frigate, but Captain Waring did not for a moment hesitate to continue in pursuit of her. A stern chase, however, is a long chase. The day wore on, and still the French ship kept ahead of the *Foxhound*.

The crew were piped to dinner to obtain fresh strength for renewing the fight.

"Well, lads," said Green, who was a bit of a wag in his way, as he looked at the powder-boys still seated on their tubs, "as you have still got your heads on your shoulders, you may put some food into your mouths. Maybe you won't have another opportunity after we get up with the big 'un we are chasing. I told you, mates," he added, turning to the crew of his gun, "the captain knew what he was about, and would make the Frenchmen haul down their flags before we hauled down ours. I should not be surprised if we got the whole lot of them."

The boys, having returned their powder to the magazine till it was again wanted, were glad enough to stretch their legs, and still more to follow Green's advice by swallowing the food which was served out to them.

The rest of the enemy's squadron were still in sight, scattered here and there, and considerably ahead of the *Mènager*; the frigate was, however, gaining on the latter, and if the wind held, would certainly be up with her some time in the afternoon.

Every stitch of canvas she could carry was set on board the *Foxhound*.

It was already five o'clock. The crew had returned to their quarters, and the powder-monkeys were seated on their tubs. Both the pursuer and pursued were on the larboard tack, going free.

"We have her now within range of our guns," cried Captain Waring. "Luff up, master, and we'll give her a broadside."

Just as he uttered the words a squall struck the frigate. Over she heeled, the water rushing in through her lower deck ports, which were unusually low, and washing over the deck.

The crews of the lee guns, as they stood up to their knees in water, fully believed that she was going over. In vain they endeavoured to run in their guns. More and more she heeled over, till the water was nearly up to their waists. None flinched, however. The guns must be got in, and the ports shut, or the ship would be lost.

"What's going to happen?" cried Tom Fletcher. "We are going down! we are going down!"

Chapter Three.

Bill does good service.

The *Foxhound* appeared indeed to be in a perilous position. The water washed higher and higher over the deck. "We are going down! we are going down!" again cried Tom, wringing his hands.

"Not if we can help it," said Jack. "We must get the ports closed, and stop the water from coming in."

"It's no use crying out till we are hurt. We can die but once," said Bill. "Cheer up, Tom; if we do go to the bottom, it's where many have gone before;" though Bill did not really think that the ship was sinking. Perhaps, had he done so, he would not have been so cool as he now appeared.

"That's a very poor consolation," answered Tom to his last remark. "Oh, dear! oh, dear! I wish that I had stayed on shore."

Though there was some confusion among the landsmen, a few of whom began to look very white, if they did not actually wring their hands and cry out, the crews of the guns remained at their stations, and hauled away lustily at the tackles to run them in. The captain, though on the quarter-deck, was fully aware of the danger. There was no time to shorten sail.

"Port the helm!" he shouted; "hard a-port, square away the yards;" and in a few seconds the ship, put before the wind, rose to an even keel, the water, in a wave, rushing across the deck, some escaping through the opposite ports, though a considerable portion made its way below.

The starboard ports were now speedily closed, when once more the ship hauled up in chase.

The *Foxhound*, sailing well, soon got up again with the *Mènager*, and once more opened her fire, receiving that of the enemy in return.

The port of Ferrol could now be distinguished about six miles off, and it was thought probable that some Spanish men-of-war lying there might come out to the assistance of their friends. It was important to make the chase a prize before that should happen.

For some minutes Captain Waring reserved his fire, having set all the sail the *Foxhound* could carry.

"Don't fire a shot till I tell you," he shouted to his men.

The crews of the starboard guns stood ready for the order to discharge the whole broadside into the enemy. Captain Waring was on the point of issuing it, the word "Fire" was on his lips, when down came the Frenchman's flag, and instead of the thunder of their guns the British seamen uttered three joyful cheers.

The *Foxhound* was hove-to to windward of the prize, while three of the boats were lowered and pulled towards her. The third lieutenant of the *Foxhound* was sent in command, and the *Mènager's* boats being also lowered, her officers and crew were transferred as fast as possible on board their captor.

As the *Mènager* was a large ship, she required a good many people to man her, thus leaving the *Foxhound* with a greatly diminished crew.

It took upwards of an hour before the prisoners with their bags and other personal property were removed to the *Foxhound*. Captain Waring and Lieutenant Saltwell turned their eyes pretty often towards the harbour. No ships were seen coming out of it. The English frigate and her two prizes consequently steered in the direction the other vessels had gone, the captain hoping to pick up one or more of them during the following morning. Her diminished crew had enough to do in attending to their proper duties, and in looking after the prisoners.

The commanders of the two ships were received by the captain in his cabin, while the gun-room officers invited those of similar rank to mess with them, the men taking care of the French and American crews. The British seamen treated them rather as guests than prisoners, being ready to attend to their wants and to do them any service in their power. Their manner towards the Frenchmen showed the compassion they felt, mixed perhaps with a certain amount of contempt. They seemed to consider them indeed somewhat like big babes, and several might have been seen feeding the wounded and nursing them with tender care.

During the night neither the watch below nor any of the officers turned in, the greater number remaining on deck in the hopes that they might catch sight of one of the ships which had hitherto escaped them.

Note: This action and the subsequent events are described exactly as they occurred.

The American commander, Captain Gregory, sat in the cabin, looking somewhat sulky, presenting a great contrast to the behaviour of the Frenchman, Monsieur Saint Julien, who, being able to speak a little English, allowed his tongue to wag without cessation, laughing and joking, and trying to raise a smile on the countenance of his brother captive, the American skipper.

"Why! my friend, it is de fortune of war. Why you so sad?" exclaimed the volatile Frenchman. "Another day we take two English ship, and then make all right. Have you never been in England? Fine country, but not equal to 'la belle France;' too much fog and rain dere."

"I don't care for the rain, or the fog, Monsieur; but I don't fancy losing my ship, when we five ought to have taken the Englishman," replied the American.

"Ah! it was bad fortune, to be sure," observed Monsieur Saint Julien. "Better luck next time, as you say; but what we cannot cure, dat we must endure; is not dat your proverb? Cheer up! cheer up! my friend."

Nothing, however, the light-hearted Frenchman could say had the effect of raising the American's spirits.

A handsome supper was placed on the table, to which Monsieur Saint

Julien did ample justice, but Captain Gregory touched scarcely anything. At an early hour he excused himself, and retired to a berth which Captain Waring had courteously appropriated to his use.

During the night the wind shifted more to the westward, and then round to the south-west, blowing pretty strong. When morning broke, the look-outs discovered two sail to the south-east, which it was evident were some of the squadron that had escaped on the previous evening. They were, however, standing in towards the land.

Captain Waring, after consultation with his first lieutenant and master, determined to let them escape. He had already three hundred and forty prisoners on board, while his own crew amounted to only one hundred and ninety. Should he take another prize, he would have still further to diminish the number of the ship's company, while that of the prisoners would be greatly increased. The French and American captains had come on deck, and were standing apart, watching the distant vessels.

"I hope these Englishmen will take one of those fellows," observed Captain Gregory to Monsieur Saint Julien.

"Why so, my friend?" asked the latter.

"They deserve it, in the first place, and then it would be a question who gets command of this ship. We are pretty strong already, and if your people would prove staunch, we might turn the tables on our captors," said the American.

"Comment!" exclaimed Captain Saint Julien, starting back. "You forget dat we did pledge our honour to behave peaceably, and not to interfere with the discipline of the ship. French officers are not accustomed to break their parole. You insult me by making the proposal, and I hope dat you are not in earnest."

"Oh, no, my friend, I was only joking," answered the American skipper, perceiving that he had gone too far.

Officers of the U.S. Navy, we may here remark, have as high a sense of honour as any English or French officer, but this ship was only a privateer, with a scratch crew, some of them renegade Englishmen, and the Captain was on a level with the lot.

The Frenchman looked at him sternly. "I will be no party to such a proceeding," he observed.

"Oh, of course not, of course not, my friend," said Captain Gregory, walking aside.

It being finally decided to allow the other French vessels to escape, the *Foxhound's* yards were squared away, and a course shaped for Plymouth, with the two prizes in company.

Soon after noon the wind fell, and the ships made but little progress. The British crew had but a short time to sleep or rest, it being necessary to keep a number of men under arms to watch the prisoners.

The Frenchmen were placed on the lower deck, where they sat down by themselves; but the Americans mixed more freely with the English. As evening approached, however, they also drew off and congregated together. Two or three of their officers came among them.

Just before dusk Captain Gregory made his appearance, and was seen talking in low whispers to several of the men.

Among those who observed him was Bill Rayner. Bill's wits were always sharp, and they had been still more sharpened since he came to sea by the new life he was leading. He had his eyes always about him to take in what he saw, and his ears open whenever there was anything worth hearing. It had struck him as a strange thing that so many prisoners should submit quietly to be kept in subjection by a mere handful of Englishmen. On seeing the American skipper talking to his men, he crept in unobserved among them. His ears being wide open, he overheard several words which dropped from their lips.

"Oh, oh!" he thought. "Is that the trick you're after? You intend to take our ship, do you? You'll not succeed if I have the power to prevent you."

But how young Bill was to do that was the question. He had never even spoken to the boatswain or the boatswain's mate. It seemed scarcely possible for him to venture to tell the first lieutenant or the captain; still, if the prisoners' plot was to be defeated, he must inform them of what he had heard, and that without delay.

His first difficulty was how to get away from among the prisoners. Should they suspect him they would probably knock him on the head or strangle him, and trust to the chance of shoving him through one of the ports unobserved. This was possible in the crowded state of the ship, desperate as the act might seem.

Bill therefore had to wait till he could make his way on deck without being remarked. Pretending to drop asleep, he lay perfectly quiet for some time; then sitting up and rubbing his eyes, he staggered away forward, as if still drowsy, to make it be supposed that he was about to turn into his hammock. Finding that he was unobserved, he crept up by the fore-hatchway, where he found Dick, who was in the watch off deck.

At first he thought of consulting Dick, in whom he knew he could trust; but second thoughts, which are generally the best, made him resolve not to say anything to him, but to go at once to either the first lieutenant or the captain.

"If I go to Mr Saltwell, perhaps he will think I was dreaming, and tell me to 'turn into my hammock and finish my dreams,'" he thought to himself. "No! I'll go to the captain at once; perhaps the sentry will let me pass, or if not, I'll get him to ask the captain to see me. He cannot eat me, that's one comfort; if he thinks that I am bringing him a cock-and-bull story, he won't punish me; and I shall at all events have done my duty."

Bill thought this, and a good deal besides, as he made his way aft till he arrived at the door of the captain's cabin, where the sentry was posted.

"Where are you going, boy?" asked the sentry, as Bill in his eagerness was trying to pass him.

"I want to see the captain," said Bill.

"But does the captain want to see you?" asked the sentry.

"He has not sent for me; but he will when he hears what I have got to tell him," replied Bill.

"You must speak to one of the lieutenants, or get the midshipman of the watch to take in your message, if he will do it," said the sentry.

"But they may laugh at me, and not believe what I have got to say," urged Bill. "Do let me pass,—the captain won't blame you, I am sure of that."

The sentry declared that it was his duty not to allow any one to pass.

While Bill was still pleading with him, the door of the inner cabin was opened, and the captain himself came out, prepared to go on deck.

"What do you want, boy?" he asked, seeing Bill.

"Please, sir, I have got something to tell you which you ought to know," said Bill, pulling off his hat.

"Let me hear it then," said the captain.

"Please, sir, it will take some time. You may have some questions to ask," answered Bill.

On this the captain stepped back a few paces, out of earshot of the sentry.

"What is it, boy?" he asked; "you seem to have some matter of importance to communicate."

Bill then told him how he came to be among the prisoners, and had heard the American captain and his men talking together, and proposing to get the Frenchmen to rise with them to overpower the British crew.

Captain Waring's countenance showed that he felt very much disposed to disbelieve what Bill had told him, or rather, to fancy that Bill was mistaken.

"Stay there;" he said, and he went to the door of the cabin which he had allowed the American skipper to occupy.

The berth was empty! He came back and cross-questioned Bill further. Re-entering the inner cabin, he found the French captain seated at the table.

"Monsieur Saint Julien," he said; "are you cognisant of the intention of the American captain to try and overpower my crew?"

"The proposal was made to me, I confess, but I refused to accede to it with indignation; and I did not suppose that Captain Gregory would make the attempt, or I should have informed you at once," answered Saint Julien.

"He does intend to make it, though," said Captain Waring, "and I depend on you and your officers to prevent your men from joining him."

"I fear that we shall have lost our influence over our men, but we will stand by you should there be any outbreak," said the French captain.

"I will trust you," observed Captain Waring. "Go and speak to your officers while I take the steps necessary for our preservation."

Captain Waring on this left the cabin, and going on deck, spoke to the first lieutenant and the midshipmen of the watch, who very speedily communicated the orders they had received to the other officers.

The lieutenant of marines quickly turned out his men, while the boatswain roused up the most trustworthy of the seamen. So quickly and silently all was done, that a strong body of officers and men well armed were collected on the quarter-deck before any of the prisoners were aware of what was going forward. They were awaiting the captain's orders, when a loud report was heard. A thick volume of smoke ascended from below, and the next instant, with loud cries and shouts, a number of the prisoners were seen springing up the hatchway ladders.

Chapter Four.

The frigate blown up.

The Americans had been joined by a number of the Frenchmen, and some few of the worst characters of the English crew—the jail-birds chiefly, who had been won over with the idea that they would sail away to some beautiful island, of which they might take possession; and live in independence, or else rove over the ocean with freedom from all discipline.

They had armed themselves with billets of wood and handspikes; and some had got hold of knives and axes, which they had secreted. They rushed on deck expecting quickly to overpower the watch.

Great was their dismay to find themselves encountered by a strong body of armed men, who seized them, or knocked them down directly they appeared.

So quickly were the first overpowered that they had no time to give the alarm to their confederates below, and thus, as fresh numbers came up, they were treated like the first. In a couple of minutes the whole of the mutineers were overpowered.

The Frenchmen who had not actually joined them cried out for mercy, declaring that they had no intention of doing so.

What might have been the case had the Americans been successful was another matter.

All those who had taken part in the outbreak having been secured, Captain Waring sent a party of marines to search for the American captain. He was quickly found, and brought on the quarter-deck.

"You have broken your word of honour; you have instigated the crew to mutiny, and I should be justified were I to run you up to the yard-arm!" said Captain Waring, sternly.

"You would have done the same," answered the American captain, boldly. "Such acts when successful have always been applauded."

"Not, sir, if I had given my word of honour, as you did, not to interfere with the discipline of the ship," said Captain Waring. "You are now under arrest, and, with those who supported you, will remain in irons till we reach England."

Captain Gregory had not a word to say for himself. The French captain, far from pleading for him, expressed his satisfaction that he had been so treated.

He and the officers who had joined him were marched off under a guard to have their irons fixed on by the armourer.

After this it became necessary to keep a strict watch on all the prisoners, and especially on the Americans, a large proportion of whom were found to be English seamen, and some of the *Foxhound's* crew recognised old shipmates among them.

Captain Waring, believing that he could trust to the French captain and his officers, allowed them to remain on their parole, a circumstance which greatly aggravated the feelings of Captain Gregory.

The captain had not forgotten Bill, who, by the timely information he had given, had materially contributed to preserve the ship from capture. Bill himself did not think that he had done anything wonderful; his chief anxiety was lest the fact of his having given the information should become known. The sentinel might guess at it, but otherwise the captain alone could know anything about it. Bill, as soon as he had told his story to the captain, and found that it was credited, stole away forward among the rest of the crew on deck, where he took very good care not to say a word of what had happened; so that not till the trustworthy men received orders to be prepared for an outbreak were they aware of what was likely to occur.

He therefore fancied that his secret had been kept, and that it would never be known; he was, consequently, surprised when the following morning the ship's corporal, touching his shoulder, told him that the captain wanted to speak to him.

Bill went aft, feeling somewhat alarmed at the thoughts of being spoken to by the captain.

On the previous evening he had been excited by being impressed with the importance of the matter he was about to communicate, but now he had time to wonder what the captain would say to him.

He met Tom and Jack by the way.

"Where are you going?" asked Tom.

Bill told him.

"I shouldn't wish to be in your shoes," remarked Tom. "What have you been about?"

Bill could not stop to answer, but followed his conductor to the cabin door.

The sentry, without inquiry, admitted him.

The captain, who was seated at a table in the cabin, near which the first lieutenant was standing, received him with a kind look.

"What is your name, boy?" he asked.

"William Rayner, sir," said Bill.

"Can you read and write pretty well?"

"No great hand at either, sir," answered Bill. "Mother taught me when I was a little chap, but I have not had much chance of learning since then."

"Should you like to improve yourself?" asked the captain.

"Yes, sir; but I have not books, or paper, or pens."

"We'll see about that," said the captain. "The information you gave me last night was of the greatest importance, and I wish to find some means of rewarding you. When we reach England, I will make known your conduct to the proper authorities, and I should like to communicate with your parents."

"Please, sir, I have no parents; they are both dead, and I have no relations that I know of; but I am much obliged to you, sir," answered Bill, who kept wondering what the captain was driving at.

"Well, my boy, I will keep an eye on you," said the captain. "Mr Saltwell, you will see what is best to be done with William Rayner," he added, turning to the first lieutenant. "If you wish to learn to read and write, you can come and get instruction every day from my clerk, Mr Finch. I will give him directions to teach you; but remember you are not forced to do it."

"Thank you, sir," said Bill. "I should like to learn very much."

After a few more words, the captain dismissed Bill, who felt greatly relieved when the formidable interview was over.

As he wisely kept secret the fact of his having given information of the mutiny, his messmates wondered what could have induced the captain so suddenly to take an interest in him.

Every day he went aft for his lesson, and Mr Finch, who was a good-natured young man, was very kind. Bill, who was remarkably quick, made great progress, and his instructor was much pleased with him.

He could soon read easily, and Mr Finch, by the captain's orders, lent him several books.

The master's assistant, calling him one day, told him that he had received orders from the captain to teach him navigation, and, greatly to his surprise, put a quadrant into his hands, and showed him how to use it.

Bill all this time had not an inkling of what the captain intended for him. It never occurred to him that the captain could have perceived any merits or qualifications sufficient to raise him out of his present position, but he was content to do his duty where he was.

Tom felt somewhat jealous of the favour Bill was receiving, though he pretended to pity him for having to go and learn lessons every day. Tom, indeed, knew a good deal more than Bill, as he had been at school, and could read very well, though he could not boast much of his writing.

Jack could neither read nor write, and had no great ambition to learn; but he was glad, as Bill seemed to like it, that he had the chance of picking up knowledge.

"Perhaps the captain intends to make you his clerk, or maybe some day you will become his coxswain," observed Jack, whose ambition soared no higher. "I should like to be that, but I suppose that it is not necessary to be able to read, or write, or sum. I never could make any hand at those things, but you seem up to them, and so it's all right that you should learn."

Notwithstanding the mark of distinction Bill was receiving, the three young messmates remained very good friends.

Bill, however, found himself much better off than he had before been. That the captain patronised him was soon known to all, and few ventured to lay a rope's-end on his back, as formerly, while he was well treated in other respects.

Bill kept his eyes open and his wits awake on all occasions, and thus rapidly picked up a good knowledge of seamanship, such as few boys of his age who had been so short a time at sea possessed.

The *Foxhound* and her prizes were slowly making their way to England. No enemy appeared to rob her of them, though they were detained by contrary winds for some time in the chops of the Channel.

At length the wind shifted a point or two, and they were able to get some way up it. The weather, however, became cloudy and dark, and no observation could be taken.

It was a trying time, for the provisions and water, in consequence of the number of souls on board, had run short.

The captain was doubly anxious to get into port; still, do all he could, but little progress was made, till one night the wind again shifted and the sky cleared. The master was aware that the ship was farther over to the French coast than was desirable, but her exact position it was difficult to determine.

The first streaks of sunlight had appeared in the eastern sky, when the look-out shouted—

"A ship to the southward, under all sail."

As the sun rose, his rays fell on the white canvas of the stranger, which was now seen clearly, standing towards the *Foxhound*.

Captain Waring made a signal to the two prizes, which were somewhat to the northward, to make all sail for Plymouth, while the *Foxhound*, under more moderate canvas, stood off shore.

Should the stranger prove an enemy, of which there was little doubt, Captain Waring determined to try and draw her away from the French coast, which could be dimly seen in the distance. He, at the same time, did not wish to make an enemy suppose that he was flying. Though ready enough to fight, he would rather first have got rid of his prisoners, but that could not now be done.

It was necessary, therefore, to double the sentries over them, and to make them clearly understand that, should any of them attempt in any way to interfere, they would immediately be shot.

Jack, Tom, and Bill had seen the stranger in the distance, and they guessed that they should before long be engaged in a fierce fight with her. There was no doubt that she was French. She was coming up rapidly.

The captain now ordered the ship to be cleared for action. The men went readily to their guns. They did not ask whether a big or small ship was to be their opponent, but stood prepared to fight as long as the captain and officers ordered them, hoping, at all events, to beat the enemy.

The powder-monkeys, as before, having been sent down to bring up the ammunition, took their places on their tubs. Of course they could see but little of what was going forward, but through one of the ports they at last caught sight of the enemy, which appeared to be considerably larger than the *Foxhound*.

"We have been and caught a Tartar," Bill heard one of the seamen observe.

"Maybe. But whether Turk or Tartar, we'll beat him," answered another.

An order was passed along the decks that not a gun should be fired till the captain gave the word. The boys had not forgotten their fight a few weeks before, and had an idea that this was to turn out something like that. Then the shot of the enemy had passed between the masts and the rigging; but scarcely one had struck the hull, nor had a man been hurt, so they had begun to fancy that fighting was a very bloodless affair.

"What shall we do with the prisoners, if we take her, I wonder?" asked Tom. "We've got Monsieurs enough on board already."

"I daresay the captain will know what to do with them," responded Bill.

"We must not count our chickens before they're hatched," said Jack. "Howsumdever, we'll do our best." Jack's remark, which was heard by some of the crew of the gun near which he was seated, caused a laugh.

"What do you call your best, Jack?" asked Ned Green.

"Sitting on my tub, and handing out the powder as you want it," answered Jack. "What more would you have me do, I should like to know?"

"Well said, Jack," observed Green. "We'll work our guns as fast as we can, and you'll hand out the powder as we want it."

The talking was cut short by the voices of the officers ordering the men to be ready for action.

The crews of the guns laid hold of the tackles, while the captains stood with the lanyards in their hands, waiting for the word of command, and ready at a moment's notice to fire.

The big ship got nearer and nearer. She could now be seen through the ports on the starboard side.

"Well, but she's a whopper!" exclaimed Ned Green, "though I hope we'll whop her, notwithstanding. Now, boys, we'll show the Monsieurs what we can do."

Just then came the word along the decks—

"Fire!"

And the guns on the starboard side, with a loud roar, sent forth their missiles of death.

While the crew were running them in to re-load, the enemy fired in return; their shot came crashing against the sides, some sweeping the upper deck, others making their way through the ports.

The smoke from the guns curled round in thick eddies, through which objects could be but dimly seen.

The boys looked at each other. All of them were seated on their tubs, but they could see several forms stretched on the deck, some convulsively moving their limbs, others stilled in death.

This was likely to be a very different affair from the former action.

Having handed out the powder, Jack, Tom, and Bill returned to their places once more.

The *Foxhound's* guns again thundered forth, and directly after there came the crashing sound of shot, rending the stout sides of the ship.

For several minutes the roar was incessant. Presently a cheer was heard from the deck.

One of the Frenchman's masts had gone over the side; but before many minutes had elapsed, a crashing sound overhead showed that the *Foxhound* had been equally unfortunate.

Her foremast had been shot away by the board, carrying with it the bowsprit and maintopmast.

She was thus rendered almost unmanageable, but still her brave captain maintained the unequal contest.

The guns, as they could be brought to bear, were fired at the enemy with such effect that she was compelled to sheer off to repair damages.

On seeing this, the crew of the *Foxhound* gave another hearty cheer; but ere the sound had died away, down came the mainmast, followed by the mizenmast, and the frigate lay an almost helpless hulk on the water.

Captain Waring at once gave the order to clear the wreck, intending to get up jury-masts, so as to be in a condition to renew the combat should the French ship again attack them.

All hands were thus busily employed. The powder in the meantime was returned to the magazine, and the guns run in and secured.

The ship was in a critical condition.

The carpenters, before anything else could be done, had to stop the shot-holes between wind and water, through which the sea was pouring in several places.

It was possible that the prisoners might not resist the temptation, while the crew were engaged, to attempt retaking the ship.

The captain and officers redoubled their watchfulness. The crew went steadily about their work, as men who knew that their lives depended on their exertions. Even the stoutest-hearted, however, looked grave.

The weather was changing for the worse, and should the wind come from the northward, they would have a hard matter to escape being wrecked, even could they keep the ship afloat.

The enemy, too, was near at hand, and might at any moment bear down upon them, and recommence the action.

The first lieutenant, as he was coming along the deck, met Bill, who was trying to make himself useful in helping where he was wanted.

"Rayner," said Mr Saltwell, "I want you to keep an eye on the prisoners, and report to the captain or me, should you see anything suspicious in their conduct—if they are talking together, or look as if they were waiting for a signal. I know I can trust you, my boy."

Bill touched his hat.

"I will do my best, sir," he answered; and he slipped down to where the prisoners were congregated.

They did not suspect that he had before informed the captain of their intended outbreak, or it would have fared but ill with him.

Whatever might have been their intentions, they seemed aware that they were carefully watched, and showed no inclination to create a disturbance.

The greatest efforts were now made to set up the jury-masts. The wind was increasing, and the sea rising every minute. The day also was drawing on, and matters were getting worse and worse; still Captain Waring and his staunch crew worked away undaunted. If they could once get up the jury-masts, a course might be steered either for the Isle of Wight or Plymouth. Sails had been got up from below; the masts were ready to raise, when there came a cry of, "The enemy is standing towards us!"

"We must beat her off, and then go to work again," cried the captain.

A cheer was the response. The powder-magazine was again opened. The men flew to their guns, and prepared for the expected conflict.

The French ship soon began to fire, the English returning their salute with interest. The round shot, as before, whistled across the deck, killing and wounding several of the crew.

The sky became still more overcast; the lightning darted from the clouds; the thunder rattled, mocked by the roaring of the guns.

Bill saw his shipmates knocked over on every side; but, as soon as one of the crew of a gun was killed, another took his place, or the remainder worked the gun with as much rapidity as before.

The cockpit was soon full of wounded men. Though things were as bad as they could be, the captain had resolved not to yield.

The officers went about the decks encouraging the crew, assuring them that they would speedily beat off the enemy.

Every man, even the idlest, was doing his duty.

Jack, Tom, and Bill were doing theirs.

Suddenly a cry arose from below of "Fire! fire!" and the next moment thick wreaths of smoke ascended through the hatchways, increasing every instant in density.

The firemen were called away. Even at that awful moment the captain and officers maintained their calmness.

Now was the time to try what the men were made of. The greater number obeyed the orders they received. Buckets were handed up and filled with water to dash over the seat of the fire. Blankets were saturated and sent down below.

The enemy ceased firing, and endeavoured to haul off from the neighbourhood of the ill-fated ship. In spite of all the efforts made, the smoke increased, and flames came rushing up from below. Still, the crew laboured on; hope had not entirely abandoned them, when suddenly a loud roar was heard, the decks were torn up, and hundreds of men in one moment were launched into eternity.

Jack, Tom, and Bill had before this made their escape to the upper deck. They had been talking together, wondering what was next to happen, when Bill lost all consciousness; but in a few moments recovering his senses, found himself in the sea, clinging to a piece of wreck.

He heard voices, but could see no one. He called to Tom and Jack, fancying that they must be near him, but no answer came.

He must have been thrown, he knew, to some distance from the ship, for he could see the burning wreck, and the wind appeared to be driving him farther and farther away from it.

The guns as they became heated went off, and he could hear the shot splashing in the water around him.

"And Jack and Tom have been lost, poor fellows!" he thought to himself. "I wish they had been sent here. There's room enough for them on this piece of wreck.

"We might have held out till to-morrow morning, when some vessel might have seen us and picked us up."

Curiously enough, he did not think much about himself. Though he was thankful to have been saved, he guessed truly that the greater number of his shipmates, and the unfortunate prisoners on board, must have been lost; yet he regretted Jack and Tom more than all the rest.

The flames from the burning ship cast a bright glare far and wide over the ocean, tinging the foam-topped seas.

Bill kept gazing towards the ship. He could make out the Frenchman at some distance off, and fancied that he saw boats pulling across the tossing waters.

On the other side he could distinguish another vessel, which was also, he hoped, sending her boats to the relief of the sufferers.

The whole ship, however, appeared so completely enveloped in fire, the flames bursting out from all the ports and rising through every hatchway, that he could not suppose it possible any had escaped.

He found it a hard matter to cling on to the piece of wreck, for the seas were constantly washing over him. Happily it was weighted below, so that it remained tolerably steady. Had it rolled over and over he must inevitably have lost his hold and been drowned.

Though he had had very little of what is called enjoyment in life, and his prospects, as far as he could see, were none of the brightest, he still had no wish to die, and the instinct of self-preservation made him cling to the wreck with might and main.

The tide, which was setting towards the shore, had got hold of his raft, which was also driven by the wind in the same direction, and he found himself drifting gradually away from the burning ship, and his chance of being picked up by one of the boats diminishing.

He remembered that land had been in sight some time before the action, but how far the ship had been from it when she caught fire he could not tell, and when he turned his eyes to the southward he could see nothing of it.

Some hours had passed away, so it seemed to him, when, as he turned his eyes towards the ship, the flames appeared to rise up higher than ever. Her stout hull was a mass of fire fore and aft—she was burning down to the water's edge. Then came the end—the wild waves washed over her, and all was dark.

"There goes the old ship," thought Bill. "I wonder how many on board her a few hours ago are now alive. Shall I reach the shore to-morrow morning? I don't see much chance of it, and if I don't, how shall I ever live through another day?"

Chapter Five.

Picked up by a fishing-vessel.

After a time, Bill began to feel very hungry, and then he recollected that at dinner he had clapped a biscuit into his pocket. He felt for it. It was soaked through and through, and nearly turned into paste, but it served to stay his appetite, and to keep up his strength. At length he became somewhat drowsy, but he did his best to keep awake. Feeling about, he got hold of a piece of rope, with which he managed to secure himself to the raft. Had he found it before, it would have saved him much exertion.

The feeling that there was now less risk of being washed away, made him not so anxious as at first to withstand the strong desire which had attacked him, and yielding to it, his eyes closed, and he dropped off to sleep.

How long he had been in that state he could not tell, when he was aroused by the sound of human voices. Opening his eyes, he found that the sun was shining down upon him, and looking round, he saw a small vessel approaching. He soon made her out to be a fishing craft with five people on board.

They hailed him, but he was too weak to answer. He managed, however, to wave one of his hands to show that he was alive.

The fishing-vessel came on, and hove-to close to him. The sea had considerably gone down. A boat was launched from her deck, and pulled up to the raft, with two men in her.

They said something, but Bill could not understand them. One of them, as they got up alongside, sprang on to the raft, and casting off the lashings which held Bill to it, the next instant was safe in the boat with him in his arms.

The man having placed him in the stern-sheets, the boat quickly returned to the cutter.

Bill was lifted on board, and the boat was then hauled up again on the cutter's deck. His preservers, though rough-looking men, uttered exclamations in kind tones which assured Bill that he had fallen into good hands. One of them then carried him down into the little cabin, and stripping off his wet clothes, placed him between the blankets in a berth on one side.

In a few minutes the same man, who appeared to be the captain of the fishing-vessel, returned with a cup of hot coffee and some white bread. Stirring the coffee and blowing to cool it, he made signs to Bill that he must drink some of it.

This Bill very gladly did, and he then felt able to eat some of the bread, which seemed very sweet and nice. This greatly restored his strength.

He wished, however, that he could answer the questions which the men put to him. He guessed that they were Frenchmen, but not a word of French did he know.

At last another man came into the cabin.

"You English boy?" asked the man.

"Yes," said Bill.

"Ship burn; blow up?" was the next question put to Bill, the speaker showing what he meant by suitable action.

"Yes," said Bill, "and I am afraid all my shipmates are lost. Though you are French, you won't send me to prison, I hope?"

"Have no fear," answered the man, smiling; and turning round to his companions, he explained what Bill had said. They smiled, and Bill heard them say, "Pauvre garçon."

"No! no! no! You sleep now, we take care of you," said the interpreter, whose knowledge of English was, however, somewhat limited.

Bill felt a strong inclination to follow the advice given him. One of the men, bundling up his wet clothes, carried them to dry at the little galley fire forward. The rest went on deck, and Bill in another minute fell fast asleep. Where the cutter was going Bill could not tell. He had known her to be a fishing-vessel by seeing the nets on deck, and he had guessed that she was French by the way in which the people on board had spoken. They had given evidence also that they intended to treat him kindly.

Some hours must have passed away when Bill again awoke, feeling very hungry. It was daylight, and he saw that his clothes were laid at the foot of his berth.

Finding that his strength had returned, he got up, and began dressing himself. He had just finished when he saw that there was some one in the opposite berth. "Perhaps the skipper was up all night, and has turned in," thought Bill; but as he looked again, he saw that the head was certainly not that of a man, but the face was turned away from him.

His intention was to go on deck, to try and thank the French fishermen, as far as he was able, for saving his life, but before he did so curiosity prompted him to look again into the berth.

What was his surprise and joy to recognise the features of his shipmate, Jack Peek! His face was very pale, but he was breathing, which showed that he was alive. At all events, Bill thought that he would not awake him, eager as he was to know how he had been saved.

He went up on deck, hoping that the man who had spoken a few words of English might be able to tell him how Jack had been picked up. On reaching the deck he found that the vessel was close in with the land. She was towing a shattered gig, which Bill recognised as one of those belonging to the *Foxhound*. He at once conjectured that Jack had managed somehow or other to get into her.

As soon as he appeared, the Frenchmen began talking to him,

forgetting that he was unable to understand them. As he made no reply, they recollected themselves, and began laughing at their own stupidity.

One of them shouted down the fore-hatchway, and presently the interpreter, as Bill called him, made his appearance.

"Glad see you. All right now?" he said, in a tone of interrogation.

"All right," said Bill, "but I want you to tell me how you happened to find my shipmate Jack Peek;" and Bill pointed down into the cabin.

"He, friend! not broder! no! We find him in boat, but he not say how he got dere. Two oder men, but dey dead, so we heave dem overboard, and take boat in tow," answered the man.

Jack himself was probably not likely to be able to give any more information than the Frenchman had done. Suddenly it struck his new friends that Bill might be hungry, and the interpreter said to him, "You want manger," pointing to Bill's mouth.

Bill understood him. "Yes, indeed I do; I am ready for anything you can give me," he said.

The fire was lighted, while a pot was put to boil on it, and, greatly to Bill's satisfaction, in a few minutes one of the men, who acted as cook, poured the contents into a huge basin which was placed on the deck, and smaller basins and wooden spoons were handed up from below.

One man remaining at the helm, the remainder sat down and ladled the soup into the smaller basins.

Bill eagerly held out his.

The mess, which consisted of fowl and pork and a variety of vegetables, smelt very tempting, and as soon as it was cool enough, Bill devoured it with a good appetite.

His friends asked him by signs if he would have any more.

"Thank you," he answered, holding out his basin. "A spoonful or two; but we must not forget Jack Peek. When he awakes, he will be glad of some;" and he pointed into the cabin.

The Frenchmen understood him, and made signs that they would keep some for his friend, one of them patting him on the back and calling him "Bon garçon."

Bill, after remaining some time on deck, again felt sleepy, and his head began to nod.

The Frenchmen, seeing this, told him to go below. He gladly followed their advice, and descending into the cabin, lay down, and was once more fast asleep.

The next time he awoke he found that the vessel was at anchor. He got up, and looked into Jack's berth. Jack at that moment turned round, and opening his eyes, saw his shipmate.

"Why, Bill, is it you!" he exclaimed. "I am main glad to see you; but where are we?—how did I come here? I thought that I was in the captain's gig with Tom Nokes and Dick Harbour. What has become of them? They were terribly hurt, poor fellows! though they managed to crawl on board the gig."

Bill told him what he had learned from the Frenchman.

"They seem kind sort of fellows, and we have fallen into good hands," he added; "but what they're going to do with us is more than I can tell."

Just then the captain of the fishing-vessel came below, and seeing that Jack was awake, he called out to one of the men to bring a basin of the soup which had been kept for him.

While he was swallowing it, a man brought him his clothes, which had been sent forward to dry. The captain then made signs to him to dress, as he intended taking them both on shore with him.

Bill helped Jack, who was somewhat weak, to get on his clothes. They then went on deck.

The vessel lay in a small harbour, protected by a reef of rocks from the sea. Near the shore were a number of cottages, and on one side of the harbour a line of cliffs running away to the eastward.

Several other small vessels and open boats lay at anchor around.

The captain, with the interpreter, whose name they found was Pierre, got into the boat, the latter telling the lads to come with them.

They did as they were directed, sitting down in the stern-sheets, while the captain and Pierre took the oars and pulled towards the shore.

It was now evening, and almost dark. They saw the lights shining in the windows of several of the cottages.

Pierre was a young man about nineteen or twenty, and, they fancied, must be the captain's son. They were right, they found, in their conjectures.

Pierre made them understand, in his broken language, that he had some short time before been a prisoner in England, where he had been treated very kindly; but before he had time to learn much English, he had been exchanged.

This had made him anxious to show kindness to the young English lads.

"Come along," said Pierre, as they reached the shore. "I show you my house, my mère, and my soeur. They take care of you; but mind! you not go out till dey tell you, or de gendarmes take you to prison perhaps. Do not speak now till we get into de house."

Bill and Jack followed their guide while the old man rowed back to the vessel.

Pierre led them to a cottage a little distance from the shore, which appeared to be somewhat larger than those they had passed. He opened the door, telling them to come in with him, when he immediately again closed it.

A middle-aged woman and a young girl, in high white caps with flaps over the shoulders, were seated spinning. They started up on seeing the two young strangers, and began inquiring of Pierre who they were. His explanation soon satisfied them, and jumping up, Madame Turgot and Jeannette took their hands, and began pouring out in voluble language their welcomes.

"You say 'Merci! merci!'" said Pierre, "which means 'Thank you! thank you!'"

"Merci! merci!" said Jack and Bill.

It was the first word of French they learned, and, as Jack observed, came in very convenient.

What the mother and her daughter said they could not make out, but they understood well enough that the French women intended to be kind.

"You hungry?" asked Pierre.

"Very," answered Jack.

Pierre said something to his mother and sister, who at once set about spreading a cloth and placing eatables on the table—bread and cheese, and pickled fish, and some salad.

"Merci! merci!" said Jack and Bill, as their hostess made signs to them to fall to. Pierre joined them, and in a short time Captain Turgot himself came in. He was as hospitably inclined as his wife and daughter, and kept pressing the food upon the boys.

"Merci! merci!" was their answer.

At last Jeannette began to laugh, as if she thought it a good joke.

Jack and Bill tried hard to understand what was said. Pierre observed them listening, and did his best to explain.

From him they learned that they must remain quiet in the house, or they might be carried away as prisoners of war. He and his father wished to save them from this, and intended, if they had the opportunity, enabling them to get back to England.

"But how will you manage that?" asked Bill.

Pierre looked very knowing, and gave them to understand that smuggling vessels occasionally came into the harbour, and that they might easily get on board one of them, and reach the English coast.

"But we do not wish to get rid of you," said Pierre. "If you like to remain with us, you shall learn French, and become French boys; and you can then go out and help us fish, and gain your livelihood."

Pierre did not say this in as many words, but Jack and Bill agreed that such was his meaning.

"He's very kind," observed Bill; "but for my part, I should not wish to become a French boy; though I would not mind remaining for a while with the French dame and her daughter, for they're both very kind, and we shall have a happy time of it."

This was said a day or two after their arrival.

Captain Turgot had fitted them up a couple of bunks in a small room in which Pierre slept, and they were both far more comfortable than they had ever been in their lives.

Captain Turgot's cottage was far superior to that of Jack's father; and as for Bill, he had never before slept in so soft a bed. They had to remain in the house, however, all day; but Captain Turgot or Pierre took them out in the evening, when they could not be observed, to stretch their legs and get a little fresh air.

They tried to make themselves useful by helping Madame Turgot, and they rapidly picked up from her and her daughter a good amount of French, so that in a short time they were able to converse, though in a curious fashion, it must be owned.

They soon got over their bashfulness, and asked the name of everything they saw, which Jeannette was always ready to tell them. Their attempts at talking French afforded her vast amusement.

Though kindly treated, they at length got tired of being shut up in the house, and were very well pleased when one day Captain Turgot brought them each a suit of clothes, and told them that he was going away to fish, and would take them with him.

Next morning they went on board the cutter, and sail being soon afterwards made, she stood out of the harbour.

Chapter Six.

Taken prisoners.

Jack and Bill made themselves very useful in hauling the nets, and cleaning the fish when caught. Jack was well up to the work, and showed Bill how to do it. Captain Turgot was highly pleased, and called them "bons garçons," and said he hoped that they would remain with him till the war was over, and as much longer as they liked. When the cutter returned into the harbour to land her fish, Jack and Bill were sent below, so that the authorities might not see them and carry them off. Captain Turgot was much afraid of losing them. They were getting on famously with their French, and Bill could chatter away already at a great rate, though not in very good French, to be sure, for he made a number of blunders, which afforded constant amusement to his companions, but Pierre was always ready to set him right.

Jack made much slower progress. He could not, he said, twist his tongue about sufficiently to get out the words, even when he remembered them. Some, he found, were wonderfully like English, and those he recollected the best, though, to be sure, they had different meanings. One day the cutter had stood out farther from the shore than usual, her nets being down, when, at daybreak, a strange sail was seen in the offing. The captain, after taking one look at her, was convinced that she was an enemy.

"Quick! quick! my sons," he shouted: "we must haul the nets and make sail, or we shall be caught by the English. They are brave people, but I have no wish to see the inside of one of their prisons."

All hands worked away as if their lives depended on their exertions.

Jack and Bill lent a hand as usual. They scarcely knew what to wish. Should the stranger prove to be an English ship, and come up with them, they would be restored to liberty; but, at the same time, they would feel very sorry that their kind friends should lose their vessel and be made prisoners; still, Jack wanted to let his mother know that he was alive, and Bill wished to be on board a man-of-war again, fighting for Old England, and getting a foot or two up the ratlines.

His ambition had been aroused by what the captain had said to him, and the assistant master had observed, though he had spoken in joke, that he might, some day or other, become an admiral.

Bill had thought the subject over and over, till he began to fancy that, could he get another chance, the road to fame might be open to him. The loss of the ship with the captain and officers seemed, to be sure, to have overthrown all his hopes; but what had happened once might happen again, and by attending to his duty, and keeping his eyes open, and his wits awake, he might have another opportunity of distinguishing himself.

No one could possibly have suspected what was passing in Bill's mind, as he worked away as energetically as the rest in stowing the nets and making sail.

The stranger was now made out to a certainty to be an English frigate, and a fast one, too, by the way she slipped through the water.

The wind was from the south-east, and being thus partially off shore, would enable the frigate to stand in closer to the land than she otherwise might have ventured to do. This greatly diminished the chances of the cutter's escape.

Captain Turgot, however, like a brave man, did not tear his hair, or stamp, or swear, as Frenchmen are sometimes supposed to do, but, taking the helm, set every sail his craft could carry, and did his best, by careful steering, to keep to windward of the enemy.

Could he once get into harbour he would be safe, unless the frigate should send her boats in to cut his vessel out. The cutter possessed a couple of long sweeps. Should it fall calm, they would be of use; but at present the breeze was too strong to render them necessary.

The crew kept looking astern to watch the progress made by their pursuer, which was evidently coming up with them. What chance, indeed, had a little fishing craft with a dashing frigate?

An idea occurred to Jack which had not struck Bill.

"Suppose we are taken—and it looks to me as if we shall be before long—what will they say on board the frigate when they find us rigged out in fisherman's clothes? They will be thinking we are deserters, and will be hanging us up at the yard-arm."

"I hope it won't go so hard as that with us," answered Bill. "We can tell them that the Frenchmen took away our clothes, and rigged us out in these, and we could not help ourselves."

"But will they believe us?" asked Jack.

On that point Bill acknowledged that there was some doubt; either way, he would be very sorry for Captain Turgot. One thing could be said, that neither their fears nor wishes would prevent the frigate from capturing the cutter. They looked upon that as a settled matter. As long, however, as there was a possibility of escaping, Captain Turgot resolved to persevere.

Matters began to look serious, when a flash and wreath of smoke was seen to issue from one of the bow guns of the frigate, and a shot came jumping over the water towards them. It did not reach them, however.

"You must get nearer, monsieur, before you hurt us," said the captain, as he watched the shot fall into the water.

Shortly afterwards another followed. It came close up to the cutter; but a miss is as good as a mile, and the little vessel was none the worse for it.

Another shot, however, might produce a very different result.

"I say, Bill, I don't quite like the look of things," observed Jack. "Our skipper had better give in, or one of those shot will be coming aboard us, and carrying somebody's head off."

"He doesn't look as if he had any thoughts of the sort," said Bill; "and as long as there is any chance of keeping ahead, he'll stand on."

Soon after Bill had made this remark, another shot was fired from the frigate, and passed alongside the cutter, falling some way ahead.

Had it been better aimed, the effect might have been somewhat disastrous. Still Captain Turgot kept at the helm.

Some of the crew, however, began to cry out, and begged him to heave to. He pointed to the shore.

"Do you want to see your wives and families again?" he asked. "Look there! How smooth the water is ahead. The wind is falling, and the frigate will soon be becalmed. She'll not think it worth while to send her boats after us. Come! out with the sweeps, and we shall soon draw out of shot of her. Look there! now her topsails are already flapping against the masts. Be of good courage, my sons!"

Thus incited, the crew got out the sweeps.

Jack and Bill helped them with as much apparent good-will as if they had had no wish to be on board the frigate.

The little vessel felt the effects of the powerful sweeps, and, in spite of the calm, continued to move ahead.

Again and again the frigate fired at her, but she was a small object, and each shot missed.

This encouraged the French crew, whose spirits rose as they saw their chance of escaping increase.

Farther and farther they got from the frigate, which, with the uncertainty from what quarter the wind would next blow, was afraid of standing closer in shore.

By nightfall the cutter, by dint of hard rowing, had got safe into harbour.

When Dame Turgot and Jeannette heard what had occurred, they expressed their delight at seeing their young friends back.

"We must not let you go to sea again, for it would be a sad thing to hear that you had been captured and shot for being deserters," said Jeannette.

She had the same idea which had occurred to Jack.

The English frigates were at this time so frequently seen off the coast, that Captain Turgot, who had several boats as well as the cutter, thought it prudent to confine his operations to inshore fishing, so as not to run the risk of being captured.

Jack and Bill sometimes went out with him, but, for some reason or other, he more generally left them at home.

Pierre, who was a good swimmer, induced them to come down and bathe with him in the morning, and gave them instruction in the art.

Jack could already swim a little. Bill took to it at once, and beat him hollow; in a short time being able to perform all sorts of evolutions. He was soon so perfectly at home in the water, that he declared he felt able to swim across the Channel, if he could carry some food with him to support himself on the way.

Jack laughed at the idea, observing that "nobody ever had swum across the Channel, and he did not believe that anybody ever would do so."

Pierre advised Bill not to make the attempt.

"No fear," said Jack. "He'll not go without me, and I am not going to drown myself if I can help it."

Bill, however, often thought over the matter, and tried to devise some plan by which he and Jack might manage to get across. His plans came to nothing; and, indeed, the Channel where they were was much too wide to be crossed except in a small vessel or in a large boat. Jack was beginning to speak French pretty well, and Bill was able to gabble away with considerable fluency, greatly to the delight of Jeannette, who was his usual instructress. He tried to teach her a little English in return, but she laughed at her own attempts, and declared that she should never be able to pronounce so break-jaw a language.

Bill thought that she got on very well, but she seemed more anxious to teach him French than to learn English herself.

Several weeks more passed by. Well treated as they were, still the boys had a longing to return to England, though the opportunity of doing so appeared as far off as ever.

They were in the house one afternoon, laughing and joking merrily with Jeannette, while Dame Turgot was away at the neighbouring town to market, when the door opened, and she entered, with a look of alarm on her countenance.

"Quick, quick, come here!" she said; and seizing them both by the arms, she dragged them into the little inner room.

"Pull off your clothes and jump into bed!" she exclaimed. "Whatever you hear, don't move or speak, but pretend to be fast asleep."

They obeyed her; and snatching up their jackets and trousers, she hurried from the room, locking the door behind her.

She had just time to tumble their clothes into a chest, when a loud knocking was heard at the door. She opened it, and several soldiers, under the command of a sergeant, entered.

The boys guessed who they were by their voices, and the noise they made when grounding their muskets.

"Well, messieurs," said Dame Turgot, with perfect composure, "and what do you want here?"

"We come in search of prisoners. It is reported that you have some concealed in your house," said the sergeant.

"Ma foi! that is a good joke! I conceal prisoners indeed!" exclaimed the dame, laughing. "Pray who are these notable prisoners?"

"That's for you to say. We only know that you have prisoners," answered the sergeant.

"Then, if you will have it so, one may possibly be a general, and the other an admiral, and the sooner they are lodged in the Bastille, the better for the safety of France," answered the dame, laughing. "I am a loyal Frenchwoman, and can cry 'Vive le Roi!' 'Vive la France!' with all my heart."

Jack and Bill, who had quaked at the thoughts of being made prisoners by the soldiers, now began to have better hope of escaping.

The sergeant, however, was not to be deceived by Dame Turgot's manner.

"Come, come, I must search your house, notwithstanding. For that purpose I was sent, and I must perform my duty," he said; and he hunted round the room.

"Now let us look into your room;" and the soldiers, entering, began poking about with their bayonets, running them under the bed, and through the bedding, in a way likely to kill anybody concealed.

Jeannette's little room was visited and treated in the same manner.

"And what's this room?" asked the sergeant, pointing to the boys' room.

"That? That is a closet," answered the dame; "or if you like it, the general and admiral are both there fast asleep, but I am unwilling to disturb them."

She said this in a laughing tone, as if she were joking.

"Well, open the door," said the sergeant, not expecting to find anybody.

"But I tell you the door is locked. Who has got the key, I wonder?" said the dame.

"Come, come, unlock the door, or we must force it open," said the sergeant, making as if he was about to prise it open with his bayonet.

On this the dame pulled the key out of her pocket, and opening the door, exclaimed—

"There in one bed you will find the general, and in the other the admiral; or, without joking, they are two poor boys whom my good man picked up at sea, and already they are more French than English."

The sergeant, looking into the beds, discovered the boys.

"Come, get up, mes garçons," he said; "you must come with me, whoever you are, and give an account of yourselves."

Neither of the boys made any reply, deeming it wiser to keep silence.

"Come along," he said; and he dragged first one, and then the other, out of bed.

"Bring the boys' clothes," he added, turning to the dame, who quickly brought their original suits.

They soon dressed themselves, hanging their knives round their necks.

"I told you the truth. You see who and what they are!" exclaimed the dame.

Jeannette, too, pleaded eloquently on their behalf, but the sergeant was unmoved.

"All you say may be right, but I must take them," he answered. "Come—quick march!"

He allowed them, however, to take an affectionate farewell of the dame and Jeannette, the latter bursting into tears as she saw them dragged off by the soldiers.

Chapter Seven.

Shut up in a tower.

Jack and Bill marched along in the middle of the party of soldiers, endeavouring, as well as they could, to keep up their spirits, and to appear unconcerned. Where they were going they could not tell.

"Jack," whispered Bill, "don't let these fellows know that we understand French. We may learn something from what they say to each other; and they are not likely to tell us the truth, if we were to ask them questions."

"Trust me for that," answered Jack. "One might suppose, from the way they treat us, that they take us for desperate fellows, who would make nothing of knocking them down right and left, if it were not for their muskets and bayonets."

"All right," responded Bill; "we'll keep our wits awake, and maybe we shall find an opportunity of getting away."

"I am ready for anything you propose," said Jack. "We might have found it more easy to make our escape if Madame Turgot had brought us back our French toggery; but still, for my part, I feel more comfortable-like in my own clothes."

"So do I," said Bill. "Somehow I fancy that I am more up to work dressed as an English sailor than I should be as a French boy. I only hope our friends will not get into any scrape for having concealed us. They are wonderfully kind people, and I shall always be ready to do a good turn to a Frenchman for their sakes."

"So shall I after I've thrashed him," said Jack. "If the French will go to war with us, they must take the consequences."

The soldiers did not interfere with the lads, but allowed them to talk on to each other as much as they liked. The road they followed led them to the eastward, as far as they could judge, at no great distance from the shore.

After marching about a couple of miles, they reached a small town, or village rather, the houses being scattered along the shores of another bay much larger than the one they had left. A river of some size ran into the bay, and on a point of land near the mouth, on a height, stood an old tower, which had been built, apparently, for the purpose of guarding the entrance.

It was in a somewhat dilapidated condition, and seemed now very unfit for its original object, for a few round shot would have speedily knocked it to pieces. It might, however, afford shelter to a small body of infantry, who could fire from the loopholes in its walls down on any boats, attempting to ascend the river.

"I wonder if they are going to shut us up there!" said Jack, as the sergeant led the party in the direction of the tower.

"No doubt about it," replied Bill; "but it doesn't seem to be a very terrible place; and, by the look of the walls, I have a notion that I could climb to the top, or make my way down them, without the slightest difficulty."

They had time to make their observations before they reached the entrance gate.

A small guard of soldiers were stationed in the tower, to whose charge the prisoners were handed over.

The officer commanding the party was a gruff old fellow, who seemed to have no feeling of compassion for his young prisoners.

After putting various questions to the sergeant who had brought them, he made signs to them to accompany him to the top of the building, and led the way, attended by two soldiers who followed close behind, up a flight of exceedingly rickety stairs, which creaked and groaned as they ascended.

On reaching the top the officer opened a door, which led into a small room, the highest apparently in the building; he then signed to the boys to go in, and without saying a word closed the door and locked it. They soon afterwards heard him and his men descending the stairs.

"Here we are," said Jack. "I wonder what's going to happen next!"

"Why, if they leave us here long enough, the next thing that will happen will be that we'll make our way out again," replied Bill. "Look at those windows! Though they are not very big, they are large enough for us to squeeze through, or it may be more convenient to make our way out by the roof. I can see daylight through one or two places, which shows that the tiles are not very securely fastened on."

"And if we do get out, where shall we go?" asked Jack.

"It won't do to return to the Turgots; we might be getting them into trouble. We must make our way down to the sea shore, and then travel on till we can reach some port or other, and when there try to get on board a smuggling lugger, as Captain Turgot at first proposed we should do," replied Bill.

"It may be a hard job to do that," said Jack; "and I should say it would be easier to run off with a boat or some small craft which we two could handle, and make our way in her across Channel. I know where to find the polar star. I have often been out at night when father steered by it, and we should be sure, some time or other, to make the English coast."

"I should not like to run away with a poor man's vessel. What would he say in the morning when he found his craft gone?" observed Bill. "It would be taking what is not ours to take. I never did and never would do that."

Jack argued the point.

"The French are enemies of the English," he said, "and therefore Englishmen have a perfect right to best them either afloat or on shore."

Bill said he would consider the subject, and in the meantime they made a further survey of their prison. It could not be called luxuriantly furnished, considering that there was only a bench of no great width running along the side of one of the walls, and the remains of a table. One of the legs had gone, and part of the top, and it was propped up by a couple of empty casks.

There were neither bedsteads nor bedding of any description, but the bench was of sufficient length to allow both the boys to lie down on it.

The sun was on the point of setting when they reached the tower, and darkness soon stole on them.

"I wonder whether they intend to give us any supper," said Jack, "or do they expect us to live on air?"

"I can hold out till to-morrow morning, but I should be thankful if they would bring us up something to-night; and we should be the better able to make our escape, if we have the opportunity," observed Bill.

"Then I propose that we make a tremendous row, and that will bring some one up to sea what's the matter. We can then point to our mouths to show that we are hungry, and perhaps they will take compassion on us," said Jack.

Bill agreeing to Jack's proposal, they began jumping and stamping about the room, and singing at the top of their voices, in a way which could scarcely fail to be heard by the men in the guard-room below.

They were in a short time convinced that their proceedings had produced the desired effect; for when they ceased to make the noise, they heard the heavy step of a man ascending the creaking stairs. It had not occurred to them that he might possibly come with a thick stick in his hand, to thrash them for making a row. The idea, however, flashed across Jack's mind by the time the man was half-way up.

"We may get more kicks than ha'pence for what we've been doing," he observed; "however, it cannot be helped; we must put a good face on the matter, and let him fancy that it is the way English boys have of showing when they are hungry. If he does not make out what we mean, we'll say, 'manger, manger,' and he'll then know what we want."

Bill laughed. He was not much afraid of a beating. He reminded Jack that he must not say anything more than he proposed, or the Frenchmen might find out that they understood their language.

The man came slowly up the steps, which creaked and groaned louder and louder.

"I'll tell you what," said Bill. "If those steps are as rotten as they appear to be, we might pull some of them up, and so prevent the guard from reaching this room, and finding out that we have made our escape."

"We should have to get the door open first," observed Jack, "and that would be no easy matter."

"More easy than you may suppose," said Bill. "I'll try and shove something into the catch of the lock while the Frenchman is in the room."

Just then the door opened, and a soldier entered, with a lantern in one hand, and, as Jack expected, a stick in the other. It was not, however, a very thick one, and Jack thought, as he eyed it, that its blows, though they might hurt, would not break any bones; however, neither he nor Bill had any intention of being thrashed if they could help it.

The soldier began at once to inquire, in an angry tone, why they had made so much noise.

They pretended not to understand him; but as he lifted his stick to strike at them, they ran round the room, Jack shouting "Manger! manger!" and pointing to his mouth.

He could easily manage to keep out of the Frenchman's reach, but at last he allowed himself to be caught for a minute at the farther end of the room, thus giving Bill time to reach the door.

Bill made good use of the opportunity, while the Frenchman's back was turned, to carry out his intention.

"All right," he cried out; and as soon as Jack heard him, he skipped out of the Frenchman's way, as he had no wish to receive more blows than he could avoid. The soldier, on seeing Bill, attacked him next, but he easily evaded most of the blows aimed at him, till the soldier grew weary of the chase.

"Manger! manger!" cried both the boys at once, in various tones, sometimes imploring, at others expostulating, and then as if they were excited by anger and indignation that they should be so treated.

The soldier understood them clearly enough, and probably thought to himself that unless he could bring some food to keep the young prisoners quiet, he might have frequent trips to make to the top of the tower.

"Ma foi! I suppose that you have had nothing to eat for some hours," he observed, in French. "I'll see what I can get for you; but remember, you must be quiet, or you will be left to starve."

They were well pleased to hear this; but still pretending not to understand him, they continued crying out, "Manger! manger!"

At last the soldier took his departure, locking the door, as he supposed, behind him.

As soon as they knew, by the sounds he made descending the steps, that he had got some distance down, the boys ran to the door, and, to their satisfaction, found that they could easily open it, though it appeared to be securely locked.

From the remarks the Frenchman had made, they had some hopes that he would bring them food; they therefore lay down on the bench to await his return.

Greatly to their satisfaction, in a short time they again heard a step on the stair, and the soldier who had before paid them a visit entered, carrying a basket with some bread and cheese, dried figs, and some wine in a bottle. He also brought up a piece of candle, and a lump of wood with a spike in it, which served as a candlestick.

He placed these on the table with the contents of the basket.

"There," he said, "eat away; you may have a long march to-morrow, and if you haven't strength we may have to carry you."

The boys pretended not to understand him; but both exclaimed, as they saw the viands, "Merci! merci!" and put out their hands to shake that of the soldier, who seemed, while performing a kind action, to be in much better humour than before.

"Mangez! mes braves garçons," he remarked. "What is over you can have for breakfast to-morrow morning, as maybe you'll get nothing else brought you."

"Merci! merci!" answered Jack and Bill, as they escorted the soldier to the door, letting him suppose that these were the only two words they understood.

As soon as he had turned the key in the door, they hurried to the table, and eagerly devoured some of the bread and cheese.

"It's fortunate we've got so large a stock of food," said Bill; "there's enough here, if we are careful of it, for a couple of days."

There was in the bottle but a small allowance of wine, which was excessively sour; but it served to quench their thirst, though they agreed that they would much rather have had fresh water.

Having finished their supper, they divided the remainder of the food into two portions, which they stowed away in their pockets. They then waited till they had reason to suppose, from hearing no noise ascending the stairs, that the soldiers in the guard-room had gone to sleep.

Having cautiously opened the door, they next examined the steps, and found that they could wrench up those of the upper part of the flight without making much noise. They had to be quick about it, as their candle would soon burn out.

First, having closed the door, they got up seven of the steps, beginning at the uppermost one, till they formed a gap which it would be impossible for a man to spring over. The boards they carried down as they descended, when they found themselves in another storey, the whole of which was occupied by one large room without doors, the reason, of course, why it had not been made their prison.

Their candle had now nearly burned out. Having hung their shoes round their necks, they were able to step softly. Hunting about, they discovered an empty space under the stairs, in which they stowed the pieces of wood.

"Perhaps we might get down by the stairs," whispered Jack.

"The chances are that we should find a door to stop us at the bottom," returned Bill. "We must try to get down the outside. The walls are so full of holes that we might manage it, and I am ready to go first and try."

The question was, on which side should they attempt to make their descent? On looking through the narrow windows, they observed a gleam of light coming out below them on one side; probably that was from the guard-room, and they accordingly fixed on the opposite side, where all was dark. They ran no little chance of breaking their necks, but about that they did not trouble themselves. If a cat could get up, they believed that they could get down, by clinging with toes and fingers, and teeth, if necessary, to the wall.

They, however, made the fullest examination in their power to ascertain the best spot for their descent; they looked out of every window in succession, but at last arrived at the conclusion that the attempt to scramble down a perpendicular wall was too hazardous to be made. They now began to fear that their enterprise must be abandoned, and that they should be compelled to make their way first to a lower storey, which, for what they could tell, might be inhabited; or else that they must descend the creaking stairs, and run a still greater chance of being discovered.

"Here's another window," said Bill; "let's look through that."

He climbed up to it, and gazed out. Great was his satisfaction to perceive the top of a massive wall a few feet below him. The tower had been a portion of an old castle, and the end of this wall was a mass of ruins, but quite thick enough to enable them to scramble along the top of it, and Bill had no doubt that they thence could easily descend to, the level ground.

Chapter Eight.

The escape—Concealed in a cavern.

Bill drew his head in from the window, and beckoned to Jack, who followed him up; and as there was no time to be lost, he at once dropped down on to the top of the wall. Jack came next, fortunately without dislodging any stones, which might have rattled down and betrayed their proceedings. Bill leading, they made their way on hands and knees along the top of the wall, which, being fringed in most places with bushes, contributed to conceal them from any passers-by. They had to move cautiously for the reason before given, and also to avoid the risk of falling down any gap in the wall which time might have produced.

As Bill had expected, the further end of the wall was broken gradually away, forming an easy descent. Down this they climbed, feeling their way with their feet, and not letting go of one mass of ruin till they had found a foothold on a lower. Thus they at length had the satisfaction of standing on the firm ground outside the walls.

They had now to consider in which direction they should direct their flight.

The river was on one side of them, and though they might swim across they would run the risk of being discovered while so doing. They finally decided to make for the sea shore, to the westward of the bay, and to lie hid among the rocks till the search for them should be given up.

They accordingly stole round the building, keeping on the side away from the guard-room, till they got into a lane which led at the back of the village down towards the shore. If they could once get there they hoped to be safe.

Few lights in the village were burning, as the inhabitants retired early to bed; but two or three still twinkled from some cottages at the farther end. Possibly the owners had gone out fishing, and had only lately returned.

They had got some distance from the tower, and no cottage was near, when Jack stopped.

"I've been thinking that we might get on board one of the fishing-boats, which have just come in, and go off in her," he whispered.

"I could not do it," said Bill. "I have said before—what would the poor fishermen think in the morning when they found their boat gone, the only means they may have of supporting their wives and families?"

Jack did not agree with Bill in this, but it was not a time to argue the point, so they set off again, and continued running till they reached a gap in the cliff, down which the road led. They then made their way to the left, under the cliffs, in the direction of the village where they had so long resided.

The tide was out, and they wisely kept close down to the water, so that the returning sea might obliterate their footsteps.

Jack proposed returning to Captain Turgot's, but Bill observed that that would not be fair to their friends, who would, of course, be exposed to great danger by again harbouring them, and who yet would not like to deliver them up.

"No, no, we must not do that," he said. "The sooner we can find a place to hide in the better. The cliff hereabouts appears to be broken, and full of hollows, and perhaps, if we search for it, we shall discover some spot fit for our purpose."

While they were talking the moon rose; and, though on the decrease, afforded a good deal of light, and greatly assisted them in their search.

The sea where they were would, they saw, at high tide, completely cover the whole beach, so they must take care to find a place beyond its reach.

They anxiously searched about. The night was drawing on, and they must find concealment before daylight, which would expose them to the view of any boats passing near the beach, or to people looking for them from the cliffs above.

They climbed up at several places without discovering any hollow sufficiently deep to conceal them effectually; still they persevered, and at last they reached a black rock which projected out from the cliff, and ran some way down the beach. From its appearance they saw that it must be covered at high-water. They made their way round it, as the sides were too smooth to climb over, and then once more reached the foot of the cliff.

The tide was now rising rapidly, and they saw that they would be exposed to the danger of being caught by the sea, could they not get some distance up the cliff. They were hurrying on when Bill exclaimed —

"There's a cave, and it may perhaps run some way back in the cliff. We shall soon find out by the feel of the rock whether the water fills it up, and if not, we couldn't have a better hiding-place."

They climbed up the slippery rock, and found themselves in a cavern with a low arched entrance. This looked promising. They groped their way onwards. As they advanced, their ears caught the gentle sound of a tiny streamlet, which issued from the rock, while the ground beneath their feet was perfectly dry, consisting in some places of hard rock, in others of soft, warm sand.

Looking back, they could distinguish the ocean, with the moonlight shining on it.

"We shall be safe here, I think," said Bill. "When daylight comes, we shall be able to find our way farther in, and perhaps discover some nook in which we may remain hidden, even were people to come to the mouth of the cave to look for us."

Jack agreed that there was no risk of the tide rising to the place where they then were, so they sat down on the dry sand, and being tired from their exertions, very soon fell fast asleep.

Jack was not much addicted to dreaming. When he went to sleep he did so in right earnest, and might have slept through a general engagement, if he had not been called to take a part in it.

Bill had a more imaginative mind, which was seldom altogether at rest. He fancied sometimes that he was escaping from the top of the tower, and tumbling head over heels to the bottom; at others that he was running along, with the Frenchmen shouting after him to stop. Then he fancied that one with a long pair of legs had overtaken him, and was grasping him tightly by the arm.

He awoke with a start, and found that Jack was trying to arouse him. Daylight was streaming through the mouth of the cavern; beyond could be seen the blue sea shining brightly in the rays of the sun, with a chasse-marée, or some other small vessel, gliding swiftly across it, impelled by a smart breeze off shore.

Jack had taken it into his head that the people on board might see them.

"I don't think there's much chance of that," said Bill. "Even if they happen to turn their glasses this way, depend on it, if we sit quiet, they'll not discover us."

The vessel soon disappeared, and they then looked about to examine more carefully the cavern in which they had taken refuge.

The tide was still at its highest, and the water washed up to the ledge in front of the cavern. The ground rose considerably above that point to where they sat, and on looking round they saw that it continued to rise behind them for some distance.

Bill advised that they should at once explore it, observing that though, even at spring-tide, with the wind off shore, the water might not reach to where they sat; yet should a gale blow from the northward, it might drive the waves far up the cavern, and expose them to great danger.

"We cannot tell what may happen," he said, "and it's as well to be prepared for the worst. Besides, if the soldiers come to look for us, they may find the mouth of the cavern, and make their way some distance in, but if they do not discover us they'll fancy we are not here, and go away again as wise as they came."

Jack saw the wisdom of this proposal. They accordingly groped their way on, aided by the light, which, though dim, pervaded the part of the cavern they had reached. Every now and then they stopped, and, on looking back, could still see the entrance, with the bright sea beyond it.

At length they came to a rock, which seemed to stop their further progress; but, feeling about them, found that the cavern made a turn here to the left. They now proceeded with the greatest caution, for fear of coming to some hole down which they might fall.

"If we had a torch we might see what sort of a place we have got to," observed Jack.

"But we haven't got a torch, and no chance of getting one; and so we must find out by making good use of our hands," answered Bill. "We must move slowly on, and feel every inch of the way, putting out one hand before we lift up the other."

They were groping forward on their hands and knees, and were in total darkness; still, as they looked back, there was a faint glimmer of light, which appeared round the corner of the rock, and this would enable them to find their way back again. Hitherto they had met only with smooth rock, gently inclining upwards; possibly it might lead them, if they went on long enough, to the top of the cliff, though they hoped that there was no opening in that direction.

Here, at all events, they thought that they should be secure, even should their pursuers enter the cavern.

As they were getting hungry, they agreed to go back and eat their breakfast in daylight near the spring, which would afford them a draught of cool water. They returned as they had come, feeling their way along the rock.

Just before they reached the turning in the cavern, they discovered a recess which would hold both of them; and they agreed to make it their hiding-place should the soldiers by any chance come to look for them.

Without much difficulty they got back to the spot where they had slept, which was close to the stream. Here they sat down, and produced the provisions which they had brought from the tower. On examining their stock, they calculated that they had sufficient to last them for a couple of days.

"When that's gone, what shall we do?" asked Jack.

"We must try to pick up some shell-fish from the rocks," answered Bill. "The soldiers by that time will have got tired of looking for us, and if any persons from the top of the cliffs see us they won't know who we are, and will fancy we are fisher-boys getting bait. Perhaps before that time a smuggling lugger may come off here, and we may manage to hail her before we run short of food; at all events, there's no use being frightened about what may happen."

Every now and then one or the other went towards the mouth of the cave to look out. As long as the tide remained high there was no danger of their being discovered; but at low water the French soldiers were very likely to come along the sands, and could scarcely fail to see the mouth of the cavern.

The tide was now rapidly going down, black rocks appearing one by one above the surface.

They accordingly determined to retire to the inner part of the cavern, and to wait there till they calculated that the tide would once more have come in.

"We must make up our minds to enjoy six hours of daylight, and to endure six of darkness," observed Bill.

"I sha'n't care much about that; we can but go to sleep and amuse ourselves the best way we can think of while the tide is in," said Jack.

"If we had some hooks and lines we might fish," said Bill.

"We should only catch rock fish, and they are not fit to eat," replied Jack.

The boys carried out their plan. It was an easy matter to get through the sleeping-time, but they became somewhat weary from having nothing to do during the period that the tide was in. They could do little more, indeed, than sit looking at the sea, and watching the few vessels which appeared in the offing. Now and then they got up and walked about to stretch their legs. They were afraid of bathing, lest while swimming about they might be seen from any part of the cliff above.

Whether the soldiers had come to look for them they could not tell; one thing was certain, they had not been discovered, and there were no signs of any persons having approached the mouth of the cavern.

They husbanded their food, but it was rapidly diminishing. At night they therefore, when the tide had gone out, crept down on the sands, and managed to cut off some limpets and other shell-fish with their knives from the rocks. These would have sustained them for some days had they been able to cook them, but they had no means of lighting a fire. Though limpets may help to keep body and soul together for a short time, they are not wholesome food, especially when raw. Their bread was all gone, but as long as they had some figs and cheese they got down the limpets very well; but both figs and cheese came to an end, and they both felt that they were getting very weak.

"If we don't take care we shall starve," said Bill.

"We must do something or other. I don't see anything but trying to get on board a lugger, as we talked of; but then in searching for her we should run the chance of being made prisoners again."

"You must come round to my plan, and run off with a boat of some sort," said Jack.

"That's just what I cannot do," said Bill

"It's either that or starving," said Jack.

"We should have to get food first, even if we did run off with a boat," observed Bill. "It would never do to put to sea without something to eat. I'll tell you what I'll do. I'll try and make my way back to Captain Turgot's. It cannot be far from this. I'll ask them to give us some food. They are sure to do that, though they might not like hiding us; and perhaps they might tell us of some boat in which we could get off without the owner being the worse for the loss. If you'll stay here, I'll go this very evening as soon as the tide is out. I calculate that I should have time to get there and back before the flood is up; and I'm not afraid of being refused, at all events." Jack wanted to go too; but Bill urged that one was less likely to be discovered than two, and that it would be better for him to go alone. Jack at last agreed to this, and directly the sand appeared below the mouth of the cavern, Bill set out.

Chapter Nine.

Visit to Captain Turgot's cottage.

As it was growing dusk, Bill had no fear of being seen as he made his way from the cavern. He felt rather weak, but he had a brave heart, and pushed on. He had some rough rocks to climb over, and others he managed to get round, walking through the water where it was not too deep. Sooner than he expected he reached the bay near which the Turgots' cottage was situated. To avoid the other cottages and huts he had to make a wide circuit.

He cautiously crept up towards the back of his friends' dwelling; then, keeping close to the wall, he looked in through the window of the room in which the family generally sat.

Jeannette was alone, spinning as usual, but looking somewhat pensive.

Bill tapped at the window, and Jeannette looked up.

"May I come in?" he asked in French.

Jeannette came to the window.

"Who are you?" she inquired.

"What! don't you know me?" said Bill.

"Ah! one of the young Englishmen!" she exclaimed; and she opened the window.

Bill jumped in.

"I am so happy to see you!" she cried. "Where have you come from? And your friend Jack, where is he? Have you both escaped from the soldiers? We thought you were in prison long ago;" and Jeannette put so many questions that Bill had great difficulty in answering them. He, however, soon contrived to let her know all that had happened, and then inquired for her father and mother and brother.

"Mother is in bed, quite ill," she said; "she was so frightened by the soldiers, expecting to be carried off to prison, that she has not got over it. My father and Pierre are out fishing. I expect them home before midnight, but they said that they should be out later than usual."

"I should like to stop and see them," said Bill; "but in the meantime, can you give me something to eat? I am nearly starved."

"Of course," cried Jeannette; and she quickly placed some food before Bill, which he as quickly attacked.

"Well, you are hungry!" she observed, "but eat away. I wish I had known before how near you were to us, and I would have brought you provisions."

"Can you bring them to us now?" asked Bill. "If we do not manage to get off, we shall soon be hungry again."

"Of course I will," she answered; "but it would not be safe for me to bring them all the way to the cave. I know, however, a place much nearer this where I could hide them, and you can come and fetch them."

"But how am I to know the place?" asked Bill.

"I will describe it to you," answered Jeannette. "You remarked, as you came along, a break in the cliff, with a stream running down the bottom. On the right side of the stream, about ten feet from high-water mark, there is a small hollow just large enough for one person to creep in. I took shelter there once when I was a little girl, having been caught in a storm as I was rambling along the sands so I remember it well."

Bill thought he could find the place, and would look for it as he went back. Jeannette promised to bring a basket every other day, directly the morning tide went down, so that Bill would know exactly when to go and fetch the food. He thanked her very much, and promised to follow her directions.

He then asked her about a boat, but she could say nothing till her father and Pierre returned. They might know of one, but as there was very small chance of her ever being restored to her owner, while the boys were not likely to have the means of paying for her, she was doubtful.

"As to that," said Bill, "we shall have plenty of prize-money. I hope to pay for her over and over again; and I will promise most faithfully to do so."

Jeannette smiled, for she thought that there was very little probability of the two young ship-boys ever getting prize-money sufficient to pay for such a boat as they required, to make a voyage across the Channel.

Bill was anxious to get back to poor Jack, who he remembered was well-nigh starving. Jeannette would have accompanied him part of the way, but she had to remain at home to receive Captain Turgot and Pierre. She had, in the meantime, packed a basket with provisions for Jack and himself, that they might be independent for a couple of days. He therefore jumped up, and, begging her to remember him very kindly to the others, he bade her farewell, and, with the basket on his arm, slipped out of the house as cautiously as he had entered.

He had noted every object as he came along, so that he had no difficulty in making his way back. He also easily discovered the small cave described by Jeannette. It was at a convenient distance from the large cavern, and, as a path led near it, should Jeannette be perceived, it might be supposed that she was making her way to the top of the cliff.

Bill did not stop longer than was necessary to examine the place to be certain of being able to find it again, as he knew that Jack would be anxiously waiting for him. He hurried on, therefore, and in a short time reached the beach below the cavern. Climbing up, he called out, "All right, Jack!" But Jack did not answer. He called again, but still there was no reply, and he began to feel very anxious.

Had the soldiers been there and carried off his companion? or had Jack died of starvation?

Jeannette had thoughtfully put a tinder-box, flint and steel, and a couple of candles into the basket. After feeling his way on for some distance, he stopped and lighted one of the candles.

The faint light gave the cavern a wild, strange appearance, so that he could scarcely have known where he was. He looked round on every side, but could nowhere see Jack; he became more and more alarmed; still he did not give up all hope of finding him.

Again and again he called out "Jack!"

At length a faint voice came from the interior. He hurried on. There lay Jack on the ground.

"Is that you, Bill?" he asked, in a low voice. "I was afraid you were caught. I fancied I heard voices, and crept away, intending to get into our hiding-place, when I fell down, and I suppose I must have gone to sleep, for I remember nothing more till I heard you calling to me. Have you brought any food?"

"Yes," said Bill; "sit up and eat as much as you can; it will do you good, and you will soon be all to rights."

Jack did not require a second invitation, but munched away at the bread and cheese, and dried fish and figs, with right good will, showing that he could not have been so very ill after all. He quickly regained his strength and spirits, and listened eagerly to what Bill had to tell him.

"Well, it's a comfort to think that we are not likely to be starved," he observed; "and I will bless Miss Jeannette as long as I live. I wish we could do something to show her how much obliged we are. And now, Bill, what about the boat? Is there a chance of our getting one?"

"A very poor chance at present, I am afraid," answered Bill. "Jeannette, however, will let us know if her father and brother can find one to suit our purpose, or if a smuggling lugger comes into the harbour."

"We'll have, after all, to do as I proposed, and take one without asking the owner's leave," said Jack. "I tell you it will be perfectly fair. The French are at war with us, and we have a right to take any of their property we can find, whether afloat or on shore."

"That may be, but I can't get it out of my head that we shall be robbing some poor fellow who may have to depend on his boat for supporting himself and his family," answered Bill.

They argued the point as before, till Bill proposed that they should lie down and go to sleep, as he felt tired after his long walk.

They allowed two days to pass, when Bill set off as agreed on to obtain the provisions he hoped Jeannette would have brought.

She had not deceived him; there was an ample supply, and two or three more candles.

Several more days passed by. Jeannette regularly brought them provisions, but she left no note to tell them of any arrangements which her father had made. They were becoming very weary of their life, for they had nothing whatever to do—no books to read, and not even a stick to whittle.

The weather had hitherto been fine, the cavern was warm and comfortable, and the dry sand afforded them soft beds. They might certainly have been very much worse off.

Bill always went to fetch the food from the cave where Jeannette left it. He had hitherto not met her, which he was anxious to do, to learn what chance there was of obtaining a boat. She, however, was always before him, the fact being that the path from her house to the cave was practicable before that from the large cavern was open.

"I don't quite like the look of the weather," observed Bill one day to Jack, just before the time Jeannette was due at the little cave, and all their provisions were expended. "If it comes on very bad she may be stopped, and we shall be pressed. I'll slip down the moment the water is shallow enough, and try to get along the shore; and if she has not reached the cave, I'll go on and meet her."

Bill at once put his resolution into practice. He did not mind wetting his feet; but he had here and there a hard job to save himself from being carried off by the sea, which rolled up the beach to the very foot of the cliff. Twice he had to cling to a rock, and frequently to wade for some distance, till he began to regret that he had ventured so soon; but having made up his mind to do a thing, he was not to be defeated by the fear of danger; so waiting till the wave had receded, he rushed on to another rock. The sky had become overcast. The leaden seas, foam-crested, came rolling in with increasing force, and had not the tide been on the ebb his position would have been perilous in the extreme.

He knew, however, that every minute would make his progress less difficult; so with a brave heart he pushed on. At last he reached the little cave by the side of the gorge. It was empty! He knew, therefore, that Jeannette had not been there.

According to his previous determination, he went on to meet her, hoping that before this she might have set out.

The rain now began to fall, and the wind blew with fitful gusts. He did not care for either himself, but he was sorry that Jeannette should be exposed to the storm. He felt nearly sure that she would come, in spite of it. If not, he made up his mind to wait till dark, and then to go on to her cottage. There was no great risk in doing so, as the soldiers would long before this have given up their search for him and Jack.

He had gone some distance, and the fishing village would soon be in sight, when he saw a figure coming towards him, wrapped in a cloak. Hoping that it was Jeannette, he hurried forward to meet her. He was not mistaken.

Bill told her that he had come on that she might be saved from a longer exposure to the rain than was necessary.

"Thank you," she answered. "I was delayed, or I should have set off earlier, but a party of soldiers came to the village pretending that they wanted to buy fish. I, however, suspected that they came to look for you, and I waited till they had gone away again. We sold them all the fish they asked for, and put on an unconcerned look, as if suspecting nothing, I saw them, however, prying about, and I recognised one of them as the sergeant who came in command of the party which carried you off. I am not at all certain, either, that they will not return, and I should not have ventured out, had I not known that you must be greatly in want of food, and that, perhaps, should the storm which is now beginning increase, many days might pass before I could supply you."

The information given by Jeannette made Bill very glad that he had come on to meet her. He, of course, thanked her warmly, and then asked what chance there was of obtaining a boat.

"My father wishes you well, but is afraid to interfere in the matter," she answered. "He does not, perhaps, enter into your feelings about getting back to England, because he thinks France the best country of the two, and sees no reason why you should not become Frenchmen. As the detachment of soldiers quartered in the neighbourhood will soon, probably, be removed, you may then come back without fear, and resume the clothes you before wore, and live with us, and help my father and brother; then who knows what may happen? You will not have to fight your own countrymen, and the war may some day come to an end, or perhaps the French may conquer the English, and then we shall all be very good friends again."

"Never! Jeannette; that will never happen," exclaimed Bill. "You are very kind to us, and we are very fond of you, and would do anything to serve you, and show our gratitude, but don't say that again."

Jeannette laughed. "Dear me, how fiery you are!" she exclaimed. "However, it's foolish to stop talking here, and I ought to hurry home, in case the soldiers should pay us another visit and suspect something. Do not be angry, my dear Bill. I did not wish to offend you; only, you know, we each think our own country the best."

Bill assured Jeannette that he was not angry, and again thanked her very much, though he could not help saying that he was sorry her father would not obtain the boat for them.

"Well, well, you must have patience," she answered. "Now go back to your cave as fast as you can, or you will be wet to the skin."

"I am that already," answered Bill, laughing; "but it's a trifle to which I am well accustomed."

Once more they shook hands, and exchanging baskets. Jeannette, drawing her cloak around her, hurried back to the village, while Bill made the best of his way to the cavern.

He was now able, in spite of the wind, to get along where he had before found it difficult to pass. In one or two places only did the waves rolling up wash round his feet, but the water was not of sufficient depth to carry him off, and he gained the mouth of the cavern in safety. Jack was eagerly looking out for him, and both of them being very sharp set, they lost no time in discussing some of the contents of the basket.

As they looked out they saw that the wind had greatly increased. A heavy north-westerly gale was blowing. It rushed into the cavern filled with spray from off the now distant foam-tipped waves. What it would do when the tide was again high was a matter of serious consideration.

"We shall have to go as far back as we can," observed Bill, "and the sooner we pick out a safe berth the better. I should like, too, to get my wet clothes off, for the wind makes me feel very cold."

Jack was of the same opinion, and he taking up the basket, they groped their way to the inner cave round the rock, where it turned, as before described, to the left. Here they were completely sheltered from the wind, and had it not been for the loud roar of the waves beating on the shore, and the howling of the gale in the outer cavern, they would not have been aware that a storm was raging outside.

They had, it should have been said, collected a quantity of drift wood, which Jack had thoughtfully employed himself in carrying to the spot where they were now seated. As they could not possibly run any risk of being detected, they agreed to light a fire, which they had hitherto avoided doing.

They soon had a cheerful one blazing up, and it made them feel much more comfortable. Bill was able to dry his wet clothes, and by its light they could now take a better survey of their abode than they had hitherto done.

The cavern was here not more than eight or ten feet in height, but it was nearly thirty broad, and penetrated, so it seemed to them, far away into the interior of the cliff.

"I vote we have a look and see where the cave leads to," said Bill, taking up a long piece of fir-wood which burnt like a torch.

Jack provided himself with another of a similar character, and, by waving them about, they found that they could keep them alight. They also took one of their candles and their match-box in case their torches should go out.

Having raked their fire together, so that it might serve as a beacon to assist them in their return, they set out.

The ground rose as they had before supposed when they explored it in the dark, but the roof continued of the same height above it.

Suddenly Jack started.

"What is that?" he exclaimed, seizing his companion's arm. "There's a man! or is it a ghost? Oh Bill!"

Chapter Ten.

Discovery of the smugglers' treasure.

Bill waved his torch on one side and peered forward. "It looks like a man, but it doesn't move. It's only a figure, Jack," he answered. "I'm not afraid of it. Come on! we'll soon see what it is."

Jack was ashamed of lagging behind, and accompanied him.

The object which had frightened Jack was soon discovered to be merely a stalactite—a mass of hardened water. Similar formations now appeared on both sides of the cavern, some hanging from the roof, others in the form of pillars and arches; indeed, the whole cavern looked like the interior of a Gothic building in ruins.

Other figures still more strange were seen, as if starting out from recesses or doorways on both sides.

"Well! this is a strange place. I never saw or heard of anything like it," exclaimed Jack, when he found how harmless all the ghosts really were.

In many places the roof and sides shone and glittered as if covered with precious stones. Even Bill began to fancy that they had got into some enchanted cavern. The ground was covered in most places with the same substance, and so rough that they could make but slow progress.

They were about to turn back for fear of their torches going out when they reached a low archway. Curiosity prompted them to enter, which they could do by stooping down. After going a short distance they found themselves in a still larger cavern, almost circular, like a vast hall, the roof and sides ornamented by nature in the same curious fashion, though still more profusely.

"It won't do to stop here," said Bill, "but we'll come back again and have another look at it with fresh torches. Hallo! what's that?"

Jack started as he had before done, as if he were not altogether comfortable in his mind. He had never heard anything about enchanted caverns, but a strange dread had seized him. He had an idea that the place must be the abode of ghosts or spirits of some sort, and that Bill had seen one.

Bill hurrying forward, the light of his torch fell on a pile composed of bales and chests, and casks, and various other articles.

The place had evidently been used as a store-room by persons who must have considered that it was not likely to be discovered.

As their torches were by this time nearly burnt out, they could not venture to stop and examine the goods, but had to hurry back as fast as they could. They had managed to get through the narrow passage, and had made some progress in their return, when both of them were obliged to let their torches drop, as they could no longer hold them without burning their hands. They might have lighted their candles, had they been in any difficulty, but their fire enabled them to find their way along, though they stumbled frequently over the inequalities of the ground, and once or twice Jack clutched Bill's arm, exclaiming, "Sure! there's some one! I saw him move! Can any of the soldiers have come to look for us?"

"Not with such a storm as there is now raging outside," answered Bill. "It was only one of the marble figures."

Presently Jack again cried out, "There! I saw another moving. I'm sure of it this time. It's a ghost if it isn't a man."

"Well! if it is a ghost it won't hurt us," answered Bill; "but the only ghosts hereabouts are those curious figures, which can't move from their places. For my part, I don't believe there are such things as ghosts at all going about to frighten people. The only one I ever heard tell of was 'The Cock Lane Ghost', and that was found out to be a sham long ago."

Jack regained his courage as they approached the fire, and both being pretty well tired, they were glad to sit down and talk about the wonderful store of goods they had discovered. Jack was afraid that the owners might come back to look for their property and discover them, but Bill was of opinion that they had been placed there by a party of smugglers, who had gone away and been lost without telling any one where they had stowed their goods.

From the appearance of the bales and chests he thought that they had been there for some time. Another visit would enable them to ascertain this, and they resolved to make it without delay.

They were becoming very sleepy, for they had been many hours on foot and the night was far advanced. Before lying down, however, Bill said he wished to see how the storm was getting on.

It was making a dreadful uproar in the cavern, and he wanted to ascertain what chance there was of the waves washing in. There was not much risk, to be sure, of their reaching as far as they then were, but it was as well to be on the safe side, and if there was a likelihood of it they would move farther up and carry their provisions and store of fuel with them, the only property they possessed.

They set out together, Jack keeping a little behind Bill for though he was as brave as any lad need be in the daylight, or out at sea, he did not somehow, he confessed, feel like himself in that dark cavern, filled with the roaring, howling, shrieking noises caused by the gale.

They got on very well till they rounded the rock, when they met a blast, driving a sheet of fine spray in their faces, which well-nigh blinded them, and forced them back. They notwithstanding made their way for some distance, till Bill began to think that it would be wise to go no farther.

Every now and then a bright glare filled the cavern, caused by the flashes of lightning darting from the clouds; while, as each sea rolled in, the whole mouth was filled as it were by a sheet of foaming water, part of which, striking the roof, fell back into the ocean, while a portion rushed up the floor, almost to where they were standing.

"It's bad enough now," shouted Jack, for they could only make each other hear by speaking at the top of their voices. "What will it be when it's high tide?"

"Perhaps it won't be much worse than it is now," answered Bill. "We shall be safe enough at our hiding-place, and if it gets up much higher it will give us notice of its coming, and allow us to retreat in good time."

They accordingly got back to their fire, the embers of which enabled them to dry their clothes. They then lay down, and, in spite of the storm and the hubbub it was creating, were soon fast asleep.

Had it not been for feeling very hungry, they might have slept on till past noon of the next day. Awaking, they found their fire completely gone out. What o'clock it was they could not tell. They were in total darkness, while the tempest roared away as loudly as ever.

They, however, lighted a candle, and ate some breakfast. To wash it down they had to get water from the spring, which was so much nearer the entrance of the cavern. They accordingly put out their candle, and groped their way round the rock. On seeing light streaming through the entrance, they knew that at all events it was no longer night.

The sea was rising over the ledge at the mouth, tossing and tumbling with foam-topped billows, and rolling up along the floor of the cavern in a seething mass of froth.

They saw how high it had come, and had no reason to fear that it would rise farther.

They now made their way to the spring, and drank heartily.

"We ought to be thankful that we are in so snug a place," observed Bill; "but I tell you, we must take care not to eat up all our food in a hurry, or we may find it a hard matter to get more. The wind appears to have driven the sea over on this shore, and I doubt whether we shall be able to make our way along the beach even at low water."

Jack did not at all like the idea of starving, but he saw that it would be wise to follow Bill's advice.

They had food enough to last them for three days, as Jeannette had put up a double allowance; but the gale might blow much longer than that, and then what should they do?

"It's no use troubling ourselves too much about the matter till the time comes," observed Bill; "only we must be careful not to eat more than is necessary to keep body and soul together."

As they had found a fire very useful and pleasant, they went down as close as they could venture to the water, and employed themselves in collecting all the driftwood and chips they could find. They agreed that they would do the same every day, so as to have a good stock of fuel. They wanted also to secure some pieces which might serve as torches, so that they could examine the smugglers' store as they called it, which they had discovered.

They carried their wood and placed it on the soft warm sand, where it would dry more rapidly, for in its present state it would not serve to kindle a fire. They had, however, some dry pieces which would answer that purpose, and they judged rightly that they might place the damp wood on the top of their fire, when it would burn in time.

Most of the day was employed in this manner. Even after the tide went out they found a number of pieces washed up along the sides of the cavern. The seas, however, rolled so far up the beach that they were afraid of descending, or they might have obtained much more.

When it grew dark they returned to their camp, lighted the fire, and made themselves comfortable.

It was difficult to keep to their resolution of eating only a very little food, and Bill had to stop Jack before he thought he had had half enough.

"I don't want to stint you," he said, "but recollect you will be crying out when our stock comes to an end, and wishing you had not eaten it."

As they had had so long a sleep, neither of them was inclined to turn in; and Bill proposed that they should examine the smugglers' store.

They had several pieces of wood which they thought would burn as the first had done, and each taking three, with a candle to be used in case of emergency, they set out.

They found their way easily enough; but Jack, as before, did not feel quite comfortable as he saw the strange figures, which seemed to be flitting about the sides of the cavern; sometimes, too, he fancied that he detected faces grinning down upon him from the roof, and more than once he declared positively that he had caught sight of a figure robed in white stealing along in front of them.

Bill each time answered with a laugh.

"Never mind. We shall catch it up if it's a ghost, and we'll make it carry a torch and go ahead to light us."

As they moved on more rapidly than before, they were able to reach the inner cavern before either of their torches was much more than half burned through. They thought it wiser to keep both alight at a time, in case one should accidentally go out, and they should be unable to light it again with a match.

With feelings of intense curiosity they approached the smugglers' store. Both agreed, as they examined it, that the goods must have been there for some time; but the place being very dry (probably it was chosen on that account), they did not appear to be much damaged. The goods, as far as they could judge, were English.

There were many bales of linen and cloth. One of the cases which they forced open contained cutlery, and another was full of pistols; and from the weight of several which they did not attempt to open, they judged that they also contained firearms.

There were two small chests placed on the top of the others. They were strongly secured; but by means of a sharp stone, which served as a chisel, and another as a hammer, they managed to break one of them open. What was their surprise to find the case full of gold pieces! They had little doubt that the other also contained money. They, neither of them, had ever seen so much gold before.

"What shall we do with it?" cried Jack. "There's enough here to let mother live like a lady till the end of her days, without going to sell fish at the market."

"It is not ours, it belongs to somebody," said Bill.

"That somebody will never come to claim it," answered Jack. "Depend on it, he's gone to the bottom, or ended his days somehow long ago, or he would have come back before this. These goods have been here for months, or years maybe, by the look of the packages; and depend on it the owners would not have let them stay where they are, if they could have come back to fetch them away."

"But gold pieces won't help us to buy food while we are shut up in the cavern. A few Dutch cheeses, with a cask of biscuits, would have been of more value," observed Bill.

"You are right," said Jack. "Still, I vote that we fill our pockets, so that if we have to hurry away, and have no time to came back here, we may carry some of the gold with us."

Bill could not make up his mind to do this. The gold was not theirs, of that he felt sure, and Jack could not persuade him to overcome the principle he had always stuck to, of not taking, under any circumstances, what was not lawfully his own. If the owners were dead, it belonged to their heirs.

Jack did not see this so clearly. The money had been lost, and they had found it, and having found it, they had a right to it.

They must not, however, lose time by arguing the point. Jack put a handful or two of the money into his pocket.

Bill kept his fingers out of the box; he did not want the money, and he had no right to it.

There were several other articles they had not examined, among which were some small casks. Jack, finding that his torch was almost burning his fingers, was obliged to let it drop. Before he lighted another, however, Bill's torch affording sufficient light for the purpose, he managed to knock in the head of one of the small casks, which he found filled with little black grains. He tasted them.

"Keep away, Bill—keep away!" he shouted, in an agitated tone, "This is gunpowder!"

Had Jack held his torch a few seconds longer in his hand, he and Bill would have been blown to atoms—the very cavern itself would have been shattered, to the great astonishment of the neighbouring population, who would, however, never have discovered the cause of the explosion, although Jeannette Turgot might have guessed at it.

"It's a mercy we didn't blow ourselves up," said Jack. "I was just going to take my torch to look at these casks."

He hunted about for all of the same description, and rolled them into a place by themselves.

"We must take care what we are about if we come here again with torches," he said.

Bill agreed with him.

After all, of what use to them was the treasure they had discovered. The cloth and linen were much more serviceable, as they could make bedding of them.

"I don't see why we should not try to make jackets and trousers for ourselves," observed Bill. "This cloth will be fine stuff for the purpose, and as the cold weather is coming on we shall be glad of some warm clothing."

"But how are we going to make them?" asked Jack.

"The linen will serve us for thread, and I must see about making some needles of wood if we can't get anything better," answered Bill. "However, we'll think about that by-and-by; it's time to return to our camp, we may be left in the dark."

They accordingly loaded themselves with as much of the linen and cloth as they could carry, cutting off pieces with their knives. They could return, they agreed, for more if this was not enough.

Bill was not quite consistent in taking the cloth when he would not touch the money, but it did not occur to him for a moment that he was wrong in appropriating it, or he would have refused to do so. Had he argued the point, he would have found it very difficult to settle. One thing was certain, that the owners were never likely to make any complaint on the subject.

They got back to their fire without much difficulty, and having raked it together, and put on fresh wood, they made their beds with the cloth they had brought, said their prayers in a thankful spirit, and slept far more comfortably than they had done since they had taken possession of the cavern.

Chapter Eleven.

The wreck.

By the roaring sound they heard when they awoke, the lads knew that the storm was still raging.

They ate sparingly of their store of food for breakfast; and then calculating that it must be once more daylight, they made their way towards the mouth of the cavern. They were not mistaken as to its being day, but how long the sun had risen they could not tell, as the sky was still thickly overcast with clouds.

The sea was washing, as before, heavily into the cavern, throwing up all sorts of articles, among which were a number of oranges, melons, and other fruits of a southern clime.

The melons were mostly broken, but they got hold of two unbroken, and very welcome they were. The oranges were mostly green, though a few had turned sufficiently red to be eaten.

"I would rather have had more substantial food," observed Jack; "but I am glad enough to get these."

"What's that?" asked Bill, pointing to the opposite side of the cavern, where a creature was seen struggling in a hollow half filled with water.

Jack dashed across at the risk of being carried off by the receding sea; and, grasping a large fish, held it up as he rushed away to escape from the following wave, which came rolling in with a loud roar.

"Here's a prize worth having," he shouted. "Hurrah! we may spend another week here without fear of starving."

He carried his prize well out of the reach of the water, and a knock on the head put an end to its struggles.

The lads piled up their various waifs, contemplating them with infinite satisfaction; but it was evident that what was their gain was somebody else's loss.

"Some unfortunate ship has gone on shore, or else has thrown her cargo overboard," observed Bill.

He went first to one side of the cavern, and then to the other, so as to obtain as wide a prospect as possible.

"See! there's a vessel trying to beat off shore," he exclaimed; and just then a brig with her foretopmast gone came into view, the sail which she was still able to carry heeling her over till her yard-arms seemed almost to touch the foaming summits of the seas.

"She'll not do it, I fear," said Jack, after they had been watching her for some time. "It's a wonder she doesn't go right over. If the wind doesn't fall, nothing can save her; and even then, unless she brings up and her anchors hold, she's sure to be cast on shore."

They watched the vessel for some time. Though carrying every stitch of canvas she could set, she appeared to be making little headway, and to be drifting bodily to leeward.

The lads uttered a cry of regret, for down came her mainmast, and immediately her head turned towards the shore.

In a few minutes she struck, though no rock was visible, and the sea swept over her deck, carrying her remaining mast, boats, caboose, and round-house overboard, with every person who could be seen. In an instant, several human forms were discernible struggling in the seething waters alongside, but they quickly disappeared.

"They are all gone," cried Jack; "not one that I can see has escaped."

"Perhaps some were below," observed Bill. "If they were, it won't much matter, for in a few minutes she will go to pieces."

He was mistaken as to the latter point, for another sea rolling in, lifted the vessel, and driving over the ledge on which she had first struck, carried her between some dark rocks, till she stuck fast on the sandy shore. Had the people been able to cling to her till now, some might possibly have been saved, but they had apparently all been on deck when the vessel struck, and been swept away by the first sea which rolled over her. The seas still continued to sweep along her deck, but their force was partly broken by the rocks, and being evidently a stout vessel, she hung together.

It was at the time nearly high-water, and the lads longed for the tide to go down, that they might examine her nearer.

"Even if anybody is alive on board, we cannot help them," observed Jack; "so I vote that we take our fish to the camp, and have some dinner. I am very sharp set, seeing that we had no breakfast to speak of."

Bill, who had no objection to offer, agreed to this; so carrying up their newly-obtained provisions, they soon had a fire lighted, and some of the fish broiling away before it.

The fate of the unfortunate vessel formed the subject of their conversation.

"I have an idea," cried Bill. "It's an ill wind that brings no one good luck. If we can manage to get on board that craft which has come on shore, we might build a boat out of her planking, or at all events a raft; and should the wind come from the southward, we might manage to get across the Channel, or be picked up by some vessel or other. We are pretty sure to find provisions on board. Perhaps one of her boats may have escaped being knocked to pieces, and we could repair her. At all events, it will be our own fault if that wreck doesn't give us the opportunity of escaping."

Jack listened to all Bill was saying.

"I cannot agree with you as to the chance of getting off," he observed. "As soon as the wreck is seen, the Frenchmen are sure to be down on the shore, and we shall be caught and carried back to prison instead of getting away. The boats are pretty certain to have been knocked into shreds before this, and as to building a boat, that is what neither you nor I can do, even if we had the tools, and where are they to come from?"

"Perhaps we shall find them on board," said Bill. "The vessel has held together till now, and I don't see why she should not hold together till the storm is over. 'Where there's a will there's a way,' and I don't see that we have so bad a chance of getting off."

"Well, I'll help you. You can show me what we had best do," said Jack. "I am not going to draw back on account of the risk. All must depend on the weather. If the wind comes off shore, and the sea goes down, I should say that our best chance would be to build a raft. We can do that, if we can only find an axe and a saw, and we might get launched before the Frenchmen find out the wreck. The first thing we have to do is to get on board, and when we are there, we must keep a bright lookout to see that none of the natives are coming along the shore to trap us."

The lads, having come to this resolution, hurried back to the entrance of the cave.

They forgot all about the smugglers' stores, and their intention of making clothes for themselves; indeed, they only thought of getting on board the vessel. They watched eagerly for the tide to go down. The day passed by and the night came on, but the clouds clearing away, a bright moon shed her light over the scene. The wind had also sensibly decreased, and the waves rolled in with far less fury than before.

The water, however, seemed to them a long time moving off; still it was evidently going down. Rock after rock appeared, and looking over the ledge they could see the sand below them.

Knowing full well that the water would not again reach the beach it had once left till the return of the tide, they leaped down without hesitation, and began to make their way in the direction of the vessel. They had again to wait, however, for, as they pushed eagerly forward, a sheet of foam from a wave which came rolling up nearly took them off their legs.

They retreated a short distance, and in a few minutes were able to pass the spot over the uncovered sand. On and on they pressed, now advancing, now having to retreat, till they stood abreast of the vessel. The water still surrounded her, and was too deep to wade through.

They looked round on every side, but not a trace of a boat could be discovered, though fragments of spars and the bulwarks of the vessel strewed the beach. Among the spars they found two whole ones, which they secured.

"These will help us to get on board if we find no ropes hanging over the side," observed Bill; "or they will enable us to withstand the sea should it catch us before we can climb up." They now advanced more boldly.

The vessel lay over on her bilge, with her deck partly turned towards the shore, the sea, after she struck, having driven her round.

They waded up to her, for their impatience did not permit them to wait till the water had entirely receded. The risk they ran of being carried off was considerable, but, dashing forward, they planted the spars against the side.

Bill swarmed up first, Jack followed, and the deck was gained.

Scarcely were Jack's feet out of the water, when a huge sea came rolling up, which would inevitably have carried him off.

They knew that they had no time to lose, for the wreck once seen from the shore, crowds of people were certain to visit it to carry off the cargo.

The after-part of the vessel was stove in, and nothing remained in the cabin; but the centre part, though nearly full of water, was unbroken. The water, however, was rushing out like a mill-stream, both at the stern and through some huge holes in the bows. Nothing whatever remained on deck.

The lads plunged down below, and gained the spar-deck, which was already out of the water. Here the first object their eyes alighted on was a chest.

It was the carpenter's, and contained axes, and saws, and nails, and tools of all sorts.

There were a good many light spars and planks stowed on one side.

"Here we have materials for a raft at hand!" cried Bill. "We must build one; for I agree with you, Jack, that there's no use in attempting a boat. It would take too much time, even if we could succeed in making her watertight."

"I said so," replied Jack. "I wish we had some grub, though; perhaps there's some for'ard. I'll go and find it if I can."

Jack made his way into the forepeak, while Bill was cutting free the lashings, and dragging out the spars. Jack returned in a short time with some cold meat, and biscuit, and cheese.

"See! we can dine like lords," he exclaimed; "and we shall be better able to work after it."

They sat down on the chest, and ate the provisions with good appetites.

Bill cast a thought on the fate of the poor fellows to whom the food had belonged; their bodies now washing about in the breakers outside.

Every now and then they alternately jumped up, and looked east and west, and to the top of the cliff, to ascertain if any one was coming. The vessel had been driven on shore out of sight of both the villages, or they would not have been left long alone. It was to be hoped that no one would come along the cliff and look down upon the wreck.

Their meal over, they set to work to plan their raft.

They were obliged to labour on deck, as they could not hoist it up through the hold, or they would have preferred keeping out of sight. It would be a hard job to launch it, but that they hoped to do by fastening tackles at either side leading to the ring bolts on deck.

As there were no bulwarks to stop them, they laid the foundation, or, as they called it, the keel, projecting slightly over the side. They would thus have only to shove it forward and tip it up to launch it.

Their plan was to form an oblong square, then to put on bows at one end; and two pieces crossing each other with a short upright between them, on which to support the steering oar. The interior of the framework they strengthened by two diagonal braces. They lashed and nailed a number of crosspieces close together, and on the top of the whole they nailed down all the planks they could find, which were sufficient to form a good flooring to their raft.

They discovered also a number of small brandy casks, which they immediately emptied of their contents, letting the spirits flow without compunction into the water, and then again tightly bunged them down.

They fastened ropes around the casks, with which, when the raft was launched, they could secure them to either side, to give it greater buoyancy. They also brought up a couple of sea-chests, which they intended to lash down to the centre, so as to afford them some protection from the sea, and at the same time to hold their provisions.

Bill was the chief suggester of all these arrangements, though Jack ably carried them out.

They worked like heroes, with all the energy they could command, for they felt that everything depended on their exertions.

The night being bright, they were able to get on as well then as in the daytime.

Chapter Twelve.

A raft built—Mysterious disappearance of Jack Peek.

Not till their raft was complete did the two boys think of again eating. They had been working, it must be remembered, for several hours since the meal they took soon after they got on board. Having finished the beef and cheese, they lighted a couple of lanterns which they found hung up in the forepeak, and hunted about for more food.

They discovered some casks of salt beef, and another of biscuits, a drum of cheese, and several boxes of dried fruit. They had thus no lack of provisions, but they did not forget the necessity of supplying themselves with a store of water.

Hunting about, they found two small vessels, which they filled from one of the water-casks.

There were several oars below, three of which they took and placed in readiness on deck—one to steer with, and the other two for rowing.

They had, lastly, to rig their raft. A fore-royal already bent was found in the sail-room, and a spar served as a mast. How to step it, and to secure it properly, was the difficulty, until Bill suggested getting a third chest and boring a hole through the lid, and then, by making another hole through the bottom, the mast would be well stepped, and it was easy to set it up by means of a rope led forward and two shrouds aft.

Knowing exactly what they wanted to do, they did it very rapidly, and were perfectly satisfied with their performance.

The tide must come up again, however, before they could launch their raft. It would not be safe to do that unless the wind was off shore and the water smooth. Of this they were thoroughly convinced. Some hours must also elapse before the hitherto tumultuous sea would go down; what should they do in the meantime?

Bill felt very unwilling to go away without wishing their friends the Turgots good-bye. He wanted also to tell Jeannette of the smugglers' store. The Turgots, at all events, would have as good a right to it as any one else, should the proper owners not be in existence.

Jack did not want him to go.

"You may be caught," he observed, "or some one may come down and discover the vessel, and if I am alone, even should the tide be high, I could not put off."

"But there is no chance of the tide coming up for the next three hours, and I can go to the village and be back again long before that," answered Bill.

At last Jack gave in.

"Well, be quick about it," he said; "we ought to be away at daylight, if the wind and the sea will let us; and if we don't, I'm afraid there will be very little chance of our getting off at all."

Bill promised without fail to return. There was no risk, he was sure, of being discovered, and it would be very ungrateful to the Turgots to go away without trying to see them again. He wished that Jack could have gone also, but he agreed that it was better for him to remain to do a few more things to the raft. Before he started they arranged the tackles for launching it; and they believed that, when once in the water, it would not take them more than ten minutes or a quarter of an hour to haul the empty casks under the bottom and to step and set up the mast. They might then, should the wind be favourable, stand boldly out to sea.

This being settled, Bill lowered himself down on the sand by a rope, and ran off as fast as he could go.

Jack quickly finished the work he had undertaken; then putting his hand into his pocket, he felt the gold pieces.

"It's a pity we shouldn't have more of these," he said to himself. "I don't agree with Bill in that matter. If he does not care about them for himself, I do for him, and he shall have half."

As he said this he emptied his pockets into one of the chests.

"I shall want a lantern by-the-bye," he said; and springing below, he secured one with a fresh candle in it.

Having done this, he forthwith lowered himself, as Bill had done, down on the sand, and quickly made his way to the cavern.

He had left the basket with the tinder-box, and the remnant of their provisions at their camp, which he soon reached.

His desire to obtain the gold overcame the fears he had before entertained of ghosts and spirits.

Having lighted his lantern he took up the basket, which had a cloth in it, and pushed forward. The pale light from his lantern, so different from that of a couple of blazing torches, made the objects around look strange and weird. He began not at all to like the appearance of things, and fancied at last that he must have got into a different part, of the cavern; still he thought, "I must have the gold. It would be so foolish to go away without it. It belongs to us as much as to anybody else, seeing that the owners are dead. Their ghosts won't come to look for it, I hope. I wish I hadn't thought of that. I must be going right. It would have been much pleasanter if Bill had been with me. Why didn't I try to persuade him to stop?"

Such were the thoughts which passed through Jack's mind; but he was a bold fellow, and did not like giving up what he had once determined on.

He saw no harm in what he was doing; on the contrary, he was serving his friend Bill as well as himself, or rather his mother, for he wanted the gold for her. In the meantime, Bill was hurrying on towards the Turgots' cottage. He should astonish them, he knew, by waking them up in the middle of the night, or rather so early in the morning; but they would appreciate his desire to wish them good-bye, and would be very much obliged to him for telling them of the treasure in the cavern.

It would make their fortunes, and Jeannette would be the richest heiress in the neighbourhood; for, of course, he would bargain that she should have a good share. There might be some difficulty in getting the goods away without being discovered, which would be a pity, as they were of as much value as the boxes of gold. However, he was doing what was right in giving them the opportunity of possessing themselves of the treasure, though he considered that he could not take it himself.

He got round to the back door, under the room where Pierre slept. He knew that he would not be out fishing then, as the weather would have prevented him.

He knocked at once. No answer came. The third time, and he heard some one moving, and presently Pierre sang out, "Who's there?"

"It's one you know; let me in," answered Bill, in a low voice, for he was afraid of any one who might by chance be in the neighbourhood hearing him.

Pierre came downstairs and opened the door. Bill explained all that had happened, except about the treasure.

"You going away!" cried Pierre. "It would be madness! You will only float about till another storm arises and you will be lost."

"You don't know what we can do," answered Bill. "We shall probably be picked up by one of our ships before we reach England; and, if not, we shall get on very well, provided the wind holds from the southward, and after the long course of northerly gales there's every chance of its doing that."

"I must consult my father before I let you go," said Pierre.

"You would not keep us prisoners against our will," said Bill, laughing, as if Pierre could only be in joke. "Come, call your mother and father and Jeannette, and let me wish them good-bye. I haven't many minutes to stop, and I've got something to tell them, which I've a notion will be satisfactory."

Pierre went to his father and mother's and Jeannette's rooms, and soon roused them up. They appeared somewhat in *deshabille*, and looked very astonished at being called out of their beds by the young Englishman.

"What is it all about?" asked Captain Turgot.

"We are going away," replied Bill, "but we could not go without again thanking you for all your kindness; and to show you that we are not ungrateful, I have to tell you how you can become a rich man in a few hours, without much trouble."

On this Bill described how they had found the smuggler's treasure.

Captain Turgot and the dame held up their hands, uttering various exclamations which showed their surprise, mixed with no little doubt as to whether Bill had not been dreaming.

He assured them that he was stating a fact, and offered, if Captain Turgot and Pierre would accompany him, to show them the place, as he thought that there would be time before daylight, when he and Jack had determined to set sail.

"I am sure he's speaking the truth," cried Jeannette; "and it's very kind and generous of you, Bill, to tell us of the treasure, when you might have carried it off yourself. I know of the cave, for I saw it once, when I was very nearly caught by the tide and drowned, though I don't think many people about here are acquainted with it; and very few, if any, have gone into the interior."

Captain Turgot and Pierre confessed that they had never seen it, though they had gone up and down the coast so often; but then, on account of the rocks, they had always kept a good distance out.

At last Bill and Jeannette persuaded them that there really was such a cave; but on considering the hour, they came to the conclusion that the tide would come in before they could make their escape from it, and they would prefer going when the tide had again made out. Bill, they thought, would only just have time to get on board the vessel, if he was determined to go.

"But if you have so much gold, you could purchase a good boat," said Captain Turgot; "and that would be much better than making your voyage on a raft."

Bill acknowledged that such might be the case, but he was unwilling to risk any further delay. He trusted to his friends' honour to let him go as he had determined. He had come of his own accord to bid them farewell, and they would not really think of detaining him against his will.

The fact, however, was that Captain Turgot doubted very much the truth of Bill's story. Had any band of smugglers possessed a hiding-place on that part of the coast, he thought that he should have known it, and he fancied that the young Englishman must in some way or other have been deceived.

"Where is the gold you speak of?" he asked. "You surely must have secured some for yourself."

Bill replied that Jack had, but that he had not wished to touch it.

"Then you give it to us, my young friend," said Captain Turgot; "where is the difference?"

"No! I only tell you of it, that you may act as you think right. If you find out the owners, I hope you will restore it to them; but, at all events, it's Frenchmen's money, and a Frenchman has more right to it than I have."

Captain Turgot did not quite understand Bill's principles, though perhaps Jeannette and Pierre did.

"Well, well, my young friend, if go you must, I will not detain you. You and your companion will run a great risk of losing your lives, and I wish you would remain with us. To-morrow, as soon as the tide is out, Pierre and I will visit the cavern, which, I think, from your description, we can find; and we will take lanterns and torches. Again I say I wish you would wait, and if there is a prize to be obtained, that you would share it with us."

Jeannette and Pierre also pressed Bill to remain, but he was firm in his resolution of rejoining Jack, and setting off at once.

He was so proud of the raft they had made, that he would have been ready to go round the world on it, if it could be got to sail on a wind, and at all events he had not the slightest doubt about its fitness to carry him and Jack across the Channel.

Bill had already delayed longer than he intended, and once more bidding his friends good-bye, he set off for the wreck. He hurried along as fast as he could go, for he felt sure that at daybreak it would be seen, if not from the shore, from the sea, and that people would come and interfere with his and Jack's proceedings.

As he knew the way thoroughly, he made good progress. On getting abreast of the wreck, he looked out for Jack, but could nowhere see him.

The water was already coming round the vessel, and in a short time would be too deep to wade through. He thought that Jack must have gone below, but he was afraid of giving a loud shout, lest his voice might be heard. He accordingly, without stopping, made his way on board.

Great was his alarm when he could nowhere discover Jack.

Could he have gone to the cavern? or could he have been carried off?

The latter was not probable, for had the stranded vessel been discovered, people would have remained in her.

"He must have gone to the cavern, and to save time, I must follow him," he said to himself; and sliding down the rope, he made his way as fast as he could towards its mouth.

He quickly climbed up, and hurried on as fast as he dare move in the dark, holding out his hands to avoid running against the sides, or to save himself should he fall.

He knew that there were no pitfalls or other serious dangers, or he could not have ventured to move even so fast as he did.

He shouted out as he went Jack's name.

"How foolish I was not to bring a lantern with me," he said. "Jack is sure to have taken one if he went to get more gold, and that I suspect is what he has been after; if he has a light, I shall see it, but I don't."

"Jack! Jack!" he again shouted out; but the cavern only echoed with his voice.

Bill was a fine-tempered fellow, but he felt very much inclined to be angry with Jack. All their plans might be upset by his having left the wreck. Even should he soon find him, they would have to swim on board, and set off in their wet clothes; but that was of little consequence compared with the delay.

At last his hands touched the rock near their camping-place, and he thence groped his way on; for having so often traversed the cavern in the dark, he found it as easily as a blind man would have done.

He soon felt his feet treading on the ashes of their former fires, and feeling about, he discovered the things which Jack had thrown out of the basket.

Among them was a candle and the tinder-box. Jack having a lighted lantern, had not troubled himself to bring it.

The basket was gone! This convinced him that Jack had been there. He quickly lighted the candle, and as there was not a breath of air, he was able to walk along with it in his hand.

The stalactite formations, which appeared on both sides, looked as weird and strange to him as they had to Jack, but he, knowing perfectly well what they were, did not trouble himself about their appearance.

He went on, keeping his gaze ahead, in the hopes of meeting Jack. He was sorry that he had not made more determined attempts to persuade Captain Turgot and Pierre to accompany him; for if anything should have happened to his companion, they would have assisted him. But what could have happened? that was the question.

Sometimes he thought that Jack might, after all, not have come to the cavern; but, then, who could have carried away the basket?

Brave as he was, the strange shadows which occasionally seemed to flit by made him feel that he would much rather not have been there all alone.

Suppose, too, the smugglers should have returned, and, perhaps, caught Jack; they would seize him also, and it would be impossible to persuade them that he had not come to rob their store. Still, his chief anxiety was for Jack.

He thought much less about himself, or the dangers he might have to encounter.

Bill was a hero, though he did not know it, notwithstanding that he had been originally only a London street boy.

"I must find Jack, whatever comes of it," he said to himself, as he pushed on.

At last he reached the low entrance of the smugglers' store-room, as Jack and he had called it. He crept on carefully, and as he gained the inner end of the passage, he saw a light burning close to where the goods were piled up, but no voices reached his ear.

If the smugglers were there, they would surely be talking. He rose to his feet, holding out the candle before him. Seeing no one, he advanced boldly across the cavern. There lay a figure stretched upon the ground!

It was Jack!

Chapter Thirteen.

The raft launched and voyage commenced.

Could Jack be dead? What could have happened to him? Bill, hurrying forward, knelt down by his side, and lifted up his head. He still breathed.

"That's a comfort," thought Bill. "How shall I bring him to? There's not a drop of water here, and I can't carry him as far as the spring."

Bill rubbed his friend's temples, while he supported his head on his knee.

"Jack! Jack! rouse up, old fellow! What's come over you?"

Bill held the candle up to Jack's eyes. Greatly to his joy they opened, and he said, "Where am I? Is that you, Bill! Is it gone?"

"I am Bill, and you are in the cavern; but there is nothing to go that I know of. It's all right. Stand up, old fellow, and come along," replied Bill, cheeringly.

"Oh, Bill," said Jack, drawing a deep sigh, "I saw something."

"Did you?" said Bill; "the something did not knock you down, though."

"No; but I thought it would," responded Jack.

"That comes of wanting to take what isn't your own," said Bill. "However, don't let's talk about that. If we are to get off with this tide, we must hurry on board as fast as we can. Don't mind the gold; I suppose that's what you came for. Our friends the Turgots will get it, I hope; and they have more right to it than we have."

Bill's voice greatly re-assured Jack, who, fancying that he saw one of the ghosts he was afraid of, had fallen down in a sort of swoon. How long it would have lasted if Bill had not come to him it is impossible to say; perhaps long enough to have allowed his candle to be extinguished. Had this happened, he would never have been able to find his way out of the cavern. He, however, with Bill by his side, soon felt like himself again.

"Let me just fill my pockets with these gold pieces," he exclaimed. "I have taken so much trouble that I shouldn't like to go away without them."

"Perhaps the ghost will come back if you do," Bill could not help saying. "Let them alone. You have got enough already, and we must not stop another moment here."

Saying this, he dragged Jack on by the arm.

"Come, if we don't make haste, our candles will go out, and we shall not be able to see our way," Bill continued.

Jack moved on. He was always ready to be led by Bill, and began to think that he had better not have come for the gold.

Bill did not scold him, vexed as he felt at the delay which had occurred. They might still be in time to get on board the wreck and to launch their raft, but it would be broad daylight before they could get to any distance from the shore, and they would then be sure to be seen. Bill only hoped that no one would think it worth while to follow them.

Having two lights, they were able to see their way pretty well, though they could not run fast for fear of extinguishing them.

Every now and then Jack showed an inclination to stop. "I wish I had got the gold," he muttered.

Bill pulled him on.

"The gold, I say, would not do us any good. I don't want it for myself, and you have got enough to make your mother independent for the rest of her days."

On they went again. Bill was thankful, on reaching the mouth of the cavern, to find that it was still night. It seemed to him a long time since he had quitted the wreck. He did not remember how fast he had gone. They jumped down on the beach, and began to wade towards the wreck, but had to swim some distance.

"If we had had our pockets full of gold we could not have done this," observed Bill. "We should have had to empty them or be drowned. We are much better without it."

They soon reached the side of the vessel, and climbed up on deck. There was plenty of water alongside to launch the raft, and to get the casks under it. The wind, too, if there were any, was off shore, but here it was a perfect calm. They had one advantage through having waited so long; they were beyond the influence of the wave which breaks even on a weather shore, especially after a gale, although the wind may have changed.

The tackles having been arranged, they lost no time in launching their raft, which they did very successfully, easing it with handspikes; and in a couple of minutes it floated, to their great satisfaction, safely alongside. Their first care was to lash the casks under the bottom. This took some time, but they were well repaid by finding the raft float buoyantly on the very surface of the water.

The cargo had, however, to be got on board, consisting of the three chests, which, of course, would bring it down somewhat. They lowered one after the other, and lashed them in the positions they had intended. The foremost chest was secured over all by ropes, as that had not to be opened, and was to serve only as a step for their mast; the other two chests were secured by their handles both fore and aft and athwartships, the lashings contributing to bind the raft still more securely together.

Daylight had now broken, and they were in a hurry to get on with their work, but this did not prevent them from securing everything effectually.

They next had to get their stores into the chests; and lastly they stepped and set up the mast, securing the sail ready for hoisting to the halyards, which had been previously rove.

They surveyed their work when completed with no little satisfaction, and considered, not without reason, that they might, in moderate weather, run across Channel, provided the wind should remain anywhere in the southward.

They well knew that they must run the risk of a northerly wind or a gale. In the first case, though they need not go back, they could make little or no progress; but then there was always the hope of being picked up by an English craft, either a man-of-war or a merchant vessel.

They might, to be sure, be fallen in with by a Frenchman, but in the event of that happening, they intended to beg hard for their liberty.

Should a gale arise, as Jack observed, they would look blue, but they hoped that their raft would even weather that out. That it would come to pieces they had no fear; and they believed that they could cling on to it till the sea should again go down.

They had put on board a sufficient supply of spare rope to lash themselves to the chests.

Jack climbed up for the last time on deck, and handed down the three sweeps, taking a look round to see that nothing was left behind.

"All right," he said; "we may shove off now, Bill. You are to be captain, and take the helm, and I'll pull till we get out far enough to find a breeze. It seems to me, by the colour of the sea, that it's blowing in the offing, and we shall then spin merrily along."

"All right," said Bill; "cast off, Jack."

Jack hauled in the rope which had secured the raft to the wreck, and give a hearty shove against it with his oar, he sent the raft gliding off some way ahead. He then got out the other oar, and standing between the two chests, pulled lustily away.

The raft floated even more lightly than they had expected. They had so well noted all the rocks, that they could easily find their way between them, and there was ample space, especially thereabouts where the brig had been driven in.

Their progress was but slow, though they worked away with all their might; every now and then looking back to ascertain whether they were observed from the shore. No one, however, could be seen on the cliffs above; and people, unless they had discovered the wreck, were not likely at that early hour to come down to the beach.

It took them more than half an hour to get clear of the rocks. When once out on the open sea, they began to breathe more freely. They pulled on and on; still, unless they should get the wind, they could not hope to make much progress. The day was advancing. Bill wetted his finger and held it up.

"There's a breeze," he cried out; "hoist the sail, Jack."

The sail filled as Bill sheeted it home, and the raft began to glide more rapidly over the water.

Jack took in the oars, for he wanted to rest, and there was but little use rowing, though it might have helped the raft on slightly.

He could now look about him, and as the two harbours to the east and west opened out, he turned his eyes anxiously towards them.

If they were pursued, it would be from one or the other. He had little fear from that on the west, as there was no one likely to trouble himself about the matter; but there were officials living near the larger harbour, and they might think it their duty to ascertain what the small raft standing off shore under sail could be about.

"I wish that we had got away a couple of hours ago," said Bill; but he did not remind Jack that it was through his fault they had not done so. He blamed himself, indeed, for having gone to see the Turgots, much as he would have regretted leaving the country without paying them a visit.

The farther the raft got from the shore the more rapidly it glided along, the sea being too smooth in any way to impede its progress.

Bill's whole attention was taken up in steering, so as to keep the raft right before the wind.

Presently Jack cried out, "There's a boat coming out of the harbour. She's just hoisted her sail, and a whacking big sail it is. She's coming after us. Oh! Bill! what shall we do?"

"Try to keep ahead of her," answered Bill, glancing round for a moment. "The Frenchmen may not think it worth while to chase us far, even if they are in chase of us, and that's not certain. Don't let us cry out before we are hurt. Get out the oars, they'll help us on a little, and we'll do our best to escape. I don't fancy being shut up again, or perhaps being carried off to a prison, and forced into a dungeon, or maybe shot, for they'll declare that we are escaped prisoners."

Jack did not, however, require these remarks to make him pull with all his might; still he could not help looking back occasionally. He was standing up, it should be understood, rowing forward, with the oars crossing, the larboard oar held in the right hand, and the starboard in the left.

"The boat's coming on three knots to our one," he cried out. "It won't take her long to be up with us."

"Pull away," again cried Bill. "We'll hold on till the Frenchmen begin to fire. If their bullets come near us, it will be time to think whether it will be worth running the risk of being shot."

Jack continued to row with might and main, and the raft went wonderfully fast over the water. It was too evident, however, that the boat was in pursuit of them, and in a few minutes a musket ball splashed into the water a short distance astern of the raft.

"That shows that they are in earnest," said Jack. "We had better lower the sail, another might come aboard us."

"Hold all fast, perhaps they are getting tired of chasing us, and may give it up when they see that we are determined to get away," replied Bill; not that he had much hope that this was the case, but he stuck to the principle of not giving in as long as there was a chance of escape.

Jack had plenty of courage, but he did not like being fired at without the means of returning the compliment.

Another shot from the boat came whistling close to them.

"It's of no use," cried Jack, "we must lower the sail."

"If you're afraid, take in the oars and lie down between the chests; you'll run very little risk of being hit there; but for my part, I'll stand at the helm till the boat gets up with us," said Bill.

Jack would not do this, but pulled away as stoutly as at first.

Presently another shot struck one of the oars, and so splintered it that the next pull Jack gave it broke short off. He was now compelled to take in the other.

"The next time the Frenchmen fire they may aim better," he said. "Come, Bill, I'm ready to stand by you, but there's no use being killed if we can help it."

"The boat isn't up with us yet," answered Bill. "Till she gets alongside I'll hold on, and maybe at the very last the Frenchmen will give up."

"I don't see any hope of that," said Jack. "In ten minutes we shall be prisoners. By-the-bye, I turned all my gold into this chest. If the Frenchmen find it they'll keep it, so I'll fill my pockets again, and they may not think of looking into them, but they're sure to rummage the chest."

Saying this, Jack opened the chest, and soon found his treasure, which he restored to his pockets. He asked Bill to take some, but Bill declined on the same ground that he had before refused to appropriate it.

Bill again advised Jack to lie down, and, to induce him to do so, he himself knelt on the raft, as he could in that position steer as well as when standing up.

Thus they presented the smallest possible mark to the Frenchmen.

Shot after shot was fired at them. Their chances of escape were indeed rapidly diminishing.

At last the Frenchmen ceased firing.

They were either struck by the hardihood of the boys, or had expended their ammunition; but the boat came on as rapidly as before, and was now not half a cable's length from them.

"We must lower the sail," cried Bill, with a sigh, "or the Frenchmen maybe will run us down;" and Jack let go the halyards.

In another minute the boat was up to them.

Besides her crew, there were five soldiers on board.

A volley of questions burst from the people in the boat; and all seemed jabbering and talking together.

As she got alongside the raft, two men leaped out, and seizing Jack and Bill, hauled them into the boat, while another made fast the raft, ready to tow it back to the harbour.

Jack and Bill were at once handed aft to the stern-sheets, where they were made to sit down. Immediately the officer in command of the boat put various questions to them, as to who they were, where they had come from, and where they were going.

According to their previous agreement they made no reply, so that their captors might not discover that they understood French; still, as far as Bill could make out, the Frenchmen were not aware that they were the lads who had escaped from the old tower.

They had no reason to complain of the way they were spoken of by the Frenchmen, who were evidently struck by their hardihood and determination in their persevering efforts to escape. They remarked to each other that their young prisoners were brave boys, and expressed their satisfaction that they were not hurt.

When the officer found, as he supposed, that they could not answer him, he forbore to put any further questions.

The crew did not appear to be angry at the long pull that had been given them back; indeed, Jack and Bill suspected, from what they heard, that the seamen, at all events, would not have been sorry if they had escaped altogether.

On reaching the landing-place in the harbour, they found a party of soldiers, with an officer, who, from what Bill made out, had sent the boat in pursuit of them.

As soon as they stepped on shore the officer began to question them, in the same way as the commander of the boat had done.

Bill shrugged his shoulders and turned to Jack, and Jack shrugged his and turned to Bill, as much as to say, "I wonder what he's talking about?"

"The lads do not understand French, that is evident," said the officer to a subordinate standing near him; "I shall get nothing out of them without an interpreter. They do not look stupid either, and they must be bold fellows, or they would not have attempted to made a voyage on that raft. I must have a nearer look at it;" and he ordered the boatmen to bring it in close to the shore, so that he might examine it.

He again turned to Bill, and said, "What were you going to attempt to cross the Channel on that?"

Bill, as before, shrugged his shoulders, quite in the French fashion, for he had learnt the trick from Pierre, who, when he was in doubt about a matter, always did so.

"I forgot; the boy doesn't understand French," observed the officer.

Bill had some little difficulty in refraining from laughing, as he understood perfectly well everything that was said around him, except when the Frenchmen talked unusually fast.

"Let the raft be moored close to the shore, just in its present state," said the officer; "the general may wish to see it. How could the lads have contrived to build such a machine?"

The commander of the boat explained that a wreck had occurred on the shore, and that they had evidently built it from the materials they found on board her, but anything further about them he could not say.

"Well, then, I'll take them up at once to the general, and the interpreter attached to our division will draw from them all we want to know. Come, lads! you must follow me," he said. "Sergeant, bring the prisoners along with you."

On this Jack and Bill found themselves surrounded by the soldiers; and thinking it possible, should they not move fast enough, that their movements might be expedited by a prick from the bayonets, they marched briskly forward, keeping good pace with the men.

Chapter Fourteen.

Again shut up.

"I say, Bill, I wonder what the mounseers are going to do with us," whispered Jack, as they marched along. "Will they put handcuffs on our wrists and throw us into a dungeon, do you think?"

Bill acknowledged that he feared such might be the fate prepared for them. They were not, however, ill-treated during their walk. Naturally they felt very much disappointed at being recaptured, but they tried as before to put as bold a face as they could on the matter, and talked away to each other in an apparently unconcerned manner.

They found from the remarks of the soldiers that they had a march of a couple of miles or more inland to the place where the troops were encamped, and that they were not to be carried to the old tower.

On one account they were sorry for this, as, having made their escape once, they thought that they might make it again, though, of course, they would be more strictly guarded if it was discovered who they were.

From a height they reached they saw the camp spread out on a wide level space a short distance off. As they got nearer to it they observed a party of officers on horseback riding towards them, one of whom, from the waving plume in his hat, and from his taking the lead, they supposed was the general.

They were right in their conjecture. As he approached with his staff, the officer who had charge of them ordered his men to halt and draw on one side.

The general reined in his horse and inquired who they were.

The captain explained that two foreign lads, supposed to be English, had been discovered, endeavouring to leave the shore on a small raft of curious construction, such as no sane people would have wished to go to sea on; that there was something very suspicious about their movements, as they had persisted in trying to escape, although fired at by the soldiers, and that he had considered it his duty to bring them up for examination, as he could not understand them or make them understand him.

"You acted rightly, Captain Dupont," said the general. "Let them be brought to my quarters, and I'll send for Colonel O'Toole to cross-question them." Bill and Jack understood every word that was said. "We are in for it," said Bill; "but we must put a bold face on the matter, and speak the truth. We can say that we were living in the cavern for some time, and that when the brig was wrecked, we resolved at once to build a raft, and get back to our own country."

"It would save a great deal of trouble if we were to say that we were wrecked in the brig, and then it would be but natural that we should try to escape from her," replied Jack.

"It would not be the truth, and we should not be believed," answered Bill. "I would say just what happened—that our ship caught fire and blew up, that we were saved by the fishermen, that some French soldiers got hold of us and carried us off prisoners, and that we made our escape from them. We need not mention the names of our friends, and perhaps the interpreter won't be very particular in making inquiries."

Bill finally persuaded Jack to agree that they should give a true account of themselves, leaving out only such particulars as were not necessary to mention, such as their visit to the Turgots, and their discovery of the smugglers' stores.

The general, who was making a survey of the country around the camp, rode on with his staff, while Captain Dupont and his men conducted their two young prisoners to head quarters, there to await his return.

The general was residing in an old chateau, with a high-peaked roof, and towers at each of the angles of the building.

The party passed through the gateway, and proceeded to a room near the chief entrance, which served as a guard-room.

The soldiers remained outside, while the captain, with two men to guard the prisoners, entered. Jack and Bill had to wait for some time, during which they were allowed to sit on a bench by themselves.

Jack began to make observations on the people around them.

"Hush!" whispered Bill, "some one here may understand English better than we suppose, and we shall be foolish to let our tongues get us into a worse scrape than we are in already."

Jack took Bill's advice, and when he made any remark it was in a whisper.

They saw several of the officers who entered looking at them, and they were evidently the subject of their conversation. Jack and Bill had reason to consider themselves for a time persons of some importance, though they had no wish to be so.

At last an officer in a handsome uniform entered. He was a red-haired man, with queer twinkling eyes, and a cock-up nose, anything but of a Roman type.

Captain Dupont spoke to him, when the lads saw him eyeing them, and presently he came up and said, "Hurroo! now me boys, just be afther telling me what part of the world you come from!"

Bill, as agreed on, began his narrative in a very circumstantial manner.

"All moighty foine, if thrue," observed Colonel O'Toole, for he was the officer who had just arrived, having been sent for to act as interpreter.

"It's true, sir, every word of it," said Bill.

"Well! we shall see, afther you repeat it all over again to the gineral, and moind you thin don't made any changes," said the colonel.

Bill wisely did not reply. Presently the general with his staff appeared, he and a few officers passing on into an inner room. A few minutes afterwards Jack and Bill were sent for.

They found the general with Colonel O'Toole and several other persons seated at a table.

The general spoke a few words, when the colonel again told the prisoners to give an account of themselves.

Bill did so exactly in the words he had before used, Colonel O'Toole interpreting sentence by sentence.

"Good!" said the general. "And what could induce you, when you were once safe on shore, to venture out to sea on so dangerous a machine?"

The colonel interpreting, turned to Jack.

"I wanted to get home and see my mother, for she must fancy I am lost," answered Jack.

"Well, and a very right motive too," said the colonel; and he explained to the general what Jack had said.

"And what induced you to attempt the voyage?" asked the colonel, turning to Bill. "Did you want to get back to see your mother?"

"No, sir; I have no mother to see," answered Bill. "I wanted to get back to do my duty, and fight the enemies of my country."

The general laughed when this was interpreted to him; and observed to the officers around him, "If such is the spirit which animates the boys of England, what must we expect from the men? I must, however, consider whether we shall allow these boys to return home. They are young now, but in a short time they will grow into sturdy fellows."

"They've got tongues in their young heads," remarked the colonel. "I'm not altogether certain that they are quite as innocent as they look. Maybe they were sent on shore as spies, and perhaps are midshipmen disguised as common seamen."

"Let them be searched, then, and ascertain whether they have any papers about them which may show their real character," said the general.

Jack and Bill clearly understood these remarks, and began to feel very uncomfortable.

Bill remembered that Jack had got his pockets filled with gold, and Jack remembered it too, and wished that he had left it behind in the cavern as Bill had advised.

The colonel, who was in no wise particular as to what work he performed, at once took hold of Bill.

"Come, young gintleman," he said, "let me see what you have got in your pockets, and next your skin; or, if you will save me the throuble, just hand out your orders or any papers you may have about you."

"I have got none, sir," answered Bill. "I told you the truth, that we are mere ship-boys, and as to being spies as you seem to think, we had nothing to spy out that I know of."

"Well, we will soon see all about that," said the colonel, beginning to search Bill; but, greatly to his surprise, he found nothing whatever about him, except his knife, the whole of Bill's worldly wealth, "I told you so, sir," said Bill, when he had finished. "I spoke only the truth about myself and my companion." Bill said this, hoping that Jack would escape the search; but the colonel was far too knowing, and presently he seized upon Jack, who, in spite of his efforts to appear unconcerned, began to quake.

The first plunge the colonel made with his hand into one of Jack's pockets brought forth a number of gold pieces. "Hurroo! now, this is your innocence is it, young gintlemen?" he exclaimed, exhibiting a handful of gold to the general. "Let me be afther seeing what your other pocket contains;" and as he spoke he quickly drew forth another handful of gold, some of which, observing that the general and the other officers were examining the first which he had produced, he slipped into his own pocket.

"Troth! you're an arrant young rogue," he exclaimed. "You either stole these, or they were given you to bribe the people to betray their country."

"They were not given me to bribe any one, and I didn't steal them," answered Jack, boldly; "I took them out of the chest which was on our raft, and there was no harm in doing that, I should think."

Bill was somewhat surprised to hear Jack say this. It was the truth, and the idea must have at that moment occurred to him. He was thus saved from having to betray the existence of the boxes of gold in the cavern, which the colonel would not have long allowed to remain unvisited, he suspected, from the little incident which has just been described.

The colonel translated fairly enough to the general what Jack had just said.

"It is probably the truth," he remarked; "however, let the boys be detained till we can ascertain more about them. I don't wish to have them ill-treated. There is a room in the western turret where they can be shut up securely till to-morrow. Colonel O'Toole, see that my orders are carried out; but you can first let them have a view of the army, that they may tell their friends, if they get home, of the mighty force prepared for the conquest of England, and impress on the minds of their countrymen how hopeless is their attempt to resist the armies of France."

Bill understood every word of these remarks, and they raised his hopes that they might be set at liberty and allowed to return home; still, the Irish colonel did not look very amiably at them; perhaps he did not quite like Bill's observations.

"Come along," he said, turning to them; and, bowing to the general and to the other officers, he conducted them from the room, when the two soldiers, who stood ready outside, again took charge of them.

They were led along to a terrace, from whence a view extended over the surrounding country. Here they saw an almost countless number of white tents pitched, with soldiers in various uniforms moving among them.

"Can you count those tents?" asked the colonel. "Each tent contains eleven or thirteen men, and one spirit animates the whole—that is, the conquest of perfidious Albion."

"They'll have a tough job, sir, let me tell them," observed Bill. "I haven't seen much of English sojers except the Guards in London, and our Marines on board ship, but I know that one of our Guardsmen would lick a whole tentful of the little chaps I see about here; and I would advise the general to stay quietly at home, and not attempt to take our tight little island."

"The French have wrongs to revenge, as have my gallant people, and bitterly will they revenge them some day, when your king and his nobles are brought in chains to France."

"That won't be just yet, and may be never," answered Bill, who was growing bold, and inclined to speak his mind. "I'll not bandy words with you, boy. Take care what you are about!" exclaimed the colonel, who did not like Bill's boldness, especially when he saw a broad grin on Jack's countenance. "If you ever get back to England—and I don't say you ever will get back—remember what you have seen to-day, and tell those wretched slaves your countrymen what they are to expect."

"We'll not forget it, sir," answered Bill, thinking it wiser to be civil; "and I hope the general won't think it necessary to keep in prison two poor sailor boys who never did any harm to the French, and never wished to do any harm, except to thrash them well in a fair stand-up fight; and you will allow, sir, that that's all right and fair play."

"Or receive a thrashing from them," answered the colonel; "however, come along. I must see you stowed safely in the tower, where the general has ordered you to be placed, and moind you kape quiet and don't kick up a row, as you midshipmen are apt to do."

"We are not midshipmen, sir," said Bill, who had not forgotten what the colonel had before said. "We are humble boys serving before the mast. Jack, there, is a fisherman's son, and I am a poor boy out of the London streets. I am only telling you the truth, sir."

"You are a very sharp boy, then," responded the colonel, looking at Bill.

"Yes, sir," said Bill, "the school I went to is a place where boys are apt to get their wits sharpened. They have little else to depend on."

The colonel still seemed to doubt whether Bill was speaking the truth, and, perhaps fortunately for them, was fully impressed with the idea that he had charge of a couple of midshipmen. Possibly Bill was a lord's son; and though he railed against English lords, yet, when brought into contact with them, he was inclined to pay them the deepest respect.

Owing to the colonel's idea, Bill and Jack were treated with far more attention than they otherwise would have received.

The room into which they were put, though small, had a table and chairs in it, and a bed in one corner.

"You will remain here for the present," said the colonel, as he saw them into the room; "probably before long the general may wish to examine you again, and I would advise you to take care that you tell him only the truth, and confess your object in coming to the country."

Bill made no answer; and the colonel, after again surveying the room, took his departure, locking the door behind him.

Chapter Fifteen.

The escape.

Jack and Bill heard Colonel O'Toole descending the stairs, and, listening, were convinced that he had gone away without leaving a sentry at the door.

"We are in luck," said Bill, as he looked round the room. "This is a better place than the old tower, and I don't see that it will be much more difficult to escape from."

They went to the window. It was long and narrow, but there was ample space for them to creep out of it. It was, however, a great height from the ground; three or four storeys up they calculated; and should they attempt to drop down, they would break every bone in their bodies.

"It cannot be done, I fear," said Jack.

"It can be done, and we'll do it before to-morrow morning, too," answered Bill. "When the general ordered us to be shut up here, he was thinking that we were just like a couple of French boys, without a notion of going aloft, or of finding their way down again."

"But I don't see how we can manage to get down here," said Jack, peeping through the window, cautiously though, for fear of being seen. "There is nothing to lay hold of, and the door is locked and bolted. I heard that traitor Irishman shoot a bolt before he went away."

"Look here," replied Bill, pointing towards the bed.

"Why, that's a bed," said Jack. "It was very good-natured in the mounseers to give it us to sleep on."

"What do you think it's made of?" asked Bill. "Why, sheets and blankets and ticking," replied Jack. "Yes," said Bill, "you are right; and with those selfsame sheets and blankets, and maybe a fathom or two of rope besides, underneath, I intend that we shall try to lower ourselves down to the ground; and when we are once outside, it will be our own fault if we do not get back to the harbour, and when there, that we do not get on board our raft again. The French captain said it was to be left just as it was for the general to see it to-morrow morning. Before that time comes, I hope that we shall be out of sight of land, if we get a fair breeze, or, at all events, out of sight of the people on shore."

"I'm always ready for anything you propose, Bill," said Jack. "I see now well enough how we are to get away. If all goes smoothly, we shall do it. But suppose we are caught?—and there are a good many chances against us, you'll allow."

"We can but be shut up again. Even if they were to flog us, we could stand it well enough; and as to the pain, that would be nothing, and it would not be like being flogged for breaking the articles of war, or doing anything against the law. I should call it an honourable flogging, and should not mind showing the scars, if any remained," said Bill.

"I'm your man, and the sooner we set about turning our sheets and blankets into a rope the better," exclaimed Jack, enthusiastically. "If we are caught and punished ever so much, we must not mind it."

"Stop a bit," said Bill. "Perhaps the red-haired colonel may pay us a visit before nightfall. We must not be caught making preparations for our escape; that would be a green trick."

"I hope if they come they'll bring us some supper," said Jack. "I am pretty sharp set already; and if the mounseers should have stolen the grub out of our chest, we should have nothing to eat on our voyage."

"I have been thinking too much about going away to feel hungry," said Bill. "But now you talk of it, I should like some food, and I hope they'll bring enough to last us for a day or two. Now, I say, it's getting dark, and we must fix upon the best spot to lower ourselves down to. You listen at the door lest any one should come up suddenly, and I'll examine the windows and settle the best plan."

Bill, however, first went to the bed, examined the blankets and sheets and mattress, and found, to his satisfaction, that below all were two thick pieces of canvas, drawn together by a rope. The rope, though rather thin, would, he was satisfied, bear their light weights. It might take them half an hour or so to twist the various materials up into a rope, and altogether would give them one of ample length for their purpose.

This discovery greatly raised the boys' spirits and hopes of success.

Bill now went to the window, and found that the grass came close up to the walls of the tower underneath. Even should they fall from a considerable height, they might have the chance of not breaking their bones, and that was some satisfaction. An iron bar extended from the top of the window to the bottom in the centre. He felt it, and it was strong as need be. It would do well for securing their rope. As far as he could judge, there was no window under them. This was of consequence, as had there been, they might have been seen by any person within during their descent, rapidly as they might make it. Bill considered whether it would be possible to withdraw the rope after they had descended, but he doubted whether they had sufficient materials to enable them to do that.

"Well, it cannot be helped," Bill said to himself. "The Frenchmen will see how we escaped, but they won't find it out till daylight, and it won't matter much then."

He had finished his survey, and settled his plan, when Jack cried out, "Hist! there's some one coming!" and they ran back and sat themselves down near the table with their heads on their hands, as if they were feeling very melancholy and disconsolate.

"I wish I could squeeze out a tear," said Jack; "but I can't for the life of me. I feel so jolly at your idea of getting off."

Presently the door opened, and an old woman entered with a basket.

"I have brought you some food and a bottle of wine, mes garçons," she said, in a kind tone. "The general gave me permission, and I was very glad to bring it, as I knew that you must be hungry. Poor boys! I heard of your attempt to get away. You would have been drowned to a certainty if you hadn't been caught, and that would have been sad, for one of you, they say, wanted to get back to see his mother. I have got a son at sea, so I can feel for her. I wish he was safe back again. I don't know what they will do with you, but I hear that you are to be tried to-morrow, and the Irish officer here says you are spies, and if so, you will run a great chance of being hung, or, at all events, shut up in a prison till you confess what you have been about. Ah! but I forgot. They say you don't speak French, and you may not have understood a word I have said."

Jack and Bill could scarcely refrain from laughing as the old woman ran on, but they restrained themselves, and when she showed them the contents of the basket, they merely said, "Bon! bon! merci! merci!" several times, and looked very well pleased, as indeed they were, for there was food enough to last them two or three days, full allowance— cheese and sausages, bread, figs, raisins, and butter, besides the bottle of wine.

They were afraid of drinking much of that, not knowing how weak it was, lest it should get into their heads, for they wanted no Dutch courage to do what they intended—they had pluck enough without that.

The old woman—not that she was so very old, but she was small and thin, with a high white cap and a brown dress fitting closely, which made her look older than she was—stood by, after she had covered the table with the provisions, that she might have the pleasure of seeing the boys eat. They were very willing to give her that pleasure, and set to with a good appetite.

She smiled benignantly, and patted them on their heads, as she watched them stowing away the various things. They were not very particular as to which they took first.

"Bon! bon!" said Jack, every now and then, as he saw that his saying so pleased her. "Merci! merci!"

She poured them out some wine; it was dreadfully sour, so Bill thought, and he made signs to her that he would drink it by-and-by, as he did not like to show her how much he disliked it.

Jack was not so particular, but he was content with a mouthful or two, and then began again on the sausages and figs.

"I hope she is not going to stop till we have done," said Bill, "or she may take away the remainder. I'll try and make her understand that we should like a little more by-and-by. I vote we stop now and put the things into the basket. We'll then show her that we do not wish her to take them away."

The kind old housekeeper of the chateau—for such she was—seemed to understand the boys' wishes. Bill even ventured to say a few words in French, which would show her what they wanted; and at last, wishing them good-night, she took her departure.

They heard the door locked and bolted after she went out, as if by some other person; and it made them fear that a sentry was placed there, who might, should they make any noise, look in to see what they were about. It would be necessary, therefore, to be extremely cautious as to their proceedings.

"There's no one moving," said Bill, who had crept to the door to listen. He, of course, spoke in a low whisper. "I vote we set to work at once and make our rope. It will take some time, and we ought to be off as soon as the people have turned in, as we must try to get a good distance from the shore before daylight."

"Suppose any one was to come, and find us cutting up our bed-clothes," said Jack, "it would be suspected what we were going to do."

"We'll keep the coverlid till the last, so as to throw it over the bed should we hear a step on the stair; we must then sit down on the edge, and pretend that we are too sorrowful to think of going to bed," said Bill.

"That will do," replied Jack; "I never was a good hand at piping my eye, but I know that I should be inclined to blubber if I thought there was a chance of being found out."

"There's no use talking about that. We must run the risk," observed Bill; "so here goes." And he forthwith turned back the coverlid, and began measuring the sheets. They were of strong and tough material, and by dividing each into four lengths, he calculated that a rope formed of them would be of sufficient strength for their purpose, and they were quickly cut through with their knives, and each length was then twisted tightly up.

The bed-ticking was treated in the same manner; but that being of less strength, gave them only six much shorter lengths. The sacking and rope at the bottom of the bed would, Bill was sure, reach, at all events, to a short distance from the ground.

As they twisted and bent one piece to another, they surveyed their work with satisfaction, and were convinced that it would bear their weight, though it would hardly have borne that of a man of moderate size. To try it, they tugged away against each other, and it held perfectly firm.

"It will do famously," exclaimed Bill, after they had joined all the pieces together. "Even if it does not quite reach to the ground, I should not mind dropping a dozen feet or so."

"But if we do that, the noise we make in our fall may be heard," said Jack. "Hadn't we better bend on the coverlid? It's not so strong as the sheets, but we can put it at the lower end."

Bill agreed to this, and, as it was of considerable width, it formed three lengths.

"We have enough almost for a double rope, I expect," said Bill, as he coiled it away ready to carry to the window at the opposite side of the room.

"Oh, no; I don't think we've enough for that," said Jack; "even if we had, it won't matter leaving the rope behind. The Frenchmen will see by the disappearance of the bed-clothes how we got out. I advise that we make only one rope, and just get down to the ground as quietly as we can manage to do."

Bill made another trip to the door to listen.

"No one is coming," he whispered, as he returned. "Now let's carry the rope to the window."

They did so, and Bill leant out to listen again. No sounds reached his ear, except the occasional barking of a dog.

"The people go to bed early in this country," he observed, "and I am very much obliged to them. We may start, Jack, without much fear of being stopped."

"But don't let us forget our grub," said Jack; and they filled their pockets with the provisions the old woman had brought them, tying up the remainder in their handkerchiefs, which they fastened to the lanyards of their knives. "Now let's bend on the rope," said Bill.

They secured it round the iron bar.

"I'll go first," said Jack; "if the rope bears me, it's certain to bear you."

"No; I proposed the plan, and I ought to go first," answered Bill. "It's of no use wasting words. Don't begin to come down till you feel that I am off the rope. So here goes."

Bill, on saying this, climbed through the narrow opening between the bar and the side of the window, and then, first grasping the bar with his hands, threw his legs off straight down, and began descending the thin rope. Jack stretched out his head to watch him, but Bill soon disappeared in the darkness.

The rope held, however, though, as he felt it, it appeared stretched to the utmost. He could with difficulty draw a breath, while he waited till, by finding the rope slacken, he should know that Bill had safely reached the bottom. At last he ascertained that Bill was no longer hanging to the rope, while, from not hearing a sound, he was sure that his companion had performed the feat in safety.

As Bill had charged him not to lose a moment, he, following his example, commenced his descent.

Down and down he went, but had he not been thoroughly accustomed to suspend himself on thin ropes, he could not have held on. It seemed to him that he should never reach the bottom; how much further he had to go he could not tell.

All at once he felt a hand grasping him by the leg. A sudden fear seized him.

Could the Frenchmen have got hold of Bill, and were they about to recapture him?

He could with difficulty refrain from crying out; still, as there would be no use in attempting to get up the rope again, he continued to lower himself.

The hand was withdrawn, and presently he found that he had reached the ground.

"All right," whispered Bill in his ear; "I caught hold of your ankle to let you understand that you were close to the bottom. Now let's be off! The harbour lies directly under yonder star. I marked its position during daylight, and again just before I began to descend the rope."

Chapter Sixteen.

Voyage on the raft.

Bill and Jack remained for a few seconds in the dark shade caused by the tall wall of the chateau, listening attentively for any sounds of people moving about. None reached their ears, and only here and there, in the more distant part of the building, were any lights to be seen gleaming from the windows.

"We may run for it now without much chance of being seen," said Bill. "We must step lightly, though, or we may be heard by some of the sentries. Keep your eye on the star, it's the best guide we have for the harbour. Now for it! let's start."

They set off, treading as lightly as they could on the ground with their bare feet, the soles of which were pretty well hardened. For some distance they had only grass to run over, and a couple of phantoms could scarcely have produced less sound.

In a short time, however, they reached a fence. It was somewhat rotten, and as they were climbing over it, a part gave way and came down with a crash.

"Quick!" said Bill, as he was helping over Jack, who followed him; "we must run on like the wind; somebody may be coming to find out what's the matter."

They did not stop, as may be supposed, to repair the damage they had caused, but soon reaching a road which led in the direction they wished to take, they scampered on at full speed.

Tall trees grew on either side of the road, which, casting a dark shadow over it, would have effectually concealed them from view, even if anybody had been looking out for them. The darkness, however, also prevented them from seeing any one who might be ahead.

Sometimes indeed they had a difficulty in keeping in the middle of the road.

"I hope we're going in the right direction," said Jack; "I can't see the star, and the road seems to me to have twisted about."

"We must, at all events, go on," answered Bill. "Perhaps we shall catch sight of the star again before long, and we must steer our course accordingly. There's no use stopping still."

They went on and on.

"There it is at last," cried Jack.

The trees which lined the road were much lower, being indeed mere pollards, and allowed them to see the sky overhead.

Presently they heard a dog bark; then another and another. Could the brutes be barking at them?

It was a sign that there were dwellings near, and the inhabitants might be looking out to ascertain what made their dogs bark.

"Never mind," whispered Bill; "the chances are that the dogs are tied up, and if we keep moving the people won't see us."

They passed through the village or hamlet.

They were still, they knew, some distance from the harbour.

Here and there only could they see a light twinkling from a window, probably of some sick-chamber. It was pretty evident that most of the people had gone to bed, still some one or other might be up who would give the alarm.

They found themselves verging to the right; it was better, however, than keeping to the left side, which might lead them away from the harbour. Presently they came to some grassy downs, and the regular road they had been pursuing turned sharp off to the left.

"We had better keep straight on," said Bill; "we shall be more exposed on the open downs; but then it isn't likely that anybody will be there to see us, so that won't matter."

Jack, as usual, was ready to do whatever Bill proposed. They got quickly over the grass, which was cropped short by sheep feeding on it, and they could manage to see somewhat better than they had done on the road. Presently Jack, whose eyesight was even keener than Bill's, having been well practised at night from his childhood, caught his companion's arm, exclaiming, "Hold back; it seems to me that we have got to the edge of the downs."

They crept cautiously forward. In another instant they would have leapt down a cliff some hundred feet in height, and been dashed to pieces.

They turned away from it, shuddering at the fearful risk they had run, and kept along on somewhat lower ground, still having the star which had before guided them ahead.

Once more they found themselves approaching buildings, but they were low and scattered; evidently only in the outskirts of the village.

"We must be close to the harbour now," said Jack.

"The greater reason that we should be cautious," observed Bill. "This road, I suspect, leads right down to the part of the harbour we want to reach."

They ran on, their hope of escape increasing.

Suddenly they heard the voice of a man shouting out, "Who goes there?"

Bill seized Jack's arm, and pulled him down in the shadow of a high wall, near which they happened at that moment to find themselves.

Some minutes they waited, scarcely daring to draw breath.

The shout was not repeated.

"We may go on now," whispered Jack; and getting up, they crept forward. Presently, below them, they caught sight of the harbour, with the stars reflected on its surface.

The most difficult part of their undertaking was now to be performed. They had to find out exactly where their raft lay.

Bill had not failed to observe the shape of the harbour, and to take note of the various objects on shore, as he and Jack were brought in prisoners by the French boat; but the partial survey he was then able to make did not enable him to settle positively in what direction they ought to proceed to find their raft.

By keeping on as they were then going they believed that they should make the shore of the harbour at no great distance from the mouth. They might then keep along up it until they reached the place where they landed, near which they hoped to find their raft moored.

"I am only afraid that we may meet some guards or patrols, or fishermen coming on shore or going off to their vessels," observed Jack.

"If we do we must try to hide ourselves," answered Bill. "We'll keep along as close as we can under the cliffs, or any walls or houses we are passing, so that we may see people before we are seen ourselves."

They acted as Bill suggested, and pushed boldly onwards. Not a sound was heard coming either from the land side or from the harbour. The water was as smooth as glass.

They were still going forward when Jack seized Bill's arm. "That's the place," he whispered. "I can make out the raft, moored outside a boat at the end of a slip."

Bill, creeping forward, assured himself that Jack was right, and, as nothing could be gained by waiting a moment, they hurried on, and in a few seconds were on board their raft. Jack plunged his hand into one of the chests, to ascertain that the articles it had contained were still there. They had not been taken away.

He could scarcely refrain from shouting out for joy.

Even the oars had not been removed.

They got another from the boat alongside to supply the place of the one which had been splintered.

"Cut the warps," cried Bill. "We'll paddle on till we find the breeze."

The raft was quickly cast loose, and, getting out the oars, they began to paddle silently down the harbour. They could not avoid making some slight noise, but they hoped that there was no one on the watch to hear it. Very frequently they turned their glances astern to ascertain if they were followed, but they could see nothing moving. There were several vessels lower down the harbour, so they steered a course which would carry them past at some little distance from them.

The raft moved easily over the smooth surface, and they made good way. There was only one vessel more which they had to pass before they reached the harbour's mouth. They both earnestly hoped that her crew were fast asleep, and that no watch was kept on deck.

They paddled slowly by, and more than half a cable's length from her, moving their oars as gently as possible, and scarcely daring to breathe. The slightest sound might betray them.

At length they got outside her, and there was nothing now between them and the open channel.

Again Jack could hardly refrain from shouting.

Just then a voice came from the vessel.

Bill looked back. He judged by the distance the vessel was off that the character of the raft could not be discovered. He answered in very good French, "We are going out early this morning, and if we have good luck in fishing, we'll bring you some for breakfast."

"Thank you, my friend, thank you," answered the man on board the vessel.

Bill had been paddling on all the time he was speaking. He was certain that the man did not suspect who he and Jack were, and in a few minutes they lost sight of the vessel altogether.

They now gave way with might and main. They were rowing for life and liberty; for if again caught, they fully believed that they should be shot. How anxiously they wished that a breeze would spring up!

For fully an hour they rowed on, till the shore faded from sight.

They were steering by the polar star, which both Jack and Bill knew well.

"If there's a breeze from the southward, we ought to feel it by this time," observed Jack.

"Never fear; we shall find it before long," answered Bill. "We are not so far away from the cliffs as you suppose, and it would be as well not to speak loud, or our voices may reach any boat passing, or even people on shore."

"I hope there will be none there at this hour, though they will come down fast enough in the morning from the chateau, when they find we have taken French leave," said Jack.

"A very proper thing to take, too, seeing we were in France," remarked Bill, with a quiet chuckle. "I hope we shall never set foot on its shores again."

"So do I; but I'm afraid we have a great chance of doing so, unless we get a breeze pretty soon. I am inclined to whistle for it," said Jack.

"It won't come the faster for that," answered Bill. "We shall do more good by working our oars. We are sending the raft along at three knots an hour at least, and as it will be three hours or more before daylight, we shall be ten miles or so away from the shore, even if we do not get a breeze, before the Frenchmen find out that we have got off."

As Bill advised, he and Jack continued pulling away as lustily as at first.

The smoothness of the water was a great advantage to them, for had there been any sea their progress would have been much slower.

An hour or more passed away, when Bill exclaimed, "Here comes the wind, and right aft, too! It's not very strong yet, but it will freshen soon, I hope. Stand by, Jack, to hoist the sail!"

"Ay, ay!" answered Jack, taking hold of the halyards and feeling that all was clear.

"Hand me the sheet; and now hoist away," said Bill.

Jack, with right good will, hauled away at the halyards, and the sail was soon set.

The raft felt the influence of the breeze and glided on at an increased speed. It was cheery to hear the water rippling against the bows.

"We must take care not to capsize the raft if the wind increases much," observed Bill. "Keep the halyards ready to let go in a moment; the sail is full large for our craft, and it would not take long to capsize it."

"Trust me for that," said Jack; "I have no wish to be drowned, and I feel wonderfully jolly at the thought of having got away. Are you steering a right course, Bill? It seems to me that the sail must be between you and the polar star."

"No; I can see it directly over the yard when I stand up and keep well aft," answered Bill. "The wind, too, won't let us go in any other direction."

"How about the tide?" asked Jack.

"Why, as it was just on the ebb when we came out of the harbour, and helped us along, it is, I calculate, making to the westward. It won't, however, run much longer in that direction, and it will then carry us to the eastward for a good six hours. We'll be well out of sight of land by that time, and, I hope, may fall in with an English cruiser, though, for my part, I would rather run right across the Channel. It would be fine fun to land, and tell the people how we managed it. They would think more of our raft than the Frenchmen did, though there are not many boys afloat who would not try to do as we have done."

Jack was of the same opinion, and as there was no necessity for rowing, while Bill steered, Jack sat on a chest with his arms folded. Suddenly he exclaimed, "I say, Bill, I am getting very peckish; I vote we have some supper."

"Well, we have not far to go for it," observed Bill, "seeing we have got enough in our pockets to last us for the whole of to-morrow."

As Bill could not well manage to steer and tend the sheet and eat his supper, too, he let Jack finish his; after which they changed places, and Bill fell to with a good appetite on some of the old Frenchwoman's provisions.

"I hope the kind old creature won't get into any scrape for supplying us," said Bill.

"I don't see how it will be found out that she gave us so much," said Jack. "When she finds that we are gone, she'll keep her own counsel, depend on that."

"We must not expend the food too fast, though," remarked Bill. "It will take us several days to get across Channel; and it won't do to run short of provisions."

"You forget those we have in the chest," said Jack.

"Are you certain that the Frenchmen allowed them to remain there," asked Bill, opening the lid of one of them, and feeling about. "Yes! here's a piece of beef or pork and some biscuit. All right, we shall do now. I'll take the helm again if you like; I feel more comfortable when I'm at it, though you steer well enough, I dare say."

"As you like," said Jack. "I'd just as soon stand by the halyards."

They again changed places.

Bill kept his eye on the polar star, while Jack peered under the sail ahead, that they might not, as he said, run down any craft.

Thus the night passed away. The breeze slightly increased, but Bill considered that they might still carry their whole sail with safety. Perhaps they did not move along quite so fast as he supposed. He told

Jack that he thought they were running through the water at five knots an hour; but four, or even three, knots was a good deal for a raft to make, with flat bows, light and well put together as it was.

They were too much excited to feel the slightest inclination to sleep, and being both in capital spirits, did not trouble themselves with thinking of the possibility that the weather might change before they could get across to the English coast. A fast lugger would take nearly two days to do the distance.

The dawn now broke, and they eagerly looked out on every side for a sail. As the light increased they were greatly disappointed, on gazing astern, to discover the French coast still in sight, though blue and indistinct, like a cloud rising out of the water. No sail, however, was to be seen in that direction. That was a comfort; they were not pursued by any large craft, and could certainly not be seen from the shore.

To the northward, however, they caught sight of a sail just rising above the horizon, and soon afterwards another was seen to the eastward, but which way she was standing they could not determine.

As the sun rose the wind decreased, and before long it became perfectly calm.

"We must lower the sail and take to our oars again," said Bill. "It won't do to stop where we are."

"I am ready to pull on as long as I have any strength in me," answered Jack, as he stowed the sail, and got out his oar.

Chapter Seventeen.

A narrow escape—The fugitives picked up by a frigate.

The rest Jack and Bill had obtained while their raft was under sail enabled them to row with as much vigour as at first; and row they did with might and main, knowing that their liberty might depend upon their exertions.

The calm was very trying, for they had expected to be wafted quickly across the Channel, and row as hard as they could, their progress must be slow. After rowing for a couple of hours or more, they found themselves apparently no nearer the ship ahead than they had been at first.

At length hunger compelled them to lay in their oars and take some breakfast. They ate a hearty one, for they had plenty of provisions; but on examining their stock of water they found that they must be very economical, or they might run short of that necessary of life.

After a short rest, Bill sprang to his feet.

"It won't do to be stopping," he observed. "If we only make a couple of miles an hour it will be something, and we shall be so much nearer home, and so much farther away from the French shore."

"I'm afraid that when the mounseers find out that we have escaped, they will be sending after us," said Jack. "They will be ashamed of being outwitted by a couple of English boys, and will do all they can to bring us back."

"I believe you are right, Jack," replied Bill; "only, as they certainly will not be able to see us from the shore, they won't know in what direction to pull, and may fancy that we are hid away somewhere along the coast."

"They'll guess well enough that we should have pulled to the nor'ard, and will be able to calculate by the set of the tide whereabouts to find us," said Jack. "We mustn't trust too much to being safe as yet. I wonder what that vessel to the eastward is. She's a ship, for I can see her royals above the horizon, and she's certainly nearer than when we first made her out."

"She must be standing to the westward, then, and will, I hope, pass inside of us, should the breeze spring up again from the same quarter," observed Bill. "She's probably French, or she would not be so close in with the coast."

"As to that, our cruisers stand in close enough at times, and she may be English notwithstanding," answered Jack.

"Unless we are certain that she's English we shall be wiser to avoid her," remarked Bill, "so we'll pull away to the nor'ard."

"But what do you think of the ship out there?" asked Jack, pointing ahead.

"I cannot help believing that she's English," said Bill. "We must run the chance of being seen by her. We shall have to pull on a good many hours, however, first, and when the breeze springs up, she'll pretty quickly run either to the eastward or westward."

The boys, however, after all their remarks, could arrive at no conclusion. They rowed and rowed, but still appeared not to have moved their position with regard either to the shore or the two vessels in sight.

The sun rose high above their heads and struck down with considerable force; but they cared little for the heat, though it made them apply more frequently than they otherwise would have done to their water-cask. Bill had more than once to warn Jack not to drink too much.

The day was drawing on, and at last Jack proposed that they should have another rest and take some dinner. "There's no use starving ourselves, and the more we eat the better we shall be able to pull," he said.

Bill was not quite of this opinion. At the same time he agreed to Jack's proposal, as his arms were becoming very weary.

They had just finished their dinner when Jack, getting up on the chest in which the mast was stepped, so that he might have a better look-out, exclaimed, "I see a sail between us and the land. The sun just now glanced on it. There's a breeze in shore, depend on it, and it will reach us before long."

Bill jumped up to have a look-out also. He could not distinguish the sail, but he thought by the darker colour of the water to the southward that a breeze was playing over it, though it had not as yet got as far as they were. They again took to their oars and pulled on. Jack, however, occasionally turned round to look to the southward, for he entertained the uncomfortable idea that they were pursued.

They were now, they agreed, nearer the ship to the northward. Her lofty sails must have caught a light westerly air, which did not reach close down to the water, and had sent her along two or three knots an hour. They could see half-way down her courses, and Jack declared his belief that she was a frigate, but whether English or French he could not determine.

Unless, however, they were to hoist their sail, they might pass very close to her without being discovered, and the course she was steering would take her somewhat to the eastward of them.

They would have to settle the point as to whether she was a friend or foe, and in the former case whether it would be advisable to hoist their sail, and made every signal in their power to attract her attention, or to keep the sail lowered until she was at a distance from them. Bill had not been convinced that Jack had seen a sail to the southward.

"Whether or not I saw one before, there's one now," cried Jack, "and pretty near, too, and what's worse, it's a boat, so that they have oars, and will be coming up with us in spite of the calm."

"They must have had a breeze to get thus far," remarked Bill.

"Yes, but it has failed them now; see, they are lowering down the sail." As Jack spoke, a light patch of white like the wing of a wild-fowl was seen for a moment glancing above the water landward.

"Yes, there's no doubt that was a sail, which must have come from the shore; but it is a question whether the Frenchmen will have the pluck to pull on in the hopes of finding us, or will turn back. One thing is certain, that we had better try to keep ahead, when they will have farther to come if they still pursue us."

Once more the boys got their oars out, and laboured away as energetically as before. They every now and then, however, looked back to ascertain if the boat were coming after them. Meantime a light breeze played occasionally over the water, but it was so light that it would not have helped them much, and they thought it wiser not to hoist their sail, as it would betray their position should a French boat really be in pursuit of them.

The ship, which they supposed to be a frigate, was in in the meantime drawing nearer to them from the north-east.

"I cannot help thinking that the boat is still coming after us," cried Jack. "I fancy I caught sight of the gleam of the sun on the men's hats; if I were to swarm up the mast I should be more certain."

"You will run the chance of capsizing the raft if you do," observed Bill.

"I'll just go a little way up," retorted Jack; and he jumped on the chest, and hoisted himself three or four feet only up the mast, while Bill sat down on the deck to counterbalance his weight.

"Yes, I was right," said Jack, coming down. "I made out a boat, as sure as we are here, and a large one, too, or I should not have seen her so clearly. She's a good way off still, so that it will be some time before she can get up with us. The French fellows in her must take yonder ship to be a countryman, or they would not pull on so boldly."

"They may think that they have time to pick us up and be off again before the ship can get near them," said Bill; "but whatever they think, we must try to disappoint them, so we'll pull away as long as we can stand, and then we'll row on our knees."

The sun was by this time sinking towards the west; and should darkness come on, their chances of escape would be increased. The wind had shifted slightly to the south-west, and should it freshen sufficiently to make it worth while hoisting the sail, they might stand away to the north-east. It still, however, wanted two or three hours before it would be perfectly dark, while the boat would be up to them before that time. After rowing for the greater part of an hour, Jack again took a look-out, and reported that he could distinctly see the boat.

"So I suspect by this time can the people on board the ship," observed Bill, "and probably they can see us also; but the crew of the boat well know that with this light wind they can easily row away from the ship should she prove to be English."

In a short time they could both see the boat when only standing up on the raft. They had now too much reason to fear that, in spite of all their efforts, they should be overtaken. Still, like brave boys, they pulled on, though their arms and backs were aching with their exertions.

The Frenchmen, who must by this time have seen the raft, appeared determined to re-take them.

Presently a report was heard, and a bullet flew skimming over the water, but dropped beneath the surface somewhere astern.

Another and another followed.

"Their shot won't hurt us as yet," observed Bill. "They fancy that they can frighten us, but we'll show them that they are mistaken;" and he pulled on as steadily as he had before been doing.

Jack, however, could not resist jumping up once more on the chest, and looking towards the ship.

"Hurrah! there's a boat coming off from the ship!" he cried out. "If she's English, she'll soon make the Frenchmen put about."

Jack was right as to a boat coming from the ship, but the Frenchmen still pulled on. Perhaps they did not see the boat, or if they did, thought that she also was French.

Again and again the pursuers fired, the bullets now falling close to the raft.

"A miss is as good as a mile," cried Bill, rowing on.

But the French boat was evidently getting terribly near.

If any tolerable marksman were on board, he could easily pick off the two occupants of the raft. They knew that well enough, but they kept to their resolution of pulling on till the last.

They were encouraged, too, by seeing the boat from the stranger making towards them. Presently three or four bullets together flew close to their ears, and fell into the water ahead.

"Pull on! pull on!" cried Bill; "the fellows fired to vent their spite. They are going to give up the chase."

He looked round as he spoke, and, sure enough, the stern of the boat was seen.

The Frenchmen were rowing back to the shore.

The boat of the stranger, instead of steering, as she had been, towards the raft, was now seen directing her course after the French boat, the crew of which were evidently straining every nerve to escape.

"Hurrah!" cried Jack, standing up and waving his cap, "that's an English frigate."

"No doubt about it," exclaimed Bill; "I can see her ensign blowing out;" and he could scarcely refrain from throwing up his cap, but remembered that it might chance to fall overboard if he did.

Directly afterwards a gun was heard, fired by the frigate.

It was a signal to recall the boat.

She would have had a long pull before she could over take the Frenchmen.

The signal was not to be disobeyed, and she was seen to pull round and steer for the raft.

The boys eagerly watched her approach.

She was soon up to them.

"Hallo, my lads! where do you come from?" asked the officer, who was standing up in the stern-sheets.

"We are running away from the Frenchmen, sir," answered Bill.

"A curious craft you have chosen for the purpose," observed the officer.

"It was the best we could get, sir," said Bill. "We twice have managed to make our escape, and the first time were caught and carried back."

"Well, we'll hear all about it by-and-by. Come, jump on board. I should like to tow your raft to the frigate, but we must not delay for that purpose," exclaimed the officer.

Jack and Bill quickly tumbled into the boat, though, as soon as they were on board, they cast wistful glances at their raft.

The officer ordered the men to give way, and steered the boat towards the frigate. He now asked the lads how they came to be in France.

Bill briefly described how the *Foxhound* had blown up, and the way in which they had been taken on board a French fishing-vessel, and their various adventures on shore.

"That's curious enough," observed the lieutenant, "for we have on board the frigate most of those who escaped."

The officer, who was the third lieutenant of the frigate, had learned the greater part of their history by the time the boat got up to her.

He and most of the crew quickly climbed on board, followed by the boys.

The falls were hooked on, and the boat hoisted up.

Whom should Jack and Bill see standing on the deck, and issuing his orders to the crew to "brace round the yards," but Mr Saltwell, the first lieutenant of their former ship.

They stood for some minutes by themselves, for everybody was too much engaged to attend to them. The frigate's head was now turned in the direction of the stranger they had seen to the eastward, towards which they observed that the glasses of several of the officers were directed.

"Though she has not shown her colours, I feel positive that she's French," observed the captain to Mr Saltwell.

"I hope that you are right, sir," was the answer; "but we shall scarcely get up to her before dark."

"We shall get near enough to make the private signal," said the captain, "and if she does not answer it we shall know how to treat her when we do get up to her."

All the sail the frigate could carry was set, and as the breeze had increased, she ran rapidly through the water.

Chapter Eighteen.

The frigate in action—Bill shows that he can be of use.

The stranger, which had apparently been beating down Channel, now put up her helm, and setting studden sails stood to the eastward before the wind. She failed also to answer the private signal; no doubt, therefore, remained that she was French, and wished to avoid an action, though, as she appeared to be as large as the English frigate, if not larger, this was somewhat surprising.

"Perhaps she has some consorts to the eastward, and wishes to lead us into their midst during the night," observed Mr Saltwell.

"She will find that she's mistaken. We will keep too bright a look-out to be so caught," said the captain.

The first lieutenant, as he was walking forward, caught sight of Bill and Jack.

"Why, lads, where do you come from?" he asked.

As he spoke he recognised Bill.

"Are you not the lad who gave notice of the plot of the American captain to capture our ship?" he asked.

Bill acknowledged that such was the case.

"I am truly glad that you have escaped. I promised our late captain that I would keep an eye on you," he continued, "and I shall now have the opportunity. I thought you, with the rest of our poor fellows, had been lost when our ship blew up."

Bill briefly described their adventures, and the lieutenant seemed much interested. He said he would have them at once entered on the ship's books, for as they were likely soon to be engaged with the enemy, it might be of importance to them.

He accordingly sent for the purser, to whom he gave the proper directions. Bill and Jack then made their way below.

On passing the galley they saw a boy busily employed, assisting the cook's mate in cleaning pots and pans. He looked up at them and started, letting drop the pot at which he was scrubbing.

"What! Bill! Jack! I thought you had gone to Davy Jones's locker," he exclaimed. "Are you really yourselves?"

"No doubt about it, Tom," answered Bill and in a few words they again told their adventures.

Tom soon recovered from his astonishment. He appeared somewhat ashamed of his present occupation. He had got into a scrape, he acknowledged, and had been ordered to assist the cook's mate.

"I wish you would tell him, Tom, that we are very hungry, as we have had a long pull, and that if he would give us something to eat we should be very much obliged to him. If he's a good-natured fellow, I daresay he will."

Tom undertook to plead for them with the cook himself, who just then put his head out of the galley. The cook, without hesitation, on hearing their story, gave them each a basin of broth and a handful of biscuit.

While they were eating they asked Tom to tell them how he had escaped.

"I've no very clear notion about the matter," he answered; "I must have been in the water, for I found myself lying at the bottom of a boat wet to the skin, and more dead than alive. There were a dozen or more of our fellows in her, and Mr Saltwell, our first lieutenant, who had been picked up, I supposed, as I had been. They thought I was done for, and, as the boat was overloaded, they were about to heave me overboard, when I opened my eyes, and sang out, 'Don't;' so they let me remain, and after some time pulled alongside a cutter, on board which we were taken and looked after below. Shortly afterwards we went in chase of a French craft of the same rig as ours, but she got away, and we then steered for Plymouth. We were at first taken on board the guardship, where we remained some time, and then I was transferred with others to this frigate, the *Thisbe*, of which, to my great satisfaction, I found that Mr Saltwell had been appointed first lieutenant. Thinking that, as we had shared a common misfortune, he would stand my friend, I went up to him, and telling him that I was a gentleman's son, begged he would have me put on the quarter-deck. He told me that if I did my duty I should have as good a chance as others; but here I am set to scrape potatoes and clean pots and pans. It's a shame, a great shame, and I can't stand it."

Bill and Jack had a tolerably correct notion why Tom was not better off, but they did not say so, as they did not wish to hurt his feelings, and were grateful to him for having obtained for them the broth and biscuits.

They had scarcely finished their meal when the order came to extinguish the galley fire.

A short time afterwards the drum beat to quarters, and every one was employed in getting the ship ready for action.

Jack and Bill expected that they would be employed in their former occupation of powder-monkeys, though, having been awake all the previous night, and in active exertion the whole of the day, notwithstanding the expectation of a battle, they could with difficulty keep their eyes open. They were going with the rest of the boys to the powder-magazine, when they heard their names called out, and the ship's corporal appearing, told them that the first lieutenant had directed that they should turn in below and take some sleep.

A couple of hammocks were slung for them forward, and they very gladly obeyed the order.

Bill made an effort to keep awake, that he might turn out again should the ship go into action, but in less than two minutes drowsiness overtook him, and he went fast asleep.

He dreamed, however, that he heard the guns firing, and the crew shouting, and that he got up and found that the frigate had taken the Frenchman.

Meantime, however, the wind falling light, the frigate made but slow progress, though she still kept the enemy in sight.

When Bill really awoke, the light was streaming down through the fore-hatchway. He roused up Jack, as there was no one below to call them, and on going on deck they discovered the crew at their quarters, and the French frigate almost within range of their guns.

She was to leeward, for the wind was still in its former quarter, and she had just then hauled up and backed her main-topsail to await their coming.

She was now seen to carry four more guns than the *Thisbe*, and to be apparently considerably larger, her bright, polished sides showing that she had not been long out of harbour.

When a ship goes into action, sail is generally shortened, but Captain Martin kept all the *Thisbe's* set, and stood on, bearing down directly for the enemy.

Jack had been sent to join the other boys, who were employed in bringing up the powder as required from the magazine, but the first lieutenant directed Bill to remain near him.

Jack took his seat as a matter of course on his tub, and, as it happened, next to Tom.

"How are you feeling?" asked Tom, who looked rather pale.

"Much as I generally do, only I am rather peckish," answered Jack. "I wish we had had time for breakfast before thrashing the mounseers, but I hope that won't take us very long."

"I hope not," said Tom; "only they say that the French ship is the bigger of the two."

"What's the odds of that, provided we can work our guns twice as fast as they can?" observed Jack; "that's the way we licked the Frenchmen before, and, of course, we shall lick them again; but I say, Tom, what makes you look so melancholy?"

"Do I? Well, if you want to know, I was thinking of home, and wishing I had not run off to sea. I've had a miserable life of it since I came on board this frigate. It was my own fault that I did not go back when I was last on shore. I had the chance, but was ashamed to show my face."

"There's no use thinking about that sort of thing now," said Jack. "We shall be fighting the Frenchmen in a few minutes, and the round and grape shot and bullets will be flying about our ears."

"That's what I don't quite like the thoughts of," replied Tom. "I hope neither you nor I will be hit, Jack."

"Of course not," said Jack; "it wouldn't be pleasant, though we must do our duty, and trust to chance, or rather trust in Providence, like the rest."

"I don't envy Bill up on deck there," remarked Tom. "I wonder what the first lieutenant wants with him."

"Perhaps he intends to turn him into a midshipman," suggested Jack.

"Into a midshipman! a London street boy, who scarcely knows who his father was," ejaculated Tom. "I should think he would have made me one before him."

"The first lieutenant doesn't care a rap what he or his father was. He remembers only the way Bill saved the ship from being taken by the American skipper, and he seemed highly pleased at our having escaped from France. I tell you I shouldn't be at all surprised if Bill is placed on the quarter-deck," said Jack.

Tom gave a grunt of dissatisfaction. The conversation had a good effect, as far as he was concerned, as it made him forget the fears he had entertained about his personal safety.

In the meantime Bill remained on deck watching what was going forward. He heard Captain Martin tell the first lieutenant that he intended to engage the enemy to leeward, in order to prevent her escape; but as the *Thisbe* approached the French ship, the latter, suspecting his intention, so as to frustrate it, wore round on the starboard tack.

After much skilful seamanship on both sides, Captain Martin, finding that he could not succeed, ranged up to windward of the enemy within pistol shot, both ships being on the larboard tack, two or three points off the wind.

They now simultaneously opened their broadsides, the shot of the

Thisbe telling with considerable effect, while not a few of those of the enemy came on board in return, cutting up her rigging, and laying low three or four of her men.

The French ship now passed under the stern of the *Thisbe*, firing her larboard broadside with great precision. A second time she attempted to repeat the manoeuvre, but the crew of the *Thisbe*, having quickly rove new braces, her sails were thrown aback, and gathering sternway, her starboard quarter took the larboard bow of the French frigate.

The French on this made several attempts to board, but the marines, who were drawn up on deck, opened so warm a fire that they were driven back with considerable loss.

The *Thisbe* had now her enemy fast to her quarter. In order to keep her there, Captain Martin and some of his crew endeavoured to lash her bowsprit to his mizenmast; while others were engaged in bringing a gun to bear, out of a port which the carpenters quickly cut through the stern windows and quarter gallery.

While they were thus engaged, the enemy kept up a hot fire on them, several men being killed and wounded; but the gun was at length brought into position.

"Now fire, my lads!" cried the second lieutenant, who was superintending the operation.

After the first, discharge, no sooner had the smoke cleared away, than full twenty Frenchmen were seen stretched on the deck.

Bill had been standing near the first lieutenant. A marine had just loaded his musket, but was knocked over before he had time to fire it. Bill at that moment saw a French seaman run along the bowsprit with a musket in his hand. Bill, springing forward, seized that of the marine, and, as he did so, he observed the Frenchman taking aim at the head of Mr Saltwell, whose eyes were turned in a different direction.

There was not a moment for deliberation. Without ceremony pushing the lieutenant aside, he fired at the Frenchman, who, as he did so, discharged his musket, but immediately fell overboard, the ball tearing away the rim of Mr Saltwell's hat, but without hurting him.

The first lieutenant, turning round, perceived the way by which his life had been saved.

"Thank you, my lad," he said, "I see how you did it, and I'll not forget the service you have rendered me."

There was no time just then for saying more, for a party of Frenchmen were attempting to fire a carronade on their forecastle. Before they could succeed, the marines had picked off the greater number. Others took their places, but every man of them was treated in the same manner. At last the attempt to fire the gun was abandoned.

The French ship now getting a breeze, began to forge ahead. This enabled the *Thisbe's* crew to bring their aftermost gun on the starboard side to bear, the first discharge from which cut away the gammoning of the French frigate's bowsprit.

The two ships now separated, but were soon again abreast of each other exchanging broadsides; but so rapidly did the English crew work their guns that they managed to fire three to the Frenchman's two.

A loud cheer burst from their throats as they saw the enemy's maintopmast go over the side. The *Thisbe* now forged ahead clear of her adversary, and the breeze dying away, the firing ceased on both sides. Still the Frenchmen kept their colours flying.

The English crew were busily employed in knotting and splicing the rigging which had been cut away, and repairing other damages.

"I hope they've had enough of it, and that the fighting is over," exclaimed Tom.

"Not so sure of that," said Jack. "The French take a good deal of drubbing, and don't always know when they are beaten."

Tom felt, at all events, that he had had enough of it, as he looked along the deck and saw numbers of the men who had been slightly hurt binding up each other's wounds. Several lay stiff and stark, whose bodies were dragged on one side, while not a few, severely hurt, had been carried below to the cockpit, where the surgeon and his mates had ample employment.

Among the killed was the second lieutenant, a master's mate, and two young midshipmen; altogether of the two hundred and fifty men who that morning were in health and strength, forty were either killed outright or were severely wounded.

Just then, however, the survivors were too much occupied to think about the matter; every man and boy was wanted to get the ship to rights, and all were eagerly looking out for a breeze that they might again attack the enemy. Bill was as eager as any one for the fight. He felt that he was somebody, as he could not help reflecting that he had done good service in saving the life of the first lieutenant, though he did not exactly expect any reward in consequence. It seemed to him that he had grown suddenly from a powder monkey into a man. Still the calm continued, and the two ships lay with their sails against the masts, the water shining like a polished mirror.

The calm was to the advantage of the French, who had thus longer time to repair their damages. The English were soon ready to renew the action.

What, however, might not happen in the meantime?

Both the captain and Mr Saltwell thought it possible that the French squadron might be to the eastward, and should the firing have been heard, and a breeze spring up from that direction, which it was very likely to do, the Frenchmen in overwhelming force might be down upon them.

The captain walked the deck, looking anxiously out in every direction for signs of a breeze. Occasionally reports were brought to him of the way the wounded men were getting on. The surgeons had as much work as they could get through, cutting off arms and legs, setting broken limbs, and binding up flesh wounds. Such are the horrors of war! How many might be added ere long to the number of the killed and wounded!

It was nearly noon when the captain exclaimed, "Here comes a breeze! Trim sails, my lads!" The men flew to the braces. The canvas blew out, and the frigate began slowly to move towards her antagonist.

Chapter Nineteen.

The "Thisbe" victorious—An enemy's squadron heaves in sight.

The crew of the *Thisbe* stood at their guns, ready to open fire at the word of command. Several who had, at the commencement of the action, been among them, were missing; and though the survivors mourned their loss, that was not the time either to think or talk about them. Not a word, indeed, was spoken fore and aft; not even the usual jokes passed between the men. The Frenchman showed no inclination to avoid the combat. He could not have got away even had he wished, for his foretopmast was gone, and he had not fully repaired the other damages he had received aloft.

Nearer and nearer the *Thisbe* drew to the enemy, still the looked-for word of command did not come. The captain resolved to wait till he got close up to her. The French, also, for some time refrained from firing, though the *Thisbe* was within range of their guns. They were the first to lose patience, or perhaps they thought that they could knock away the spars and rigging of their antagonist, and thus be able to make their escape.

The *Thisbe*, however, was coming up on their larboard quarter. Their guns which they could bring to bear were trained high for the purpose mentioned. The shot came whistling about her masts and rigging; but though some of her sails were shot through, and a few ropes cut away, no material damage was received. The breeze at that instant freshened, and the *Thisbe* glided rapidly on.

"Give it them, my lads!" cried the captain, as the helm being put to starboard the whole of the *Thisbe's* broadside was brought to bear with terrible effect on the enemy.

The Frenchman again fired. The *Thisbe's* guns were quickly run in and reloaded. The breeze at that instant blew aside the smoke, and as it did so the enemy's foremast was seen to fall with a crash overboard.

Loud cheers rang forth from the decks of the *Thisbe*. Again her broadside was fired, but no return came. The next instant, through the smoke, the Frenchman's ensign was seen in the act of being lowered, just in time to save them from another broadside.

The British crew had cheered lustily when they saw the foremast fall. They now redoubled their shouts, turning round and shaking each other heartily by the hand; some throwing up their caps, and others, mostly the Irishmen of the crew, leaping and dancing with delight.

Two of the *Thisbe's* boats being uninjured, they were lowered; and the third lieutenant, with a master's mate and a party of seamen, was sent on board to take possession of the prize.

As they were about to shove off, Mr Saltwell inquired whether any one could speak French.

"I can, sir," said Bill, touching his hat.

"Then go and assist Mr Sterling; you will be of much use," said the first lieutenant.

Bill, who had been longing to visit the prize, obeyed with no small satisfaction.

As they reached her deck, an officer advanced with his sword in his hand, and presented it to Mr Sterling, who, receiving it, handed it to Bill.

The French officer announced that he was the second lieutenant of the *Diana* frigate, which it was his misfortune now to yield into the possession of her British conquerors.

Mr Sterling bowed in return.

"Tell him, Rayner," he said, "that we acknowledge how bravely he and his countrymen have fought their ship, and that though they have lost her, they have not lost their honour."

The French lieutenant looked highly gratified at this remark when Bill interpreted it, and desired him to express his obligation to the English lieutenant.

The captain and first lieutenant had been killed, as were no less than thirty of the crew, including other officers, while fifty were wounded.

The deck, indeed, presented a dreadful scene—strewed in every direction with corpses, while many poor fellows were so fearfully injured that their shipmates had been unwilling to move them.

The other officers presented their swords, while the seamen unbuckled their cutlasses, and the marines piled their arms. Many wry faces were made, though most of the Frenchmen merely shrugged their shoulders, observing that what had happened to them was the fortune of war. Bill made himself very useful in communicating with the French officers and crew.

One of the *Diana's* boats had escaped injury, and she, being lowered, assisted the other boats in carrying the prisoners on board the *Thisbe*. They far outnumbered the English, and much vigilance was required to keep them in order.

The prize crew sent on board the *Diana* set to work, under the command of Mr Sterling, to stop the shot-holes in her sides, and to repair her other more serious damages. A jury-mast was rigged forward, to supply the place of the foremast carried away. In the meantime, a hawser being conveyed on board the *Thisbe*, the prize was taken in tow, and sail was made for Plymouth.

It was of the greatest importance to get away from the French coast without delay, for a northerly wind might spring up and drive the two ships upon it; or if, as Captain Martin suspected, a French squadron was in the neighbourhood, the sound of the firing might have reached them, and they would very probably come up to ascertain what had taken place, when the prize would be recaptured, and the *Thisbe* herself might find it very difficult to escape.

Everybody on board had, therefore, ample work to do; besides which the prisoners in both ships had to be watched. Several had been allowed to remain on board the prize to assist the surgeons in attending to the wounded men. An eye had also to be kept on them.

Mr Saltwell sent for Bill, who had returned to the *Thisbe*.

"I remember well how you behaved on board the *Foxhound*, and I want you to keep a watch on the prisoners, and let me know if you hear or see anything suspicious. They will probably remain quiet enough, as they must know that they would have very little chance of success should they attempt to rise upon us. At the same time it is better to be on the safe side, and not to trust them too much."

"They have heard me talking French to the officers, and will be careful what they say when they see me near them," answered Bill; "but there's my messmate, Jack Peek, who was in France with me, and knows their 'lingo' as well as I do; and as they have not heard him talking, they'll not suspect him; and if you will allow me, sir, I will tell him to go among them, and he'll soon find out if they have any thoughts of mischief."

Mr Saltwell approved of Bill's proposal, and gave him leave to employ Jack as he suggested.

Bill, going below, soon found out his messmate.

Jack was well pleased at the confidence placed in him, and promised to keep his eyes and ears well open.

There was no time for conversation just then, for every man in the ship was busy, and the boys were wanted to assist them.

The frigate and her prize had made some way to the northward before night came on. A bright look-out was kept for any enemy which might heave in sight; but when darkness gradually stole over the ocean, none had appeared.

During that night none of the English officers or men turned in. The most tired snatched a few moments of sleep at intervals as best they could when off watch.

The Frenchmen were allowed to lie down on deck between the guns, with sentries placed over them. It was very evident that, had they chosen to rise, they might have overpowered the sentries at the cost of a few of their own lives. Fortunately none of them liked to run the risk of being shot, and remained quiet.

The wind was light, and the *Thisbe* and her prize made but slow progress.

The captain anxiously waited the return of morning.

At early dawn look-outs were sent aloft to ascertain if any vessels were in sight. They reported three to the south-east, and one to the westward; but what they were it was impossible at that distance to say, as their loftier sails could but indistinctly be seen rising above the horizon.

The *Thisbe* had already as much sail set as she could carry, but Lieutenant Sterling was making an effort to get up a maintopmast on board the prize.

When Jack and Bill met at breakfast, Jack reported that he had been frequently among the prisoners, but had failed to hear anything which showed that they had the slightest thoughts of attempting to regain their liberty.

"What would you know about the matter even if they had been talking treason?" observed Tom. "I doubt if either of you fellows know much about French."

"As to that," said Bill, "we managed to talk to Frenchmen, and to understand what they said to us. That, at least, shows that we do know something about French; not that I wish to boast, only I think I should do much better if I could get hold of some French books."

Tom laughed. "Oh! I dare say you are going to become a great scholar, and to beat us all," he observed, with a sneer. "Jack was even declaring that you were likely to be placed on the quarter-deck. That would be a good joke."

"It would be a good reality for me, though I don't think it's what is very likely to happen," answered Bill, without getting at all angry.

"Nor do I," said Tom, in the same tone as before. "Just fancy a chap like you turned into an officer. You can jabber a few words of French, and may have picked up a smattering of navigation on board the *Foxhound*, though I've a notion you must pretty well have forgotten all you knew by this time, and you may be fond of books, but all that won't turn a fellow who has come out of the gutter, as one may say, into a gentleman, as I suppose those on the quarter-deck call themselves."

"And what do you call them?" exclaimed Jack, not liking to hear such remarks made to Bill. "I wonder you dare to speak in that way."

"I call myself the son of a gentleman, and I'm thinking when I get into port of writing to my father and asking him to have me placed on the quarter-deck."

"I wonder you didn't do that before you ran away from home," said Jack. "They'll have forgotten all about you by this time, and maybe, if you do manage to write a letter, your father won't believe that it comes from you."

"Let him alone, Jack," said Bill; "I don't mind what he says about me. If his father gets him made a midshipman, I shall be as glad as any one."

"Thank you," said Tom; "I flatter myself I shall know how to strut about the quarter-deck and order the men here and there as well as the rest of them."

Just then a voice was heard shouting, "Tom Fletcher, the cook wants you in the galley. Be smart, now, you've been long enough at breakfast."

Tom, bolting his last piece of biscuit, hurried away, as he had no fancy for the rope's-ending which would have been bestowed upon him had he delayed obeying the summons.

The mess-tins were stowed away, and the watch hastened on deck. The wind by this time had somewhat freshened, and the frigate and her prize were making better progress than before. The strangers, however, which had appeared in sight in the morning were considerably nearer. A fourth was now seen beyond the three which had been made out to the eastward. The ship to the westward which was considerably farther off than the others, was evidently a large vessel, and the captain declared his belief that she was a line-of-battle ship, but whether English or French, it was impossible to decide. He hoped, as did everybody on board, that she was English, for should she prove to be French, as undoubtedly were the vessels to the eastward, the *Thisbe* would lose her hard-won prize, even though she might manage to escape herself. Still, Captain Martin was not a man to give up hope while there was a chance of escape.

The *Thisbe*, followed by her prize, kept on her course with every stitch of canvas she could carry set.

"I'm afraid if we don't outrun those fellows there, we shall get boxed up again by the Frenchmen," observed Jack, pointing to the approaching ships.

"If we do we must manage to get out somehow or other, as we did before," answered Bill; "but even if they do come up with us, that's no reason why we should be taken. We must try and beat them off, and the captain and Mr Saltwell are the men to do it. They are only four to our two ships, for the lieutenant in charge of the prize will fight his guns as well as we do ours."

"But what do you say to that big ship coming up Channel out there?" asked Tom. "We shall be made mincemeat of if she gets up to us, for I heard the boatswain's mate say that she's a seventy-four at least, and may be an eighty-gun ship, or still larger."

"She hasn't come up with us yet," answered Bill. "We shall have time to beat off the others and stand away to the northward before she gets us within range of her guns. Perhaps, too, the wind will shift to the eastward, and throw her to leeward. We shall then be well in with Plymouth by the time she can manage to beat up to us. We are not going to give in while the tight little frigate keeps above water."

Bill expressed the sentiments of most of the crew. Still, the odds were greatly against the *Thisbe* and *Diana*. The latter had but forty hands on board to work the guns and manage the sails, while the crew of the *Thisbe* was thus far diminished, besides which they had to look after their prisoners.

The two leading ships of the enemy had been made out to be frigates, as it was thought probable were their consorts astern; and even though they might fail to capture the *Thisbe*, they might knock away her masts and spars, and so maul her that she would be compelled to succumb to the line-of-battle ship coming up from the westward.

Not, however, by his manner, or anything he said, did the captain show the least apprehension of such a result. The crew were at their stations, ready to shorten sail should the breeze freshening render it necessary. The men joked and laughed as usual, as ready for action as if they were only expecting one opponent of equal size.

The morning wore on, the hands were piped down to dinner, the prospect of hot work not at all damping their appetites, though perhaps they got through their meal rather faster than was their wont; when they again hurried on deck to see how things were going on. The two French frigates were approaching. The headmost in a short time fired a bowchaser, but the shot fell short. It served, however, as a signal to prepare for action. Once more the guns were cast loose, and their crews stood ready to fire as soon as they received the looked-for word of command.

A few of the French prisoners who had been allowed to remain on deck were now ordered below. They went willingly enough, exhibiting in their countenances the satisfaction they felt at the expectation of being soon restored to liberty. They were, of course, narrowly watched, and well knew that they would be pretty severely dealt with should they show any signs of insubordination.

Chapter Twenty.

The "Thisbe's" narrow escape—Tom hopes to be made a midshipman.

Half an hour or more passed, when again the leading French frigate fired, the shot falling close to the counter of the *Diana*, which by this time, having got up a fresh maintopmast, was able to make more sail.

Captain Martin now ordered Lieutenant Sterling to cast off the tow rope and to stand on ahead of him, while, to allow the *Diana* to do so, he clewed up the *Thisbe's* topsails.

"Make the best of your way to Plymouth," he shouted, as the *Diana* passed the *Thisbe*; "we'll keep these two fellows in play, and shall, I hope, be soon after you."

As soon as the prize had got some distance ahead, Captain Martin, who had been watching the two frigates coming up on the starboard quarter, ordered the *Thisbe's* helm to be put to port; at the same moment, her starboard broadside being fired, the shot raked the two Frenchmen fore and aft. The helm was then immediately put over, and the frigate coming up on the other tack, her larboard broadside was poured into her antagonists. The shot told with considerable effect. The foretopmast of the leading frigate was shot away, and the mizenmast of the one following was seen to go by the board. This, however, did not much alter their rate of sailing, as, the wind being aft, all the canvas they required continued set. They also opened their fire, and their shot came crashing on board the *Thisbe*, killing and wounding two or three men, but not doing any material damage to her spars or rigging. She having shortened sail, her antagonists were compelled to do the same; and while they poured their broadsides into her, she returned them as rapidly as the crew could run the guns in and out.

Captain Martin's great object was to keep them engaged, and, if possible, to knock away their masts, so as to enable the *Diana* to escape, for although he might hope to get off himself, he could not expect to capture either of the enemy's ships.

The *Thisbe* had been several times hulled, and her sails were already completely riddled, while many more of her crew had fallen.

"It is going hard with us, I fear," said Jack to Tom, who was seated next him on his powder tub. "There's well-nigh a score of poor fellows killed or wounded within the last half-hour. It may be the lot of one of us before long."

"Oh, dear! I hope not," cried Tom. "I wish the skipper would try and get away instead of fighting the Frenchmen. Two to one is fearful odds against us, and we shall have the two other ships blazing away at our heads before long."

"We haven't much to fear from them," said Jack. "I have just heard they're corvettes, and they won't be up to us until we've given the other two a drubbing, and have made sail again to the northward."

The two corvettes were, however, likely to prove no despicable opponents, and Captain Martin was only watching until he had knocked away the masts or spars of one or both of the frigates, to make sail and escape, for it would have been madness to have continued the fight longer than was necessary to accomplish that object.

The Frenchmen, however, fought bravely, and evidently did not intend to let him get off if they could help it. Each had just fired another broadside into the *Thisbe*, when they were seen to haul their wind, the two ships coming up astern doing the same. The reason of this was evident: the line-of-battle ship to the westward, now approaching under a pressure of sail, had hoisted British colours, and any longer delay would have enabled her quickly to capture one or both of them. The brave crew of the *Thisbe* expressed their satisfaction by giving a loud cheer, which was joined in even by many of the wounded.

Captain Martin had accomplished his object; he had secured the safety of his prize, and his crew, now swarming aloft, set to work rapidly to knot and splice the rigging which had been shot away.

As soon as this had been accomplished sufficiently to make sail, the *Thisbe*, brought to the wind, stood after the flying enemy, firing her bow chasers as she did so; but it was soon seen that she had little chance of coming up with them. Still her captain persevered; but, with both masts and spars wounded, it was impossible to carry as much sail as would otherwise have been done. Consequently, before long the line-of-battle ship, which made the signal *Terrible*, seventy-four, overtook her.

A cheer rose from the deck of the big ship, which came gliding slowly by. Her captain hailed, "Well done, Martin!"

The pursuit was continued for some time, but night was approaching, and the coast of France was not far off. The seventy-four therefore threw out the signal to bear up and a course was shaped for Plymouth.

A sharp look-out was kept during the night for the *Diana*. Soon after sunrise she was seen steering for Plymouth, into which harbour Captain Martin and his gallant crew had the satisfaction of conducting her the following day. Although it was a day of triumph to the surviving crew, it was one of mourning to many who had lost relatives and friends. The dead were carried on shore to be buried, the wounded conveyed to hospitals, the Frenchmen were landed and marched off under an escort of marines to the prisons prepared for them, and press-gangs were soon busy at work to obtain fresh hands to supply the places of those who had fallen, although many prime seamen volunteered to serve on board a frigate which had already won a name for herself.

Tom Fletcher, as soon as the ship got into harbour, managed to procure a pen and some ink and paper, and indited a letter to his father. It was not over-well written, but he contrived to make it pretty clearly express that he was serving on board H.M.S. *Thisbe*, and that having already seen a great deal of service, he felt sure that if his father would apply to the Admiralty and make him an allowance of thirty or forty pounds a year, he should be placed on the quarter-deck, and in due course of time become an admiral.

"We are sure to make lots of prize-money," he added; "and if I were a midshipman now, I should be receiving a hundred pounds or more, so that you may be sure, father, that I will pay it all back with interest."

"Father likes interest," he observed to Bill, who was sitting by him at the time, and helping him in his somewhat unaccustomed task; "that'll make him more ready to do what I want, though whether he'll ever get the money is neither here nor there."

"But if you promise to pay him, you are bound to do so," observed Bill. "You need not have made the promise, then you could have waited to know whether he required interest."

"Well, I've written it, and can't scratch it out now," said Tom. "It will come to the same thing in the end."

Bill had some doubts whether Tom's father would make the allowance Tom asked for; but if he were a rich man, as Tom asserted, he might do so, and therefore he said nothing.

The letter, after being folded several times and creased all over, was at length closed, sealed, and addressed, by which time it had assumed a somewhat grimy appearance. Tom got the cook's mate, who was going on shore, to post his letter, having told him that he expected to receive a good sum of money by return, and promising him a part of the proceeds. Bill and Jack looked forward to the reply with almost as much interest as Tom himself, neither of them feeling that they should be at all jealous, should it produce the satisfactory result he anticipated.

Meantime, every possible exertion was made to get the ship ready for sea. Mr Saltwell was very busy superintending all the operations. Bill, however, found that he was not forgotten, from a kind word or two which on several occasions the first lieutenant bestowed upon him. As Tom was not aware of this, he amused himself by telling Bill that Mr Saltwell would not trouble himself more about him—that he must be content to remain a powder monkey until he got big enough to be rated as an ordinary seaman.

"Better than being cook's boy," cried Jack, who could never stand hearing Bill sneered at. "He's a precious deal more likely to be made a midshipman than you are, even though your father is a rich man and rides in his carriage, as you say."

Tom retorted, and Jack looked as if he was much inclined to knock him over, when the quarrel was cut short by the appearance of the cook's mate, who dragged off Tom to help him clean the galley and scrub the pots and pans.

Day after day went by. The frigate was reported ready for sea, and her complement of men having been filled up, she only waited for her captain to come on board to continue her cruise.

Still Tom had received no reply from his father. "Perhaps he or the Admiralty may have written to the captain, and when he comes aboard I shall be placed in my proper position," he observed in confidence to Bill.

"I hope so, but I'm afraid there will be but little time for you to get a proper uniform and an outfit," was the answer.

"I'm not much afraid of that; the tailors won't take long in rigging me out," answered Tom.

Soon after this the captain came on board, and Tom, greatly to his disappointment, was not sent for. Just, however, as the ship was going out into the Sound, the mail-bag arrived, and a letter addressed, "Thomas Fletcher, H.M.S. *Thisbe*," was handed him. He eagerly broke the seal. As he was no great hand at reading writing, he was obliged to ask Bill to assist him in deciphering the contents. He had, however, to rub his eyes several times before he could make them out, even with his messmate's help.

"It's not from father at all," he observed, after looking at the paper all over. "S. Fletcher must be my biggest brother, and he always gave me more kicks than ha'pence."

The letter began:—

"Dear Tom,—Our father received yours of the third instant, as the first intimation of your being alive since your unaccountable disappearance. You have caused us by your wicked proceeding no end of grief and trouble, and, as far as we can make out by your wretchedly written epistle, you do not seem to be at all ashamed of yourself, or sorry for what you have done; and our father bids me to say, that as you have made your bed, you must lie in it. As to making you an allowance of thirty or forty pounds a year, and getting you placed on the quarter-deck, the notion is too ridiculous to be entertained. I must tell you, too, our father has failed, smashed up completely, won't pay sixpence in the pound. As we find it a hard matter to live, he is not likely to make you an allowance of thirty pounds, or thirty pence a year, or to trouble himself by going to the Admiralty with the certainty of being sent away with a flea in his ear; so you see, Tom, you must just grin and bear it. If you don't get killed, I would advise you—should you ever wish to come home—to make your appearance with your pockets full of the prize-money you talk of, and you will then perhaps receive a welcome, and be well entertained as long as it lasts by the rest of the family, as also by—

"Your affectionate brother—

"S. Fletcher.

"P.S. Until then I would advise you not to show your nose in this neighbourhood."

"He always was an ill-natured fellow, was my brother Sam," exclaimed Tom, not seeming concerned at the news of his father's ruin, while, crumpling up the letter, he thrust it into his pocket. "I feel inclined to hang myself or jump overboard."

"Don't think of doing anything so bad," said Bill. "You are no worse off than you were before. All you've got to do is to attend to your duty, and try to please those above you."

"The cook and the cook's mate," growled poor Tom. "It isn't a pleasant task to have to scrub saucepans and clean out the galley."

"But it is your duty, and while you have to do it it would be best to try and do it as well as you can," observed Bill. "Neither the cook nor the cook's mate are bad fellows, and you will gain their good-will by showing a pleasant temper, and working as hard as you can."

"All very well for you to preach," said Tom; "but there's no help for it, I suppose, and so I must make the best of my hard lot."

"That's just what I'm advising," said Bill; though he did not add, "You must remember you brought it upon yourself by running away from home."

The boatswain's pipe summoned all hands on deck to make sail, and the frigate, standing down the Sound, at once put to sea.

A bright look-out was kept for enemies; all hands, from the captain downwards, being eager to secure another prize, even though they might have to fight a tough battle to win her. The captain's orders were to capture, sink, burn, destroy, or drive on shore any of the enemy's vessels he could come up with. With this object in view the *Thisbe* continued to cruise, now down the Channel, now up again, keeping as much as possible in sight of the French coast. She had been some time at sea, however, without having made any prizes; for although she had chased several vessels, they, having espied her in time, had managed to escape by running close in shore, under strong batteries, or getting up harbours where they could not be followed. At last one morning, as the frigate had just made the land, from which she had been standing off during the night, a sail was seen inside of her—that is, between her and the French coast, steering to the eastward, apparently bound down Channel.

Chapter Twenty One.

A cutting-out expedition—Bill discovers an old friend.

The wind being very light, every stitch of canvas the *Thisbe* could carry was packed on her, and her course altered so as to cut off the stranger. As the sun rose, and its beams lighted up the white canvas of the latter, she was pronounced to be a full-rigged ship, either a man-of-war or privateer, or a large merchantman, but at the distance she was off it was difficult to determine whether she was a frigate or a flush-decked vessel. Captain Martin hoped that she would prove to be a frigate, and an antagonist worthy of engaging. She must have seen the *Thisbe* approaching, but either took her for a friend or believed that she was well able to cope with her, as she did not alter her course. Captain Martin calculated that the *Thisbe* would be up with the stranger before noon. Every telescope on board was directed towards her. Bill wished that he had one, that he might form an opinion as to what she was. He heard some officers talking, and they declared that she was undoubtedly French, and was either a large man-of-war corvette, or a privateer. If such were the case, and the *Thisbe* could get up to her, she would be captured to a certainty, though she would probably fight, and try to knock away some of the *Thisbe's* spars, so as to effect her escape. The wind, which had hitherto been blowing from the southward and south, suddenly shifted to the east. As soon as the stranger felt it, she was seen to haul her tacks on board, brace up her yards, and stand away towards the land.

"She's going to run on shore," exclaimed Jack, who had been watching her as eagerly as any one, when his duty would allow him to take a look-out.

"More likely she knows of a harbour or battery in there, and is running in for shelter," answered Bill.

"We shan't be able to take her then," said Jack. "I was making sure we should have her as our prize."

"I won't say we shan't take her, notwithstanding," observed Bill. "Perhaps we shall fight the battery and her too, if she brings up under one. Or if she runs into a harbour, the boats may be sent in after her to bring her out."

As soon as the stranger was seen standing to the southward, the *Thisbe* also hauled up to continue the pursuit, but the chase was still beyond the reach of her guns.

"We shan't catch her after all," said Jack, who had taken another look at the stranger some time after she had altered her course.

"I don't see that we have not still a chance of coming up with her," answered Bill. "The captain thinks so, or he would not be keeping after her. Perhaps she may be becalmed closer in with the land, or we may draw near enough to knock away her masts. We have gained a mile on her during the last hour. I would always try to succeed while a single chance remains, and I would never knock under to an enemy while I had a stick standing, or a plank beneath my feet."

Still, notwithstanding Bill's sanguine hopes of success, as the day wore on there seemed every probability that the French ship would make good her escape. It was now seen that she was steering for a harbour, the mouth of which could be distinguished from the deck of the *Thisbe*, with a battery on one side.

"Our bow chasers will reach her, Mr Saltwell," cried the captain, at length.

The order to fire was eagerly obeyed. The frigate, however, had to yaw for the purpose. One of the shot was seen to go right through the sails of the chase, but the other fell on one side.

The guns were quickly reloaded, and were fired immediately the ship was kept away sufficiently for the purpose. Again one of the shot took effect, but what damage was done it was impossible to say, and the chase stood on as before.

The manoeuvre was repeated several times, causing the frigate to lose ground; but a fortunate shot would have enabled her quickly to regain it. Though several of the *Thisbe's* shot took effect, the chase continued her course, firing in return from a gun run out astern; but none of the shot struck her pursuer. At last, however, the chase ran past the battery, which shortly afterwards opened fire. Captain Martin returned it with such effect that two of the guns were silenced, when the frigate's head was put off shore, and she stood away to avoid the risk of being becalmed should the wind fall, as was very likely, towards evening.

"I say, Bill, I really believe that's the very place we got away from on our raft," said Jack.

"No doubt about it," answered Bill. "I remember the look of the land to the eastward, and I feel pretty sure I could find my way up the harbour."

Bill had scarcely said this when he heard his name called, and he was told to go to the first lieutenant.

"Do you recollect anything about the harbour up there?" asked Mr Saltwell.

"Yes, sir," answered Bill. "I remember it was the one from which Peek and I got off, and I was thinking I could make my way up it at night, if I had to do so."

"You will have an opportunity to-night, I hope, of showing your knowledge. The captain intends to send up the boats to try and cut out the vessel we chased into the harbour. I am to command the expedition, and I will take you with me."

"Thank you, sir," said Bill, touching his hat. "I feel pretty sure that I know my way up to the landing-place, and I do not suppose that a ship the size of the chase could get up higher."

"You can go forward now, and be ready to accompany me when you are summoned," said Mr Saltwell.

Bill felt highly gratified by the confidence placed in him, and was thankful that he had so thoroughly observed the harbour before he and Jack had made their escape. The frigate, meantime, was standing out to sea, so that by the time the sun went down she could not be perceived from the shore. She was then hove-to, and preparations were made for the intended expedition.

Lieutenant Saltwell went in the barge, the third lieutenant in the launch, and the lieutenant of marines, with the senior mate, in the cutter, the oars of all the boats being muffled, so that no sound would betray their approach to the enemy.

The frigate then again stood in, taking care to show no lights, when in perfect silence the boats shoved off, carrying among them about fifty officers and men. Lieutenant Saltwell called Bill aft to take a seat by his side. Before leaving the frigate, the captain had directed the first lieutenant to return should he find the ship so moored as to render it impossible to bring her out. Bill, however, told him that he had observed a vessel at anchor some way below the landing-place, and that he supposed no large craft could get up higher on account of the shallowness of the water. The wind, which had hitherto been east and north-east, again shifting to the southward, blew directly down the harbour, which would enable the ship, should she be captured, to be brought down without difficulty.

Bill's heart beat quicker than usual as he thought of the work in hand, and recollected that the success of the undertaking might considerably depend upon him. The night was very dark, but as the boats got up to the mouth of the harbour the lights on shore could be distinguished, as well as several on board vessels at anchor. The boats kept clear of the latter, lest any of their people might discover them and give the alarm. The barge led, the launch and cutter following in succession. The success of the undertaking would depend on their being able to take the enemy by surprise.

As yet no signs had been perceived that their approach was discovered, and Bill advised that they should keep over to the west shore, where there were no vessels at anchor, but where he was sure there was water for the boats, from having seen a good-sized craft keeping that course at low tide.

As they got higher up, the sound of voices came off the shore, as if the people were laughing and making merry. This gave Mr Saltwell hopes that many of the crew were landed, and that those on board would be totally unprepared for an attack. He intended to board on the starboard quarter, and he had given directions to the other officers, one to board on the larboard quarter and the other at the main chains, his object being to overpower the resistance the officer's would make aft, then to sweep the decks until the forecastle was gained. One of the boats was immediately to shove ahead and cut the cable, while certain of the men had been directed to hoist the headsails, so that the prize might, without an instant's delay, be making her way down the harbour before any assistance could come off to her from the land.

The moment for action was approaching. The ship was seen at the spot where Bill thought she would be found, lying silent and dark, her tall masts and the tracery of her rigging just to be distinguished against the sky. No one was observed moving on her deck. Eagerly the boats dashed forward to the posts allotted to them. The bows of the barge had just hooked on when the sentry on the gangway, who had evidently not been attending to his duty, shouted out, and fired his musket.

The rest of the watch came rushing aft, but it was to encounter the crew of the barge, who, having climbed up her side, had already gained her deck. Their officers at the same moment sprang up the companion-hatch, sword in hand, but were knocked over before they could strike a blow.

The crews of the other boats had, in the meantime, gained the deck, but not before the rest of the Frenchmen came tumbling up from below armed with cutlasses and pikes, or such weapons as they could lay their hands on. Though they made a bold stand, and endeavoured to defend the fore part of the ship, they had to retreat before the desperate charge of the boarders, who, with cutlasses flashing and cutting, soon hewed a way for themselves to the forecastle, leaving the deck on either side covered with dead or wounded men. Not a word had been spoken, and scarcely a shout uttered, but the clashing of steel and flashing of pistols must have showed the people on shore what was going forward.

The mate, to whom the duty had been assigned, having in the meantime carried his boat under the bows, quickly cut the cable, then allowing her to drift alongside, he sprang on to the forecastle, where he took charge of the party engaged in making sail.

The third lieutenant, though he was severely wounded, went aft to the helm, and in less than three minutes from the time the boats got alongside, the prize, under her foresail and foretopsail, was standing down the harbour.

Bill, having got hold of a pistol, kept close to Mr Saltwell, that he might be ready to assist him or obey any orders he might receive. A few only of his men were standing round the lieutenant when a party of the French crew, who had already yielded, led by the boatswain, a big, sturdy fellow, whose cutlass had already brought two of the English seamen to the deck, suddenly attacked him, hoping to regain the ship. The sailors had enough to do to defend themselves, and the big boatswain was making a desperate blow at the lieutenant's head, when Bill, who thought it a time to use his pistol with effect, fired, and the boatswain fell, his cutlass dropping from his hand. His followers on this sprang back, and, throwing down their weapons, cried for mercy.

"I saw you do it, my lad," said the lieutenant. "The second time you have saved my life. I'll not forget it."

The English sailors now had work enough to do to prevent the Frenchmen from rising. While sail was being made, numerous boats also were seen coming off from the shore full of armed men, evidently with the intention of attempting to board the prize. Sail after sail was let drop, and the ship ran faster and faster through the water. She was not, however, as yet entirely won. Her crew, though beaten down below, were still very numerous, and might, should they find the boats of their friends coming alongside, at any moment rise and try to regain her. The fort also had to be passed, and the garrison were sure to have heard the uproar and would open fire as soon as she got within range of their guns.

Notwithstanding this, the British seamen performed their various duties as steadily as if they were on board their own ship. Some were aloft, loosing sails; others ran out the guns, ready to give the boats a warm reception, and others kept an eye on the prisoners.

The breeze freshened, and the prize in a short time reached the mouth of the harbour. No sooner had she done so than the guns from the fort, as had been expected, opened fire, and their shot, thick as hail, came crashing on board. Several men were struck, and the sails shot through and through. None of the yards, however, were carried away, and the canvas stood filled out with the breeze.

A number of prisoners had remained on deck, with sentries over them, as the shot struck the ship. Several, to avoid it, endeavoured to escape below. Some succeeded, not waiting to descend by the ladders, but leaping down, to the no small risk of breaking their arms and legs. There was still more sail to be set, and Bill was pulling and hauling, when he saw a shot come plump in among a party of prisoners. Three fell; the rest, in spite of the sentries, making a desperate rush, leapt down the main hatchway.

Bill at that moment saw a young Frenchman, who had been struck, struggling on the deck, and a voice crying out which he thought he recognised.

He sprang towards the sailor, and lifted him up. He was not mistaken; it was his friend Pierre.

"Are you badly hurt?" he asked in French.

"I'm afraid so, in my side," was the answer. "My poor mother, and Jeannette, I shall never see them more."

"I hope that things are not so bad as that," responded Bill. "I will try and get you below. Here!" and he called to one of the prisoners who had remained on deck, and who, being very glad to get out of the way of the shot, willingly assisted Bill in dragging the wounded man to the companion-hatchway, down which the two together lifted him, and placed him in the gun-room.

Fortunately the French surgeon had been ill in his berth, but had now got up, prepared to attend to his professional duties. As yet, however, none of the wounded prisoners had been brought aft, and Pierre, who had been placed on the gun-room table, was the first man the surgeon took under his care.

"He is not badly hurt, I hope," said Bill, rather anxiously.

"That's more than I can say, my young friend," answered the surgeon, "but I will attend to him. I shall have patients enough on my hands directly, I fear."

Bill felt that he ought not to remain a moment longer below, though he greatly wished to learn how much Pierre had been injured. All he could do, therefore, was to press his friend's hand, and spring up again on deck.

The battery was still firing away at the prize, and every now and then a crashing sound, as the shot struck her, showed that she was within range of its guns; but she was rapidly distancing the boats, which could now only be dimly seen astern.

The British crew raised a cheer when they found that they had to a certainty secured their prize. Still the battery continued firing, but not another shot struck her, and at length the dim outline of the *Thisbe* was seen ahead. Shortly afterwards the prize, rounding to under the frigate's quarter, was received with hearty cheers by her crew.

Chapter Twenty Two.

The powder monkey gets his first step up the ratlines.

The British wounded, and the French prisoners captured in the prize, were forthwith taken on board the *Thisbe*, when both ships made sail to get a good offing from the coast before daylight. Mr Saltwell remained in command of the prize with the crew which had so gallantly won her. The wounded Frenchmen were also allowed to continue on board under charge of their surgeon, with an English assistant-surgeon to help him, for there were upwards of forty poor fellows who required his care.

Bill was glad to find that he had not to go back to his own ship, as he wanted to look after Pierre, and as soon as his duty would allow him he went below to learn how his young French friend was getting on. When he asked for the man whom he had brought down, the doctor pointed to one of the officer's cabins in the gun-room, observing, "He is somewhat badly hurt, but there are others still more cruelly knocked about who require my care, and I have not been able to attend to him for some time."

Bill hurried into the cabin. A faint voice replied to him.

"*Merci, merci*! It is very kind of you to come and see me, but I fear that I shall not get over it," said Pierre. "Is there no chance of our returning to France? I should like to die under my father's roof, and see my mother and Jeannette once more."

"There's no chance of your getting back for the present, but I hope you will see your mother and sister notwithstanding," answered Bill. "We are running across the Channel, and shall be in an English port in a day or two, when you will be landed, and I will ask the captain to let me take care of you. I should like to prove how grateful I am for all your kindness to me and Jack Peek, and I will tell Mr Saltwell, the lieutenant who commands this ship, how you and your family treated me. But I don't think you ought to talk; I came to see if I could do anything for you."

"My lips are parched; I am very thirsty; I should like something to drink," answered Pierre.

"I will see what I can find," said Bill; and making his way to the steward's pantry outside the captain's cabin, he hunted about until he discovered some lemons. He quickly squeezed out the juice of a couple of them, and mixing it with water, brought the beverage to Pierre, who drank it eagerly. It much revived him.

"I was very unfortunate to be on board the *Atlante* when you captured her, for I had no wish to fight the English," said Pierre. "Only ten days ago I was persuaded to come on board to see a friend, and the crew would not let me return on shore. However, I was determined to make the best of it, hoping before long to get back to my family, and be able to assist my father. And now to be cut down by my own countrymen, for it was a shot from the battery on shore which wounded me. It is more than I can bear!"

"Don't think about it," said Bill; "you are safe from further harm, and will be well taken care of; and when you have recovered, and the war is over, you will be able to go back. I must leave you now, but I will come and see you as often as I can. I have placed the jug of lemonade close to your head, where it cannot slip. When that is gone I will get some more; it is the best thing you can take at present."

Saying this, Bill hurried back to attend to his duty on deck, for, young as he was, as the prize was short-handed, he had plenty of work to do. Several times he passed Mr Saltwell, who gave him a kind look or said a word or two of encouragement, but did not allude to the service Bill had done him.

"He probably has forgotten all about my having shot the French boatswain," thought Bill. "I only did my duty, and if anybody else had been in his place I should have done the same."

The frigate and her fresh prize were meantime making the best of their way across the Channel. As the latter, a fast sailor, was not materially injured, all sail was made on her, and she kept good way with the *Thisbe*. At the same time there was still the risk of either one or both being taken by a French ship of superior force, though neither was likely to yield without making every effort to escape. A constant lookout was kept from the mast-head, but as the ships got farther and farther from the French coast, the hope of escaping without having again to fight increased.

Several sail were seen in the distance, but it was supposed that they were either merchantmen, standing up or down Channel, in spite of the enemy's cruisers on the watch to pick them up, or privateers, and, seeing that the *Thisbe* was a frigate, took good care to keep out of her way.

At length the entrance to Plymouth Sound was descried, and the *Thisbe* and her prize stood up it triumphantly with colours flying, creating considerable astonishment at her quick return with another capture. Both were soon moored in Hamoaze, when the *Atlante*, a fine little ship, carrying twenty guns on one deck, was handed over to the prize agents with the full expectation that she would be bought into the service. The prisoners were carried on shore, the wounded men were taken to the hospital, and the prize crew returned on board their own ship.

Bill had been very anxious to accompany Pierre, that he might watch over him with more care than strangers could do, but he had had no opportunity of asking leave of Mr Saltwell.

He had not been long on board the frigate, and was giving an account of the boarding expedition to Jack and Tom, when he heard his name called along the decks.

"Boy Rayner, the captain has sent for you into the cabin," said the master-at-arms.

"What can you be wanted for!" exclaimed Tom. "Look out for squalls. I shouldn't like to be in your shoes."

"No fear of that," said Jack. "Maybe the first lieutenant has told the captain how Bill saved his life. I wish that I had had a chance of doing something of the sort."

Bill, however, did not stop to hear the remarks of his two friends, but hurried aft, thinking that now would be the time to say something in poor Pierre's favour.

The sentry, who knew that he had been sent for, allowed him to pass without question, and he soon found himself in the presence of the captain and Mr Saltwell, who were seated at the table in the main cabin. Bill stood, hat in hand, ready to answer any questions which might be put to him.

"William Rayner," said the captain, "you have, I understand, behaved remarkably well on several occasions, twice especially, by saving Mr Saltwell's life through your coolness and presence of mind. You are also, I find, a fair French scholar, and the first lieutenant reports favourably of your conduct in your former ship. I wish to reward you. Let me know how I can best do so in a way satisfactory to yourself."

"I only did my duty without thinking of being rewarded," answered Bill; "but I have been wishing since we took the prize that something could be done for a young Frenchman who was badly hurt on board her by a shot from the battery which fired at us. He and his father saved Jack Peek and me from drowning when we were blown up in the *Foxhound*, and his family were afterwards very kind to us, and did their utmost to save us from being carried off to prison, and when we were hid away in a cave, his sister, at great risk, brought us food. He will now be amongst strangers, who do not understand his lingo, and the poor fellow will be very sad and solitary; so I think he would like it, if I could get leave to go and stay with him while the frigate remains in harbour. I'll take it as a great favour, sir, since you ask me what reward I should like, if you can let me go and be with him at the hospital, or if that cannot be, if he may be removed to some lodging where he can be well looked after until he recovers and is sent back to his own home."

"There may be some difficulty in doing as you propose," replied the captain. "Mr Saltwell will, however, I have no doubt, try to make a satisfactory arrangement, for a person behaving as the young Frenchman has done deserves to be rewarded; but that is not what I meant; I want you to choose some reward for yourself, and wish you to let me know how I can best serve you."

"Thank you, sir," answered Bill. "I cannot think just now of anything I require, though I should be very glad if I could get Pierre sent back to his family."

"Your parents, perhaps, will be able to decide better than you can do, then. Your father or mother," observed the captain.

"I have neither father nor mother, sir," answered Bill. "They are both dead."

"Your relatives and friends might decide," said the captain.

"I have no relatives or friends, nor any one to care for me that I know of," said Bill, in a quiet voice.

"Then Mr Saltwell and I must settle the matter," said Captain Martin. "Should you like to be placed on the quarter-deck? If you go on as you have begun, and let duty alone guide you on all occasions, you will, if you live, rise in the service and be an honour to it."

Bill almost gasped for breath as he heard this. He knew that the captain was in earnest, and he looked at him, and then at Mr Saltwell, but could not speak.

"Come, say what you wish, my lad," said Captain Martin, in an encouraging tone.

Still Bill was silent.

"You will have opportunities of improving your education, and you need not fear about being well received by the young gentlemen in the midshipmen's berth," observed Mr Saltwell. "Captain Martin and I will make arrangements for giving you an outfit and supplying you with such funds as you will require, besides which you will come in for a midshipman's share of prize-money."

The kind way in which the captain and first lieutenant spoke greatly assisted Bill to find his tongue and to express himself appropriately.

"I am grateful, sirs, for your offer, and hope that I always shall be grateful. If you think that I am fit to become a midshipman, I will try to do my duty as such, so I accept your offer with all my heart."

Bill, overpowered by his feelings, could say no more.

"The matter is settled, then," said the captain; and sending for the purser, he at once entered the name of William Rayner as a midshipman on the ship's books, the only formality requisite in those days, though his rank would afterwards have to be confirmed at the Admiralty.

The purser observed that he had a suit of clothes belonging to one of the midshipmen killed in the action with the French frigate, which would, he thought, exactly fit Mr Rayner.

Bill felt very curious at hearing himself so spoken of.

The purser said that he would debit him with them at a moderate price.

The captain approving of this proposal, Bill, in the course of a few minutes, found himself dressed in a midshipman's uniform. He could scarcely believe his senses. It seemed to him as if by the power of an enchanter's wand he had been changed into some one else.

The first lieutenant then desired him to accompany him, and leading the way down to the berth, in which a number of the young gentlemen were assembled for dinner, he stopped at the door.

"I wish, young gentlemen, to present a new messmate to you," he said, looking in. "Mr William Rayner! He has gained his position by exhibiting those qualities which I am sure you all admire, and you will, I have no doubt, treat him as a friend."

The members of the mess who were present rose and cordially put out their hands towards Bill, whom the first lieutenant, taking by the aim, drew into the berth.

Mr Saltwell then returned on deck.

Bill naturally felt very bashful, but his new messmates did their best to set him at ease, and no one alluded to his former position. They spoke only of the late action, and begged him to give a description of the way in which he had saved Mr Saltwell's life, a vague account of which they had heard.

Bill complied, modestly, not saying more about himself than was necessary. What he said gained him the applause of his new messmates, and raised him greatly in their estimation; he therefore found himself far more at his ease than he had expected would be possible; no one by word or deed showing that they recollected that he had been just before a ship's boy, but all treated him as an equal.

His only regret now was that he could no longer talk with Jack and Tom as he had been accustomed to do, though he hoped that he should still be able, without doing anything derogatory to his new position, to speak to them in a friendly way. Thinking highly of Jack as he did, he regretted more than ever that his former messmate could neither read nor write. He felt sure that he would, should he have an opportunity, do something to merit promotion.

Bill commenced his new duties with a spirit and alacrity which was remarked by his superior officers. He had narrowly observed the way the midshipmen conducted themselves, and was thus able to behave as well as the best of them. He was a little puzzled at first at dinner, but by seeing what others did he soon got over the slight difficulty he had to encounter.

Next day Mr Saltwell called him up as he was walking the quarter-deck.

"I have been making inquiries as to what can be done for your friend Pierre Turgot," he said. "As you told me he was not willingly on board the privateer, I was able to state that in his favour, and I have obtained leave for him to be removed to a private house, where he can remain until he has recovered, and he will then, I hope, be allowed to return to France without waiting for an exchange of prisoners. Were he to be sent back with others, he would probably at once be compelled to serve afloat, and his great desire is, I understand, to return to his own family, to follow his former occupation of a fisherman."

"Thank you, sir," exclaimed Bill, "I cannot be too grateful to you for your kindness."

"Don't talk of that, my lad; if it hadn't been for your courage and coolness I should not have been here. I am now going on shore, and wish you to accompany me. I have seen the widow of an old shipmate of mine who is willing to receive Pierre into her house, and to attend to him. We will have him removed at once, so that when we sail you will know he is placed under good care."

Chapter Twenty Three.

William Rayner is enabled to show his gratitude to Pierre.

Will at once got ready to attend the first lieutenant. The boat being alongside, they were soon on shore. Their first visit was to the hospital, which, being overcrowded, the authorities were glad to get rid of one of their patients. Pierre was placed in a litter and conveyed, accompanied by Mr Saltwell and Bill, to the residence of Mrs Crofton, a neat cottage standing by itself in a small garden. A pretty little girl about thirteen years of age opened the door, and on seeing the strangers summoned her mother, who at once appeared, and led the way to the room she had prepared for Pierre's reception. It was on the ground-floor, and contained a dimity-covered bed, and a few other simple articles of furniture, quite sufficient for all the young French sailor's wants.

Pierre again and again thanked Bill for having brought him to so delightful a place.

"Ah!" he said, "that lady," looking at Mrs Crofton, "reminds me of my mother, and the little girl is just like Jeannette, when she was younger. And they are so kind and gentle! I shall get well very soon, though I think I should have died if I had remained at the hospital, where I was nearly stifled, while day and night I heard the oaths and groans of my wounded compatriots, who abuse the English as the cause of their suffering, regardless of the care that is being taken of them."

"I was very sure you would recover sooner in a quiet house by yourself, and therefore I begged my officer to have you removed," said Bill.

It was not for some time that Pierre remarked the new midshipman's uniform.

"Why, you told me you were a ship's boy, now I see you dressed as an officer!" he exclaimed, in a tone of astonishment. "The gendarmes were right after all."

"No, they were wrong," answered Bill. "I was then what I told you, but I am now a midshipman."

He then gave an account to Pierre of how he had been promoted. Their conversation was interrupted by the return of Mrs Crofton and Mary with some food for their patient, as the doctor had told Mr

Saltwell that he should be fed often, though with but little at a time. As Mrs Crofton could speak French, she did not require Bill to interpret for her.

He was glad to find that Pierre would be able to converse with his kind hostess Mr Saltwell, who had gone into the drawing-room, now told Bill that he might stay with Pierre until the evening, and that he should have leave to visit him every day while the frigate remained in harbour.

The first lieutenant now took his leave, and Mrs Crofton observing that "Pierre would be the better for some sleep, after the excitement of being moved," invited Bill into her sitting-room, she naturally wishing to hear more about his adventures in France than Mr Saltwell had been able to tell her. Bill himself was perfectly willing to talk away on the subject as long as she wished, especially when he found so ready a listener in Mary. He began with an account of the blowing up of the *Foxhound*; and when he had finished, Mrs Crofton wished to know how it was that he first came to go to sea, and so he had to go back to tell her all about himself, and the death of his mother, and how he had been left penniless in the world.

"And now I find you a midshipman with warm friends; in a few years you will be a lieutenant, then a commander, and next a post-captain, I hope, and at length a British admiral, and you will have gained your promotion without the interest of relatives or born friends, simply by your own good conduct and bravery."

"I don't know what I may become, ma'am," said Bill, inclined to smile at Mrs Crofton's enthusiasm. "At present I am but a midshipman, but I will try, as I always have, to do my duty."

This conversation made Bill feel perfectly at home with Mrs Crofton. Indeed, it seemed to him as if he had known her all his life, so that he was willing to confide in her as if she were his mother.

He was equally willing to confide in Mary. Indeed, all the reserve he at first felt quickly wore off, and he talked to her as if she had been his sister. If he did not say to himself that she was a perfect angel, he thought her what most people would consider very much better—a kind, good, honest, open-hearted girl, with clear hazel, truthful eyes, and a sweet smile on her mouth when she smiled, which was very frequently, with a hearty ring in her laughter. She reminded him, as she did Pierre, of Jeannette, and Bill felt very sure that, should she ever have the opportunity of helping any one in distress, she would be ready to take as much trouble and run as many risks as the French girl had in assisting Jack and him.

"Do you know, Mr Rayner, I like midshipmen very much?" she said, in her artless way. "My brother Oliver is a midshipman, and as I am very fond of him, I like all midshipmen for his sake. At first I was inclined to like you because you were a midshipman, but now I like you for yourself."

"I am much obliged to you," said Bill; "and I like you for yourself, I can tell you. I didn't know before that you had a brother Oliver. Where is he serving?"

"On board the *Ariel* corvette in the West Indies," answered Mary.

"Perhaps some day we may fall in with each other," said Bill; "and I am very sure, from what you say about him, we shall become good friends, for I shall be inclined to like him for your sake."

"Then I'm sure he will like you; he could not help doing so. He is only three years older than I am; just about your age I suppose. He went to sea when he was a very little fellow with poor dear papa, who was killed in action. Oliver was by his side at the time, and wrote us home an account of the sad, sad event, saying how brokenhearted he was. The people were very kind to him. Papa was lieutenant of the ship, and was loved by all the men, as I am sure he would have been, remembering how good and kind and gentle he was with us."

The tears came into Mary's bright eyes as she spoke of her father.

"Whenever we hear of a battle out there, poor mamma is very anxious until the particulars come home, and she knows that Oliver is safe," said Mary. "We are nearly sure to get a letter from him, for he always writes when he can, and I hope that you'll write also when you are away, and tell us all that you are doing; then we shall receive two letters instead of one, and we shall always be so very, very glad to hear from you."

Bill promised that he would write constantly, saying that he should be pleased to do so, especially as he had not many correspondents; indeed, he might have said that he had none, as he was, in truth, not acquainted with anybody on shore. Mary and her mother were the first friends he had ever possessed, so that he very naturally valued them the more. They were of very great service to him in many respects, for Mrs Crofton was a ladylike and refined person, though her means were small, and she was able to give him instruction in the ways and manners of people of education; though Bill was so observant, and anxious to imitate what was right, that he only required the opportunity to fit himself thoroughly for his new station in life.

Mr Saltwell lent him books, and he read during every spare moment, to make amends for his want of early education.

When he came on shore, Mrs Crofton assisted him, and as she knew French very well, helped him to study it with a grammar and dictionary, which he found very easy, as he already understood so much of the language, and he was able to practise speaking with Pierre.

The young Frenchman slowly recovered, but the doctor, who came to visit him from the hospital every day, said that it would be a long time before he would regain strength and be able to return to France.

Bill had written, at Pierre's dictation, to Madame Turgot, to tell her where he was, what had happened to him, and how well he was treated. It was rather a funny composition, as Pierre was no great scholar, and could not say how the words should be spelt, but Bill showed it to Mrs Crofton, who assured him that it would be understood perfectly well, which was the great object required, and that Madame Turgot would be satisfied, from the tone and expression, that it came from her son.

There was no regular post in those days between the two countries. Pierre, however, at length got an answer from his mother, directed to the care of Mrs Crofton, expressing her heartfelt thanks to Lieutenant Saltwell and Bill, and the kind lady who had befriended him. She sent also many messages from Captain Turgot and Jeannette.

The letter arrived just as the *Thisbe* was ready for sea. Mary could not help bursting into tears when Bill took his leave for the last time.

"It's just like Oliver going away," she said. Indeed, it was evident that she looked upon Bill as another Oliver, and even Mrs Crofton showed how sincerely sorry she was to part with her young visitor, who had so greatly won on her affections.

She promised to write again to Madame Turgot to let her know how Pierre was getting on; but there appeared no probability of his being able to move until the frigate came back, when Mr Saltwell would be able to make arrangements for his return to France.

Though sorry to leave his kind friends, Bill was very glad to be at sea again, and engaged in the active duties of his profession. His messmates treated him with much kindness, and remarked among themselves the improvement in his manners, while two or three fresh members of the mess, when they heard how he had gained his promotion, looked upon him with evident respect. He did not, however, forget his old friends, and Jack was always pleased when he came forward to talk to him, and did not appear at all jealous, which could not be said of Tom, who, though he did not venture to show his feelings, was inclined to keep out of his way, and sometimes answered in rather a surly tone when spoken to, always taking care to bring in the "sir" after every sentence, and touching his hat with mock respect, of which Bill, though he could not fail to observe, took no notice.

The *Thisbe* had been several weeks at sea, and had during that time captured, without firing a shot, three of the enemy's merchantmen, which she had sent into Plymouth, the more pugnacious of the crew grumbling at not having encountered an enemy worthy of their prowess, and which would have afforded them a larger amount of prize-money.

Captain Martin was about to return to port to take on board his officers and men when he was joined by the *Venus* frigate. Her captain told him that he had just before made out two French frigates to the south-east, and the *Thisbe* bore up with the *Venus* in chase, with every stitch of canvas they could carry set.

A stern chase is proverbially a long chase, and the French frigates, which had been seen to the eastward, had a considerable start of their pursuers. Still, as they had been under moderate canvas, it was hoped that they would set no more sail, and might thus be overtaken.

A sharp look-out was kept, and the officers were continually going aloft with their glasses, and sweeping the horizon from north to south, in the hopes of espying the enemy.

"I say, Jack, do you think if we come up with those two Frenchmen we are chasing they'll turn round and fight us?" asked Tom, who thought it much pleasanter to capture unarmed merchant vessels than to have to fight an enemy which sent round shots and bullets on board in return.

"No doubt about that, youngster," answered Ben Twinch, the boatswain's mate, who overheard Tom's remark. "What do you think we come to sea for? If we can take a man-of-war of our own size she's worth half a dozen merchant craft, though, to be sure, some of us may lose the number of our mess; but we all know that, and make no count of it. Maybe you'll have your head taken off one of these days, and if you do, you'll only share the fate of many another fine fellow."

"I hope not!" cried Tom, mechanically putting up his hand to his head as if to hold it on, and turning from Ben.

"Never fear!" said Jack, wishing to console him; "the chances are that you will escape and live to fight another day."

If Tom had any fear, it was not the time to show it. He heard all around him speak of fighting as if it were fun, and of death with seeming levity. It is the way of the young and the thoughtless. Old sailors and old soldiers seldom talk thus, and think more of duty than of glory. For young or for old the loss of life is not a matter for light talk, as if death were only the end of it. Those that cause war will have much to reckon for hereafter. But there is no time for such thoughts in sight of the enemy. So we must go on with our story.

The midshipmen aft were universally anxious to come up with the vessels of which they were in chase. It was supposed that they were frigates of the same size as their own and the *Venus*; but should they prove much larger, they were equally ready to engage them.

Still, hour after hour went by, and no enemy appearing, they began to fear that the Frenchmen would get into port before they could be overtaken. At length, just before the sun reached the horizon, his rays fell on the royals and topgallantsails of two ships right ahead. As the sun sank lower they were again lost to view, but their appearance revived the hopes of all on board. It was not likely that they would alter their course during the night, and it was hoped, therefore, that before morning they would be overtaken. It was not likely that the *Thisbe* and *Venus*, being in the shadow, would have been perceived.

"The chances are that we shall be upon them in the dark," said Jack to Tom; "and we'll surprise them, I've a notion. The captain thinks so, or he wouldn't have given the order to prepare for action."

"I would rather fight in daylight," said Tom, "and I hope they'll manage to keep ahead till then."

Jack laughed, for he suspected that Tom would rather not fight at all.

The watch below were ordered to turn in as usual, but most of the officers kept on deck, too eager for the work to be able to sleep.

Chapter Twenty Four.

Action between the "Thisbe" and a French frigate.

Rayner—for such he ought now to be called—who was in the middle watch, was standing forward on the look-out, and, as may be supposed, he did not allow an eye to wink. Several times he thought that he could see two dark objects rising above the horizon, but his imagination might have deceived him, for they, at all events, grew no larger. When his watch was over, he came aft into the midshipmen's berth, where several of his messmates were collected. He might have turned in, for the night was drawing on, but there were still two hours to daylight. He, as well as others, dropped asleep with their heads on the table.

They were aroused from their uncomfortable slumbers by the boatswain's call, piping the hammocks up, and on coming on deck the first thing they saw were the two ships they had been chasing all night directly ahead, their topsails just rising above the water. Their hopes revived that they would come up with them before the day was many hours older; still the strangers were a long way out of range of their bow chasers.

As the sun rose and shone on their own canvas they knew that they must be clearly seen, and it was hoped that the two ships would, if their captains were inclined to fight, heave to and await their coming.

Such, however, it was evidently the intention of the Frenchman not to do, for it was seen that studding-sails were being set below and aloft.

"Still they may not have the heels of us," observed Captain Martin to the first lieutenant; "and before they get into Cherbourg we may be up to them."

It was thought that as the day advanced the wind might increase, but in this Captain Martin was disappointed. At length, towards evening, Cape La Hogue and the coast of France, to the westward of Cherbourg, appeared in sight. In a few hours it was too probable that the French ships would get safe into port.

Remarks not over complimentary to the valour of the Frenchmen were made by the crews of the English frigates, when they saw that the enemy had escaped them; but as Jack observed, "There's no use grumbling; the mounseers have got away from us because they knew the tremendous drubbing we would have given them."

"Perhaps we may see them again before long," said Tom, his courage returning now that all danger of an encounter had passed. "Depend on it, our captain will do his best to give them a taste of our quality."

Tom was right; for although the *Thisbe* and *Venus* had to haul their wind, and stand off shore, a bright look-out was kept, in the hopes that the French frigates might again put to sea.

Day after day passed, and at length the *Venus* parted company from the *Thisbe*. The latter frigate was standing across Channel when a lugger was sighted, to which she gave chase. The stranger at first made all sail, as if to escape. She was at length seen to heave to. On coming up with her, it was at first doubtful whether she was English or French, but as the frigate approached she hoisted English colours and lowered a boat, which in a short time came alongside, and a fine, intelligent-looking man stepping upon deck, announced himself as master of the lugger. He had, he said, at first taken the *Thisbe* for a French frigate which was in the habit of coming out of Cherbourg every evening, picking up any prizes she could fall in with, and returning next morning with them into port. He had, indeed, narrowly escaped once before.

This was valuable information, and Captain Martin determined to act upon it, in the hopes of capturing the marauder. Being engaged in particular service, the master of the lugger was allowed to proceed on his way, and the *Thisbe* stood back towards Cherbourg.

The day passed, and no enemy appeared. Next morning, however, a sail was seen to the northward. Captain Martin immediately bore up to ascertain her character. As the daylight increased, all felt confident that she was a frigate, and probably French. The stranger was seen to be carrying a press of canvas, and apparently steering for Cherbourg. To re-enter that port she must encounter the *Thisbe*, on board which preparations were made for the expected engagement. The stranger, too, continuing her course, hauled her wind, and stood down Channel, as if anxious to escape. Why she did so it was difficult to say, except on the possibility that she had seen another English ship to the northward, and was unwilling to encounter two enemies at once.

It was the general opinion that she was a powerful frigate, considerably larger than the *Thisbe*; but even if such were the case, Captain Martin was not the man to be deterred from engaging her. The stranger sailed well, and there appeared every probability that she would distance the *Thisbe*, and if she wished it, get back to port without coming to action.

In a short time the weather became very thick, and, to the disappointment of all, the stranger was lost sight of. Still the *Thisbe* continued her course, and many a sharp pair of eyes were employed in looking out for the Frenchman, it being difficult to say, should the fog lift, in what direction she might next be seen. She might tack and run back to Cherbourg, or she might, trusting to her superior sailing, stand across the *Thisbe's* bows to the southward.

A couple of hours passed. As at any moment the fog might clear away, and the stranger might appear close aboard her, the *Thisbe* prepared for immediate action. The men had been sent below to dinner, and the prospect of a fight did not damp their appetites.

The midshipmen had finished theirs, and Rayner, who had just relieved one of his messmates on deck, was on the look-out when he espied, away on the larboard bow, a sail through the fog, which had somewhat dispersed in that quarter. A second glance convinced him that she was a large ship. He instantly shouted out the welcome intelligence. Every one hoped that she was the vessel they were in search of. The drum beat to quarters, and scarcely were the guns run out than the fog clearing still more discovered a large frigate standing under all sail to the eastward, about half a mile away. If she were the one they had before seen, she had evidently acted as Captain Martin had supposed might be the case, and having crossed the *Thisbe's* course, had then kept away, hoping to get in shore of her and back to Cherbourg. At once the *Thisbe* was put about, and then stood so as to cross the stranger's bows. The latter, on seeing this, hoisting French colours, rapidly shortened sail and hauled up to the northward, the two ships crossing each other on contrary tacks. The *Thisbe* fired her starboard broadside, receiving one in return, and then going about, endeavoured to get to windward of her antagonist. This, however, she was unable to do, and was compelled to continue the engagement to leeward. Her crew fought with the usual courage of British seamen, but the enemy's shot were making fearful havoc on her masts and rigging. Her three lower masts and bowsprit were in a short time wounded in several places, most of her stays were shot away, and much damage was done to the main rigging.

At length her main-topsail yard was shot away in the slings by a double-headed shot, and the yard-arms came down in front of the mainyard, the leech ropes of the mainsail were cut to pieces and the sail riddled. All the time, also, whenever the ships were within musket-range, showers of bullets came rattling on board, and several of the men were laid low.

Still Captain Martin did not attempt to escape from his opponent, which was seen to have twenty guns on a side, besides quarter-deck guns, and a number of men armed with muskets. He hoped, by perseverance, to knock away her masts or inflict such other serious injury as might compel her to give in.

This was Rayner's first action since he had attained his present rank. He endeavoured to maintain his character, and though it was trying work to see his shipmates struck down on either side of him, he did not for a moment think of himself or the risk he ran of meeting the same fate. All the time spars, rigging, and blocks were falling from aloft, shot away by the hot fire of the enemy. He endeavoured to keep himself cool and composed, and to execute the orders he received.

Jack and Tom were employed as powder-monkeys on the maindeck, when Rayner was sent by the captain to ascertain what was going on. As he went along it he passed his two friends.

Jack was as active as ever, handing up the powder required; poor Tom looked the picture of misery.

"Ain't the enemy going to strike yet, Mr Rayner?" he asked, in a melancholy tone; "we've been a long time about it, and I thought they would have given in long ago."

"I hope they soon will have enough of it and give in, and we must blaze away at them until they do," answered the midshipman, hurrying on.

Just then a shot came crashing in through the side, passing just where Rayner had been standing, sending the splinters flying about in all directions. He had not time to look round, but thought he heard a cry as if some one had been hit, and he hurried on to deliver his message to the second lieutenant.

On his way back he took a glance to see how it fared with his two friends. Tom was seated on his tub, but poor Jack lay stretched on deck. Rayner, hastening to him, lifted him up.

"I'm only hit in the leg," answered Jack to his inquiries. "It hurt me very much, and I fell, but I'll try to do my duty." How barbarous is war!

Rayner, however, saw that this was impossible, as the blood was flowing rapidly from the wounded limb, and calling one of the people appointed to attend those who were hurt, he ordered him to carry Jack below. "Tell the surgeons he's badly wounded, and get them to attend to him at once," he said.

He longed to be able to go himself, but his duty compelled him to return to the upper deck. Scarcely had he got there than he saw, to his grief, that the enemy had dropped under the stern, and the next instant, discharging her broadside, she raked the *Thisbe* fore and aft. In vain the latter tried to escape from her critical position; before she could do so she was a second time raked, the gaff being shot away, the mizenmast injured, and the remaining rigging cut through and through. Fortunately, the *Thisbe* still answered her helm, and the crew were endeavouring to make sail, when the enemy ranged up on the starboard quarter, her forecastle being covered with men, evidently intending to board.

Captain Martin, on seeing this, sent Rayner below with orders to double shot the after-maindeck guns, and to fire them as the enemy came close up. The next he shouted the cry which British seamen are always ready to obey, "Boarders, repel boarders;" and every man not engaged at the guns hurried aft, cutlass in hand, ready to drive back the foe as soon as the ships should touch; but ere that moment arrived, an iron shower issued from the guns beneath their feet, crashing through the Frenchman's bows and tearing along her decks. Instead of coming on, she suddenly threw all her sails aback, and hauled off out of gunshot. On seeing this, the British crew uttered three hearty cheers, and Rayner, with others who had hurried from below, fully believed that the enemy had hauled down her flag, but instead of that, under all the sail she could carry, she continued standing away until she had got two miles off. Here she hove-to, in order, it was evident, to repair damages. These must have been very severe, for many of her men were seen over the sides engaged in stopping shot-holes, while the water, which issued forth in cascades, showed that the pumps were being worked with might and main to keep her from sinking.

The *Thisbe* was in too crippled a condition to follow. Several shot had passed between wind and water on both sides. One gun on the quarter-deck and two on the maindeck were dismounted, and almost all the tackles and breachings were cut away. The maindeck before the mainmast was torn up from the waterway to the hatchways, and the bits were shot away, as was the chief part of the gangways. Not an officer had been killed, but two midshipmen, the master, and gunner, were wounded. Twenty men were wounded and eleven lost the number of their mess.

The wind, which had been moderate when the action began, had now greatly increased. Not a moment was lost in commencing the repair of damages. The sky indicated the approach of bad weather, and a westerly or south-westerly gale might be expected. Before all the shot-holes could be stopped it came on to blow very hard. Plymouth being too far to the westward, the nearest shelter the *Thisbe* could reach was Portland, towards which she steered.

The moon coming forth, she had light sufficient to run in and anchor, protected by the projecting headland from the furious gale now blowing.

Many a brave man on board besides the captain breathed more freely than they had done for some hours when the anchor was dropped and the torn canvas furled. Still the *Thisbe* would be in a critical position should the wind shift more to the southward, as she would be exposed to the seas rolling into the bay.

Chapter Twenty Five.

The shipwreck.

As soon as Rayner could obtain a spare moment, he hastened below to visit poor Jack. He met Tom on the way.

"Jack's very bad, Mr Rayner," answered Tom to his inquiries. "He didn't know me just now; he's talking about his mother, and fancying she's nursing him."

This news made our hero feel very sad, and he hurried on to the lower deck, where the wounded lay in their hammocks, sheltered by a canvas screen.

He inquired of one of the attendants where Jack Peek was, and soon found him, the surgeon being by his side dressing his wound.

"I'm much afraid that he will slip through our fingers unless we can manage to quell the fever. He requires constant watching, and that is more than he can well obtain, with so many men laid up, and so much to do," said the doctor as he finished his task. "However, Rayner, if you can stay by him, I'll be back in a few minutes to see how he's getting on. In the meantime give him this medicine; if he comes to his senses, a word or two from you may do him good."

Though Rayner himself could scarcely stand from fatigue, he undertook to do as the doctor requested. He waited until he saw, by the light of the lantern hung up from a beam overhead, that Jack had come somewhat to himself, when he got him to take the draught he held in his hand.

"How do you feel, Jack?" he asked in a low tone; but poor Jack did not reply. After waiting a little time longer, Rayner again spoke. "We've beaten off the enemy, you know, and are safe under shelter of the land. Cheer up now, you'll soon get round."

"Is that you, Bill?" asked Jack, in a faint voice. "I thought mother was with me, and I was on shore, but I'm glad she's not, for it would grieve her to see me knocked about as I am."

"You'll do well now, the doctor said so, as you've come to yourself," observed Rayner, much cheered at hearing Jack speak. "I'll stay by you while it is my watch below, and then I'll get Tom to come. Now go to sleep, if the pain will let you."

"The pain isn't so very great, and I don't mind it since we have licked the enemy," answered Jack; "but I hope you won't be angry at me calling you Bill; I quite forgot, Mr Rayner, that you were a midshipman."

"No, I didn't remark that you called me Bill," answered Rayner; "if I had, I shouldn't have thought about it. I just feel as I did when I was your messmate. However, I must not let you be talking, so now shut your eyes and get some sleep; it will do you more good than the doctor's stuff."

Rayner was very glad when the doctor came back, accompanied by Tom, and having observed that Jack was going on as well as he expected, told him to go to his hammock. This he gladly did, leaving Tom in charge of their friend.

Rayner felt that he greatly needed rest; but as he had expended part of his watch below, he could not have three hours' sleep.

On coming on deck he found the gale was blowing harder than ever, though the frigate lay sheltered by the land.

Almost immediately the sound of a distant gun reached his ear. It was followed rapidly by others, and the sound appeared to come down on the gale.

"There's a ship in danger on the other side of Portland," observed the second lieutenant, who was the officer of the watch. "Rayner, go and tell the captain. He desired to be called if anything happened."

Captain Martin, who had only thrown himself down on his bed in his clothes, was on his feet in a moment, and followed Rayner on deck.

After listening a minute. "It's more than possible she's our late antagonist," he observed. "If the gale caught her unprepared, her masts probably went by the board, and, unable to help herself, she is driving in here. Get a couple of boats ready with some coils of rope, and spars, and rockets, and we'll try and save the lives of the poor fellows."

Rayner was surprised to hear this, supposing that the captain intended to pull out to sea, whereas he had resolved to go overland to the part of the coast which probably the ship in distress was approaching. Although where the frigate lay was tolerably smooth water, yet, from the white-crested seas which broke outside, and the roaring of the wind as it swept over the land, it was very evident that no boat could live when once from under its shelter.

The captain, accompanied by three gun-room officers, Rayner and another midshipman, and twenty men, landed at the nearest spot where the boats could put in, and proceeded overland in the direction from which the sound of the guns had come.

Again and again they boomed forth through the midnight air. Solemnly they struck on the ear, telling of danger and death. Scarcely, however, had the party proceeded a quarter of a mile than they ceased. In vain they were listened for. It was too evident that the ship had struck the fatal rocks, and if so, there was not a moment to be lost, or too probably the whole of the hapless crew would be lost.

The western shore was reached at last. As they approached the cliffs they saw a number of people moving about, and as they got to the bay and looked down over the foaming ocean, they could see a dark object some fifty fathoms off, from which proceeded piercing shrieks and cries for help. It was the hull of a large ship, hove on her beam-ends, her masts gone, the after-part already shattered and rent by the fierce seas which dashed furiously against her, threatening to sweep off the miserable wretches clinging to the bulwarks and stanchions. To form a communication with her was Captain Martin's first object. As yet it was evident that no attempt of the sort had been made, most of the people who had collected being more eager apparently to secure the casks, chests, and other things thrown on shore than to assist their perishing fellow-creatures. It was vain to shout and direct the people on the wreck to attach a line to a cask and let it float in towards the beach. The most stentorian voices could not make themselves heard when sent in the teeth of the gale now blowing. On descending the cliffs, Captain Martin and his party found a narrow strip of beach, on which they could stand out of the power of the seas, which, in quick succession, came foaming and roaring in towards them. He immediately ordered a couple of rockets to be let off, to show the strangers that there were those on shore who were ready to help them. No signal was fired in return, not even a lantern shown, but the crashing, rending sounds which came from the wreck made it too evident that she could not much longer withstand the furious assaults of the raging ocean. Captain Martin inquired whether any of his crew were sufficiently good swimmers to reach the wreck.

Rayner longed to say that he would try, but he had never swum in a heavy sea, and felt that it would be madness to make the attempt.

"I'll try it, sir," cried Ben Twinch, the boatswain's mate, one of the most powerful men in the ship. "I'd like, howsomdever, to have a line round my waist. Do you stand by, mates, and haul me back if I don't make way; there are some ugly bits of timber floating about, and one of them may give me a lick on the head, and I shan't know what's happening."

Ben's offer was accepted. While the coil of line was being got ready, a large spar, to which a couple of men were clinging, was seen floating in towards the beach, but it was still at some distance, and there was a fearful probability that before it touched the shore the reflux of the water might drag them off to destruction.

"Quick, lads, quick, and I'll try to get hold of one or both of them, if I can," cried Ben, fastening the rope round his body. His example was followed by another man, who, in the same way, secured a rope round himself, when both plunged in and seized the well-nigh drowning strangers, just as, utterly exhausted, they had let go their hold. They were able, however, to speak, and Rayner discovered that they were French.

By the captain's directions he inquired the name of the ship.

"The *Zenobie* frigate, of forty guns and three hundred and forty men," was the answer. "We had an action yesterday with an English frigate, which made off while we were repairing damages, but truly she so knocked us about that when we were caught by the gale our masts went over the side, and we were driven utterly helpless on this terrible coast."

Rayner did not tell the *Thisbe's* men, who were trying to assist the hapless strangers, that they were their late antagonists. He merely said, "They are Frenchmen, lads; but I'm sure that will make no difference to any of us."

"I should think not, whether they're Mynheers or Mounseers," cried Ben. "They're drowning, and want our help; so, whether enemies or friends, we'll try to haul as many of the poor fellows ashore as we can get hold of, and give them dry jackets, and a warm welcome afterwards. Slack away, mates!" And he plunged into the foaming billows.

His progress was anxiously watched as he rose now on the top of a roaring sea, now concealed as he sank into the hollow to appear again on the side of another, all the time buffeting the foaming breakers, now avoiding a mass of timber, now grasping a spar, and making it support him as he forced his way onward, until he was lost to sight in the gloom.

After a considerable time of intense anxiety it was found that the line was taut. Ben had, it was supposed, reached the forechains of the frigate. Then the question rose, whether he would be able to make himself understood by the Frenchmen. One of the men, however, who had been washed on shore said that he believed one or two people on board understood English; but it was doubtful whether they were among those who had already perished.

Some more minutes passed, and then they felt the line shaken. It was the signal for them to haul in. Rapidly pulling away, they at length had the satisfaction of finding the end of a stout hawser, with a smaller line attached to it. The hawser was made fast round a rock, then, knowing the object of the line, they hauled away at it until they saw a cradle coming along with a couple of boys in it. The moment they were taken out the cradle was hauled back, and then a man appeared, and thus, one after another, about sixty of the French crew were dragged on shore.

Every time the cradle appeared, his shipmates hoped to see Ben in it; but Rayner learned from one of the persons in it that he had remained on the wreck, assisting those who were too benumbed or bewildered with fear to secure themselves.

As the poor Frenchmen were landed, they were placed under charge of some of the men appointed for the purpose, while two of the officers supplied the most exhausted with such restoratives as they required.

Many, they said, had already been washed off the wreck and been lost, while others were too much paralysed by fear even to make their way to where Ben was standing, lashed to a stanchion, ready to help them into the cradle.

Great fears were now entertained lest he should suffer by his noble exertions to save others. The crashing and rending sounds increased in frequency. Every instant some huge portion of the wreck was rent away, and the whole intervening mass of seething waters was covered by dark fragments of timber, tossing and rolling as they approached the beach, or were floated out to sea, or cast against the rocks. Still the Frenchmen kept arriving. Now one more daring than the others would crawl along the cable in spite of the risk of being washed off by the hungry breakers into which it was occasionally plunged.

Rayner, who stood on the rock with a party engaged in assisting the people as they arrived in the cradle, inquired whether there were many more to come.

"I think so, monsieur," was the answer; "we mustered nearly four hundred souls, but of those, alas! numbers have already been washed away."

Again and again those fearful crashings, mingled with despairing shrieks, were heard above the roar of wild breakers. Rayner felt serious apprehensions about the safety of brave Ben.

At any moment the wreck might break up, and then it would be scarcely possible for a human being to exist amidst the masses of timber which would be hurled wildly about.

Again the cradle was to be hauled in. In came with greater difficulty than before, as if it carried a heavier weight. It seemed as if the cable would not bear the additional strain.

The British seamen exerted all their strength, for at any moment, even if the cable did not break, it might be torn from its holdfast on the wreck. As the cradle came in, two men were seen seated in it, one holding another in his arms. Rayner heard the words, "Vite, vite, mon ami, ou nous sommes perdu."

"Haul away, lads, haul away!" he shouted out, though his men required no urging.

Just as the cradle was reaching the rock, a crash, even louder than its predecessors, was heard. Several men sprang forward to grasp the occupants of the cradle. The outer end of the rope had given way, and in another instant they would have been too late.

Again the wild shrieks of despair of the helpless wretches who still remained on the wreck echoed along the cliffs.

"Poor Ben! has he gone?" exclaimed Rayner. "No, sir, he's one of those we've just got ashore," answered a quarter-master who, with several others, had rushed down to help the two men taken out of the cradle, and who were now bearing the apparently inanimate body of the boatswain's mate up the rock; "the other's a Frenchman by his lingo."

Rayner hurried to the spot, when what was his surprise, as the light of the lantern fell on the countenance of the Frenchman last landed, to see Pierre's father, Captain Turgot!

Putting out his hand, he warmly shook that of his old friend, who opened his eyes with a look of astonishment, naturally not recognising him.

"Don't you know me, Captain Turgot?" said Rayner. "I am one of the boys you saved when our frigate was blown up."

"What! are you little Bill?" exclaimed the honest fisherman. "That is wonderful. Then you escaped after all. I am indeed glad."

There was no time just then, however, for explanations. Rayner thanked his old friend for saving Ben's life.

"I could do nothing else," was the answer. "He was about to place another man in the cradle who had not the courage to get into it by himself, when a piece of timber surging up struck both of them, the other was swept away, and the brave English sailor would have suffered the same fate had I not got hold of him; and then, though I had made up my mind to remain to the last, I saw that the only way to save him was to bring him myself in the cradle to the shore, and I am thankful that I did so. But my poor countrymen! There are many still remaining who must perish if we cannot get another hawser secured to the wreck."

This was what Captain Martin was now endeavouring to do, but there was no one found willing or able to swim back to the wreck. The danger of making the attempt was, indeed, far greater than at first.

Ben was regaining his consciousness; but even had he been uninjured, after the exertions he had gone through, he would have been unfit to repeat the dangerous exploit.

Captain Turgot offered to try; but when he saw the intermediate space through which he would have to pass covered with masses of wreck, he acknowledged that it would be impossible to succeed.

The final catastrophe came at last. A tremendous wave, higher than its predecessors, rolled in, apparently lifting the wreck, which, coming down again with fearful force upon the rocks, split into a thousand fragments.

As the wave, after dashing furiously on the shore, rolled back again, a few shattered timbers could alone be perceived, with not a human being clinging to them.

Shrieks of despair, heard above the howling tempest, rose from the surging water, but they were speedily hushed, and of the struggling wretches two men alone, almost exhausted, were thrown by a succeeding wave on the shingly beach, together with the bodies of several already numbered among the dead.

When Captain Martin came to muster the shipwrecked men saved by his exertions, he found that upwards of three hundred of the crew of his late antagonist had perished, seventy alone having landed in safety. Leaving a party on the beach to watch lest any more should be washed on shore, he and the magistrate led the way up the cliff. The Frenchmen followed with downcast hearts, fully believing that they were to be treated as prisoners of war. Some of them, aided by the British seamen, carried those who had been too much injured to walk.

After they had arrived at a spot where some shelter was found from the fury of the wind, Captain Martin, calling a halt, sent for Rayner, and told him to assure the Frenchmen that he did not look upon them as enemies or prisoners of war, but rather as unfortunate strangers who, having been driven on the English coast by the elements, had a right to expect assistance and kind treatment from the inhabitants, and that such it was his wish to afford them.

Expressions of gratitude rose from the lips of the Frenchmen when Rayner had translated what Captain Martin had said. The magistrate then offered to receive as many as his own house could accommodate, as did two gentlemen who had accompanied him, their example being followed by other persons, and before morning the whole of the shipwrecked seamen were housed, including three or four officers, the only ones saved. The poor fellows endeavoured by every way in their power to show how grateful they were for the kindness they were receiving.

Captain Martin's first care was to write an account of the occurrence to the Admiralty, stating what he had done, and expressing a hope that the shipwrecked crew would be sent back as soon as possible to

France.

By return of post, which was not, however, until the end of three or four days, Captain Martin had the satisfaction of receiving a letter from the king himself, highly approving of his conduct, and directing that the Frenchmen should each receive as much clothing and money as they required, and as soon as a cartel could be got ready, sent back to Cherbourg or some other French port.

News of the battered state of the *Thisbe* having been received at the Admiralty, a frigate was ordered round to escort her into port, as she was not in a position to put to sea safely by herself. The Frenchmen having been received on board the two frigates, and a light northerly breeze springing up, they sailed together for Plymouth. The pumps were kept going on board the *Thisbe* during the whole passage, when the Frenchmen, at the instigation of Captain Turgot, volunteered to work them.

Rayner had many a talk about Pierre with his old friend, who longed to embrace his son, and was profuse in his expressions of gratitude for the kindness he had received.

Directly he returned on board, Rayner went to Jack, whom he found going on well. Captain Turgot, on hearing that Jack had been wounded, begged permission to see him, and from that moment spent every instant he could by his side, tending him as if he had been his own son.

It was curious to see the way the English sailors treated their French guests who had so lately been engaged with them in a desperate fight. Several were suffering from bruises and exposure on the wreck. These were nursed with a tender care, as if they had been women or children, the sailors carrying those about whose legs had been hurt, and feeding two or three, whose hands or arms had been injured, just as if they had been big babies.

The rest of the Frenchmen who had escaped injury quickly recovered their spirits, and might have been seen toeing and heeling it at night to the sound of Bob Rosin's fiddle; and Bob, a one-legged negro, who performed the double duty of cook's second mate and musician-general of the ship, was never tired of playing as long as he could get any one to dance. The style of performance of the two nationalities was very different, but both received their share of applause from one another. The Frenchmen leapt into the air, whirled, bounded and skipped, while the British tars did the double-shuffle and performed the various evolutions of the hornpipe, to the admiration of their Gallic rivals.

By the time they had reached Plymouth they had won each other's hearts, and hands were wrung, and many of the Frenchmen burst into tears as they took their leave of their gallant entertainers, all protesting that they should always remember their kindness, and expressing the hope that they should never meet again except as friends.

Sad it is that men, who would be ever ready to live on friendly terms and advance their mutual interests, should, by the ambition and lust of power of a few, be compelled to slaughter and injure each other, as has unhappily been the case for so many centuries throughout the whole civilised portion of the world.

As soon as the anchor was dropped, Rayner asked for leave to go on shore with Captain Turgot, to visit Mrs Crofton, and learn how Pierre was getting on.

"You may go, but you must return on board at night, as there is plenty of work to be done," answered the first lieutenant.

"Thank you, sir," said Rayner; and he hurried below to tell Captain Turgot to get ready.

They shoved off by the first boat going on shore. They walked on quickly through the streets of Plymouth, Rayner anticipating the pleasure of seeing Mrs Crofton and Mary, and of witnessing the meeting between the honest Frenchman and his son.

"I hope that we shall find Pierre recovered; but the doctor said his wound would take long to heal, and you must not be surprised if he is still unable to move," he said to Captain Turgot. "Our friends will take very good care of him, and perhaps you would like to remain behind until he is well."

"I would wish to be with him, but I am anxious to relieve the anxiety of Madame Turgot and Jeannette, who, if they do not see me, will suppose that I am lost," answered the Captain. "I shall grieve to leave my boy behind, but I know that he will be well cared for, and I cannot tell you, my young friend, how grateful I am. Little did I think, when I picked you up out of the water, how amply you would return the service I did you."

"I certainly did not expect in any way to be able to repay it," said Rayner, "or, to say the truth, to feel the regard for Frenchmen which I do for you and your son."

Rayner found Mrs Crofton and her daughter seated in the drawing-room. After the first greetings were over, and he had introduced Captain Turgot, he inquired after Pierre, expecting, through not seeing him, that he was still unable to leave his room.

"He has gone out for a short walk, as the doctor tells him to be in the fresh air as much as possible, and he is well able to get along with the help of a stick," answered Mrs Crofton. "I hope his father has not come to take him away, for we shall be very sorry to lose him?"

"I don't know whether he will be allowed to go without being exchanged," answered Rayner; and he gave an account of the wreck of the *Zenobie* and the arrangement which had been made for sending the survivors of her crew back to France.

"That is very kind and generous of our good king. No wonder that his soldiers and sailors are so ready to fight for him," remarked Mrs Crofton.

While they were speaking, Pierre entered the house. His joy at seeing his father almost overcame him. They threw themselves into each other's arms and embraced as Frenchmen are accustomed to embrace—somewhat, it must be confessed, to Mary's amusement. After they had become more tranquil they sat down and talked away at such a rate that even Rayner could scarcely understand what they were saying. He meantime had a pleasant conversation with Mary and her mother, for he had plenty to tell them, and they evidently liked to listen to him.

After some time, during a pause in the conversation, Captain Turgot desired Pierre to tell Mrs Crofton and her daughter how grateful he felt for their kindness, his own knowledge of English being insufficient to express his wishes.

They, hearing him, replied in French, and soon the whole party was talking away in that language, though Mary's French, it must be admitted, was not of a very choice description; but she laughed at her own mistakes, and Rayner helped her out when she was in want of a word.

The afternoon passed pleasantly away, and Rayner, looking at his watch, was sorry to find it was time to return. He told Pierre that he must report his state to the Captain and Mr Saltwell, who would decide what he was to do.

Captain Turgot went back with him, having nowhere else to go.

Captain Martin lost no time in carrying out the wishes of the kind king. A brig was chartered as a cartel, on board of which the Frenchmen were at once sent. Rayner was not aware that Mr Saltwell had obtained permission for Pierre to go back with his father, and was much surprised on being directed to go to Mrs Crofton's, and to escort him on board the brig.

Pierre seemed scarcely to know whether to laugh or cry at regaining his liberty as he took leave of his kind hostess and her daughter; but his desire to see his mother and sister and la belle France finally overcame his regret at parting from them, and he quickly got ready to set off.

"We shall be happy to see you as soon as you can come again, Mr Rayner," said Mrs Crofton.

"Oh yes," added Mary, in a sweet voice, with a smile, which made our hero at once promise that he would lose no opportunity of paying them a visit. Rayner's first duty was to see Captain Turgot and Pierre on board the cartel. They embraced him with tears in their eyes as they wished him farewell, and many of the grateful Frenchmen gathered round him, several expressing their hopes that France and England would soon make up their quarrel.

"What it's all about, ma foi, is more than I or any of us can tell," exclaimed a boatswain's mate, wringing Rayner's hand, which all were eager to grasp. "We are carried on board ship and told to fight, and so we fight—more fools we! If we were wise, we should navigate our merchant vessels, or go fishing, or stay at home and cultivate our fields and gardens. We all hope that there'll be peace when we next meet, messieurs."

Many others echoed the sentiment, and cheered Rayner, who, after he had sent many kind messages to Madame Turgot and Jeannette, hurried down the side and returned on board the frigate.

Chapter Twenty Six.

The ship on fire.

Jack, with the rest of those who had been wounded, had been sent to the hospital. Rayner the next day obtained leave to visit him. He was sorry for Tom, who was thus left very much to his own resources, and he tried to find an opportunity of speaking a kind word to his former companion; but Tom, as before, sulkily kept aloof, so that he was compelled to leave him to himself. He was very sorry, soon after, to see him being led along the deck by the master-at-arms. Tom looked dreadfully downcast and frightened.

Rayner inquired what he had been doing.

"Attempting to desert, sir," was the answer. "He had got on shore and had dressed himself in a smock-frock and carter's hat, and was making his way out of the town."

Tom could not deny the accusation, and he was placed in irons, awaiting his punishment, with two other men who had also run from the ship and had been caught.

Rayner felt a sincere compassion for his old messmate, and obtained leave to pay him a visit, anxious to ascertain if there were any extenuating circumstances by which he might obtain a remission of his punishment.

"What made you try to run, Fletcher?" he asked, as he found Tom and his two companions seated in "durance vile," on the deck.

"I wanted to go back to my father and to try and persuade him to get me made a midshipman as you are," answered Tom. "It's a shame that a gentleman's son should be treated as I have been, and made a powder monkey of, while you have been placed on the quarter-deck."

"I thought that you had applied to your father before, and that he had refused to interfere," said Rayner, taking no notice of Tom's remark in regard to himself.

"I know that, well enough; but it was my brother who answered the letter; and, as my father is a clever man, I daresay by this time he has become rich again, and, for very shame at having a son of his a common ship's boy, would do as I wish. Can't you tell the captain that, and perhaps he'll excuse me the flogging? It's very hard to be prevented seeing my family, and to be flogged into the bargain. It's more than I can bear, and I've a great mind to jump overboard and drown myself when I get my wrists out of these irons."

"You'll not do that," answered Rayner, knowing very well that Tom did not dream of putting his threat into execution; "but I'll tell the first lieutenant what you say about your wish to see your family, though I fear it will not influence him in recommending the captain to remit your punishment. I would advise you, whatever happens, to submit, and to try, by doing your duty, to gain a good name for yourself," said Rayner, who gave him some other sound advice before he returned on deck.

Mr Saltwell shook his head when he heard what Rayner had to say.

"The captain won't forgive him, you may depend upon that, Rayner," he answered; "desertion must be punished, were it only as a warning to others."

Rayner, fortunately for himself, was on shore when Tom underwent his punishment, so that he was saved the pain of seeing it inflicted.

The frigate had been surveyed, but what opinion had been formed about her was not known for some time. At length the captain, who had gone on shore, returned, and, mustering the ship's company, informed them that, according to the surveyor's report, it would take some months to put her in thorough repair, and that in the meantime he had been appointed to the command of the store-ship *Bombay Castle*, of sixty-four guns, bound for the Mediterranean, and he should take his officers and crew with him. "We all of us might wish for more active service, my lads, but we shall not be long absent, and I hope by the time we come back that we shall find our tight little frigate as ready for any duty she may be sent on, as you all, I am sure, will be."

A cheer was the reply to this address, and the next day the officers and crew of the *Thisbe* went on board their new ship. They had, however, first to get her ready for sea, and then to receive the stores on board, by which time several of the wounded men, including Jack Peek, had sufficiently recovered to join her.

The *Bombay Castle* was rolling her away across the Bay of Biscay with a northerly breeze. She was a very different craft from the *Thisbe*, and though more than twice her size, not nearly so comfortable. Captain Martin had received orders to avoid an engagement, except attacked, and then to do his best to escape, as the stores she carried were of great value, and were much required by the fleet. Though several sail were sighted supposed to be an enemy's squadron, she managed to escape from them, and arrived safe at Gibraltar. Here she was joined by the *Ione* frigate, and the two ships sailed together, expecting to fall in with the fleet off Toulon.

The two ships lay almost becalmed in the Gulf of Lyons. Several officers of the *Ione*, which was only a short distance off, had come on board, when Captain Martin advised them, somewhat to their surprise, to get back to the frigate.

"I don't quite like the look of the weather," he remarked. "I've seen the masts of a ship whipped out of her, when not five minutes before there was no more wind than we have at present."

The frigate's boat left the side and was seen pulling rapidly towards her. Suddenly the cry was heard, "All hands on deck to save ship!"

Those who were below, springing up, found the ship heeling over till her yard-arms almost touched the foaming water, which came rushing over the deck, while the watch were engaged in letting fly tacks and sheets, lowering topsails, clewing up, and hauling down, blocks were rattling, sails shivering, the wind roaring, the sea leaping, hissing, and foaming. The helm was put up, the ship righted, and away she flew before the furious blast, not having suffered any material damage.

The *Ione*, however, could nowhere be seen. Struck by the squall, she might either have been dismasted or have capsized. In the former case it was very probable that she might fall into the hands of the enemy; but, much as the captain desired it, he could not return to her assistance.

Night came on, and the gale increased, the big ship tumbling and rolling about almost as much as she would have done in the Atlantic, so rapidly did the sea get up. It took some time to get everything snug, but as the ship was at a considerable distance from the land, no great anxiety was felt for her safety.

In the morning the master reported that by his calculation they were about thirteen leagues south-east of Cape Saint Sebastian, on the Spanish coast.

The wind had fallen with almost the same rapidity with which it had risen, but there was still a good deal of sea on. It had now shifted. The first lieutenant was officer of the watch, and was superintending the operation of washing decks.

Rayner, and another midshipman, also with bare feet and trousers tucked up, were paddling about, directing the men in their various duties.

Our hero had just came aft, and was addressing Mr Saltwell, when the latter looking forward, suddenly exclaimed, "What can that smoke be? Run and see where it comes from!"

As Rayner hurried forward he observed a thick volume of smoke rising out of the fore-hatchway, and immediately afterwards a similar ominous cloud ascended from the main hatchway. Before he had made a step aft to report this he saw Mr Saltwell hastening forward.

The next moment the cry of "Fire!" was raised, and the people came rushing up the hatchway in the midst of volumes of smoke ascending from the orlop deck.

"Rayner, go and inform the captain what has occurred," said Mr Saltwell, in a calm tone. "Let the drum beat to quarters!" he shouted.

The rolling sound of the drum was soon heard along the decks, and the men, springing from all parts of the ship, hurried to their respective stations, where they stood, ready for their orders.

Not a cry was heard. Not an expression of alarm escaped from one of the men. Scarcely a word was spoken as they stood prepared to do their duty.

Summoning the gunner and the boatswain, the first lieutenant ordered the former to open the ports, to give light and air below, and the latter to pipe up the hammocks. He then ascended to the orlop deck, made his way first into one tier, then into another, in both of which he found the smoke issuing exceedingly thick from forward. He was now joined by the second lieutenant and Rayner.

"We'll just go into the sail-room and ascertain if the fire is there," he said.

On reaching it, there was no appearance of fire or smoke. It was thus evident that the seat of the fire was farther forward. He and his companions next proceeded to the hold, but the dense smoke compelled them to beat a retreat, as their throats became affected as if from the fumes of hot tar. A second attempt to reach the hold was equally unsuccessful. The entire absence of heat, however, convinced them that the fire could not be in that part of the ship, but that the smoke found its way through the bulkheads.

They were returning on deck, when a cry was raised that the fire was down forward.

"I alone will go!" said Mr Saltwell. "Not a life must be risked without necessity. Remain, and render me any assistance I may require."

Having descended to the orlop deck, he was attempting to go down into the cockpit, when several men rushed by him, crying out that the fire was increasing. He endeavoured to retreat, but would have fallen before he reached the deck, had not the second lieutenant and Rayner, springing forward, assisted him up, and the next moment he sank down, apparently lifeless.

It was some minutes before the fresh air revived him.

Two poor fellows were suffocated by the smoke rolling in dense volumes along the lower deck, and others were rescued half dead by their shipmates.

Some short time was of necessity lost while the captain and master and the lieutenants were holding a consultation as to what was to be done.

In the meantime, Rayner, seeing the importance of discovering the seat of the fire, resolved at every risk to make the attempt. Without telling any of the officers of his intention, he called on Ben Twinch and Jack and Tom, whom he met on his way, to accompany him, and to bring a long rope with him. On reaching the hatchway he fastened the end round his waist.

"Haul me up if you find it becomes slack," he said. "You'll know then that I am not able to get on."

"Don't go, sir! don't go!" cried Jack. "It won't matter to any one if I get choked, but so many would be sorry if anything happened to you."

"I'll tell you what it is, Mr Rayner," exclaimed Ben; "no man who hasn't been down to the bottom of Stromboli or down Etna will be able to live two minutes in the cockpit, and I cannot help you, sir, to throw your life away. The ship's on fire somewhere forward, and what we've got to do is to pump the water over it, and try and put it out. If we can't do that, we must shut down the hatches, and see if we can't smother it."

Rayner was not inclined to listen to this well-meant and really judicious advice, but rushing forward, was attempting to make his way down the ladder. Scarcely, however, had he descended three or four steps, when the smoke filling his mouth and nostrils, he would have fallen headlong down had not Ben and Jack hauled him up again, almost in the same condition as Mr Saltwell had been.

"I told you so, sir," said Ben, as he carried him out of the way of the hose, which now began to play over the spot, under the direction of Mr Saltwell. The water, however, seemed to make no impression on the fire, or in any way to lessen the volumes of smoke, which, on the contrary, became thicker and thicker.

The men who were directing the hose were compelled to retire. The carpenters had, in the meantime, been engaged in scuttling the orlop deck, so that water might be poured down in great quantities. All their efforts were of no avail, however.

In a short time the first lieutenant was heard issuing his orders to cover in the hatchways, and to close the ports, so as to prevent the circulation of air.

With a sad heart Mr Saltwell now went on deck to report to the captain what had been done. He spoke in a low and earnest tone.

"I am afraid, Captain Martin, that we cannot hope to save the ship," he said; "the fire may be kept under for an hour or perhaps two hours, but if it once makes its way through the hatchways and gets to the lower decks, there is nothing to stop it. I would strongly advise that the boats should at once be got ready, so that as many lives as possible may be preserved."

"Were we to do that, the people would immediately fancy that the destruction of the ship is certain, and abandon themselves to despair," said the captain.

"I know our men, and can answer for their doing their duty," replied Mr Saltwell, with confidence. "If we delay getting out the boats, we may find it impossible to do so at last, and the lives of all on board may be sacrificed. We can trust to the marines, and give them directions to prevent any of the men getting into the boats until you issue the order for them to do so."

"You are right, Saltwell; send the sergeant of marines here," said the captain.

The sergeant quickly appeared and stood bolt upright, with his hand to the peak of his hat, as if on parade, ready to receive any orders which might be given.

"Call out your men, and understand that they are to load with ball and shoot any of the seamen who get into the boats without orders."

The sergeant, saluting, faced about, as if going to perform some ordinary routine of duty, and, quickly mustering his marines, stationed them as directed. The first lieutenant now gave orders to the boatswain to turn the hands up, and as soon as they appeared on deck, he shouted, "Out boats! but understand, my lads, that not one of you is to enter them without leave. The marines have received orders to shoot the first man who attempts to do so, though you do not require to be told that."

The crew hastened to the tackles and falls, and with the most perfect regularity the boats were lowered into the water when they were veered astern and secured for towing. The helm was now put down, the yards braced up, and the ship's head directed to the north-west, in which direction the land lay, though not visible from the deck.

The crew knew by this that the captain and officers considered the ship to be in great danger, and at the same time it encouraged them to persevere in their attempts to keep the fire under. They had some hopes also of falling in with the *Ione* or by firing the guns to attract her attention, should she be within hearing of them.

As the boats, however, would not carry the whole ship's company, the captain directed the carpenter and his mates to get the booms overboard for the purpose of constructing a raft large enough to support those whom the boats could not carry.

As it was now evident, from the increasing volumes of smoke which ascended through the hatchways, that the fire was working its way aft, although the flames had not yet burst out, it became of the greatest importance to get the powder out of the magazine. For this purpose the second lieutenant descended with a party of men, and succeeded in bringing up a considerable quantity, which was stowed in the stern gallery. All the other hands, not otherwise employed, were engaged under the different officers in heaving water down the hatchways; but the smoke increased to such a degree that they were compelled to desist, several who persevered falling senseless on the deck. The powder which had been got up being hove into the sea, the captain gave the order to drown the magazine. The difficulty of accomplishing this task was, however, very great, and the second lieutenant and gunner, with several of the men, were drawn up, apparently lifeless, after making the attempt. Lieutenant Saltwell now again descended to the after cockpit, where he found one man alone still persevering in the hazardous duty—Ben Twinch, boatswain's mate.

"A few more buckets, and we'll do it, sir!" cried Ben; but almost immediately afterwards he sank down exhausted.

The lieutenant, singing out for a rope, fastened it round him, though feeling that he himself would be overpowered before the gallant seaman could be drawn up. He succeeded, however, and once more returned to the deck above. Still, he knew that a large quantity of powder remained dry, and that should the fire reach the magazine, the destruction of all on board would be inevitable. Although gasping for breath, he was about again to descend, when a light, active figure, with a rope round his waist, darted passed him, and he recognised Rayner. He was about to follow, when he heard the voice of the midshipman shouting, "Haul me up, quick!"

The next instant Rayner was drawn up, too much exhausted to speak. He had succeeded in drowning a portion of the powder; but a quantity remained, sufficient at any moment to blow the ship into the air.

Although no human being could exist between the decks forward, the after-part of the lower deck remained free from smoke. In the hopes of getting at the magazine, the carpenter was directed to cut scuttles through the ward room, and gun-room, so as to get down right above it. By keeping all the doors closed, the smoke was prevented from entering, and at length it was found that the powder could be drawn, up and hove overboard out of the gallery windows. Several of the officers volunteered for this dangerous duty. Rayner, notwithstanding that he had just before escaped suffocation, again twice descended, and was each time drawn up more dead than alive. Several hours had now gone by, and the wind providentially holding fair, the ship was nearing the land. Meantime, the fire was fast gaining on them, and might at any moment triumph over all the heroic efforts of the crew to subdue it. The heat below was intense. The first lieutenant, going forward, found that the hatches had been blown off, as also the tarpaulins placed over the gratings. As it was of the greatest importance to keep them on, he directed the carpenter, with as many men as could be obtained, to replace them, while he returned once more aft, to superintend the operation of getting up the powder.

Although hitherto none of the men had attempted to shirk their duty, greatly to his annoyance he saw, on looking out of the ward-room windows, the stern ladders covered with people, who fancied that they would there be more secure, and escape discovery.

At once bursting open a window he ordered them all up, and directed Rayner to go and see that they made their appearance on deck. Among one of the first who came creeping up, our hero discovered his former messmate Tom Fletcher.

"You people have disgraced yourselves. Fletcher, I am sorry to have to say the same to you," he exclaimed.

It was the first time he had ever openly found fault with his former companion, but his feelings compelled him to utter the words.

Tom, and the whole of the men who had been on the ladders, sneaked away on either side, ashamed, at all events, of being found out, and still looking with longing eyes at the boats astern. Every now and then a seaman was brought aft and placed under the doctor's care, but of the number four were found to be past recovery, and it seemed doubtful whether several others would revive.

The greater portion of the crew, under the direction of the officers, were vieing with each other, trying to keep down the flames.

The wind shifted a point or two more in their favour. The captain immediately ordered the hands aloft, to set the topgallant sails and royals.

Seven anxious hours had passed, when while the men were still aloft, the cry arose, "Land, land, on the weather bow!"

The men on deck cheered at the announcement. In a short time it could be observed through the haze right ahead. The sight, though the land was still five leagues distant, revived the sinking spirits of the crew, and spurred them on to greater exertions. Still, notwithstanding all their efforts, the fire rapidly increased. Again and again efforts were made to clear the magazine, but the smoke as often drove the men back. By this time the whole of the fore part of the lower deck was on fire, but owing to the ports being closed and all circulation of air prevented, the flames did not rise with the rapidity which would otherwise have been the case. The fear was that, the heels of the masts being consumed by the fire, the masts themselves might fall.

Still they stood right gallantly, carrying their widespread canvas, and urging on the ship to the wished-for shore.

By this time all communication with the fore part of the ship was cut off. The crew were gathered aft, still actively employed in fighting the flames by heaving down water. But foot by foot they were driven towards the stern.

At length the devouring element burst through all control, and rushed up the fore-hatchway, rising triumphantly as high as the foreyard. Yet the ship kept on her way.

The men remained firm to their duty. Now, not only from the fore, but from the main hatchway, the flames were seen to ascend, but for some time, the courses having been thoroughly wetted, they stood still urging on the ship towards the land.

Time went on. The fire had commenced at seven in the morning, it was now several hours past noon. For all that period the crew had been fighting desperately with the fiery element for their lives. Anxiously, with straining eyes, they gazed at the land. On either side a dark mass of smoke ascended before them, and blew away to leeward, while the lurid flames rose beneath it, striving furiously for victory over the masts and spars, sails and rigging. It seemed like a miracle that the masts should stand in the midst of the hot furnace which glowed far down the depths of the ship. All were aware that at any moment one of several fearful events might occur. The wind might shift and prevent the ship reaching the land ahead, or a gale might spring up and cast the ship helplessly upon the rocks, or a calm might come on and delay her progress, or the masts, burnt through, might fall and crush those on deck, or, still more dreadful, a spark might reach the magazine, and her immediate destruction must follow.

Still the officers and crew strove on, though they well knew that no human power could extinguish the raging flames, which with sullen roar came nearer and nearer to where they stood.

An alarm was given that the mizenmast was on fire in the captain's cabin, and as Rayner looked over the side, he could see the flames burst out of the lee ports. The guns had not been loaded, but there was no necessity to fire signals of distress. The condition of the ship could be seen from far along the shore, and it was hoped that boats would, as she drew near, put off to her assistance.

The master, some time before, had brought up a chart on deck, and now pointed out to his brother officers the exact spot towards which the ship was steering. It was the Bay of Rosas. Already the ship was entering between two capes which formed its northern and southern sides. The captain stood in the midst of his officers and men, gathered on deck, for every place below was filled with smoke, and, except in the after-part of the ship, the raging flames had gained full mastery.

His wish had been to reach the shore before any one quitted the ship; he now saw that to do this was impossible.

"My lads," he said, "I am about to order up the boats. You have hitherto maintained your discipline; let me see that you are ready to obey orders to the last. And now we'll have the raft overboard, which will carry every man who cannot be stowed in the boats, even if the Spaniards don't come out to help us. Lower away."

It was no easy matter to perform this operation, with the fire raging uncontrolled not many feet off, almost scorching the backs of the men standing nearest it.

A cheer announced that it had safely reached the water, when the carpenter and his crew, with a few additional hands, were ordered on to it, to secure the booms on either side, so as to increase its power of supporting a heavy weight.

Scarcely had this been done, and the launch ordered up under the stern, than the ship struck and remained immovable, though nearly a mile from the shore. Then the tall masts seemed to sway to and fro as if they were about to fall, though it might only have been fancy.

The marines, who had faithfully performed their duty, were stationed on either side, while the sick and several of the wounded were lowered into the launch. The boys and younger midshipmen were next directed to go down the ladder, and the other men were told off. The two yawls and jolly-boat being hauled up, were then loaded with as many as they could carry.

"May I stay by you, sir?" asked Rayner of Mr Saltwell.

"No, Rayner," answered the first lieutenant; "you have done your duty well this day, and I cannot allow you to risk your life by remaining a moment longer than is necessary. We cannot tell when the ship may blow up. It may be before the captain and I quit her. I order you to go."

Rayner obeyed and descended into one of the yawls. Looking towards the shore he saw several boats coming off. He pointed them out to the officer in command of the launch. "Tell them to come under the stern of the ship and take off the remainder of the crew," said the lieutenant.

While the yawl was pulling towards the Spanish boats, he looked round to the ship. Already it appeared as if the flames were rushing from every port, while they were rising higher and higher, forming a vast pyramid of fire, as circling round and round the masts they caught hold of the canvas and rigging, and seized the spars in their embrace.

He urged the crew to pull with all their strength, that they might the sooner return to the assistance of their friends. The Spanish boats were reached, but in vain he endeavoured to persuade their crews to come near the burning ship. They were ready enough to receive on board the people in the yawl, but not to risk their lives by approaching her.

One of the officers could speak a little Spanish, and Rayner tried his French upon them, endeavouring to persuade them, and at length threatening condign punishment if they refused. But nothing that could be said had any effect. Time was precious, so, putting the men from the crowded yawl into one of the boats, Rayner, who took charge of her, urging the men to pull with all their might steered back for the ship. From the position in which the boat was, between her head and the shore, she appeared already to be one mass of flame. It seemed impossible indeed that any human being could still be alive on board. Pulling round, however, so as to approach the stern, Rayner saw that the after portion still remained free from flame, though the crew, as if they knew that there was no time to be lost, were not only descending the ladders, but sliding rapidly down the ropes hanging over the taffrail on to the raft. They had good reason for doing so, for he could see the ruddy light even through the stern windows, and from every port, except the extreme after ones, the flames were rushing out.

Three figures alone stood on the poop; they were those of the captain, the first lieutenant, and master, who had maintained their perilous position until every living man was out of the ship.

Remembering the remark Mr Saltwell had made just before he had quitted the ship, Rayner again urged on his well-nigh exhausted crew to pull up and rescue their brave officers. The raft was crowded with men. The shout rose, "Shove off! shove off!" and with broken spars and pieces of board, those on it were endeavouring to make their way to a distance from the side of the ship.

Rayner steered his boat under the stern. The master was the first to descend, Mr Saltwell came next, and the captain was the last to leave her.

"Pull away, Rayner," he said, in a calm voice. "We have reason to be thankful to Providence that she has not blown up yet, for at any moment the fire may reach the magazine, and there is still powder enough, I understand, to send the fragments far around."

The first yawl having received on board several people from the land, took the raft in tow. In a short time the other boats returned, having placed the people they carried in the Spanish boats, several of which also arrived, though they lost not a moment in pulling again towards the shore, as far as they could from the burning ship.

The captain directed Rayner to keep astern of the other boats. His eye rested on his ship as if he desired to see her as long as she existed. The moment of her destruction came at last. The rest of the crew having landed, the yawl was nearing the shore, when a loud roar was heard as if a whole broadside had been fired. The flames rose high in the air; the masts shot upwards surrounded by burning fragments of planks and timbers; the stout sides, rent asunder, rushed outwards, and in another minute a few blackened fragments of the gallant ship, which had that morning floated trim and proudly on the ocean, were alone visible.

Captain Martin looked sad and grave as he stepped on shore; but he felt that he, as well as his officers, had done their duty, and had made every possible effort to preserve the ship. Neither he nor they could discover the cause of the fire.

Fortunately, England had not then declared war against Spain, and the authorities received the British officers and men in a friendly manner, while many of the inhabitants of the neighbouring town vied with each other in rendering them all the service in their power.

Chapter Twenty Seven.

A narrow escape—Home—An action suddenly ended.

The morning after the day they landed in Spain, Rayner had gone down to the beach with Mr Saltwell, who wanted, he said, to have another look at the remains of the old barkie. The midshipman was examining the black ribs of the wreck appearing above water through the telescope which the lieutenant had lent him, when the latter exclaimed, "Do you see a sail away to the south-east?"

The sun glanced for a moment on her canvas.

"Yes, sir," answered Rayner. "She's a large craft, too, for I can only just see her royals rising above the horizon. She's standing in this direction."

"Hand me the glass," said Mr Saltwell. "You are right, youngster," he continued, looking through it. "I only hope that she may be one of our own cruisers, but it will be some time before that point can be decided."

After watching the approaching stranger for some time the lieutenant and midshipman returned with the intelligence to the farm-house where the captain and several of the other officers were quartered.

Hoping that she might be the *Ione*, Captain Martin ordered the first yawl to be got ready to go off to her. The crew were then mustered. Eight did not answer to their names. It was known how five had died, but what had become of the other three? At length it was whispered among the men that they had managed to get drinking the previous night, and had fallen below, stupefied by the smoke.

The men having breakfasted, the greater number hurried down to the shore to have a look at the stranger, now approaching under all sail.

Three cheers were uttered as the flag of England flew out at her peak. The captain immediately ordered Mr Sterling to pull off to her, and to request that his officers and ship's company might be received on board.

"You will make sure before you get near that she is English," he whispered. "The Frenchman may have a fancy to take some Spaniards prisoners, and would be better pleased to get hold of you."

Rayner went as midshipman of the boat, which made good way towards the frigate now lying hove-to about three miles from the shore.

"What do you think of her, Noakes?" asked the lieutenant of the coxswain, as they got nearer.

The old seaman took a steady glance at the stranger, surveying her from truck to water-line.

"If she doesn't carry a British crew, the Frenchmen must have got hold of her since we parted company three days ago, and I don't think that's likely, or there would be not a few shot-holes in her canvas, and a pretty good sprinkling in her hull, too," he answered, in a confident tone. "She's the *Ione*, sir, or I don't know a frigate from a Dutch dogger."

Now certain that there was no mistake, Mr Sterling steered for the frigate. Pulling alongside, he and Rayner stepped on board. Captain Dickson, with most of his officers, were on deck.

"Where is your ship?" was the first question the captain asked of the lieutenant.

"There is all that remains of her," answered Mr Sterling, pointing to the blackened ribs of the ship, which could be distinguished through a telescope near the shore; and he gave an account of what had happened.

Due regrets at the occurrence having been expressed, Captain Dickson saying that he had been induced to stand into the bay in consequence of hearing the sound of the explosion, at once ordered out all the boats, and in a few minutes they were pulling for the shore, accompanied by the yawl.

The *Ione*, meantime, was standing in somewhat nearer, to be ready to receive the crew of the store-ship on board.

No time was lost in embarking, and it was with intense satisfaction that Captain Martin and those under him found themselves again on the deck of an English frigate.

Sail was at once made for Gibraltar, Malta not having at that time been taken possession of by the English. As the two ships' companies had to be stowed away below, they were compelled to pack pretty closely, but no one minded that, as they expected a speedy passage to the Rock, while the officers and crew of the store-ship hoped immediately to be sent back to England.

It is too true a saying that "There's many a slip 'twixt the cup and the lip." The *Ione* was about midway between the Spanish coast and Majorca, when, as morning broke, a number of ships were seen standing out from the direction of Minorca. At first it was supposed that they were part of the English fleet, but after two of the lieutenants had taken a careful survey of them from aloft, it was decided that they were French.

"They have seen us, and guess what we are," observed Captain Dickson to his brother captain. "See, here come two frigates in chase. Turn the hands up and make sail!" he added, addressing the first lieutenant.

The crew were quickly aloft, and every stitch of canvas the *Ione* could set was packed upon her. There was no disgrace in running from so superior a force. The *Ione* was considered a good sailer, but the Frenchmen showed that they were still faster. Captain Dickson, however, had no intention of yielding his ship as long as he had a stick standing to escape with. Full of men as he now was, he hoped to beat off both his foes, though he could not expect to capture them in sight of an enemy's squadron. As they got nearer, a couple of guns were trained aft to serve as stern chasers, and every preparation was made to fight for life and liberty.

Another frigate and two line-of-battle ships were seen standing after the first, but they were so far astern, that should the *Ione* keep ahead, without having her masts and spars shot away, there might still be hopes of her escaping.

British seamen seldom wish to avoid a fight, but on the present occasion few on board were such fire-eaters as not to hope that they might keep well ahead of their foes.

The two frigates were rapidly gaining on the *Ione*; another half-hour, or even less, and she would be within range of their guns. To hit her, however, they would have to yaw, and this would enable her to gain on them, while she could fire without altering her course.

Jack and Tom every now and then got a glimpse of the enemy through the ports.

"I say, Jack, it isn't fair of those two fellows out there to be chasing us after all we have gone through. I was hoping to go home and see my father, and ask him to get me placed on the quarter-deck. I shouldn't like to be killed till I've been made a midshipman—not that I should like it then."

"Don't you be talking nonsense about being made a midshipman. You've about as much chance as you have of being made port-admiral off-hand," answered Jack, with more temper than he generally showed. "Of course you don't want to be killed—no more do I; but we must both be ready should it be God's will to call us in the way of duty."

At length the drum beat to quarters, by which the men knew that the captain expected before long to be engaged in a fierce fight.

Rayner was at his station forward, but he could still see what was taking place astern. Presently the frigates yawed. Two flashes were seen, and the low, booming sound of a couple of guns came across the ocean.

"We're not quite within range of the mounseers' popguns yet," observed the boatswain, with a laugh. "They must come closer before they can harm us."

"Do you think we can beat them off?" asked Rayner.

"You may be very sure that we'll try pretty hard to do so," answered the boatswain, in a confident tone. "I've heard of your doings aboard the *Thisbe*. We'll show you that the crew of the *Ione* are made of the same stuff."

As the two Frenchmen drew nearer, the desire of the British sailors to fight increased, and it was with a feeling of almost bitter disappointment, just as the *Ione* had fired her stern chasers, that the enemy were seen to haul their tacks aboard, in answer, apparently, to the signals made by the ships astern.

The general opinion was that the British fleet had appeared to the eastward. Whether or not this was the case it was impossible to say.

The *Ione* continued her course, and in a short time ran the enemy out of sight. On her arrival at Gibraltar, the first intelligence Mr Saltwell received was that he had been promoted to the rank of commander.

The very next day two ships came in from the fleet with despatches, which the *Ione* was directed to carry immediately to England.

As they were both short of hands, much to Captain Martin's annoyance, a considerable number of his men were drafted on board them. Had other ships come in, he would probably have lost many more. The *Ione* sailed immediately with the remainder, and he hoped that they would form the nucleus of a new crew for the *Thisbe*.

The *Ione* had a quick passage to Plymouth. On his arrival there, much to his disappointment, Captain Martin found that the *Thisbe* was not yet ready for sea.

Rayner was considering how to dispose of himself during the intermediate time. He did not expect that Mrs Crofton would offer him a room, but he wished, at all events, to pay her and Mary a visit, as they had always shown so friendly a feeling towards him. When, however, she heard how he was situated, she insisted that he should take up his quarters with them.

"I do not require any payment, as I have no other lodger at present, and I am only too glad to have you," she said, in a kind tone.

Rayner thanked her very warmly, and accepted her offer.

"I daresay Captain Saltwell will come and see us as soon as he has time. I was delighted to hear that he had obtained his promotion, and I hope, Mr Rayner, that you will soon get yours. You have surely served long enough to pass for a mate, and I would advise you to apply at once, that you may be ready for your lieutenancy."

"I am afraid that I should have but little chance of passing, but I'll try," said Rayner. "I am told the examinations are very stiff. If a midshipman doesn't answer every question put to him, he is turned back immediately."

"At all events, go in and try, and take a testimonial from Captain Saltwell," said Mrs Crofton, who had heard something of the way examinations were conducted in those days.

Rayner found, on inquiry, that, fortunately, a board was to sit the very next day, and, meeting Captain Saltwell, he mentioned his intention.

"The very thing I was going to advise," was the answer. "I'll write a letter to Captain Cranston, and you can take it with you."

Next morning Rayner presented himself on board the flagship, where he found several other midshipmen ready to go up. First one, and then another, was sent for, and came back with smiling faces. At last one, who certainly did not look as if he would set the Thames on fire, went in. In a short time he reappeared, grumbling and complaining that it was very hard a fellow who had been at sea six years should be turned back.

Rayner's turn came next. Comparatively but a few questions were asked in navigation. He had no difficulty in answering those put to him in seamanship. At last, Captain Cranston, knitting his brow, and looking very serious, said—

"Now, Mr Rayner, supposing the ship you are in charge of is caught on a lee shore with a hurricane blowing, and you find yourself embayed; what would you do?"

"If there was holding ground, I should let go the best bower, and make all snug aloft."

"But suppose the best bower is carried away?"

"I should let go the second bower, sir."

"But suppose you lose that?" asked the captain, looking still more serious.

"I should cut away the masts and bring up with my sheet anchor."

"But in the event of losing that, Mr Rayner, how would you next proceed?"

"I should have done all that a man can do, and should look out for the most suitable place for running the ship ashore."

"But, suppose you could find no suitable place, Mr Rayner?"

"Then, sir, I should let her find one for herself, and make the best preparations time would allow for saving the lives of her people, when she struck."

"I have the pleasure to inform you, Mr Rayner, that you have passed your examination very creditably," said Captain Cranston, handing him his papers.

Rayner, thanking the captain, and bowing, made his exit. On afterwards comparing notes with the midshipman who had been turned back, he mentioned the question which had been put to him.

"Why, that's the very one he asked me," said his companion. "I told him I would club-haul the ship, and try all sorts of manoeuvres to beat out of the bay, and would not on any account let her go ashore."

"I'm not surprised that you were turned back, old fellow," observed Rayner, with a laugh.

On returning on shore he met Commander Saltwell. "I congratulate you, Rayner," he said. "I have just received orders to commission the *Lily* sloop-of-war, and I will apply to have you with me. By-the-bye, where are you going to put up?"

"Mrs Crofton has asked me to go to her house, and as I thought that you would have no objection, I accepted her offer, sir," answered Rayner.

"I am glad to hear it; the very best thing you could do," said Commander Saltwell. "Though many would prefer the freedom of an inn, I admire your good taste in taking advantage of the opportunity offered you to pass your time in the society of refined, right-minded persons like Mrs Crofton and her daughter."

Our hero spent a few happy days with the kind widow and Mary, who both evidently took a warm interest in his welfare. It was the first time he had been living on shore, except during his sojourn in France, since he first went to sea. He was introduced to some of the few friends they possessed, and he made several pleasant excursions with them to visit some of the beautiful scenery in the neighbourhood of Plymouth. His observation, unknown to himself, enabled him rapidly to adapt himself to the manners of people of education, and no one would have recognised in the gentlemanly young midshipman the powder monkey of a short time back. It was with more regret than he supposed he could possibly have felt that he received a summons to join the *Lily*, now fitting out with all despatch for the West Indies. Though he no longer belonged to the *Thisbe*, it was with much sorrow that he heard she was pronounced unfit for sea, and that her crew had been dispersed. He made inquiries for Jack and Tom. The former, he discovered, had gone to pay his mother a visit; but, though he searched for Tom, he could nowhere hear of him.

The day after he had joined the *Lily*, he was well pleased to see Jack come on board.

"I found out, sir, that you belonged to the corvette, as I thought you would when I heard that Mr Saltwell was appointed to command her," said Jack; "so, sir, I made up my mind to volunteer for her, if I could escape being pressed before I got back to Plymouth."

"I am glad to see you, Peek," said our hero. "Have you heard anything of Tom Fletcher?"

"Well, sir, I'm sorry to say I have," answered Jack. "He has been knocking about Plymouth, hiding away from the press-gangs in all sorts of places, instead of going home to his father, as he said he would. I only found him last night, and tried to persuade him to join the *Lily* with me, but he'd still a shiner or two in his locker, and he couldn't make up his mind to come till the last had gone. I know where to find him, and I'll try again after I have entered on board the *Lily*."

"Do so," said Rayner. "He may be better off with a friend like you to look after him than left to himself."

Rayner had the satisfaction of seeing Jack rated as an A.B. Several of the *Thisbe's* crew had joined the *Lily*, and besides them Ben Twinch, who, owing to Captain Martin's recommendation, had been raised to the rank of warrant officer, was appointed to her as boatswain.

"Very glad to be with you again, Mr Rayner," said honest Ben; "and I hope before the ship is paid off to see you one of her lieutenants. We are likely to have a good ship's company; and I am glad to say my brother warrant officers, Mr Coles the gunner, and Mr Jenks the carpenter, are men who can be trusted."

Rayner's own messmates were all strangers. The first lieutenant, Mr Horrocks, a red-faced man, with curly whiskers, and as stiff as a poker, had not much the cut of a naval officer; while the second lieutenant, Mr Lascelles, who was delicate, refined, young, and good-looking, offered a great contrast to him.

They were both not only civil but kind to Rayner, of whom Commander Saltwell had spoken highly to them.

Jack had been twice on shore to look out for Tom, and had returned saying that he could not persuade him to come on board.

At last, when the ship was almost ready for sea, being still some hands short of her complement, Rayner obtained leave for Jack, with two other men who could be trusted to try and bring him off, and any others they could pick up.

Late in the evening a shore boat came off with several men in her, and Jack made his appearance on deck, where Rayner was doing duty as mate of the watch.

"I have brought him, sir, though he does not exactly know where he is coming to," said Jack.

"I found him with his pockets emptied and the landlady of the house where he was lodging about to turn him out of doors. We managed to bring him along, sir, however, and to-morrow morning, when he comes to his senses, I have no doubt he'll be thankful to enter."

"I'm glad to hear you've got him safe at last, and I know you'll look after him," said Rayner.

Next morning Tom, not knowing that Rayner was on board, or how he himself came there, entered as an ordinary seaman, which placed him in an inferior position to Jack Peek, who might soon, from his activity and good conduct, be raised to the rank of a petty officer.

Our hero paid a last visit to Mrs Crofton and Mary, promising, as they asked him to do, to write whenever he could obtain an opportunity.

At length the *Lily*, a fine corvette, carrying twenty guns on a flush deck and a complement of one hundred and twenty men, was ready for sea.

On going down the Sound she found the *Latona*, which ship she was to assist in convoying a fleet of merchantmen brought up in Cawsand Bay.

As the men-of-war approached, the merchant vessels, to the number of nearly fifty, got under way and stood down Channel. It was pretty hard work to keep them together, and the corvette was employed in continually firing signals to urge on the laggers, or to prevent the faster craft from running out of sight. What with shortening and making sail and signalling, together with getting a newly commissioned ship into trim, the time of all on board was pretty well occupied, and Rayner had no opportunity of learning anything about Tom Fletcher. A bright lookout was kept on every side, for an enemy might at any moment appear, especially at night, when it was possible some daring privateer might pounce down and attempt to carry off one of the merchantmen, just as a hawk picks off a hapless chicken from a brood watched over so carefully by the hen.

The wind was fair, the sea calm, and the traders bound for Jamaica safely reached Port Royal harbour, the remainder being convoyed to the other islands by the *Latona* and *Lily*, which were afterwards to be sent to cruise in search of the enemy's privateers. Our hero had not forgotten Tom Fletcher, but watched in the hopes of doing him a service Jack's report of him had not been favourable. He had talked of going home to his father, and had plenty of money in his pocket to do so, but instead of that he had gone to dancing-houses and similar places resorted to by seamen, where his money rapidly disappeared. He might have fallen into the docks, or died in the streets, had not Jack found him and brought him on board the *Lily*. For some neglect of duty his leave had been stopped, and, fortunately for himself, he was not allowed to go on shore at Port Royal when the ship put in there. Tom, however, still avoided Rayner, who had no opportunity, unless he expressly sent to speak to him, to give him a word of advice or encouragement.

Jack, who was really the best friend he had in the ship, did his utmost to keep him out of mischief.

"It's all very fine for you to talk that way," answered Tom, when one day Jack had been giving him a lecture. "You got rated as an able seaman, and now have been made captain of the mizen-top, too, and will, I suppose, before long, get another step; and here am I sticking where I was. It's no fault of mine, that I can see. I'll cut and run if I have the chance, for I cannot bear to see others placed over my head, as you and Bill Rayner have been, and to see him walking the quarter-deck in a brand new uniform, and talking to the officers as friendly and easy as if he had been born among them, while I, a gentleman's son, remain a foremast man, with every chance of being one to the end of my days."

"There's no use grumbling, Tom; all you have to think about is to do your duty with smartness, keep sober, and to avoid doing anything wrong, and with your education, which I wish I had, you are sure to get on."

There is an old saying that it is useless to try and make a silk purse out of a sow's ear. It is to be seen whether Tom Fletcher was like the sow's ear.

Soon after the *Lily* left Jamaica she fell in with the *Ariel*. As a calm came on while they were in company, the officers of the two ships paid visits to each other. Rayner, recollecting that Mary Crofton's brother Oliver was serving in her, got leave to go on board, for the purpose of making his acquaintance. He was much disappointed, on inquiring for him, to learn that he had been sent away a few days before, in charge of a prize, a brig called the *Clerie*, with orders to take her to Jamaica.

"She ought to have arrived before you left there," observed the midshipman who told him this.

"How provoking that I should have missed him, though I do not think any such vessel came in while we were there," answered Rayner. "His mother and sister are great friends of mine."

"They must be nice people if they are like him, for Oliver Crofton is a capital fellow. He is as kind-hearted and even-tempered as he is brave and good-looking, and he is a favourite with all on board."

"I am glad to hear that, though it makes me the more sorry that we should have missed each other, but I hope before long to fall in with him," observed Rayner.

A breeze springing up, the officers retired to their respective vessels, and the *Lily* and *Ariel* parted company, the former rejoining the frigate. While off Antigua, the wind being from the eastward, the frigate made the signal of three strange sail to the south-west, and directly afterwards to give chase.

All the canvas they could carry was set. In a short time one of the strangers was seen to haul up to the northward, and the *Lily* was ordered to go in pursuit of her. She was apparently the smallest of the three, but was still likely to prove no mean antagonist. As the *Lily* appeared to be gaining on her, the commander gave the order to prepare for action. The frigate meantime was standing after the other two vessels. Before long her topsails, and finally her royals, disappeared beneath the horizon.

"We shall have her all to ourselves, and we'll see how soon we can take her," observed Mr Horrocks to the second lieutenant. "It is some time since you smelt powder, Lascelles."

"Last time I smelt a good deal of it, when we were beating off a ship twice our size, and should have taken her, too, had she not gone down in the night," answered the second lieutenant, in his usual quiet tone. "I got my promotion in consequence."

"And wrote an ode to victory, eh?" said Mr Horrocks, who was fond of bantering his brother lieutenant on his fondness for poetry.

"And it was considered good," responded the young officer.

"You will have an opportunity of exercising your poetical talents before long on the same subject, I hope," observed the first lieutenant. "We are gaining fast on the chase."

Just then the look-out from the mast-head shouted, "Sail on the starboard bow!"

"Go and see what she is like," said the commander to Rayner.

Our hero hurried aloft, his telescope hanging by a strap at his back. He was quickly joined by the second lieutenant. They were of opinion that she was a large craft, and that the object of the chase was to draw the *Lily* away from the frigate, so that the corvette might have two opponents to contend with.

"We must manage to take her before she reaches the other, then we shall have time to prepare for a second action," observed Mr Lascelles.

"Can she be the *Ariel*?" asked Rayner. "She's very likely to be cruising hereabouts."

Mr Lascelles took another look at her through his glass.

"I think not," he answered. "The chase must have seen her, and must know her to be a friend, or she would not keep on as she is at present standing."

The two officers descended to make their report.

The *Lily* was a fast craft, and now rapidly gained on the chase, which, as she drew within range, fired a couple of shot.

Captain Saltwell ordered the two foremost guns to be fired in return. The second lieutenant took charge of one and Rayner of the other. Both, looking along the sights, gave them the proper elevation, and fired at the same moment. The effect of the shot was beyond all expectation. Down came the foreyard, shot away in the slings, causing, it was very evident, considerable confusion on board.

"Bravo, Rayner! you did it!" cried Mr Lascelles. "My shot went through the mainsail."

The enemy now opened fire from a broadside of ten guns, but not a shot damaged the *Lily*, which, ranging up on the weather side of her opponent, began blazing away as fast as the crews could run in and load their guns.

The stranger was a large flush-decked vessel, crowded with men, many of whom, stripped to the waist, were working away desperately at their guns, while others opened a heavy fire of musketry.

As Rayner, who had charge of the foremost guns, was watching her, he caught sight of a young man in the uniform of a midshipman, who sprang suddenly up through the companion-hatch, and, making his way aft, seemed to be addressing the captain with energetic action. Rayner got but a glimpse of him, for the next moment there came a fearful roaring sound. The deck of the enemy's ship rose in the air, rent into a thousand fragments. Her masts and yards and sails shot upwards, and her dark hull seemed suddenly to melt away.

The *Lily* reeled with the shock, and the crew, astounded by the awful catastrophe, for a moment forgot their discipline. Several of the men were knocked down; indeed, it seemed surprising that any should have escaped. Rayner remained at his station, and although several pieces of burning plank fell close to him, he was uninjured.

The voice of the commander was soon heard recalling the men to their duty, and ordering them to fill the buckets with water, to prevent the blazing fragments which strewed the deck from setting the ship on fire.

Chapter Twenty Eight.

A rescue.

While some of the crew were engaged on deck, others, led by the second lieutenant, the boatswain, and Rayner, ascended the rigging with buckets of water to heave over the sails, which in several places had caught fire.

It was a work of extreme peril, but it was quickly accomplished, before much damage had been done. The ship all the time was standing on, her starboard tacks aboard.

Nearly a quarter of an hour had elapsed before any one could look in the direction where their late antagonist had floated.

A few dark fragments of wreck could alone be seen in the far distance, but no one supposed that any human beings could have escaped from the fearful catastrophe. The *Lily* was quickly put to rights and stood on in chase of the stranger, which was now seen, under a press of sail, standing away to the north-west.

Evening was approaching, and it was feared that if she wished to avoid the risk of an engagement, she might manage to escape in the night.

During the first part of it the atmosphere was tolerably clear, and the chase could dimly be seen in the distance. She was carrying all sail, evidently doing her best to escape. The *Lily* had all her canvas set, but as at night a squall cannot be seen, as in the daytime, coming across the ocean, all hands were kept on deck, ready to take it in at a moment's notice.

"Are we gaining on the chase?" asked the commander, when the second lieutenant, who had just before gone forward, returned.

"I think so, sir; but unless the breeze freshens, it will be a long time before we can get her within range of our guns."

Everything that could be thought of was done to make the corvette move through the water. The sails were wetted, the hammocks were piped down, and the watch were ordered to turn in, with a couple of round shot with each, under the idea that as the hammocks swung forward with the surge of the ship, her speed would be increased.

The privateers were at that time committing so much havoc among the English merchantmen, that it was of the greatest importance to stop their career.

As the night drew on, the crescent moon, which had before been affording some light, sank beneath the horizon, and the darkness increased, a mist gradually filling the atmosphere, and obscuring all objects around. The chase was thus shut out from view. Still the *Lily* continued standing in the direction she had last been seen.

Rayner was on the forecastle near Ben Twinch, both endeavouring to pierce the veil which surrounded the supposed privateer.

"We may at any moment run through this mist, and we shall then, I hope, see the chase again," observed Ben. "It won't do for a moment to shut our eyes, for maybe we shall find her much closer than before."

"I fancy that I can even now see her, but my imagination may deceive me," said Rayner. "Can that be her out there?"

"I can't see anything," said the boatswain, putting his hands on either side of his eyes.

"What is that on the lee bow?" suddenly exclaimed Rayner.

Before the boatswain could turn his eyes in the direction the midshipman was pointing, the latter added, "I must have been mistaken. It has disappeared, for I can see nothing. Still I must go aft and report to the commander what I saw, or fancied I saw."

"It could only have been fancy," remarked Captain Saltwell. "The imagination is easily deceived in an atmosphere like this. We'll keep on as we were standing."

Rayner accordingly went forward. He was not sorry at length to be relieved, as he was growing weary from having had so long to keep a strain on his eyes.

At last, awakened by the gruff voice of the boatswain turning up the hands, he went on deck, and found that it was already daylight; but not a sail was in sight, and it was pretty evident that the chase had altered her course.

The commander, thinking it likely that she had kept to the westward, steered in that direction.

The day wore on, but still no sail appeared, nor did it seem at all likely that the chase would again be sighted. The ship was therefore put about to rejoin the *Ione*.

Soon after noon the wind fell, and the *Lily* lay motionless on the glassy ocean; the sun shining forth with intense heat, making the pitch in the seams of the deck bubble up, and every piece of metal feel as if it had just come out of a furnace. The seamen sought every spot of shade which the sails afforded, and made frequent visits to the water-cask to quench their thirst.

A few hours thus passed by, when, away to the south-east, a few clouds could be seen floating across the sky.

"The calm can only be partial, for there's wind out there," observed the commander, pointing the clouds out to the first lieutenant. "I hope we shall soon get it."

In this he was disappointed. The day went by; the ship still lay motionless on the waste of waters. Another night came on. It was not until the sun again rose that the sails were heard to give several loud flaps against the masts; a few cat's-paws were seen playing over the surface of the water, and at length the canvas swelled out to an easterly breeze. The tacks were hauled aboard, and the *Lily* stood in the direction it was supposed the *Ione* would be found, over the course she had just come.

The wind was light, and she made but little progress. It freshened, however, in the evening, and during the night the log showed that she was going at a fair rate.

Rayner was in the morning watch, and was forward when the look-out from the mast-head shouted, "A piece of wreck away on the starboard bow." As the ship would pass close by it, she was kept on her course. Rayner was examining the piece of wreck through his glass, when he saw what he supposed was a person moving on it.

He went aft, and reported this to the first lieutenant, who was on deck, and the ship was headed up towards it. "I can see four or five men!" exclaimed Rayner, "some are lying down. One man is kneeling up and waving."

By this time the commander had come on deck, and as the ship drew near, he ordered a boat to be got ready.

Two of the men were seen to rise on their knees, and wave.

"They must have belonged to the crew of the ship which blew up the other day, though how they escaped seems a miracle," observed the commander. "Poor fellows, they must have suffered fearfully! Put a beaker of water and some food in the boat. They'll want nourishment as soon as possible."

The corvette was hove-to. Rayner took charge of the boat, the crew pulling eagerly away to the rescue of the hapless men on the raft.

As they drew near, Rayner observed, to his surprise, as he stood up steering, that one of the persons kneeling on the raft was dressed in the uniform of an English midshipman.

"Give way, lads—give way!" he shouted.

The boat was quickly up to the raft, which was a portion apparently of the poop deck. Besides the young Englishman, there were five persons dressed as ordinary seamen, dark, swarthy fellows, their countenances haggard, and their whole appearance wretched in the extreme.

"Water, water! in mercy give us water!" cried the young Englishman; while the other men, who were scarcely able to move, pointed to their mouths. One lay stretched on the raft, apparently lifeless, and another seemed almost too far gone to recover.

Two of the *Lily's* crew leapt on the raft, and, lifting up the English midshipman, carried him to the stern-sheets, where Rayner stood with a cup of water ready to give him.

He grasped it with both his hands, and eagerly drank the contents. A second mug had in the meantime been filled. One of the Frenchmen, in his eagerness to reach it, stretched out his arms, and fell flat on his face. The English seamen lifted him up, and gently poured the water down his throat. He and two more were lifted on board. They then took a cup to the rest, who were too weak to make the slightest exertion. They poured some water down the throat of one; he gave one gasp, and then sank back, apparently lifeless. A sixth person was already beyond human help. On raising his arm, it fell again at his side.

"Are we to take these two bodies with us?" asked one of the men. "They don't seem to have any life in them."

"Yes, by all means," answered Rayner; "we must let the doctor judge about them—perhaps he may bring them round."

The two bodies were placed in the bows, and the crew giving way, Rayner steered for the ship. As he looked at the countenance of the English midshipman, he thought he had seen him before. He did not trouble him with questions, however; indeed, although the latter had asked for water, it was very evident that he was unable to answer them.

The boat was soon alongside. The young midshipman was the first lifted on board.

"Why, who can this be?" exclaimed the commander. "How came he among the crew of the privateer?"

Rayner explained that he had seen him spring on deck the instant before the ship blew up, but more about him he could not say, as he had not spoken a word since he was taken on board the boat.

"Carry him at once into my cabin," said the commander. "You'll do all you can for him I know, doctor," he added, addressing the surgeon, who, with the aid of the master and another officer, had already lifted up the young stranger.

"He wants nourishment more than doctoring," answered the surgeon.

While the midshipman was being carried into the cabin, the assistant-surgeon was examining the other men. He ordered some broth to be given to the three who had first been taken into the boat, observing that it was the only thing they required; and he then at once turned his attention to a fourth man, whose pulse he felt with a serious countenance.

"There's life in him still," he observed; and ordering his head to be slightly raised, he hurried down to his dispensary, and quickly returned with a stimulant, which he poured down his throat. The effect was wonderful, for scarcely had it been swallowed than the patient gave signs of returning animation. The last poor fellow, after a careful examination, he pronounced beyond human aid.

"Had we arrived half an hour sooner, his life might have been saved," he observed, "for even now he is scarcely cold."

The surgeon soon came up.

"We'll try what can be done," he said, "for I never despair in a case of this sort."

All his efforts, however, proved vain; and he at last had to acknowledge to the assistant-surgeon that the unfortunate man was beyond recovery. The yards had in the meantime been braced round, and the ship had been standing on her course.

Rayner was now sent for into the cabin, where he found the midshipman he had saved placed in the commander's cot.

"Do you see a likeness to any one you know?" asked Commander Saltwell.

"Yes," answered Rayner, looking at the countenance of the young stranger, who was sleeping calmly; "I thought so from the first; he reminds me of Mrs Crofton, or, rather, of her daughter."

"So he does me. I have little doubt that he is Oliver Crofton, and I can fully account for his being on board the privateer," said the commander. "She must have captured the prize of which he was in charge. I fear that the rest of the men who were prisoners on board have perished."

"I am thankful that he has been saved," said Rayner. "It would well-nigh have broken Mrs Crofton's and her daughter's hearts if they had heard that he had died in so dreadful a manner, though to be sure no one would have known of it unless we had fallen in with the raft."

The doctor would not allow any questions to be asked his patient until he had several times taken a small quantity of nourishment, and had passed the intermediate time in sleep; and the commander also kindly directed that he should be allowed to remain in his cot, while he had a hammock slung in his cabin for himself.

The surgeon or assistant-surgeon was in constant attendance on him during the night.

Their unremitting care was rewarded, for soon after the hammocks were piped up the young stranger opened his eyes, and exclaimed in a faint voice, with a tone of astonishment, "Where am I? What has happened?"

"You are all right, and safe among friends," said the commander, who had just turned out of his hammock, coming to his side. "You shall have some breakfast, and then I must get you to tell me all about yourself. Unless I am mistaken, we have met before. Are you not Oliver Crofton?"

"Yes, sir," answered the midshipman. "How did you know that, sir?"

"I made a shrewd guess at it," answered the commander, smiling, "and truly glad I am to have you on board my ship. However, do not exert yourself just now, but go to sleep again if you can till the steward brings you your breakfast, and you shall then, if the doctor thinks you are strong enough, tell me all that has happened."

The commander, coming on deck, told Rayner that he was right in his conjectures, and invited him to breakfast with him.

The surgeon, however, would not allow Oliver to get up, but said that he might give an account of his adventures, provided he did not spin too long a yarn.

"Thank you, sir," said Oliver. "I'll try to collect my thoughts; for, to say the truth, I find them somewhat scattered at present.

"It must have been nearly ten days ago when the *Ariel*, to which I belonged, captured a French brig. Captain Matson sent me on board to take her to Port Royal. We were just in sight of the eastern end of Jamaica, when a large privateer bore down on us. We did our best to escape, but as she sailed two feet to our one, and carried twenty-two guns, we were compelled to yield, and I and my men were taken on board, while our prize was sent away to one of the French islands.

"The privateer continued her cruise in search of our merchantmen, or any prizes our ships might have taken. A more ruffianly set of fellows I never set eyes on. My poor men were robbed of everything they had about them, and I should have had my jacket taken off my back but for the interference of the officers, who allowed me to mess with them, and to go on deck whenever I wished. Considering the style of their conversation at table, however, I should have thankfully preferred living by myself.

"When they discovered that you were English, the officers took a fearful oath that nothing should compel them to yield. They, however, did their best to escape; but when they found that you had the heels of them, they made up their minds to fight, fully expecting, I believe, to take you. Nothing could exceed the savageness of the crew as, stripped to the waist, they went to their guns. Several of them, as they cast their eyes on me, vowed that they would shoot me through the head should the day go against them. Having no fancy to be so treated, I thought it prudent to go below, knowing very well that, in spite of their boasting, they would soon get the worst of it, and that you, at all events, would fight on until you had compelled them to strike their flag or sent them to the bottom. I felt the awful position in which I was placed. I might be killed by one of your shot, even should I escape the knives and bullets of my captors.

"I considered how I could best preserve my life, as I thought it very possible that you would send the privateer to the bottom should she not yield or try to escape. I determined, should I find her sinking, to leap out through one of the stern windows of the captain's cabin. I accordingly made my way there, and was looking out for some instrument with which to force open the window when I saw smoke curling up through an opening in the deck below me. I at once knew that it must arise from a spot at no great distance from the magazine. In the hopes of inducing the commander to send some men down to try and extinguish the fire before it was too late, I sprang on deck. Scarcely had I reached it, and was telling the captain of our danger, when I felt a fearful concussion, and found myself lifted into the air, the next instant to be plunged overboard amidst the mangled crew, some few around me shrieking vainly for help, though the greater number had been killed by the explosion and sank immediately. Being a strong swimmer, I struck out, narrowly avoiding several who clutched at my legs, and swam towards a large piece of wreck which had been blown to some distance from where the ship went down. I scrambled upon it, and was soon joined by three other men, who had, they told me, been forward, and found themselves uninjured in the water.

"I saw soon afterwards two others floating at some distance from the raft. One of them shouted for help saying that he was exhausted, and could no longer support himself. The other, notwithstanding left him to his fate and swam towards us. I could not bear to see the poor fellow perish in our sight with the possibility of saving him, and as there was no time to be lost, I plunged in and made for him, picking up in my way a piece of plank. I placed it under his arms, and telling him to hold on to it, shoved it before me in the direction of the raft. The other fellow had in the meantime got hold of a piece of timber, on which he was resting, but was apparently almost exhausted. As I passed, I told him that if I could I would come to his help, and I at length managed to get back to the raft, on to which the three other men had hauled up their other shipmate.

"I was pretty well tired by this time, and had to rest two or three minutes before I could again venture into the water. While I was trying to recover my strength, the man clinging to the log, fancying that no one was coming, again shrieked out for help. Once more slipping into the water, at last by shoving the piece of plank before me, I contrived to reach him; then getting him to take hold of it, I made my way back to the raft, when we were both dragged nearly exhausted out of the water.

"At first I had hopes that you would discover us and put back to take us off; but when I perceived that you were on fire, I began to fear that we should not be observed, though I did not say so to my companions in misfortune, but endeavoured to keep up their spirits. I told them that if the ship with which they had been engaged should come back, my countrymen would not look upon them as enemies, but would treat them kindly, as people who had suffered a great misfortune. When, however, they saw you standing away, they began to abuse the English, declaring that we were a perfidious nation, never to be trusted; and I had some suspicion that they would wreak their ill-temper on my head.

"My position would have been very dreadful even had I been with well-disposed companions. The sun beat down upon our heads with terrific force; we had not a particle of food, nor a drop of water to quench our thirst. I was thankful when, the sun at length having set, the men, accustomed only to think of the present, and not suffering much as yet from the want of food or water, stretched themselves on the raft to sleep.

"I sat up, hoping against hope that you might come back to ascertain if any people had escaped, or that some other vessel might pass within hail. We had no means of making a signal, not even a spar on which to hoist our handkerchiefs or shirts. The only article which had by some means or other been thrown on the raft was a blanket. How it had fallen there I cannot tell. I secured it, and doubling it up, it served as a rest to my head. I constantly, however, got up to look about, but no vessel could I see, and at length, overpowered by weariness, I lay down and fell asleep.

"At daylight I awoke. The sea was calm. I gazed anxiously around. Not a speck was visible in the horizon. The sun rose, and its rays beat down upon us with even greater fury than on the previous day, or, at all events, I suffered more, as did my companions. They now cried out for water and food, and I saw them eye me with savage looks. I pretended not to observe this, and said that I hoped and thought that we might catch some fish or birds.

"'It will be better for some of us if we do,' muttered one of the men.

"Although I saw several coveys of flying-fish leaping out of the water in the distance, none came near us. Once I caught sight of the black fin of a shark gliding by; presently the creature turned, and as it passed it eyed us, I thought, with an evil look; but while the water was calm, there was no risk of its getting at us. Had the brute been smaller, we might have tried to catch it. I remembered having heard of several people who saved their lives, when nearly starved, by getting hold of a shark. One of the men stuck out his leg, and when the creature tried to grab it, a running bowline was slipped round its head, and it was hauled up. My companions, however, had not the spirits to make the attempt—indeed, we could not find rope sufficient for the purpose on our raft.

"The day wore on, and scarcely any of my companions spoke, but lay stretched at full length on the raft. Others sat with their arms round their knees, and their heads bent down, groaning and complaining, one or two swearing fearfully at the terrible fate which had overtaken them, regardless of that of their late shipmates, hurried into eternity. In vain I tried to arouse them. Now and then one would look at me with an ominous glance, and I confess I began to fear, as night drew on, that I should not be allowed to see another day dawn. I stood up, though it was with difficulty that I could steady myself, for my strength was already failing. Anxiously I looked round the horizon. The sky had hitherto been clear; but, as I cast my eye to the eastward, I observed a cloud rising rapidly. Another and another followed. They came on directly towards us, discharging heavy drops of rain. My fear was that they would empty themselves before they reached us. The looks of my companions brightened.

"'Now, my friends,' I said, 'we must try and catch some of that rain. Here, spread out this blanket, for if a shower falls but for ten minutes we shall have water enough to quench our thirst.'

"We got the blanket ready. The first cloud passed by, nearly saturating the blanket. The men wrung it out into one of their hats, two or three sucking at the corners. They seemed inclined to fight for the small quantity they had obtained, but did not even offer to give me any. I got no water, though the blanket was somewhat cleansed, not that I felt inclined to be particular. In a few minutes another shower fell. Each of us got an ample supply of water. My spirits rose in a way I could not have expected. For some time I did not suffer from the pangs of hunger; but they presently returned with greater force than before, and I guessed how my companions were feeling. I encouraged them as well as I was able. 'God, in His mercy, has sent us water, and He may, I trust, supply us with food.'

"Some of them stared at my remark, but others replied—

"'Yes, yes, perhaps to-morrow we shall have an ample breakfast.'

"Still I did not trust them completely, and endeavoured to keep awake until they had all dropped off to sleep.

"Another heavy shower fell during the night, and I roused them up to obtain a further supply of water. We filled all our hats, for we had nothing else to put it in. The next day was but a repetition of the former. The water we had obtained during the night was quickly exhausted. My hopes of catching some fish appeared likely to be disappointed. Twice a shark came near us, but the brute was too large to give us a chance of catching it. It was far more likely to have caught us had we made the attempt. We shouted to drive it off. At last, smaller fish of some sort approached—albicores or bonitas. It was extraordinary with what eager looks we eyed the creatures.

"While we were watching the fish, trying to devise some means of snatching them, one of the men, who lay stretched on the raft apparently asleep or in a state of stupor, suddenly sat up, uttering an exclamation of delight. We turned our heads, and saw him eagerly gnawing at a flying-fish; but he snarled and growled, eating eagerly all the time, just as a dog does when a person attempts to take a bone from him. He had managed to gulp down the larger portion before the others could snatch the prize from him. The next moment he sank back, and never spoke again. I saw no violence used, except the force they exerted to take the fragments of the fish from his hands. It appeared to me as if one of them had stabbed him, so suddenly did he fall.

"The others gave me none of the fish: indeed, my portion would have been so small that I did not miss it, though for the moment I would have been thankful for the merest scrap of food.

"I still endeavoured to keep up my spirits, and prayed for strength from above. I am sure it was given me, or I should have sunk. I did not like even to think of the pain I suffered. The Frenchmen, too, were growing ravenous, and I heard them talking together, and looking at me as if meditating mischief.

"I thought over the means by which I could best preserve my life. I knew that it would not do to show the slightest fear, so arousing myself, I said, 'My friends, you are hungry, so am I, but we can endure another day without eating. Now I want you to understand that we are more likely to be saved by an English vessel than by one of any other nation, as there are three times as many English cruisers in these seas as there are French, and ten times as many merchantmen. If we are picked up by an English vessel, you are sure to be well treated for my sake, but if any accident were to happen to me—if I were to fall overboard, for instance—there would be no one to say a word in your favour. Remember that I was the means of saving the lives of two of you, although, when I plunged into the water and swam to you at the risk of being caught by a shark, or sinking myself from fatigue, I did not expect any return. I suppose that you do not wish to be ungrateful.'

"This address seemed to have some effect on the men I had saved. Each of them uttered an exclamation of approval, while the two others, who still retained some little strength, turned aside their heads, not daring to look at me. I did not move until night came on, when I crawled from the place I had occupied, and lay down between the two men who seemed most disposed to befriend me. In the middle of the night I awoke, and finding that there was a light breeze. I endeavoured to kneel up and ascertain if providentially any vessel were approaching.

"I was raising myself on my elbow when I saw one of the men who had threatened me by their words creeping towards me. I instantly awoke my two friends, for so I will call them, by exclaiming, 'There is a breeze. Perhaps a vessel is approaching us. We should not be sleeping;' while the man whom I suspected of a design against my life drew back and lay perfectly still. I determined not again to fall asleep, if I could avoid it, until daylight. I believe, however, that I frequently dropped off, but I was preserved. When morning dawned, I discovered that the man who had, as I believed, intended to kill me was utterly unable to move. The other fellow, however, seemed to be the strongest of the party. He got up, and stretching out his arms, exclaimed, addressing his countrymen—

"'Food we must have this day at every coast, or we shall perish.'

"I also rose, and found, to my surprise, that I could stand on my feet.

"'I pray God that we may have food, and that some friendly vessel may bring it,' I exclaimed.

"As I spoke I looked round the horizon, when I need not tell you how grateful I felt to Heaven at seeing a sail standing, as I judged, directly towards us. I pointed her out to my companions; but as they were sitting down, they could not for some time make her out. I, too, could no longer support myself, and once more sank on the raft. In a short time, however, we could all distinguish her. The Frenchmen began to weep. Now they expressed their fears that she would pass us; now they tried to shout for joy at the thoughts of being saved. I at times also dreaded lest we should not be observed, but all my doubts vanished when I made you out to be an English sloop-of-war, and saw you haul up towards us."

Chapter Twenty Nine.

A shipwreck.

The *Lily* had been continuing her cruise in the Caribbean Sea for some days without falling in with the *Ariel*, or any other English ship-of-war, nor had she taken a prize. Oliver Crofton had completely recovered. As one of the midshipmen was ill, he took his duty. Our hero and Oliver soon became fast friends, and they were well able to appreciate each other's good qualities.

Commander Saltwell, not looking upon the Frenchmen he had picked up in the light of prisoners, wished to put them on shore as soon as possible. He resolved, therefore, to stand in towards the coast of San Domingo, the western portion of which island belonged to France, and to land them at some settlement where they could obtain assistance.

The *Lily* was still off the east end of the island, belonging to Spain, when a schooner was sighted running along the shore, apparently endeavouring to escape observation. The wind, however, headed her, and she was compelled to tack off the land.

"She's French, to a certainty, or she would have run in and brought up somewhere," observed Mr Horrocks.

The commander agreed with him. The ship was steered so as to cut her off. On seeing this, the schooner wore, and, setting a large square sail, ran off before the wind to the westward. Though the stranger evidently possessed a fast pair of heels, the *Lily*, making all sail, soon got near enough to send a shot skipping over the water close under her counter. The schooner, notwithstanding, still held on, when another shot almost grazed her side. Her object was probably to run on until she could steer for some port where she could obtain shelter and protection.

"If she doesn't shorten sail presently, send another shot through her canvas, Mr Coles," said the commander.

The *Lily* carried a long gun which could be run out at either of her bow ports. It was the gunner's favourite. He declared that he could shoot as true with it, and ten times as far, as he could with a tower musket. The gun was loaded and pointed through the larboard bow port.

Still the chase held on. It was time to bring her to, for the wind gave signs of dropping.

"Are you ready there, forward, with the gun?" asked the commander.

"Ay, ay, sir!" was the answer.

"Port the helm! Fire!" he shouted directly afterwards.

The gun was well aimed, for the shot went through the schooner's large squaresail. The ship was again kept on her course, when the gun was hauled in and reloaded.

"Stand by to fire again, and this time pitch it into her. All ready there, forward?"

"Ay, ay, sir!"

Again the helm was ported, but before the commander had time to shout "Fire!" the schooner was seen to haul down her flag, at the same time to take in her squaresail and clew up her foretopsail.

The corvette was soon up, when she was found to be a fine little schooner, such as was employed in the carrying trade between the islands, or in bringing the produce of the plantations to some central depôt.

"Heave to!" cried the commander; "and if you attempt to escape I'll sink you, remember that! Tell them in French what I mean," he added, turning to Rayner.

"Oui, oui; je comprende," answered one of the few white men on board —probably the master—and, the schooner's helm being put down, she came up head to wind, with her foretopsail to the mast.

The corvette, which had by this time shot a little way ahead, also hove-to, and the commander directed Rayner, with a boat's crew, to go on board the prize and take possession.

The master stood, hat in hand, at the gangway, ready to receive him.

He was bound, he said, for Martinique, in ballast, to obtain a cargo and other stores for Leogane, the principal settlement of the French in the island. The crew consisted of a Creole mate, two mulattos, and four blacks, one of the former calling himself the boatswain.

"Then you'll do me the favour of accompanying the master and mate on board the ship," said Rayner pointing to the boat.

The master seemed very unwilling to obey, but the crew soon tumbled him, with the mate and boatswain, into the boat, which returned to the corvette, while Rayner remained with two hands on board.

He now ordered the crew to haul round the fore yard, and, keeping the helm up, soon ran within speaking distance of the *Lily*.

"I intend to send you in to land the people picked up on the raft, with a flag of truce, and as soon as you put them on shore, come back and join me," said the commander.

"Ay, ay, sir," answered Rayner, very well pleased to have a separate command, although it might only last a few hours. He was still more pleased, however, when the boat came back, bringing Oliver Crofton, the four Frenchmen, and Jack and Tom, to form part of his crew. The blacks and the mulatto were kept on board to assist in working the schooner. The mulatto said he was the steward, and one of the blacks, with a low bow, introduced himself as the cook.

"Me talkee English, massa, well as French, and me cookee anyting dat buckra officer like to order," he said, with a grimace which made the midshipman laugh.

"By-the-bye, before we part company with the corvette, we may as well ascertain what Sambo here has got to cook," said Oliver.

It was fortunate that he had this forethought, for, except a supply of salt-fish, some yams and bananas, and a small cask of flour, with a half-empty case of claret, no other provisions were discovered for officers or men. Oliver accordingly returned, and obtained some beef and biscuit, and a few articles from the mess.

"And just bring five or six dollars with you, in case we want to purchase any fish or vegetables," said Rayner, as he was shoving off.

No time was lost in procuring what was necessary, when Oliver returned to the *Mouche*, for such was the name of the prize. The corvette making sail, she and the schooner ran on in company until they came off the French part of the coast. The commander then ordered Rayner to stand in, directing him, should any people be seen on shore, to hoist a white flag, and land the four Frenchmen.

Scarcely, however, had they parted company for a couple of hours, when a dead calm came on, and Rayner and Oliver believed that there was no chance of being able to land the Frenchmen that night.

"I am very sorry for it," remarked Oliver; "for from the experience I have had of them, I think it more than possible, if they can get the assistance of the black crew, they will try and play us some scurvy trick. I have not hitherto pointed out the fellow who tried to take my life, and who was so nearly dying himself; but I suspect his disposition has not altered for the better. You'll fancy me somewhat suspicious, but I cannot help thinking that should he win over the blacks, they will try and take the schooner from us."

"They'll find that rather a tough job with you and me and our four men to oppose them," answered Rayner. "However, after your warning, I'll keep an eye on the gentlemen, and I'll tell Jack Peek to let me know if he sees anything suspicious in their behaviour. He understands French almost as well as I do, and he'll soon find out what they are about."

"I do not like to think ill of other people, even though they are foreigners; but I cannot forget what a villain one of those men is," remarked Oliver.

"Forewarned, forearmed," said Rayner. "We need not, after all, be anxious about the matter; but it will be wise to keep our pistols in our belts and our swords by our sides, and not to let the Frenchmen and the black crew mix together more than is necessary." The steward now came aft, hat in hand, and speaking in a jargon of French and Spanish, interlarded with a few words of English, of which he was evidently proud, requested to know what the officers would like for supper.

"We shall not find fault, provided that the cook supplies us with the best he can," answered Rayner. "One of our men there,"—pointing to Jack Peek—"will give him the materials, unless he happens to have some ducks or fowls, or a fine fish, for which we will pay him."

The steward shrugged his shoulders, regretting that the only fish he had on board were salted; but, notwithstanding, the cook would exercise his skill upon them, and would produce a dish which even an epicure would not disdain.

While waiting for the evening meal, the young officers walked the deck, whistling for a breeze, but there seemed no chance of its coming. The land lay blue, but still indistinct, away to the northward, its outline varied by hills of picturesque form, which rose here and there along the coast.

Rayner called up Jack Peek, and told him to keep a watch not only on the black crew, but on the Frenchmen. "Notwithstanding the kind way they have been treated, they may think it a fine opportunity for obtaining a vessel in which they can carry on their former calling," he observed.

"They'll be audaciously ungrateful wretches if they do, sir," answered Jack. "To my mind they'll deserve to be hove overboard to feed one of those sharks out there;" and he pointed to a black fin which was gliding just above the surface.

"I hope that they will not prove treacherous, and it is our business to take care that they have no opportunity of being so," said Rayner. "Do you and Tom keep an eye upon them, that's all."

"Ay, ay, sir," answered Jack.

The English seamen kept together. Though there were but four of them, they were sturdy fellows, well armed, and it was not likely that either the blacks or Frenchmen would venture to attack them.

At length the mulatto steward announced supper ready, and Rayner and Oliver descended to partake of it, leaving Tom in charge of the deck.

"Call me if you see the slightest sign of a breeze," said the former, as he went below.

The cabin was not very large nor yet very clean; indeed, cockroaches and centipedes were crawling about in all directions, and every now and then dropped down on the white cloth from the beams above. The table, however, was covered with several dishes, which, from the fragrant odour ascending from them, promised to satisfy the hunger of a couple of midshipmen. It was difficult to make out the materials of which the dishes were composed, but on examination it was found that they consisted chiefly of salt beef and fish dressed in a variety of fashions, fricasséed, stewed, and grilled, and mixed with an abundance of vegetables, with some delicious fruit, such as the West Indies can alone produce.

"Me tinkee better keep on de cobers, massa," observed the steward, "or de cockroaches fall in an' drown demselves."

"By all means," said Rayner, laughing. Indeed, he and Oliver had to examine each mouthful before they raised it to their lips, lest they should find one of the nauseous creatures between their teeth.

As soon as the midshipmen had finished supper, they returned on deck.

The sun had sunk beneath the ocean in a refulgence of glory, its parting rays throwing a ruddy glow over the surface, unbroken by a single ripple.

"We must make up our minds to spend the night where we are," observed Rayner. "It will be as well for you and me to take watch and watch, and not to trust to any of the men, for although I have every confidence in Peek, I cannot say the same for the rest."

Oliver, of course, agreed to this, and took the first watch. At midnight he aroused Rayner, who had stretched himself on one of the lockers, not feeling inclined to turn into either of the doubtful-looking bunks at the side of the vessel.

"I suspect that we are going to have a change of weather," said Oliver, as he came on deck. "The air feels unusually oppressive for this time of night. There is a mist rising to the southward, though the stars overhead shine as bright as usual."

"I don't know what to think of it, having had but little experience in these seas," answered Rayner; "I must ask the oldest of the Frenchmen, but I don't see any of them on deck."

"No, they and the blacks have all turned in," said Oliver. "They did not ask my leave, but I thought it useless to rouse them up again, as there seemed no chance of their being wanted."

"Well, go and lie down and take a caulk, if the centipedes and cockroaches will let you," laughed Rayner. "They have been crawling all over me during the time I have been below, but I knew there was no use attempting to keep them off, so I let them crawl, without interfering with their pleasure. If I see any further change in the appearance of the sky, I will rouse you up, and we'll make the black fellows turn out to be ready to shorten sail."

Rayner for some time walked the deck of the little vessel alone. Jack was at the helm, and one of the men forward. The watch was very nearly out, and he determined not to call up Oliver until daylight. On looking to the southward he saw that the mist which had before remained only a few feet above the horizon was rapidly covering the sky, while beneath it he distinguished a long line of white foam.

"Turn out, Oliver!" he shouted through the cabin skylight; "I'll take the helm. Peek, run forward and rouse up the blacks and Frenchmen to shorten sail. Not a moment to be lost!"

Jack as he went forward shouted down the main hatchway, where Tom and the other men were sleeping, and then in a stentorian voice called, in French, to shorten sail.

The Englishmen were on deck in a moment, but the blacks came up stretching their arms and yawning.

"Lower away with the throat and peak halyards!" shouted Rayner.

Oliver and the two English sailors hastened to obey the order.

"Brail up the foresail. Be smart, lads! Aloft with you and furl the foretopsail, or it will be blown out of the bolt-ropes!"

The mainsail was quickly got down. The black crew were pulling and hauling at the brails of the headsails, when a fierce blast struck the vessel. She heeled over to it.

Rayner immediately put up the helm; but before the vessel had answered to it, she heeled over till the water rushed over the deck. Then there came a clap like thunder, and the main-topsail, split across, was blown out of the bolt-ropes.

"Square away the foreyard!" shouted Rayner.

The vessel, righting, flew off before the fierce gale, the water rushing and foaming round her sides. Astern, the whole ocean seemed a mass of tumultuous foam-covered waves.

The sky was as black as ink. To bring the vessel to the wind was impossible. All that could be done was to run directly before the gale, and even then it seemed that at any moment the fast rising seas might break over her stern and sweep her decks.

The schooner, however, by continuing her course, was running on destruction, unless some port could be found under her lee to afford her shelter; but even then there was a great risk of being captured by the enemy, who would not pay much attention to a flag of truce, or believe that she came for the object of landing the Frenchmen. Besides which, as the vessel was a prize, it would be thought perfectly right to detain her.

Dawn broke; for an instant a fiery-red line appeared in the eastern horizon, but was quickly obscured. The increasing light, however, enabled the crew to carry on work which could not otherwise have been performed.

Rayner and Oliver resolved that they must, at all risks, try to heave the schooner to while there was yet sea-room; and, should the weather moderate, beat off shore until the gale was over and a boat could land the people with safety on the beach. The first thing to be done was to strike the maintopmast. Peek took the helm, while the rest went aloft.

It was no easy matter to get out the fid—the pin which secured the heel of the topmast in the cross-trees—but after considerable exertions, with a fearful risk of being jerked overboard, they succeeded in lowering down the mast.

They had next to get fore and main-trysails ready to set, should it be found possible to beat to windward, though at present it was evident that the schooner could not bear even that amount of canvas.

The foretopsail had stood, being a new stout sail, and it being closely reefed, Rayner hoped that the little vessel would lay to under it. It was a dangerous experiment he was about to try, but he had to choose between two evils—that of being driven on shore, or the risk of having the decks swept by the tremendous seas rolling up from the southward before the schooner could be hove-to. She had already run a considerable distance nearer the land.

Stationing the men in readiness to brace round the yard, he looked out for a favourable opportunity to put down the helm and bring the vessel up to the wind.

That favourable opportunity, however, did not come; every sea that rolled up astern threatened to overwhelm her should he make the attempt.

The land appeared closer and closer. If the vessel was to be hove-to it must be done at once, in spite of all risks.

"Hold on, lads, for your lives!" cried Rayner, in English and French, setting the example by clinging to the larboard main rigging. "Now starboard the helm. Haul away on the larboard headbrace. Ease off the starboard."

Oliver and Jack, who were at the helm, as they put it down prepared to lash it to starboard; but as the vessel came up to the wind, a fearful sea struck her, sweeping over her deck, carrying away the caboose and the whole of the bulwarks forward; at the same moment the foretopsail split as the other had done, and the canvas, after fluttering wildly in the blast, was whisked round and round the yard.

"Up with the helm!" cried Rayner.

Oliver and Jack, knowing what was necessary, were already putting it up. Before another sea struck the vessel she was again before the gale. Her only resource was now to anchor, should no port be discovered into which they could run.

The cable was accordingly ranged ready to let go at a moment's notice; but Rayner and Oliver well knew that there was little hope of the anchor holding, or if it did, of the vessel living through the seas which would break over her as soon as her course was stopped. Still, desperate as was the chance, it must be tried. There might be time to set the foresail yet, and she might lay to under it.

The order was given to get the sail ready for setting as soon as she could be brought up to the wind. Again the helm was put down.

"Hoist away!" shouted Rayner.

But scarcely had the sail felt the wind than it was blown away to leeward, and another sea, even heavier than the first, struck the vessel, sweeping fore and aft over her deck.

Rayner, who was clinging on to the rigging, thought that she would never rise again. A fearful shriek reached his ear, and looking to leeward, he saw two of his people in the embraces of the relentless sea.

In vain the poor fellows attempted to regain the schooner, farther and farther they were borne away, until, throwing up their arms, they disappeared beneath the foaming waters.

At first he thought they were his own men, but on looking round he saw Oliver and Jack clinging to the companion-hatch, and the rest holding on to the main rigging. One of the Frenchmen had been lost, and the coloured steward.

Ere long the rest on board might have to share the same fate. Still Rayner resolved to struggle to the last.

Another attempt was made. The main-trysail was shifted to the foremast; if that would stand, the vessel might possibly be kept off shore; but scarcely had it been set, than the hurricane came down on the hapless vessel with redoubled fury. The weather rigging gave way, and down came the mast itself, killing one of the blacks, and fearfully crushing another; and, to Rayner's dismay striking down Jack Peek. He sprang forward to drag Jack out from beneath the tangled rigging and spars, calling Tom Fletcher to assist him. They ran a fearful risk of being washed away, but he could not leave Jack to perish.

"Are you much hurt?" he shouted, as he saw Jack struggling to free himself.

"Can't say, sir; but my shoulder and leg don't feel of much use," answered Jack.

Tom, with evident reluctance, had to let go his hold, but could not refuse to run the same risk as his officer.

By lifting the spars they got Jack out, and dragged him to the after-part of the vessel, where, as he did not seem able to help himself, Rayner secured him by a lashing to a stanchion.

"I'll stand by you, Peek, and, if it becomes necessary, I'll cast you off, so that you may have a chance of saving yourself," he said.

As it was now evidently hopeless to attempt heaving the vessel to, she was once more kept before the wind, while Rayner and his men, armed with two axes, which they found hanging up in the companion-hatch, and their knives cut away the rigging, and allowed the foremast, which hung over the side, to float clear of the vessel.

"We must now cut away the mainmast. We shall have to bring up presently, and it will enable her to ride more easily," cried Rayner. The standing rigging was first cut through, then that on the other side, when a few strokes sent the mast overboard. Still the schooner ran on before the wind. Had she been laden, she must have foundered. The hatches had been got on and battened down. They now, as far as practicable, secured the companion-hatch, for they all well knew that the moment they should bring up, the seas would come rolling on board, and sweep the decks fore and aft. By Rayner's advice, each man got lashings ready to secure himself to the stanchions or stumps of the masts. Nearer and nearer the vessel drew to the shore. Looking ahead, the line of breakers were seen dashing wildly on a reef parallel with the shore, beyond which there appeared to be a narrow lagoon.

Rayner, observing that the surf did not roll up the beach to any considerable height, looked out for a passage through which the vessel might be steered. The continuous line of breakers ran as far as the eye could reach along the shore. There was only one spot where they seemed to break with less fury. Towards it Rayner determined to steer the schooner. He and Oliver soon came to the conclusion that it would be useless to attempt anchoring. The water, probably, was far too deep outside the reef for their range of cable, and even if it were not, the anchor was not likely to hold.

They accordingly steered for the spot they had discovered, the only one which afforded them the slightest hope of escaping instant destruction.

On rushed the vessel, now rising on the top of a sea, now plunging into a deep hollow. Rayner and Oliver held their breaths.

"I say, what's going to happen?" asked Tom of one of the other men. "Shall we get safe on shore? I shouldn't mind if we could, although the Frenchmen made us prisoners."

"As to that, it seems to me doubtful," was the answer. "Maybe, in a few minutes we shall be floating about among those breakers there, with no more life in us than those poor fellows who were washed away just now; or it may be that this little craft will be carried clear over the reef into smooth water."

"Oh dear, oh dear!" exclaimed Tom, "I have often wished that I had stayed at home; I wish it more than ever now."

"No use wishing. It won't undo what has been done. But, see, we are getting very close. We shall know all about it presently."

The schooner was farther off than Rayner had at first supposed; and as they got nearer he saw, to his relief, that the spot for which he was steering was wider than he had fancied.

There seemed just a chance that the vessel might be thrown through without striking; at the same time, tossed about as she was, it was impossible to steer her as might be wished. He commended himself and his followers, as every wise men would do, to the care of the Almighty, and nerved himself up for whatever might happen.

The roar of the breakers sounded louder and louder. On the vessel drove, until there was a crash. She had struck, but, contrary to all expectation, another sea lifted her and flung her completely through the breakers, when, swinging round, she grounded on a sandbank just within them, heeling over with her head to the eastward, and her deck towards the shore.

Though the sea, which washed over the reef, still beat against her, she might possibly hold together for some time.

Chapter Thirty.

Rayner proves that he is a true hero.

The sea dashing over the reef, though spent of its fury, still broke with great force against the hull of the schooner. Her timbers shook and quivered as wave after wave, striking them, rolled on towards the beach, and then came hissing back, covering the surface of the lagoon with a mass of creaming foam. The coast, as far as could be seen through the masses of spray, looked barren and uninviting.

The Frenchmen and blacks, recovering from the alarm which had well-nigh paralysed them, rushed to the boat stowed amidships, and began casting adrift the lashings, and preparing to launch her.

"Keep all fast there!" cried Rayner, as he saw what they were about. "It will be best to wait till the sea goes down, when we shall be able to get the boat into the water with less risk of her being swamped than at present."

They, however, paid no attention to his orders, and continued their preparations for launching the boat.

When he found that they persisted in their attempts, he urged them to wait till they had collected a supply of provisions, and obtained some fresh water, as it was probable that they might find neither the one nor the other on shore. Calling Fletcher aft to attend to Peek, he and Oliver went into the cabin to collect all the eatables they could find, as also their carpet bags and such other articles as might be useful.

"We must get up some water before the boat shoves off," said Rayner. "I'll send one of the men to help you, while I go into the hold to search for casks."

The boat was still on the deck, and there seemed no probability that the Frenchmen and blacks would succeed in launching her.

He was some time below, hunting about for the casks of water.

He had just found a couple, and was about to return on deck to obtain some slings for hoisting them up, when he heard Jack Peek shout out, "Quick, Mr Rayner—quick! the fellows are shoving off in the boat."

Springing on deck, what was his surprise and indignation to see the boat in the water, and all the men in her, including Tom Fletcher!

"What treachery is this?" he exclaimed. "If go you must, wait until we can get our injured shipmate into the boat, and Mr Crofton will be on deck in a moment."

While he was speaking, the man named Brown, who had gone with him below, rushing on deck, leapt into the boat, intending to prevent them from shoving off. Rayner, for the same object, followed him, with a rope in his hand, which he was in the act of making fast, when one of the Frenchmen cut it through, and the boat rapidly drifted away from the side of the vessel.

In vain Rayner urged the people to pull back, and take off Oliver and Jack; but, regardless of his entreaties, one of them, seizing the helm, turned the boat's head towards the beach. They pulled rapidly away, endeavouring to keep her from being swamped by the heavy seas which rolled up astern. Now she rose, now she sank, as she neared the shore.

"Oliver will fancy that I have deserted him; but Jack Peek knows me too well to suppose that I could have acted so basely," thought Rayner. "If, however, the boat is knocked to pieces, it will be a hard matter to get back to the wreck. All I can do is to pray to Heaven that the schooner may hold together till I can manage to return on board."

These thoughts passed through his mind as the boat approached the beach. He saw that it would be utterly useless to try and induce the men to return. Indeed, the attempt at present would be dangerous. He again urged the crew to be careful how they beached the boat.

"The moment she touches jump out and try to run her up, for should another sea follow quickly on the first, she will be driven broadside on the beach, and before you can get free of her, you may be carried away by the reflux."

The Frenchmen and blacks, eager to save themselves, paid no attention to what he said. On flew the boat on the summit of a sea, and carried forward, the next instant her keel struck the sand. Regardless of his advice, they all at the same moment sprang forward, each man trying to be the first to get out of the boat. He and Tom Fletcher held on to the thwarts.

On came the sea. Before the men had got out of its influence, two of them were carried off their legs, and swept back by the boiling surf, while the boat, broaching to, was hove high up on the beach, on which she fell with a loud crash, her side stove in. Rayner, fearing that she might be carried off, leaped out on the beach, Tom scrambling after him. His first thought was to try and rescue the two men who had been carried off by the receding wave. Looking round to see who was missing, he discovered that one of them was a British seaman, the other a Frenchman. He sprang back to the boat to secure a coil of rope which had been thrown into her, and calling on his companions to hold on to one end, he fastened the other round his waist, intending to plunge in, and hoping to seize hold of the poor fellows, who could be seen struggling frantically in the hissing foam. The Frenchmen and blacks, however, terror-stricken, and thinking only of their own safety, rushed up the beach, as if fancying that the sea might still overtake them. Tom and his messmate alone remained, and held on to the rope. Rayner swam off towards the Frenchman, who was nearest to the shore. Grasping him by the shirt, he ordered Tom and Brown to haul him in, and in a few seconds they succeeded in getting the Frenchman on shore.

Ward, the other seaman, could still be seen floating, apparently lifeless, in the surf—now driven nearer the beach, now carried off again, far beyond the reach of the rope. The moment the Frenchman had been deposited on the sands, Rayner sprang back again, telling Tom and Brown to advance as far as possible into the water.

Rayner, however, did not feel very confident that they would obey his orders, but trusted to his powers as a swimmer to make his way back to the beach. A sea rolled in. He swam on bravely, surmounting its foaming crest. He had got to the end of the rope, and Ward was still beyond his reach. Still he struggled. Perhaps another sea might bring the man to him. He was not disappointed, and grasping the collar of Ward's jacket, he shouted to Brown and Tom to haul away; but the sea which had brought Ward in rolled on, and Tom, fancying that he should be lifted off his legs, let go the rope and sprang back. Happily, Brown held on, but his strength was not sufficient to drag in the rope. In vain he called on Tom to come back to his assistance. While tugging manfully away, he kept his feet on the ground, although the water rose above his waist. The next instant the sea bore Rayner and his now lifeless burden close up to where he stood. Rayner himself was almost exhausted, but with the help of Brown, and such aid as Tom was at length, from very shame, induced to give, they got beyond the influence of the angry seas Rayner lost no time in trying to restore the seaman, but with sorrow he found that it was a corpse alone he had brought on shore.

The Frenchman, Jacques Le Duc, having been less time in the water, quickly recovered, and expressed his gratitude to Rayner for having saved him.

"Mais, ma foi! those poltroons who ran off, afraid that the sea would swallow them up, should be ashamed of themselves," he exclaimed. "You had best show your gratitude, my friend, by getting them to assist us in bringing off my brother officer and the seaman from the wreck," answered Rayner. "I fear that she will not hold together many hours, and unless they are soon rescued they may lose their lives."

"I will try and persuade them to act like men," answered Jacques. "You have twice saved my life, and I feel bound to help you."

Saying this, Jacques, who had been assisted on his legs by Tom and Brown, staggered after his companions, shouting to them to stop.

On seeing him, they only ran the faster.

"Do you take me for a ghost?" he cried out, "Come back, come back, you cowards, and help the brave Englishman!"

At last they stopped, and Jacques was seen talking to them. In a short time he came back, saying that they declared nothing would induce them to return to the wreck; that the boat, they knew, could no longer float, and that there was no other means of getting off; that if they remained on the shore they should be starved, and that they must hurry away in search of food and shelter before night, which was fast approaching.

"Then we must see what we can do by ourselves," said Rayner. "We cannot allow Mr Crofton and Peek to perish while we have any means of going to their assistance. I must first see if we can patch up the boat so as to enable her to keep afloat."

On examining her, however, it was discovered that several of the planks on one side were stove in, and that they could not repair her sufficiently to keep out the water. At first Rayner thought of making a raft out of the materials of the boat; but he soon came to the conclusion that he should never be able to paddle it against the seas which came rolling in.

"It must be done," he said to himself. "I have swum as far in smooth water, with no object in view; but strength will be given me, I trust, when I am making an effort to save my fellow-creatures. Crofton might perhaps swim to the shore, but nothing would induce him to leave a shipmate alone to perish."

All this time Oliver and Jack could be seen seated on the deck, holding on to the stanchions to save themselves from being washed away by the seas which, occasionally breaking over her side, poured down upon them.

It of course occurred to Rayner that if Oliver could manage to float a cask, or even a piece of plank secured to the end of a rope, a communication might be established between the wreck and the shore; but as far as he could see, the running rigging and all the ropes had gone overboard with the masts, and the only coil saved was that which had been brought in the boat.

"Go off again I must," he said; "and I want you, my lads, to promise me, should I perish, that you will use every exertion to save the people on the wreck. Fletcher, you know our object in coming on the coast. You must go to the authorities and explain that we had no hostile intentions—that our wish was to land the Frenchmen whose lives we had saved; and if you explain this, I hope that you will all be well treated."

Even Tom was struck by his officer's courage and thoughtfulness; and he and his messmate promised to obey his orders.

Rayner, having now committed himself to the care of Heaven, prepared to swim off to the wreck. He knew that Oliver would see him coming, and would be ready to help him get on board. Waiting until a sea had broken on the beach, he followed it out, and darting through the next which rolled forward, he was soon a long way from the shore. He found he could swim much better than before, now that he had no rope to carry. Boldly he struck forward. Happily he did not recollect that those seas swarmed with sharks. On and on he went. Now and again, as a sea rushed over the reef, he was thrown back, but exerting all his strength, he struggled forward. He was nearing the wreck, and could see that Oliver, who was eagerly watching him, had got hold of a short length of rope, with which he stood ready to heave when he should be near enough. But he felt his own strength failing. It seemed almost beyond his power to reach the wreck. Still, it was not in his nature to give in, and making a desperate effort, striking out through the surging waters, he clutched the rope which Oliver hove-to him, and the next instant was clambering on board. Throwing himself down on the deck, he endeavoured to regain his strength, Oliver grasping him tightly with one hand, while he held to the stanchion with the other.

"I knew you would not desert us, Rayner," he said. "But now you have come, how are we to get this poor fellow to the shore? I could not leave him, or I would not have allowed you to risk your life by returning on board. We must try and knock a raft together sufficient to carry Peek, and you and I will swim alongside it, if we cannot make it large enough to hold us all three. There's no time to be lost, though."

Providentially the wind had by this time decreased, and the tide having fallen, the seas struck with less fury against the wreck, and enabled the two midshipmen to work far more effectually than they could otherwise have done.

Jack begged that he might try and help them, but they insisted on his remaining where he was, lest a sea should carry him off, and he might not have the strength to regain the wreck.

Fortunately the two axes had been preserved, and going below, they found several lengths of rope, though not of sufficient strength to form a safe communication with the shore. They would serve, however, for lashing the raft together.

They quickly cutaway some of the bulkheads. They also discovered below several spars and a grating. By lashing these together they in a short time formed a raft of sufficient size to carry all three. They next made a couple of paddles with which to guide the raft. They were very rough, but they would serve their purpose. It was almost dark by the time the raft was finished.

"I say, I feel desperately hungry, and I daresay so do you, Rayner, after all you have gone through," said Oliver. "I propose that we should have some of the contents of the basket we packed. I left it in the steward's pantry on the weather side."

"A very good idea," answered Rayner. "Pray get it up. Some food will do Peek good, and enable us all to exert ourselves. I'll finish this lashing in the meantime."

They were not long in discussing some of the sausages and bread which Oliver produced.

"I feel much more hearty, sir," said Jack, when he had swallowed the food. "I don't fancy there's so much the matter with me after all, only my leg and back do feel somewhat curious."

"Come," said Rayner, "we must make the attempt, for we cannot tell what sort of weather we shall have during the night."

With forethought, they had fixed some lashings to the raft with which to secure both Jack and themselves. It floated with sufficient quietness to enable them to place Jack upon it.

"We must not forget the food, though," said Oliver.

"Do you, Peek, hold the basket, and do not let it go if you can help it."

They took their seats, and lashing themselves to the raft, cast off the rope which held it to the wreck, and began paddling away with might and main. The seas rolled in with much less force than before, though there was still considerable risk of the raft capsizing.

While under the lee of the wreck they proceeded smoothly enough, but the seas which passed her ahead and astern meeting, several times washed over them. As they approached the shores they could see through the gloom three figures standing ready to receive them.

"I am glad those fellows have not deserted us, for after the way they before behaved I did not feel quite sure about the matter," said Rayner.

While he was speaking, a sea higher than the rest came rolling along in, and lifting the raft on its summit, went hissing and roaring forward.

"Be ready to cast off the lashings, and to spring clear of the raft, or it may be thrown over upon us," cried Rayner. He gave the warning not a moment too soon, for the sea, carrying on the raft, almost immediately dashed it on the beach. Springing up and seizing Jack Peek by the arm, he leapt clear of it. They would both have fallen, however, had not Tom and Brown dashed into the water and assisted them, while Le Duc rendered the same assistance on the other side to Oliver.

Before the raft could be secured the reflux carried it away, together with the basket of provisions, and it soon disappeared in the darkness. "What shall we do next?" asked Oliver. "We cannot stop on the beach all night."

Wet to the skin as they were, although the wind was not cold, it blew through their thin clothing, and made them feel very chilly.

"We must look out for food and shelter," observed Rayner. "Perhaps we shall fall in with some of the huts of the black people where we can obtain both, though the country did not look very inviting when there was light enough to see it. I, however, don't like to leave the body of that poor fellow on the beach."

"Fletcher and I will try and bury him, sir," said Jack.

"I don't see much use in doing that," growled Tom. "He can't feel the cold. It will keep us here all the night, seeing we have no spades, nor anything else to dig a grave."

"We might do it if we could find some boards," said Jack. "How would you like to be left on shore just like a dead dog?"

His good intentions, however, were frustrated, as no pieces of board could be found, and they were compelled at length to be satisfied with placing the body on a dry bank out of the reach of the water. This done, they commenced their march in search of some human habitations, Tom and Brown supporting poor Jack, who was unable to walk without help, between them.

The country, from the glimpse they had had of it, appeared more inviting to the west, but Rayner reflected that by going in that direction they would get farther and farther from the Spanish territory, but were they once to reach it, they might claim assistance from the inhabitants. How many miles they were from the border neither Rayner nor Oliver was certain; it might be a dozen or it might be twenty or thirty. Le Duc could give them no information. It was difficult to find the way in the darkness; they could indeed only guide themselves by listening to the roar of the breakers, with an occasional glimpse of the dark ocean to the right. The two officers agreed that it would be of great advantage to get into Spanish territory before daylight, as they would thus avoid being taken prisoners. Though their object in coming on the coast was a peaceable one, it would be difficult to induce the authorities to believe that this was the case. Le Duc promised that he would bear testimony to the truth of the account they intended to give of themselves; but, he observed, "My word may not be believed, and I myself may be accused of being a deserter. The people hereabouts do not set much value on human life, and they may shoot us all to save themselves the trouble of making further inquiries."

These observations, which Rayner translated to his companions, made them still more anxious to push on. He and Oliver led the way with Le Duc, whom they desired to answer should they come suddenly on any of the inhabitants.

They went on and on, stumbling among rocks, now forcing their way through a wood, now ascending a rugged slope, until they found themselves at what appeared to have been a sugar plantation, but evidently abandoned for the fences were thrown down, though the shrubs and bushes formed an almost impenetrable barrier. They discovered, however, at last, a path. Even that was much overgrown, though they managed to force their way through it.

When once out of the plantation they found the road less obstructed. Reaching a rising ground, they eagerly looked round, hoping to see a light streaming from the windows of some house, where they could obtain the rest and food they so much required.

"I think I caught sight of a glimmer among the trees. Look there!" said Oliver.

They took the bearings of the light, and descending the hill, endeavoured to direct their course towards it. At last they reached a road, which they concluded must lead towards the house where the light had been seen. They went on some way farther in darkness.

"We are all right," cried Oliver. "I caught sight of three lights from as many different windows. That shows that it is a house of some size."

"I don't know whether that would be an advantage," observed Rayner. "The owner may dislike the English, and refuse to receive us, or send off to the authorities and have us carried away to prison."

"But you and Le Duc and Peek, as you speak French, may pass for Frenchmen; and a man must be a curmudgeon if he refuses to afford assistance to sailors in distress," observed Oliver.

"I can't say much for Peek's French, or for my own either. I would rather state at once who we are," said Rayner. "Le Duc is an honest fellow, and he will explain why we came on the coast, and will tell them how we saved his life."

Le Duc, being asked, replied that he would gladly undertake whatever the English officers wished, and it was arranged that as soon as they got near the house he should go on and ascertain the disposition of the inhabitants. Should they be ill-disposed towards the English he was to return, and they would go on rather than run the risk of being detained and sent to prison.

Sooner than they had expected they got close up to what was evidently a house of considerable size, as the lights came from windows some distance above the ground. While Le Duc went forward, the rest of the party remained concealed under shelter of some thick bushes. He had not got far when a loud barking showed that several dogs were on the watch.

He advanced, however, boldly, calling to the dogs, and shouting for some one to come and receive him.

The animals, though satisfied that he was not a thief, seemed to suspect that there were other persons not far off.

"I say, here the brutes come," whispered Tom. "They'll be tearing us to pieces. The people in these parts, I have read, have great big bloodhounds to hunt the Indians with. If they come near us we must knock them over."

"That won't make the people inclined to treat us more kindly," answered Jack. "When the dogs find we are quiet, they'll let us alone."

Just then the voice of some one was heard calling the dogs, who went back to the house.

Some time passed. At last Le Duc's voice was heard. It was too dark to see him.

"It's all arranged, messieurs," he said. "There's an old lady and two young ladies in the house. I told them all about you, when they said that they were fond of the English, and would be very happy to give you shelter and food, but that you must come quietly so that no one but their old brown maître d'hôtel, and black girls who wait on them, should know that you are in the house. Follow me, then, and just have the goodness to tell the men that they must behave themselves or they may be getting into trouble."

"I'll tell them what you say," observed Rayner; and turning to the three seamen, he said—

"Remember that though you are on shore you belong to the *Lily*, and are, therefore, as much under discipline as if you were on board."

They now proceeded towards the house, led by Le Duc. The two officers going first, they mounted the steps, and getting inside the house, they saw an old mulatto carrying a couple of wax candles. He beckoned them with his head to follow, and led the way to an inner room, when an old lady advanced to meet them. Behind her came two young ladies, whom the midshipmen thought very handsome, with dark flashing eyes and black tresses, their costumes being light and elegant, and suited to that warm clime. The old lady introduced them as her daughters, Sophie and Virginie. The midshipmen advanced bowing, and Rayner, who was spokesman, apologised for appearing in their wet and somewhat torn clothes.

"We have received the invitation madame has been so kind as to afford us, and we throw ourselves on her hospitality." He then repeated what he had told Le Duc to say.

"You shall have your necessities supplied, and I will gladly do all I can to protect and help you regain your ship," she said. "I was once with my daughters taken prisoner when on a voyage from France by an English ship-of-war, and we were treated by the English officers as if we had been princesses. Ah! they were indeed true gentlemen! They won our hearts;" and she sighed. "I thought two of them would have become husbands of my daughters, but stern duty compelled them to sail away after they had landed us, and we have never heard of them since."

"We will gladly convey any message to them, if you will tell us their names, and the ships to which they belonged," said Rayner, "should we be fortunate enough to fall in with them."

"My daughters will tell you by-and-by," answered the old lady. "You, I see, require to change your dresses, which you can do while supper is preparing. My maître d'hôtel will look to your men with the help of the French sailor whom you sent up with your message."

"One of them was hurt on board the wreck, and requires some doctoring, I fear," said Rayner; "he managed to drag himself, with the assistance of his shipmates, thus far, but he must be suffering."

"Be sure that I will attend to him," answered Madame La Roche. "I have some skill in surgery, and it will be a satisfaction to exercise it on one of your countrymen; but now François will conduct you to a room, and supply you with such garments as he can collect. Your men in the meantime will be attended to."

François on this stepped forward with his candles, and, with an inimitable bow, requested the young officers to follow him. They bowing again to madame and her daughters, followed the maître d'hôtel, who led the way to a large room with two beds in it, as also a couple of cane sofas, several chairs, a table, and, what was of no small consequence, a washhand-stand.

"De best ting messieurs can do will be to get into de bed while I bring dem some dry clothes," said François.

Rayner and Oliver requested, however, that they might be allowed, in the first place, to wash their hands and faces.

This done, they jumped into their respective beds, and when once there they agreed that, if they were not so hungry, they would infinitely prefer going to sleep to having to get up again and make themselves agreeable to the ladies. As soon as François got possession of their clothes he hurried away, but shortly returned, bringing with him a supply of linen and silk stockings, and two antiquated court suits. They were, he said, the only costumes which he considered worthy of the English officers, and he begged that they would put them on without ceremony.

Though not much inclined for merriment just then, they could not help laughing as they got into the white satin small clothes offered them. They then put on the richly-embroidered waistcoats, which, being very long, came down over their hips. Their frilled shirts stuck out in front to a considerable distance, but when they came to the coats, Rayner, who had the broadest pair of shoulders, felt considerable fear lest he should split his across, while his hands projected some way beyond the ruffles which adorned the wrists.

François assisted them in the operation of dressing, and after they had tied their neckcloths, he begged, with a low bow, to fasten on their swords. When their costumes were complete he stepped back, and surveyed them with evident satisfaction.

Oliver could not keep his countenance, but laughed heartily for some time.

"It's just as well to get it over, Rayner," he said; "for otherwise I could not help bursting out every time I looked at you."

The maître d'hôtel, however, did not appear to think there was anything laughable in the appearance of the two Englishmen.

"Oh, messieurs! you are admirable. Let me have the honour of conducting you to the saloon." Saying this he took up the candles, and with stately step marched before them, until they reached a large room, in the centre of which was a table spread with a handsome repast.

Madame La Roche, coming in, took the head of the table, and the young ladies, sailing like swans into the room, placed themselves by the side of their guests, on the strangeness of whose costumes they made not the slightest remark. Rayner and Oliver had become somewhat faint from long fasting, but their spirits quickly revived after they had eaten some of the viands placed before them. At first they supposed that the repast was served up solely on their account, but from the way the girls and their mother kept them in countenance, they were satisfied that they had simply come in for the family supper.

Rayner talked away, now to the old lady, now to the young one at his side, while Oliver found that he could converse much more fluently than he had supposed.

After a time, however, they found it very difficult to keep their eyes open, and Rayner heard the old lady remark to her daughters, in pitying accents, that "Les pauvres garçons much required rest, and that it would be cruel to keep them up longer than was necessary."

She accordingly summoned François, who appeared with his huge candlesticks. Wishing them good-night, the old lady advised them to follow the maître d'hôtel to their chamber.

They bowed as well as they could, and staggered off, more asleep than awake.

"We are certainly in clover here," remarked Oliver, as they reached their room; "I question whether we shall be as well treated when we reach Spanish territory; and I propose, if Madame La Roche is willing to keep us, that we take up our quarters here until Peek is better able to travel than he is now."

"Certainly," answered Rayner, taking off his silk coat and placing his sword on the table. "We'll talk of that to-morrow."

They had not placed their heads on their pillows many seconds before they both were fast asleep.

Chapter Thirty One.

Captured.

The shipwrecked midshipmen would probably have slept far into the next day had not François appeared with their clothes, nicely brushed and carefully mended, so that they were able to make a presentable appearance in their own characters before their hostesses.

He had also brought them a cup of café-au-lait, informing them that breakfast would be ready as soon as they were dressed in the salle-à-manger.

They found an abundant meal spread out, as François had promised. The old lady and her daughters welcomed them kindly—the latter with wreathed smiles, the elder with a host of questions to which she did not wait for a reply.

They were all three thorough Frenchwomen, talking, as Oliver observed, "thirteen to the dozen."

Madame La Roche told them that she had been attending to the English sailor, who, she hoped, would, under her care, be quite well in a day or two. "I ought to warn you not to go out. People in these parts are not well affected towards the English, and should it be discovered that I am harbouring British officers I may get into trouble," she added.

The morning passed very pleasantly. The young ladies produced their guitars, and sang with good voices several French airs. Rayner and Oliver thought them charming girls, and had they not felt it was their duty to get back to their ship as soon as possible, would gladly have remained in their society for an indefinite period.

At last they begged leave to go down to see their men. They were guided to their rooms by sounds of music and uproarious laughter. They found Le Duc seated on a three-legged stool on the top of a table fiddling away, while old François, three black women, Tom and Brown, were dancing in the strangest possible fashion, whirling round and round, kicking up their heels, and joining hands, while Jack lay on a bed at the farther end of the room, looking as if he longed to get up and take a part in the dance.

On seeing the strangers, François became as grave as a judge, and hurrying up to them, observed, "I thought it as well, messieurs, just to join in for one minute to set the young people going. The poor sailors needed encouragement, and I like to make people happy."

"You succeeded well, Monsieur François," remarked Rayner. "I will not interrupt them, but I have a few words to speak to my men."

He then told Tom and Brown that it was the wish of Madame La Roche that they should remain in the house, and not show themselves by any chance to the people outside.

"In course, sir," said Brown. "We are as happy as princes here. They feed us with as much as we can eat, and give us a right good welcome too."

"Take care that you don't indulge too much," said Rayner. "We are obliged to you, Le Duc, for finding us such good quarters, and we shall be still more grateful if you will accompany us to the Spanish border. I conclude you will then desire to return home."

"I am very much at home where I am," replied Le Duc, with a grin. "If madame will accept my services, I shall be very happy to remain here. Perhaps one of the young ladies will fall in love with me, and I should prefer settling down to knocking about at sea."

Rayner and Oliver were horrified at the Frenchman's impudence.

"Pray do not be troubled at what I say, messieurs," said Le Duc, with perfect coolness. "Such things have happened before, and one Frenchman here is as good as another."

They saw that it would not do to discuss the matter with the seaman, who, it was evident, from the dishes and glasses standing on the table by the window, had been making himself merry with his companions.

The afternoon was spent very much as the morning had been. The young ladies possessed no other accomplishment than that of playing the guitar and dancing. They read when they could get books, but these were mostly French novels, certainly not of an improving character.

Rayner and Oliver could not help comparing them with Mary Crofton, and the comparison was greatly to her advantage.

The next day, François, who had been out to market returned with a troubled countenance. He hurried in to his mistress, who soon afterwards came into the room where her daughters and the young officers were seated.

"I am sorry to say that the authorities have heard of your being in the neighbourhood, and have sent the gendarmes to search for you!" she exclaimed, in an anxious tone. "I did not wish to drive you away, and am willing to try and conceal you. At present, no one knows you are in the house. You may remain in a loft between the ceiling of this room and the roof, where you are not likely to be found; but the place is low, and will, I fear, be hot in the daytime, and far from pleasant. François might manage to conduct you to a hut in the woods at no great distance from this, to which we could send you food; but there is the risk of the person who goes being seen, and your retreat being discovered."

"We are very sorry to cause you so much trouble, madame," said Rayner. "It will, I think, be safest to leave this place to-night, and to try and make our way, as we intended, into Spanish territory."

"Ah! but the distance is long—fully twenty leagues," answered Madame La Roche. "You would be recognised as strangers, and probably detained by the mayor of a large village you must pass through."

"But we must take care and not pass through any village," said Rayner. "We will try to make our way along bypaths. What we should be most thankful for is a trustworthy guide. Perhaps our good friend François here will find one for us."

"That I will try to do," said the old mulatto. "It is not, however, very easy, as few of them know much of the country to the east."

"But how was it discovered that these English officers and their men were in the country?" asked Mademoiselle Sophie, the eldest of the young ladies, turning to François.

"It appears that yesterday morning there was found on the beach the dead body of a seaman, who was supposed from his appearance and dress to be English, while the marks of numerous feet were perceived on the sand, some going to the west, others coming in this direction. Those going to the west were traced until a party of French and black sailors were discovered asleep in a wood. They stated that the vessel was French, captured by an English man-of-war; that she had been driven by the hurricane on the reef, and that it was their belief the English officers and crew had escaped as well as themselves, but they could not tell what had become of them. The mayor, on hearing this, had despatched a party of gendarmes in search of the missing people. How soon they may be here it is impossible to say."

"But they will not be so barbarous as to carry off to prison English officers who come with a flag of truce, and had no hostile intentions!" exclaimed Virginie.

"The authorities would be only too glad to get some Englishmen to exhibit as prisoners," said François. "We must not trust them; and I propose that we hide away the officers and men."

Just as François had finished giving this account, Le Duc ran into the room.

"Oh, madame, oh messieurs!" he exclaimed, "I have seen those gendarmes coming along the road towards the house; they will be here presently."

"Here, come this way, my friends!" cried Madame La Roche. "François, run and get the ladder. There may be time for you all to mount up before the gendarmes appear. Call the other sailors. The sick man is strong enough to move, or some one must help him. Vite, vite!"

The old lady hurried about in a state of great agitation. Rayner and Oliver had serious fears that she would betray herself.

François soon came with the ladder, which he placed in a dark corner of a passage, and, ascending, opened a trapdoor, and urged the party to mount without delay. Oliver went up first. Jack was able to get up without assistance. Le Duc was unwilling to go until the old lady seized him by the arm.

"Go up, my son, go up," she said. "You will not be worse off than the rest."

He at length unwillingly obeyed.

As soon as Rayner got up, by François' directions he shut down the trapdoor. There was just light sufficient, through a pane of glass in the roof, to see that the loft extended over a considerable portion of the building. Part only was covered with boards, on which, according to the instructions given them, they laid down. François had charged them on no account to move about, lest they should be heard by the people below. The planks, however, were not placed very close together, and after they had been there a minute or so, Rayner discovered a glimmer of light coming through a broadish chink.

Putting his face near it, he perceived that the old lady and her daughters had seated themselves at a table with their work before them, endeavouring to look as unconcerned as possible.

He had not been in this position many minutes, when he heard some heavy steps coming along the passage; they entered the room, and a gruff voice demanded if any Englishmen had been, or still were, in the house.

The old lady started to her feet with an exclamation of well-feigned astonishment.

"What can monsieur mean?" she asked. "Englishmen in my house! Where can they have come from? My character is well known as a true patriot. The enemies of France are my enemies. Pray explain yourself more clearly."

On this the sergeant of gendarmes began to apologise in more courteous language than he had at first used, explaining why he had been sent to look for the Englishmen who, it had been ascertained, were in that part of the country.

"Suppose you find them, what would you do with them?" asked Madame La Roche.

"No doubt send them to prison. They are enemies of France, and it would not be wise when we can catch them to allow such to wander at large and commit mischief."

"Very true, very true, Monsieur Sergeant," said the old lady. "But that does not excuse you for accusing me of harbouring them, and coming to my house as if I were a traitress."

The sergeant, however, was evidently persuaded, notwithstanding Madame La Roche's evasion, that the fugitives had been at the house, if they were not there still, and he insisted, with due respect to her, that it was his duty to make a thorough search.

"As you desire it, pray obey your orders," said Madame La Roche. "My maître d'hôtel will show you round the house and outbuildings, and wherever you wish to go. You must excuse me on account of my age, as also my daughters from their youth and delicate nerves from accompanying you."

The sergeant bowed, and said something with a laugh which Rayner did not hear, and the old lady, calling François, bade him conduct the sergeant and his gendarmes through the house. "And take care that he looks into every corner, under the beds and in them, if he likes, so that he may be thoroughly satisfied," she added.

"Oui, madame," answered François with perfect gravity. "Come along, Monsieur Sergeant. If you do not find these Englishmen of whom you speak, do not blame me."

Rayner heard them retire from the room. He now began to breathe more freely, hoping, for the sake especially of Madame La Roche, that the sergeant would be satisfied when they were not found in the house.

The ladies went on working and talking as if nothing were happening, though their countenances betrayed their anxiety. The gendarmes had been absent a sufficient time to make a thorough search through the whole of the building when Rayner heard them coming back. Suddenly the sergeant stopped, and asked, in a loud voice, "What is the object of this ladder, my friend?"

"To reach the roof from the verandah, or to enable the inmates to descend should the house be on fire," answered François, promptly.

"The roof everywhere overlaps the verandah," answered the sergeant, "and no ladder is necessary to get out of these windows to the ground. It appears to me of a length suited to reach the ceiling. Come, show me any trapdoor through which I can reach the loft over the rooms. You forgot, my friend, that part of the house."

"A trapdoor in the ceiling! What a strange thought of yours!" exclaimed François. "However, perhaps you will find it, should one exist, that you may be satisfied on that point, and let one of your men take the ladder, for I am old, and it would fatigue me to carry it."

One of the gendarmes took up the ladder, and he could be heard knocking at the ceiling in various directions. Still Rayner hoped that they would not discover the dark corner, which François evidently had no intention to show them.

"It must be found somewhere or other," he heard the sergeant say. "This ladder is exactly suited to reach it."

At last he entered the room where the ladies were seated.

"Will madame have the goodness to tell me whereabouts the trapdoor is that leads to the roof?" he asked.

"The trapdoor leading to the roof!" repeated Madame La Roche. "It is not likely that an old woman, as I am, would have scrambled up there, or my delicate daughters either. Surely, Monsieur Sergeant, you are laughing at me."

The sergeant turned away, but presently one of the men exclaimed, "I have found it! I have found it—here, up in this corner!"

Rayner heard the men ascending, the trap was lifted, but he and his companions lay perfectly still, hoping that in the darkness they might not be perceived.

But the gendarme, after waiting a few seconds to accustom his eyes to the dim light, began groping about until he caught hold of Tom's leg. Tom, dreadfully frightened, cried out in English, "Oh, dear; he's got me!"

"Come down, messieurs, come down!" exclaimed the sergeant. "Oh, Madame La Roche, you would have deceived me."

Rayner and his companions were compelled to descend. He truly felt more for his kind hostess and her daughters than he did for himself. They might be heavily fined, if not more severely punished. He and his companions had only to look forward to a prison, from which they might escape.

With the exception of Le Duc they were all soon collected in the room below. He had managed by some means to escape detection. They were allowed but a short time to take leave of Madame La Roche and her daughters. The sergeant having received no orders respecting the ladies, and satisfied at having secured his prisoners, seemed disposed to allow the former to remain unmolested. They looked very melancholy, however. The young ladies, as they shook hands, burst into tears. In vain Madame La Roche begged that their guests might be allowed to partake of some refreshment before commencing their journey. The sergeant would not hear of it. He had caught the spies, and he intended to keep them. If he allowed them to remain, some trick might be played, and they might make their escape.

He at once, therefore, ordered his men to lead his prisoners to the courtyard of the house.

"Hands off; I won't be manacled by a French jackanapes," cried Brown, turning round as one of the men seized his arm. "We are five to seven, mayn't we knock the fellows over, sir? We could do it easily enough, and get off before they came to themselves again."

"I'll join you with all my heart," said Jack, "though I can't fight as well as I could before my ribs were stove in."

"I'll tackle one of the fellows if I may take the smallest," said Tom, though he looked rather pale at the thought of the impending struggle.

"What do you advise, Rayner?" asked Oliver.

"I can advise no violence," said Rayner. "We may succeed in mastering the Frenchmen, but if we did, the kind old lady here and her daughters would certainly suffer in consequence. We must submit with a good grace, and we may possibly afterwards have an opportunity of making our escape without fighting."

Though the Frenchmen did not understand what was said, they evidently, from the looks of the seamen, suspected their intentions, and drawing their pistols presented them at the heads of their prisoners.

The ladies shrieked, fancying they were about to fire, and Tom turned pale.

"Pray don't be alarmed," said Rayner. "We yield to the sergeant, and before we go I wish, in the name of my companions and myself, to express to you the deep gratitude we feel for your kindness. Farewell!"

He and Oliver kissed their hands, and the sergeant made significant signs to them to go through the doorway.

"Have I the word of you two officers and your men that you will commit no violence?" he asked. "If you refuse it, I shall be under the necessity of binding your arms behind you."

"What shall I say, Oliver?" asked Rayner. "If we give the promise we lose the chance of attempting to make our escape; but then again, if our arms are bound no opportunity can occur."

"Say then that we will attempt no violence, and submit to any directions he may give us," answered Oliver.

Rayner spoke as Oliver advised, and the sergeant appeared satisfied, as he imposed no other promise.

Chapter Thirty Two.

In prison, and out again.

The order to march was given. The two officers went first, followed by Brown and Tom supporting Jack, and the gendarmes marched on either side of them with their bayonets fixed.

Rayner and Oliver took the bearings of the house and remarked the country as they went along. They found that they were proceeding inland, and on inquiring of the sergeant he said that they were going to a place called Le Trou, where other English prisoners were confined.

"Are there many of them?" inquired Rayner.

"Yes," answered the Frenchman, "some hundreds, I believe; for one of our frigates captured a ship of yours not long ago, and most of the officers and men who escaped death were sent there."

Rayner in vain endeavoured to ascertain what English ship was spoken of, for he had heard of none taken by the French of late years. The sergeant, however, was positive, though he did not know either the name of the ship or the exact time of the capture.

"I suspect he has heard some old story, and he repeats it for the sake of annoying us," observed Oliver.

"We must not let him suppose that we are cast down. We'll try to learn how far off this Le Trou is."

Rayner questioned the sergeant.

"He says it is three days' journey. We shall have to stop at different houses on the road. That he must first take us to the mayor, or some official, who may perhaps send us to the governor at Leogane, by whom we shall be examined, and if found to be spies, we shall be shot."

"Then Le Trou is not our first destination, and much will depend upon the character of the mayor before whom we are taken," observed Oliver.

As they still continued in a northerly direction, they knew that they were not going to Leogane, which lay to the westward, nor were they increasing their distance from the Spanish border.

Towards evening they reached a house of some size built, as are most of those in the country, on one storey, raised on a platform, with a broad veranda and wide projecting eaves. At one end, however, was a circular tower of considerable height.

"Here we shall stop, and there will be your lodging after you have been examined by Monsieur le Maire," said the sergeant, pointing to the tower.

They conducted them up the steps to a hall, at one end of which was a baize-covered table, with a large chair and several smaller chairs on either side.

After some time a little old gentleman in a red nightcap and flowered dressing-gown, with slippered feet, and spectacles on nose, entered the hall, followed by another in black, apparently his clerk. Two other persons also came in, and took their seats at the table, while the clerk began to nibble his pen and shuffle his papers.

The old gentleman, in a squeaky voice, inquired who were the prisoners now brought before him, and of what crime they were accused.

The sergeant at once stepped up to the table, and giving a military salute, informed Monsieur le Maire how he had heard of spies being in the country, and how he had captured them at the house of Madame La Roche.

"But if they are Englishmen, they cannot speak French, and we require an interpreter," said the mayor. "Do any of you, my friends, understand the language of those detestable islanders?"

No one replied. After the remark of the mayor, it might seem a disgrace even to speak English.

Rayner, anxious not to prolong the business, on hearing what was said, stepped up to the table, and observed that, as he spoke French, he should be happy to explain how he and his companions came into the country.

He then gave a brief account of the circumstances which led to the shipwreck, and what had since occurred. He was sorry anybody present should entertain ill-feelings towards the English, as for his part he liked France, and had a warm regard for many Frenchmen.

Even the mayor was impressed, and a pleased smile came over his weazened features.

"I am ready to believe the account you give me, and that you certainly are not spies," he said. "The body of your countryman found on the beach proves that you were shipwrecked. Still, as you are in the country, we must consider you as prisoners of war, and treat you as such. For this night you must remain here, and to-morrow I will consider whether I will send you to Leogane or Le Trou, where you will wait with others of your countrymen to be exchanged."

After some further remarks the examination terminated, and Rayner and Oliver, with the three seamen, were marched off under a guard to the tower.

It was nearly dark, and they were conducted by the light of a lantern up two flights of steps to a room in an upper storey. As far as they could judge, it was furnished with several pallet beds, a table, some chairs, and stools.

"You are to remain here until to-morrow morning, messieurs, when I shall know in what direction to proceed. Monsieur le Maire has ordered you some food, and you will, I hope, not complain of your treatment," said the sergeant, as he closed the door, which he locked and bolted. They heard him descending.

"We are better off than I should have expected," remarked Rayner, surveying the room by the light of the lantern which the sergeant had left.

"The point is, Are we able to escape?" said Oliver.

"You mind, sir, how we got out of the prison in France, and I don't see why we shouldn't get out of this place," observed Jack, going to one of the two narrow windows which the room contained, and looking forth. They were strongly-barred. The night was dark, and he could only see the glimmer of a light here and there in the distance. It was impossible also to ascertain the height of the window from the ground.

"We will certainly try to get out," said Rayner, joining Jack at the window. "Though I fear that you with your bruises and battered ribs will be unable to make your way on foot across the country."

"Don't mind me, sir," answered Jack. "I have no pain to speak of. If the worst comes to the worst, I can but remain behind. I shall be content if you and Mr Crofton and Tom and Brown make your escape."

"No, no, my brave fellow," said Rayner, "we will not leave you behind. But before we talk of what we will do, we must try what we can do. These bars seem very strongly fixed into the stone, and may resist our attempts to get them out."

"There's nothing like trying, however," observed Oliver. "We must get away to-night, for if the mayor decides on sending us either to Leogane or Le Trou we shall have a very poor chance afterwards."

They tried the bars, but all of them were deeply imbedded in the stone.

"Where there's a will there's a way," observed Jack. "We may dig out the lead with our knives, and if we can get one bar loose we shall soon wrench off the ends of the others, or bend them back enough to let us creep through. Brown wouldn't make much of bending one of these iron bars, would you, Sam?"

"I'll try what I can do," said the seaman, "especially if it's to get us our liberty."

"Then, not to lose time, I'll make a beginning, if you'll let me, sir," said Jack; and he got out his knife, but just as he had commenced operations, steps were heard ascending the stairs. The door opened, and one of the gendarmes appeared, followed by a negro carrying a basket of provisions.

"Monsieur le Maire does not want to starve you, and so from his bountiful kindness has sent you some supper," said the former.

"We are much obliged to Monsieur the Mayor, but we should be still more so if he would set us at liberty," said Rayner.

Meanwhile the black boy was spreading the table with the contents of the basket.

The gendarme laughed. "No, no, we are not apt to let our caged birds fly," he answered. "I hope, messieurs, you will enjoy your suppers, and I would advise you then to take some sleep to be ready to start early in the morning, as soon as it is decided in what direction you are to go."

Rayner thanked the gendarme, who, followed by the black boy, went out of the room, bolting and barring the door behind him.

The men now drew their benches to the table, and Rayner and Oliver, taking their places, fell to with the rest, there being no necessity, under such circumstances, for keeping up official ceremony.

Supper was quickly got through, and each man stowed away the remainder of the provisions in his pockets. While they went to work with their knives at the bars, Rayner and Oliver examined the beds. They were thankful to find that the canvas at the bottom was lashed by pieces of tolerably stout rope. These, with the aid of the ticking cut into strips, would form a line of sufficient length and strength to enable them to descend, should they succeed in getting out the bars. This, however, was not easily to be accomplished. When the officers went to the window, they found that Jack and his companions had made little progress. The bars fitted so closely into the holes that there was but a small quantity of lead, and without a hammer and chisel it seemed impossible to make the hole sufficiently large to move the bars so as to allow Brown to exert his strength upon them. If the two centre perpendicular bars could be got out, the lowest horizontal bar might be sent up. This would afford ample room for the stoutest of the party to get through.

"We've got out of a French prison before, sir, and we'll get out now," said Jack, working away.

"Yes, but we were small boys then, and you, Jack, and I, would find it a hard matter to get through the same sized hole now that we could then," observed Rayner.

"That's just it, sir. If two small boys could get out of a French prison, I am thinking that five well-nigh grown men can manage the job. We'll do it, sir, never fear. If this stone was granite it might puzzle us, but it's softer than that by a long way, and I have already cut out some of it with my knife, though, to be sure, it does blunt it considerably."

The progress Jack and his companions made was very small, and it was evident that unless they could work faster they would be unable to remove the bar before daylight. Rayner and Oliver searched round the room for any pieces of iron which might serve the purpose of a chisel. They examined the bedsteads—they were formed entirely of wood. There was, of course, no fireplace, or a poker might have assisted them. They had just returned to the window when their ears caught the sounds of a few low notes from a violin, played almost directly beneath them.

"Why! I do believe that's the tune Le Duc was playing to us last evening," exclaimed Jack.

All was again silent. Rayner and Oliver tried to look through the bars, but could see nothing; all was still. Again the notes were heard. Jack whistled a few bars of the same air. A voice from below, in a suppressed tone asked in French, "Have you a thin line? Let it down."

"It is Le Duc. He has got something for us. Maybe just what we want," cried Jack.

"Oui, oui," he answered. "It will quickly be ready."

The ticking of one of the mattresses was quickly cut up and formed into a line, which was lowered. Rayner, who held it, felt a gentle tug, and as he hauled it up, what was the delight of the party to find two strong files! There could be no doubt that Le Duc had formed some plan to assist them in escaping, or he would not have come thus furnished. Probably they had to thank Madame La Roche for suggesting it. They did not stop, however, to discuss the matter, but set to work immediately to file away the bars, making as little noise as possible. While two of them were thus employed, the rest walked about the room, and talked and laughed and sang, so as to drown the sound of the files. Presently they heard from the other side of the building the loud tones of a fiddle, the player evidently keeping his bow going at a rapid rate. Then came the sounds of laughter and the stamping of feet, as if people were dancing.

"Why, our guards will be kept awake and we shall have no chance of getting off, I fear," said Oliver.

"If our guards dance they will drink, and sleep afterwards, never fear," answered Rayner. "Our friend Le Duc knows what he is about. I'm sure that we can trust him, or he would not have taken the trouble to bring us these files."

The fiddle was kept going, and Brown and Jack kept time to the tunes with the files as they worked, laughing heartily as they did so.

"Hurrah!" cried Jack, "there's one bar through. Take a spell here, Tom. You've helped the armourer sometimes, and know how to use a file."

Tom, being as eager to get out as the rest, worked away better than he did on most occasions.

Jack, however, soon again took the file, and in a short time announced that both the centre bars were cut through at the bottom. They had next to file the upper bars sufficiently to enable Brown to bend them back. Losing patience, however, he at last seized one of them, when, placing his feet against the window, he bent back with all his strength. He was more successful than he expected, for the iron giving way, down he fell on the floor with a tremendous crash, which would certainly have been heard by the guards below, had not their attention been drawn off by the fiddle of Le Duc, who was scraping away with more vehemence than ever. Rayner and Oliver had in the meantime been manufacturing the rope by which they hoped to descend to the ground. They could measure the necessary length by the small line with which the files had been drawn up, and they had the satisfaction of finding that it was amply long enough for their purpose. They now secured it to one of the remaining bars. Rayner and Oliver agreed that it would be wise to descend while the fiddle was going.

"Let me go first," said Brown. "I am the heaviest, and if it bears me, it will bear any of you."

Tom said nothing. His modesty or something else prevented him from putting himself forward when any danger was to be encountered.

Rayner himself had intended to descend first, but the rest of the party begged him to let some one else go, and at last Oliver led the way.

Judging by the still louder scraping of Le Duc's fiddle, he must have suspected what they were about. Oliver could hear the notes coming round from the other side of the building. All, however, below him was silence and darkness. He could not judge, as he looked down, whether he was to alight on hard or soft ground, whether into a ditch or stream, or whether they should have a fence to climb. His chief fear was that some of the dogs allowed to go loose in every country house might discover him and his companions before they could effect their escape.

All this passed through his mind as he was letting himself down the rope, to which he clung with arms and feet as a sailor only can cling with security. He soon reached the bottom. The ground appeared to be firm, and was, as far as he could judge, perfectly level. The tower threw a dark shadow, in which he stood listening for any sounds which might indicate danger. It had been agreed, even should one or two of the gendarmes come round, to spring upon them, seize their arms, and gag them. As soon as his feet touched the ground, he pulled out his handkerchief, ready for the latter object. Presently another came down. It was Brown, the best man to tackle an enemy, as his muscular strength was equal to any two of the rest. No enemy appeared, however, and at length Rayner, who came last, reached the bottom in safety.

Chapter Thirty Three.

Travelling under difficulties.

They waited and waited. Le Duc kept fiddling away with as much vehemence as at first. But they could not ascertain whether their guards were still dancing—the scraping of the fiddle-strings drowning all other sounds.

At length the music became slower and slower, until only a low, moaning wail reached their ears. It was of a remarkably somniferous character,—the cunning Le Duc had evidently some object in playing thus. Presently the music ceased altogether. Not a sound was heard, except the soughing of the wind round the tower. Still their patience had to be tried. Something was keeping Le Duc.

At last they saw a figure coming towards the tower. Perhaps it was not Le Duc. If a stranger, they must stop his mouth. Perhaps they might have to bind him. They could cut off a sufficient length of rope for the purpose.

He appeared to be a peasant wearing a broad-brimmed hat and a shirt, with a long stick or ox-goad in his hand. They were so well concealed, crouching down against the wall, that he did not perceive them.

Rayner and Brown were on the point of springing out to seize him, when he said, in a low whisper, "Don't you know me, friends? Follow me, but bend down as low as you can, that if seen from the house you may be taken for my dogs or sheep. Pardon me for saying so."

"No necessity for that; lead on, we will follow," said Rayner.

Walking upright, staff in hand, he proceeded at a good rate across the open space at the back of the village. They could see the lights glimmering from several houses on its borders.

They soon reached a stream with a long wooden bridge thrown over it. Here, as they would be exposed to view, the sooner they could get across it the better. They hurried over, still stooping down, Le Duc walking erect. At last their backs began to ache from remaining so long in a bent position.

They were thankful when they reached the edge of a plantation, and Le Duc, stopping, said, "You have acted admirably, my friends. Come on a little farther to a spot where we shall find some clothes in which you can disguise yourselves. We can get over some leagues before daylight, and the inhabitants we shall then meet with are all blacks, and being very stupid will not discover that you are English, provided those who do not speak French hold their tongues."

"A very right precaution," said Rayner. After he had thanked Le Duc for his exertions, he added, "Remember, Brown and Fletcher, neither of you attempt to open your mouths except to put food into them. If you are spoken to, make off, or pretend that you are deaf and dumb."

After proceeding another mile or so, they reached a solitary hut, partially in ruins. Le Duc here produced five bundles from behind a heap of rubbish, covered over with bushes.

"These I brought by the desire of Madame La Roche," he said. "She and her daughters, and their black girls, and old François, worked away very hard to get them finished. They began the very moment you and the gendarmes left the house. It was Mademoiselle Sophie's idea, she's a clever young lady. Directly the dresses were completed, François and I started off on horseback, as we knew the road you had taken, I dressed as you see me, and carrying my fiddle in a bag hung round my neck. I was a strolling player once, and belonged to a circus before I became a sailor, so I was at home on horseback, and I was at home also when playing my tricks off on the gendarmes. I have keen wits and strong nerves, messieurs. One without the other is of small value. United, wonders can be worked. How I did bamboozle those stupid fellows! It was fortunate, however, that none of the black crew of the schooner or my late shipmates appeared, or I should have been discovered. Now, put on these dresses, they are such as are worn by the planters of this country, and you can pretend you are going to a fair at Goave to buy mules, that is what François advises, and he has got a good head on his shoulders. I wish that he could have come with us, but as soon as he had deposited these clothes he had to ride back as fast as he could to attend to his mistress, and I undertook the rest."

"You have indeed done your part well," said Rayner. "What shall we do with our own clothes?"

"Do your jackets and trousers up in bundles, and carry them with you. You must take care, however, not to let them out of your hands," answered Le Duc.

As they were in a solitary place, with no chance of being overheard, the men, as they looked at themselves by the light of a lantern Le Duc had carried, though he had not until now lit it, indulged in hearty laughter.

"You do look like an overseer, Brown," said Jack, "and I should be precious sorry to be a black slave when you had your whip lifted above my shoulders. You'd hit mighty hard, I've a notion."

As Rayner and Oliver surveyed each other, they expressed strong doubts whether their disguise was sufficient to enable them to pass undetected, and they agreed that it would be necessary to keep as much as possible out of the way of the inhabitants. Still, the risk must be run. The consequences of being caught would be very serious to them, yet more so to Le Duc, who would almost to a certainty be shot for having assisted in their escape.

Having done up their clothes in the handkerchiefs which had contained the dresses they now had on, they pushed forward.

Le Duc had never before been in that part of the country, but he had received minute directions from François, which helped greatly to guide them.

At length they came to a dense jungle. François had told Le Duc of this, and that he would find a path through it. They hunted about for some time in vain.

"Come this way, messieurs!" exclaimed Le Duc, at length. "This must be the path François told me of." He had gone a short distance to the southward, and now led on, feeling the way with his long stick. The others followed. The path was narrow, and the trees met overhead, so that they were in complete darkness. On they went, keeping close behind each other, for there was no room for two to walk abreast.

Le Duc walked at a good pace. The jungle seemed interminable. They must have gone on, they fancied, for two or three miles, when they found their feet splashing in water.

"I am afraid we are getting into a swamp, messieurs," said Le Duc. "It cannot be helped; we must scramble through it somehow or other. If we had daylight it would be an advantage. It won't do to stop here, however."

The water grew deeper. The ground had now become very soft, and they were often up to their knees in mud, so that their progress was greatly delayed.

"We shall cut but a sorry appearance, messieurs, if we meet any one when morning breaks," observed Le Duc. "As soon as we get to dry ground we must stop and put ourselves to rights."

"Perhaps we shall, and it would be as well if we can wash the mud off our legs," said Rayner. "But go on, my fine fellow; if this path is in general use it cannot be much worse than it is."

Rayner was right. In a short time the water became shallower, and soon afterwards they got on to firm ground. To their very great satisfaction they at last found themselves out of the jungle. Before them rose a hill, over which they had to climb.

At the foot of the hill they came to a clear, broad stream, passing over a shingly bed. Le Duc, feeling the depth with his staff, walked in. It was sufficiently shallow to enable them to ford it without difficulty; and they took the opportunity of washing off the mud which had stuck to their legs in the swamp.

All this time poor Jack never once complained, but he was suffering no small amount of pain. His great fear was that he might have to give in and delay the rest.

On the other side of the stream the country showed signs of cultivation. They passed outside several plantations, but what they were they could not tell; still, as they could manage to make their way to the eastward they went on.

"We must be near the large village François spoke of," said Le Duc. "He advised that we should go to the southward of it, as the country on that side is more easily traversed, and we may hope thus to get by without being discovered if we can pass it before daybreak."

They accordingly took the direction as advised. After going some way they heard the barking of dogs and saw a light gleaming, they supposed, from the window of a cottage, whose inmates were up early, or, perhaps, where some one lay dying or dead.

At length the bright streaks of early dawn appeared in the sky ahead.

Jack at last had to acknowledge that he could go no farther.

"If we could but reach some hut or other where the blacks would take care of me, I would be ready to stop sooner than let you be caught, sir," he said, addressing Rayner.

"No, I will never allow that," was the answer. "We'll get you along a little farther, until we can find some place to rest in. There's a wood I see ahead, and we must conceal ourselves in it until you are able to go on again. If Mr Crofton likes to lead on the rest and try to get across the frontier, he may do so, but I'll stick by you, Jack. Don't be afraid."

"Thank you, Bill, thank you!" said Jack, pressing his old messmate's hand, scarcely knowing what he was saying, but thinking somehow that they were again boys together. "You were always a brave, generous chap, and I know you'd never desert a shipmate."

Poor Jack was getting worse every moment. Rayner made no reply, but calling Brown, they helped him along between them, lifting him over the rough places as they made their way towards the wood. They reached it just as daylight burst on the world, as it does in the tropics, the hot sun rushing up immediately afterwards to blaze away with intense heat.

Oliver, with Le Duc and Tom, hurried on ahead to look for some place where they might have a chance of effectually concealing themselves. In a short time Oliver came back.

"We have discovered just the sort of place we want," he said. "The sooner we can stow ourselves away in it the better. Let me take your place and help Peek along."

Rayner would not allow this.

"I can support him a mile farther if necessary," he answered.

In a short time, making their way through the jungle, and crossing a small stream which would afford them water, they saw before them a huge tree, upturned from the roots, forming beneath it a cavern of considerable size, which Le Duc and Tom were engaged in clearing out. There was a risk of being bitten by snakes, which might have made it their abode, but that could not be avoided. Le Duc was running his stick into every hole he could see to drive out any which might be concealed. In other respects, no better place could be found.

Rayner and Brown lifted in Jack and placed him on the ground, and Rayner gave him some of the food they had brought from the tower. They had only enough, unfortunately, for one meal. Meantime it was better than nothing, and resolved to give Jack his share.

The rest of the party had collected some branches and brushwood to conceal the entrance. This done, they all crept in.

Le Duc, who had surveyed their place of concealment from the outside, declared that no person not actually searching for them would suspect that any one was there. No sooner had they swallowed their food than they all fell asleep.

Rayner was the first to awaken. He listened, but could hear no sound except the buzz of insects, and he knew, by the light which came in from the upper part of the entrance, that the sun was shining brightly.

Jack was still asleep. He was breathing easily, and appeared to be better; but still it was not probable that he would be able to continue the journey. It would be necessary, therefore, at all events, to remain in the cavern all the day, but should he be well enough they might continue their journey at nightfall. Their chief difficulty would be to procure food from the neighbouring village without exciting suspicion.

Rayner was unwilling to arouse his companions. At length, however, Oliver awoke; then Le Duc sat up rubbing his eyes.

They consulted as to what was to be done. Oliver agreed with Rayner that they must remain where they were, but Le Duc was for pushing on. When, however, Rayner reminded him that Jack could not possibly move as fast as necessary, if at all, he consented to remain.

"But should the gendarmes come in this direction to look for us, we shall probably be discovered," he observed.

"We must hope, then, that they will not come in this direction," said Oliver.

"But what about food, monsieur?" asked Le Duc.

"We must try to go without it for a few hours," answered Rayner. "We shall be well rested, and must tie our handkerchiefs tightly round our stomachs. I have got enough for the sick man, who requires it more than we do; but we must not let him know that we have none, or he will probably refuse to touch it."

"We can at all events procure some water," said Le Duc. "Give me your hats, gentlemen; they will hold as much as we want."

Though Rayner and Oliver would have preferred some other means of obtaining the water, they willingly gave their hats to Le Duc, who crept out with them, and soon returned with both full to the brim.

The thirst of the party being quenched, for a short time they suffered much less than before from the pangs of hunger.

Tom and Brown were ready to do what their officers wished, only Tom groaned at having nothing to eat.

Jack slept on while the rest again lay down. The light which came through the bushes began somewhat to decrease, and Rayner saw that the sun was sinking behind the trees in the west. He was watching Jack, who at length awoke. The moment he opened his eyes, Rayner offered him the food he had kept ready in his pocket.

"Come, Jack, stow this away in your inside as fast as you can, that you may have strength to go on as soon as it is time to start. We don't intend to spend our lives here, like mice in a hole." Jack did as he was bid, without asking questions. Just as he had finished, Tom groaned out, "I shall die soon if I don't get something to eat."

"Nonsense lad; you can hold out for a few hours longer," replied Brown. "I'm just as bad as you are, for that matter."

Le Duc guessed what they were talking about. He himself felt desperately hungry.

"I tell you what, messieurs, without food we shall make slow progress. I'll go into the village and try to procure some. I shall easily learn from some person, before I venture to enter, whether the gendarmes are there, and if they are not, we shall be safe for the present. They will, I hope, fancying that you made your way back to the house of Madame La Roche, have gone off there. We must hope for the best, and I will try and invent some reason for wishing to purchase food. The kind lady supplied me with money, so that I shall have no difficulty on that score."

Rayner, who in reality suffered more than any one, as he had had less to eat, at last consented to the proposal of Le Duc, who set off.

As soon as he had gone the bushes were drawn close again. The party sat in silence, anxiously waiting his return.

They waited and waited. Again it became dark.

Jack declared that he felt strong enough to go on.

"Yes, you may; but I could not budge an inch until I have had some food," growled Tom. "I wish that that Frenchman would come back."

"Shut up there, mate, and don't be grumbling. You're not worse than the rest of us," said Brown.

Time wore on; it was now perfectly dark. They listened eagerly for the sound of Le Duc's footsteps.

Rayner had made up his mind to go out and try to ascertain what had become of him, or at all events to obtain some food, for he felt that neither he nor the rest of the party could get through the night when travelling without it. Later on it would be still more difficult to obtain, as the inhabitants would be in bed. He thought he should be able to find his way back to their place of concealment; so, desiring the party to keep perfectly silent, he set out. He had not gone far in the wood, when he heard footsteps. He crouched down behind a tree, when, looking out, he saw a man, with something on his back, approaching. He hoped that it was Le Duc, but it might be a stranger. He kept quiet.

The person came nearer, now stopping, now turning on one side, now on the other. It must be Le Duc, thought Rayner. He has lost his way, perhaps that may account for his long absence. Stepping from behind the tree, he advanced.

"What are you searching for, my friend?" he asked, in French.

The man stopped, and seemed inclined to run away.

"Le Duc, what's the matter?" asked Rayner, in a suppressed tone.

"Ah, monsieur! is it you?" cried Le Duc. "I thought I should never find the place where I left you. I saw it only in daylight. Things look so different in the dark. I have had a narrow escape, but I have got some food now. If you follow my advice you will eat and set off immediately. Is the cave near?"

"No; but I can lead you to it," answered Rayner.

As they went along, Le Duc said, "When I got near the village I met an old black, who told me there were no strangers in the place, and that I might easily procure what I wanted. I accordingly went on boldly, until I reached a cottage just in the outskirts. I entered and found the people ready enough to sell me some bread and sausages, charging me three times as much as they were worth. I also procured this straw bag to put them in. While I was there packing them up several persons who had come in were talking, and I heard them say that a party of soldiers had just arrived, on their way from Leogane to Port Saint Louis in the bay, and that they were ordered to look out for several English spies, and that some blacks, who knew the Englishmen, had accompanied the soldiers to assist in finding them. As soon as I heard this I hastily put some of the things into my bag, not waiting for the remainder, and hurried out of the hut. As I did so, what was my dismay to see three of the soldiers, accompanied by one of the black fellows who had escaped from the wreck! Were I to have run away they would have suspected me, so I walked on whistling, as if I had nothing to fear from them.

"As mischance would have it, they were proceeding in the same direction, and it is my belief that they were even then going in search of you. Thoughtless of the consequence, I happened to whistle an air which I sang that night on board the schooner when we were becalmed. The rogue of a black recognised it, for, turning my head, I saw him coming after me. I was silent directly, and began to walk very fast. Fortunately it was almost dusk, and, reaching some thick bushes, I dodged behind them. The black passed me and went on. I lay quiet, and after a time he came back, and I heard him tell the soldiers, who had followed him, that he must have been mistaken; so they then proposed going back to the village.

"I waited until they were out of hearing, and then set off to try and find my way to the cave, but I missed it, and have been wandering about ever since."

No one troubled Le Duc with questions. They were too eager to dispose of the contents of his bag. They could not see what they were eating, but they were not inclined to be particular. As soon as they had finished their meal, being told by Rayner that soldiers were in the neighbourhood, they begged at once to continue their journey; but Rayner was very doubtful whether Jack could keep up, though he declared that he was ready.

When, however, he crept out of the cave, he was scarcely able to stand, much less to walk any distance.

"I must remain, then," said Rayner, "and you, Oliver, go on with the other two men and Le Duc, and when he has seen you safely into Spanish territory he will, perhaps, come back and assist me and Jack Peek. If he cannot, we must do our best by ourselves. We have been in a more difficult position together before now, and managed to escape."

Oliver, however, would not hear of this, and it was finally settled that the whole party should remain in their cave another night and day.

Jack was very unhappy at being the cause of their detention; but Rayner cheered him up by reminding him that it was not his fault, and perhaps, after all, it was the best thing they could do.

They accordingly all crept into the cave and went to sleep.

In the morning light enough found its way through the bushes to enable them to eat breakfast. They, of course, took care not to speak above a whisper, though listening all the time for the sound of footsteps; but as no one came near them, they hoped that their place of concealment was unknown to any of the villagers, who might otherwise have pointed it out to the soldiers.

The day went by. All the food Le Duc had brought was consumed, except a small portion kept for Jack. He offered to go for more, but Rayner judged it imprudent to let him return to the village, where he would be recognised as having come on the previous evening. They accordingly had to go supperless to sleep, Tom grumbling, as usual, at his hard fate.

When daylight streamed into the cavern, Le Duc declared that he could hold out no longer, and that, both for his own sake and that of others, he must go and get some food.

"The soldiers will have gone away by this time," he observed, "and the black people in the village can have no object in detaining me. If they do, I will bribe them to let me off, and they know if they hand me over to the soldiers that they will get nothing."

The hunger all were feeling and his arguments prevailed, and he set off, promising to be back as soon as possible, and to take care that no one followed him.

Rayner felt some misgiving as he disappeared. All they could do in the meantime was to keep close in their hole.

All day they waited, but Le Duc did not return.

Tom muttered, "The Frenchman has deserted us after all."

Even Brown expressed some doubts about his honesty.

"You never can trust those mounseers," he said in reply to Tom's remark.

"Be silent there, men," said Rayner. "Our good friend has probably thought it safer to hide himself, and will manage to get back at night."

Night came, however, and still Le Duc did not appear. Rayner and Oliver became more anxious than ever.

"I must not let you fellows starve," said Rayner at last. "I'll go out and try and get provisions of some sort. Le Duc spoke of several cottages on the outskirts of the village, and I'll call at one of them and try to bribe the inhabitants, or to move their compassion; perhaps I may get tidings of our friend."

Though either Oliver or Brown would gladly have gone instead, they knew that Rayner was the best person to undertake the expedition.

"If I do not return before midnight, you must all set out and travel eastward as fast as you can. How do you feel, Peek? Can you manage to move along."

"Yes, sir," answered Jack. "I could if you were with us, but I am afraid if you were left behind in the grip of soldiers I shouldn't do much."

"Don't let that idea weigh on your mind. If I am captured and sent to prison, there I must remain until I am exchanged for a French officer, though I don't think there's much chance of my being caught."

Having given his final directions, Rayner set off.

He went on till he saw a light streaming through a cottage window. The better sort of people were alone likely to be sitting up at that hour, as the poorer blacks, he knew, went to bed at sundown and rose at daybreak.

He went up to the door and knocked.

"May I come in?" he asked in French; and without waiting for an answer he lifted the latch.

An old mulatto woman was seated spinning. Near her sat a young girl of much lighter complexion, with remarkably pretty features, engaged in working on some pieces of female finery. She rose as he entered, and the old woman uttered an exclamation of astonishment.

He at once explained his errand. He wanted food, and was ready to pay for it. They would not be so hard-hearted as to refuse it to starving men.

The girl looked at the old woman, who was apparently her grandmother.

"Mon père will soon be back. Will monsieur object to wait?" she asked.

"I have no time to wait; here, accept this," said Rayner, holding out a dollar which he fortunately had in his pocket.

The old woman's eyes glittered.

"Give monsieur what he wants, but keep enough for your father's supper and breakfast to-morrow. It is strange that he should require food since he is so rich."

"I want sufficient for several persons—anything you have got," said Rayner.

The girl went to a shelf at the other end of the room and got down a couple of loaves of maize bread, some cakes, salt-fish, and fruit.

"You can take some of these," she said, placing them on the table; "but how are you to carry them?"

He had a silk handkerchief, which he produced, intending to tie up the provisions in. The girl looked at it with admiration.

"Perhaps you will accept this, and give me a basket, or a matting bag instead?" he said.

She quickly produced a bag large enough to hold all the things.

"Now can you give me any news of anything happening in the village?"

"Yes, some soldiers have been there, and impudent fellows they were; some of them came to our house, and if my Pierre had been present there would have been a fight. I am glad that they have gone. It is said they were in search of deserters or spies, and that they had caught one of them, but could not find the rest. If monsieur dislikes the military as much as I do, he'll keep out of their way."

The girl said this in a significant manner. Rayner thanked her and the old woman, and advised them to say nothing about his visit.

"If we know nothing we can say nothing, eh, monsieur? Bon voyage, and keep out of the way of the soldiers," whispered the girl as she let him out.

He could not help thinking, as he hurried back towards the cave, that she suspected he was one of the persons the soldiers were in search of. Although she wished to befriend him, her father might be in a different mood. There was the danger, too, that if poor Le Duc was caught, he might be tortured to make him confess where his companions were. Rayner considered, therefore, that it would be imprudent to remain longer in the cave, and that it would be safer even to carry Jack, should he be unable to walk, than to delay their journey.

He got back safely, and the food he brought soon restored the spirits of the party. Even Jack declared that he was strong enough to walk a dozen miles if necessary. They were in great hopes, therefore, of getting across the border before daybreak. They regretted greatly the loss of Le Duc, who had served them so faithfully, especially as they feared that he himself was in danger of suffering in consequence of the assistance he had given them.

Rayner led the way. The stars being as bright as on the previous night, he had no difficulty in directing his course. The country was much of the same character as that they had previously crossed. In some parts they came to plantations, and could distinguish the residences of the proprietors.

Now they had to make their way by narrow paths through jungles, now to wade through marshes.

Jack, helped by Brown and Tom, got on better than might have been expected. Rayner intended to halt for a short time at the first convenient spot they could reach.

He had for some distance observed no signs of cultivation, when he found that they were passing close to a plantation. Then there appeared a house on one side, then another and another. Barking dogs came rushing out, and they had some difficulty in keeping them at bay. The brutes followed them, however, joined by others. A voice from a gateway shouted, "Who goes there?"

"Friends!" answered Rayner.

"Advance, friends, and show yourselves, and give the countersign," said a sentry, at the same time calling out the guard.

To run would have been useless, besides which it is not a movement British officers and seamen are wont to make, except after an enemy.

Rayner therefore determined to put a bold face upon the matter, advanced with his companions, and the next instant they found themselves surrounded by a body of French soldiers, whose looks, as they held up a couple of lanterns, were anything but satisfactory.

Chapter Thirty Four.

Recaptured—An unexpected rescue.

"Whence do you come and where are you going, mes amis?" asked the sergeant of the guard, addressing Tom, who was nearest him.

"What's that you say, old chap?" said Tom, forgetting the strict orders he had received to hold his tongue.

"Ah, what language is that?" exclaimed the sergeant, holding up his lantern and examining the sailor's countenance. "You are not a Frenchman, I'll vow." He turned from one to the other, looking in the faces of each. "Why, I believe these are the very men we were ordered to search for. Seize them all. Take care that none escape. There are five of them, the very number we were told of, and one, the traitor, we have already got. Can any of you speak French? though I doubt it."

"Should you be satisfied, monsieur sergeant, if we do speak French, and better French than many of the people about here?" asked Rayner. "If so, will you let us go on our journey? do we look like English sailors?"

"I don't know how English sailors generally look," said the sergeant, gruffly, and rather taken aback at being suddenly addressed in his own language. "You certainly have the appearance of overseers, or people of that sort, but your countenances betray you. I am not to be deceived. Bring them along into the guard-room."

In vain Rayner pleaded that he and his companions were in a hurry to proceed on their journey.

They were dragged into the building, and a guard with fixed bayonets was placed over them. For the remainder of the night they had to sit on a hard bench, with their backs against the wall, sleeping as well as they could in so uncomfortable a position. At daybreak the next morning Sergeant Gabot, by whom they had been captured, entering the room, ordered the guard to bring them along into the presence of Captain Dupuis. The seamen, imitating their officers, quietly followed the sergeant, who led the way to a room in the same building. Here Captain Dupuis, a fierce-looking gentleman wearing a huge pair of moustaches, and a long sword by his side, was found seated at a table with two other officers.

He cast his eye over the prisoners and inquired their names. Here was a puzzle, for neither Rayner nor Oliver had thought of assuming French ones. They, therefore, without hesitation, gave their own, as did Jack.

"Please, sir, what does the chap say?" asked Brown, when the officer addressed him.

"He wishes to know your name," said Oliver.

Captain Dupuis, twirling his moustaches, took them down as well as he could.

"These names do not sound like those of Frenchmen," he said.

"And such we do not pretend to be," replied Rayner, stepping forward. "We found it necessary to assume these disguises for the sake of escaping from prison. We are not spies, and have no desire to injure France or Frenchmen except in open warfare."

He then gave an account of their object in approaching the coast and the way in which they had been so unwillingly compelled to land.

"I am inclined to believe you, monsieur," said Captain Dupuis, more politely than at first. "But my duty is to convey you to Port Louis, where my regiment is stationed, and the colonel will decide on your case. We will march directly."

Captain Dupuis appeared not to be ill-disposed, for he ordered some breakfast to be brought to them in the hall.

"Thank you for your kindness, monsieur," said Rayner. "With your permission we will put on our proper dresses, which are contained in these bundles."

"Assuredly you have my leave. It will show the people that we have two English officers in captivity, as well as some of their men, and probably the report will be spread that an English frigate and her crew have been taken," observed the captain, laughing.

"Well, I do feel more like myself now," exclaimed Brown, as he put on his shirt and jacket, and tied his black handkerchief in a lover's knot round his throat.

Rayner and Oliver, though they did not say so, felt very much as their men did, thankful to throw off their disguises.

As soon as they had finished breakfast, the soldiers fell in, the prisoners being placed in the centre, and with the captain at their head they commenced their march to the southward.

It was not until late in the evening that they arrived at their destination. There were three old-fashioned forts, one intended to support the other, commanding the entrance of the bay.

Rayner and Oliver, as they approached, took note of their position, and they remarked that the water appeared to be deep close up to the heights on which the forts were situated. In the largest were several buildings, the residence of the commandant, the barracks, and a small edifice with strongly-barred windows, which they soon discovered to be a prison.

They were halted in front of these buildings, while the captain went in to make his report to the commandant. After waiting some time they were marched in between guards with fixed bayonets.

Their examination was very similar to that which they had before gone through. Rayner and Oliver, however, hoped that their account of themselves would be believed, and that they would, even at the worst, only be detained as prisoners-of-war. Still, they did not quite like the looks of the commandant, who was evidently of a more savage disposition than his subordinate. He glared at the English, and declared they he believed they were capable of the most abominable acts of treachery and deceit.

Rayner replied calmly, and pointed out how improbable it was that he and his companions should have landed for any sinister object.

"If you come not as spies yourselves, you come to land French spies. Miscreant traitors to their country!" exclaimed the commandant. "One of them has been caught. Death will be the penalty of his crime. Bring forward the witnesses."

As he spoke the soldiers stepped aside and two black seamen were led forward. Rayner recognised them as the most ruffianly of the schooner's crew. First one, and then the other, swore that the vessel had been sent to the coast for the purpose of landing some French spies, that the schooner was to wait for them, and then when they had gained information as to the strength of the forts and vessels in the harbours they were to return to the frigate.

In vain Rayner explained the truth. The commandant scornfully answered that he could not believe an English officer upon his oath, that he should send a report of their capture to Leogane, and that for his part he hoped that he should have orders to shoot them all forthwith.

The mock examination terminated, they were marched away to the prison on the other side of the fort. The door being opened, they were unceremoniously thrust in, one after the other, and it was closed behind them. As it was by this time growing dusk, and there were only small, narrow windows close under the roof, they were left in almost perfect obscurity, so that they could not venture to move from the spot where they stood. As, however, their eyes got accustomed to the gloom, they found that they were in a room about twelve or fourteen feet square, the floor and sides being of roughly hewn stone. Round it ran a stone bench, just above which they could see several massive iron rings fixed in the walls.

"While we have light we had better pick out the cleanest spots we can find," said Oliver. "We shall be kept here to-night, at all events, and the surly commandant will not allow us any luxuries."

As they moved a few paces forward, they saw three persons chained to the wall at the farther end of the room.

"Who are you?"

"Alas! alas!" exclaimed one of them, leaning eagerly forward; and they recognised Le Duc's voice. "Ah, messieurs, you will understand the less said the better as to the past."

Rayner took the hint, guessing that Le Duc was unwilling to have anything said in the presence of the two other prisoners which might implicate Madame La Roche or François.

"You have heard, messieurs, that they have condemned me to death," continued Le Duc, "and the wonder is that they have not shot me already, but I know that at any moment I may be led out. I should wish to live that I may play the fiddle and make others happy as well as myself."

"I am very sorry to hear this. If the commandant would believe us, we can prove your innocence, and, surely, our word ought to be taken instead of that of the two blacks," said Rayner.

"So it would, according to law, for the evidence of the blacks is worth nothing, and is not received in a court of justice. It proves that the commandant has resolved, at all costs, to wreak his hatred of the English on your heads."

Rayner and Oliver seated themselves on the stone bench near him. The men had drawn together on the opposite corner. Le Duc narrated how he had been captured just as he was quitting the village. His great fear had been lest he should be compelled to betray them; and he declared to Rayner, who believed him, that he would have undergone any torture rather than have done so.

Le Duc whispered that the two other prisoners had been condemned for murder.

"Pleasant sort of companions," observed Oliver. "We may as well let them have their side of the prison to themselves."

The men in the meantime had scraped the seat as clean as they could with their knives.

Tom, as usual, began to grumble.

"We must take the rough and the smooth together," observed Jack. "I am hungry enough myself, and I hope the mounseers don't intend to starve us, though maybe we shan't get roast beef and plum pudding."

"Don't talk of it," cried Brown; "I could eat half an ox if I had the chance."

While they were talking the door opened, and a man appeared, carrying a lantern and a pitcher in one hand, and a basket in the other, which he placed on the bench near them.

The pitcher contained water, and the basket some very brown, heavy-looking bread, with a couple of tin mugs. Having allowed the other prisoners to drink, and given each of them a piece of bread, he handed the basket with its contents to the Englishmen.

"You Anglais like ros' beef. Here you eat this. Good enough for you," he said, in a surly tone.

They were all too hungry to refuse the bread or the water, which, in spite of its brackish taste, quenched the thirst from which they had long been suffering.

Their gaoler left them the lantern, in order that they might see how to divide the bread. It assisted them also to select places on which to stretch themselves round the room, and, in spite of the hardness of their couches, in a short time were all asleep.

Some more bread and water was brought them in the morning, and a similar unpalatable meal was provided in the afternoon. This was evidently to be their only food during their imprisonment. They had no one to complain to, no means of obtaining redress; so, like wise men, they made up their minds to bear it, though Tom grumbled and growled all day long at the way in which he was treated.

Rayner supposed that the commandant was waiting for a reply to the report he had sent to Leogane. Until that could arrive, no change either for the better or worse was likely to be made in their treatment.

Le Duc was still allowed to live; but, in spite of his high spirits, the feeling that he might at any moment be led out and shot was telling upon him. The two officers and Jack did their best to encourage him, and, under the circumstances, it was wonderful how he kept up. In the evening the gaoler appeared with their usual fare.

"There will be one less of you to feed to-morrow," he growled out, looking at Le Duc, "and I can't say but that you five others mayn't have to join him company, for while the firing party are out it is as easy to shoot six as one."

Le Duc made no answer, but bent his head down on his manacled hands. It was the first sign of deep emotion he had exhibited.

"I hope the fellow is only trying to alarm you for the purpose of exercising his own bad feelings," said Rayner, after the surly gaoler had gone.

Again left in darkness, they prepared to pass another disagreeable night. Rayner felt that their position was critical in the extreme. He and his companions, accused as they were of being spies, might be led out at any moment and shot. He therefore considered it his duty to prepare his companions as best he could for the worst. Oliver he knew was as ready to die as he was himself. He spoke earnestly and faithfully to the others, pointing out the unspeakable importance of being prepared to stand in the presence of the Judge of all men. He was thankful to hear Jack's reply, which expressed the simple hope of the Christian—faith in Christ as a Saviour; but the other two were silent.

After Rayner and his companions had talked for some time they stretched themselves on the bench to try and obtain some sleep. That was more easily sought for than found, for no sooner were they quiet than countless creatures began to sting, and bite, and crawl over them. Tom was continually slapping himself, and moaning and groaning.

But, in spite of their hard stone couches and the attacks of the insects, they did manage to drop off occasionally.

Rayner's eyes had been closed some time when he was awakened by the dull roar of a gun fired from seaward. He started up, as did his companions.

"Where did that come from?" exclaimed Oliver.

Before Rayner could answer, the sound of eight or nine guns, a sloop's whole broadside, was heard, followed by the crash of the shot as they struck the fortification.

In an instant the whole fort was in an uproar, the officers shouting their orders to the men, and the men calling to each other, as they rushed from their quarters to the ramparts. They had evidently been found napping, for before a single gun had been discharged from the fort, the shot from another broadside came plunging into it.

The game, however, was not to be all on one side. The Frenchmen's guns were heard going off as fast as they could get their matches ready. They could easily be distinguished by the far louder noise they made. Those from the two other forts at the same time could be heard firing away. Cries and shrieks rose from wounded men, and a loud explosion, as if a gun had burst, rent the air.

"The vessel attacking is a corvette," cried Rayner. "She must have run close in for her shot to strike in the way they are doing. It is a bold enterprise, and I pray she may be successful for her sake as well as ours."

"Can she be the *Ariel* or *Lily*?" asked Oliver.

"Whichever she is, the attempt would not have been made without good hope of success," remarked Rayner.

"I wish that we were out of this, and aboard her," exclaimed Jack.

"So do I," cried Brown. "I don't like being boxed up here while such work is going on. Couldn't we manage to break out?"

"We are safe here, and we'd better remain where we are," said Tom; "only I hope none of those round shot will find their way into this place."

On the impulse of the moment Jack and Brown made a rush at the door, but it was far too strongly bolted to allow them to break it open. The other prisoners sat with their hands before them, hoping probably, as Tom did, that no shot would find its way among them.

Rayner and Oliver looked up at the windows near the roof, but they were strongly-barred and too narrow to enable a grown man to squeeze through them. To sit down quietly seemed impossible. They stood therefore listening, and trying to make out by the sounds which reached their ears how the fight was going. Presently some more guns were heard coming from the sea.

"There must be another vessel!" exclaimed Rayner. "Hark! she must be engaging the upper fort. I thought that one would scarcely venture singly to attack the three forts."

The roar of the artillery continued. Suddenly there burst forth a loud thundering sound. The ground beneath their feet shook, the walls trembled, and the roof seemed about to fall on their heads, while the glare of a vivid flame penetrating through the windows lighted up the whole interior of the building, shrieks, groans, and cries echoing through the fort.

The magazine had blown up. It was a wonder that the prison itself had not been hurled to the ground.

"Thank Heaven, we have escaped!" exclaimed Oliver.

The attacking vessels still continued firing, and after a short interval the fort once more replied, but evidently with fewer guns than before.

A crash was heard over their heads, and down fell a mass of timber, plank, and tiles just above the door. Looking up, the clear sky could be seen, from out of which a crescent moon shone brightly.

No one was injured, for the shot, having torn its way through the roof, had fallen outside.

"Hurrah! thanks to that shot, we may make our escape out of this, for the Frenchmen are too much engaged at the guns to see us!" cried Jack. "Let us get down to the shore, and when we are once there we may manage to find our way aboard the ship. The chances are we shall find some fishing boat or other on the beach. May we try, sir, what we can do?"

"What do you say, Oliver? Shall we make the attempt Jack proposes?" asked Rayner. "If we go we must take Le Duc with us, I wish that we could find something to knock off his chains, and we might set the other poor fellows at liberty."

To climb out would be no difficult matter, as Brown found that by standing on Tom's and Jack's shoulders he could reach the lower part of the roof. But Rayner positively refused to go without first setting Le Duc at liberty. He told Brown to try and dislodge a piece of stone from the wall with which they might break the prisoners' chains.

Suddenly Tom recollected that he had stowed away one of the files which Le Duc himself had brought in his pocket.

"Hand it here," cried Rayner; and heat once began filing away.

In the meantime Brown managed to get hold of one of the upper stones of the wall. It was hard, and had a sharp side.

"Here it is, sir," he said, clambering down and bringing it to Rayner. A few blows on the bench served to sever the link already partly filed through.

"Oh! set us free, monsieur?" cried the other prisoners.

"What does he say?" asked Brown.

"There won't be time to set you both free, but I'll see what I can do for one of you;" and he began filing away, and with the help of the stone he managed to liberate the arm of one of the men.

"Here, take the file and see what you can do for your comrade," he said.

The rest of the party had in the meantime begun to mount the wall.

Chapter Thirty Five.

New adventures and successes.

As Oliver, who went first, had just got to the top, his attention was attracted by loud shouts coming from the rear of the fort. Above them quickly rose a hearty British cheer. Showers of bullets came flying through the air. The shouts and cries increased. Amid the clash of steel, and the sharp crack of pistols, the voices of the officers reached him calling the men to abandon the guns and defend the fort. But it was too late. Already a strong party of blue-jackets and marines were inside.

The gate in the rear, insufficiently protected, had evidently been taken by a rush. The Frenchmen, as they always do, fought bravely, but hurrying up without order, many of them without muskets, they were driven back.

Even had they been better disciplined, nothing could have withstood the fierce onslaught of the British. Numbers of the defenders were seen to fall, their officers being killed or made prisoners. Most of the remainder, taking to flight, crept through the embrasures or leapt over the parapet.

Directly Oliver announced what was going on, the rest of the party were more eager than ever to get out. Jack was the last drawn up, and they all, with Le Duc, dropped on the ground.

"Hullo! here's a firelock, and a bayonet at the end of it," said Brown, picking up a musket which the sentry had probably thrown down when making his escape. "Hurrah, boys! we'll charge the mounseers, and make them wish they'd never set eyes on us."

Brown, in his eagerness, would have set off without waiting for his companions. Three muskets were found piled close outside of the prison, and a little way off lay the body of an officer who had been shot while making his way to the rear.

Rayner took possession of his sword. The victorious assailants were now sweeping onwards towards the farther end of the fort, in which direction most of the garrison had fled.

At the other end Rayner observed a group of men, either undecided how to act or waiting an opportunity to attack the British in the rear, for they could now see by the increasing daylight that it was but a small party which had surprised the fort.

Brown had seen them also, and, excited at finding himself at liberty, rushed forward with his musket at the charge, without waiting for his companions.

They, however, coming out from behind the buildings, were following in the rear.

On seeing them approach, a French officer, stepping forward, shouted out that they surrendered. Brown, not understanding his object, still charged on, and whisking his sword out of his hand, would have run him through had he not slipped and fallen, while the rest of the party, supposing he had been killed, retreated out of the way of the bold seaman.

"Get up, old fellow, and defend yourself," cried Brown. "I'm not the chap to strike a man when he's down;" and as he spoke he picked up the officer's sword, and, helping him to his feet, presented it to him. All this was done so rapidly that Rayner and his companions arrived only just in time to prevent Brown, who had stepped back a few paces, from making a lunge with his bayonet at the astonished Frenchman, who, now seeing an officer, though he did not recognise Rayner, again cried out that he surrendered, and skipping out of Brown's way offered his sword.

The rest of the garrison, seeing the storming party, who had now swept round, coming towards them, threw down their arms, and cried for quarter, while the officers, amongst whom were Captain Dupuis and Sergeant Gabot, presented their swords to Rayner and Oliver. They, turning round, had the satisfaction of greeting Lieutenant Horrocks and other officers of the *Lily* and *Ariel.*

"Glad to see you, Rayner and Crofton. We all thought you were dead. No time to ask how you escaped. We've got to take those two other forts. If you like you can come with us. Crofton, you can take charge of the prisoners. I'll leave Sergeant Maloney and a dozen men with you. The rest follow me."

Saying this, the first lieutenant of the *Lily* led his men on to the attack of the other fort still engaged with the *Ariel,* Rushing on, they were up to the rear of it before the garrison were aware of the capture of the larger fort. By a sudden dash it was taken as the former had been, the *British* not losing a single man, though several of its defenders, attempting to stand their ground, were cut down. A rocket let off the moment they were in was the signal to the *Ariel* to cease firing.

The third fort higher up, towards which she had hitherto only occasionally fired a gun, now engaged her entire attention.

The increasing light showed the garrison the *British* flags flying above the ramparts of the two other forts, yet they showed no signs of giving in. Though the guns were well placed for defence on the west side, the rear offered a weak point.

Without halting, Lieutenant Horrocks led his men towards it.

"Lads, we must be over those ramparts in five minutes," he said, pointing to them with his sword.

"In two, if you please, sir!" shouted the men.

Rayner, who was among those leading, cheered, and springing forward, leapt into the ditch and began climbing up the bank on the opposite side.

The blue-jackets of his own ship eagerly pressed after him. He was the first at the top, and with a dozen others who had followed him closely, leapt down among a number of the garrison who, leaving their guns, had hurriedly collected to oppose them. In vain the defenders attempted to resist the impetuous attack. Fresh assailants, among the first of whom was Lieutenant Horrocks, came on, and inch by inch driven back; and seeing that all further resistance was useless, the Frenchmen threw down their arms and cried for quarter.

It was now daylight, and there was still much to be done. The prisoners had to be collected, the forts blown up, and the men embarked.

Lieutenant Horrocks gave Rayner the satisfactory intelligence that two privateers had been captured at the entrance of the harbour by the boats without firing a shot. The crews, however, had resisted when boarded, and two officers, one of whom was Lieutenant Lascelles, had been badly wounded.

"Poor fellow! if he recovers I don't think he will be fit for service for some time," said the first lieutenant. "I shall have to report the gallant way in which you assisted in the capture of the fort."

The prisoners being collected from the three forts, and assembled on the beach, Captain Saltwell came on shore and offered the officers their liberty and permission to carry away any of their private property on condition of their pledging their word of honour not to serve against the English again during the war. This they willingly gave.

The men also were to be dismissed, though it was useless to make terms which they would not have it in their power to keep. The wounded were collected, and the garrison were allowed to carry off such materials as could be easily removed for forming huts and tents to shelter them.

On going through the fort, Rayner and Oliver looked into the prison. The two captives had made their escape. Le Duc had hitherto remained with the English. He naturally feared that he should be considered a traitor should he venture among his own countrymen.

"But ah, messieurs, I love France as well as ever; and though I regard the English as brothers after the treatment I have received from them, I would not injure her or her people."

Rayner therefore proposed that he should come on board the *Lily* and remain at Jamaica until he could return home.

The last scene had now to be enacted.

The marines and parties of seamen had been employed for some hours in digging holes under the fortifications, which were then filled with casks of powder, the whole being connected by carefully laid trains. The men were next embarked. One boat alone remained under each fort, the gunner and boatswain of the *Lily* and a warrant officer of the *Ariel* being ordered to fire the trains.

Rayner had taken command of one of the *Lily's* boats. The men waited with their oars in their hands, ready to shove off at a moment's notice. Mr Coles, the gunnel, who was in Rayner's boat, ascended the bank match in hand. Presently he was seen rushing down again, faster probably than he had ever moved before.

"No time to lose, sir," he shouted, as he leapt on board. "The fuse in this hot country burns faster than I calculated on."

"Give way, lads!" cried Rayner.

The men bent to their oars. The other boats were seen pulling away at the same time. They had not got twenty fathoms from the shore, when a thundering report was heard, and up rose a portion of the large fort, filling the air with masses of stone and earth, and dust and smoke.

In another second or two the other forts followed suit. The whole atmosphere was filled with a dense black cloud and masses of lurid flame beneath, while thundering reports in rapid succession rent the air. A few seconds afterwards down came showers of stone and earth and pieces of burning timber, just astern of the boats. Had there been any delay they must have been overwhelmed. Fortunately they all escaped injury, and pulled away for their ships, which, with the prizes, had in the meantime got under way and were standing out of the harbour.

After a quick run the *Ariel* and *Lily* reached Port Royal to repair damages. Rayner was sent for on board the flagship.

"I have great pleasure in handing you your commission as lieutenant," said the admiral. "You have won it by your general meritorious conduct, as also by the gallantry you displayed in the capture of Fort Louis. I have appointed you as second lieutenant of the *Lily*, and shall be very glad in another year or two to hear that you have obtained your commander's rank."

These remarks of the admiral were indeed encouraging. Rayner, of course, said what was proper in return, and pocketing his commission, bowed and took his departure for the shore, which he had to visit to obtain a new uniform and other articles.

Lascelles had been removed to the hospital, where he was to remain until he was sufficiently recovered to go home. Rayner's only regret was being parted from Oliver, the dangers they had gone through together having united them like brothers.

While, however, their ships were refitting they were constantly in each other's society.

"I wish that I had the chance of getting appointed to your ship," said Oliver. "The *Ariel* will soon be going home, but for the sake of being with you I should be glad to remain out another year or two. I am well seasoned by this time, and have no fear of Yellow Jack."

Not many days after this the senior mate of the *Lily* was taken very ill while on shore. His shipmates declared that it was in consequence of his chagrin at finding that Rayner had obtained his promotion before him. They were heartily sorry at having made so unkind a remark, when in two days news were received on board that the poor fellow had fallen a victim to yellow fever.

Rayner at once advised Oliver to make application for the vacancy. He did so; the admiral appointed him to the *Lily*, and Captain Saltwell was very glad to have him on board.

Le Duc, who had been landed at Kingston, came on board one day while the ship was fitting out and begged to speak to the second lieutenant, Monsieur Rayner.

"Ah, monsieur, the first thing I did on landing was to purchase a violin, and the next to play it, and I have fiddled with such good effect that I have played my way into the heart of a Creole young lady whose father is wonderfully rich, and as I can turn my hand to other things besides fiddling, he has accepted me as his daughter's husband, and we are to be married soon. I propose settling at Kingston as professor of music and dancing, teacher of languages, and other polite arts; besides which I can make fiddles, harpsichords, and other instruments; I am also a first-rate cook. Indeed, monsieur lieutenant, I should blush were I to speak more of my accomplishments."

"I congratulate you heartily," said Rayner, "and I sincerely hope that you will be successful in your new condition. You will, I doubt not, be far happier living on shore with a charming young wife, than knocking about at sea with the chance of being shot or drowned."

Le Duc having communicated his good fortune to Jack and his other friends, and invited them to pay him a visit whenever they could get on shore, took his leave.

Chapter Thirty Six.

Fresh successes and perils.

Our hero had now got the first step up the ratlines as an officer. As the *Lily's* repairs were likely to occupy some time, Captain Saltwell had, by the admiral's permission, fitted out one of the prizes, a fine and fast little schooner, to which the name of the *Active* had been given. He intended to man her from his own and the *Ariel's* crews, and to send her cruising in search of the piratical craft which, under the guise of privateers, in vast numbers infested those seas.

The admiral had intended to send a *protégé* of his own in charge of the vessel, but that officer was taken ill, and both Lieutenant Horrocks and the first lieutenant of the *Ariel* were engaged in attending to their respective ships.

Rayner was sent for, and the command was offered to him. He accepted it with delight, and begged that Crofton might be allowed to accompany him. He took also Jack and Brown, and though he did not ask for Tom Fletcher, Tom was sent among the men drafted for the purpose.

The schooner was furnished with four carronades and two long six-pounders. Her crew mustered twenty men.

"We can dare and do anything in such a craft as this," he exclaimed, enthusiastically, as he and Oliver were walking the deck together, while the schooner, under all sail, was steering a course for San Domingo.

Before long they both dared and did several gallant actions. Just as they had sighted the land they fell in with three piratical feluccas, either one of which was a match for the *Active*.

One, after a desperate resistance, was captured, another was sunk, and the third, while the British crew were securing their first prize, and endeavouring to save the drowning men, effected her escape. She was, however, shortly afterwards taken, and on the return of the *Active* to Port Royal with her prizes, the thanks of the merchants of Jamaica were offered to Lieutenant Rayner for the service he had rendered to commerce.

The admiral the next day sent for Rayner, and received him with more cordiality than is generally awarded to junior officers. Having listened to his report, and commended him for his gallantry.

"How soon will you be ready to sail again?" he asked.

"Directly our damages have been repaired, and they won't take long, sir," was the answer.

"That is right. I have received information that a desperate fellow in command of a craft somewhat larger than the *Active* has been pillaging vessels of all nations, and it will be a feather in your cap if you take her."

"I'll do my best, sir," answered Rayner.

In two days the *Active* was again at sea. Within a fortnight, after a long chase, she had fought and driven on shore a large schooner, got her off again, and recaptured two of her prizes, returning in triumph with all three to Jamaica.

He and Oliver were highly complimented on their success. The admiral, who was still in the harbour, invited them to dine on board the flagship.

"Mr Horrocks has just obtained his promotion, and you are thus, Mr

Rayner, first lieutenant of the *Lily*; and, Mr Crofton, I intend to give you an acting order as second lieutenant, and I hope that before long you will be confirmed in your rank."

This was good news. With happy hearts the two friends went on board the *Lily*, which was now ready for sea. They found Lieutenant Horrocks packing up, ready to go on board a frigate just sailing for England.

"I expect to enjoy a few weeks' hunting before I get a ship, and when I do get one I shall be very glad to have you, Rayner, with me, should you be unemployed," he said as they parted.

Rayner would have preferred retaining the command of the *Active*, but an officer older than himself was appointed to her, and he could not complain.

Once more the *Lily* was at sea. She cruised for some months, during which she captured several prizes, and cut out two others in a very gallant manner under the guns of a strong battery. Oliver soon afterwards had the satisfaction of being confirmed in his rank as lieutenant.

Though Commander Saltwell made honourable mention of our hero on each occasion, he received no further recognition of his services. "I have no business to complain," he observed. "My position is only that of many others who have done more than I have, but I should like to be wearing an epaulette on my right shoulder when we get home, and obtain a command with you, Oliver, as my first lieutenant."

With this exception, Rayner never alluded to the subject.

The *Lily's* cruise was nearly up. She had lately sent away in her prizes her master and several petty officers and seamen, so that out of her establishment she could scarcely muster more than a hundred men.

It was night, a light breeze blowing, the island of Desirade bearing south-east by south, distant six or seven leagues. The two lieutenants had been talking of home. In a few months they expected to be at Plymouth, and Rayner's thoughts had been occupied, as they often were, with his brother officer's sweet sister, Mary Crofton.

Rayner had just come on deck to relieve Oliver, who had the middle watch. He had been pacing the deck, waiting for daylight, to commence the morning operation of washing decks, and was looking to windward, when, as the light slowly increased, at some little distance off he made out the dim outline of a large ship. Whether she was a friend or foe he could not determine; if the latter, the position of the *Lily* was critical in the extreme. He instantly sent the midshipman of the watch to arouse the commander, who hurried on deck. After watching the stranger for a few seconds, they both came to the conclusion that she was a frigate, and, as they knew of no English vessel of her class likely to be thereabouts, that she was French.

"Turn the hands up and make sail," said the commander. "We shall probably have to fight, but when the odds are so decidedly against us, it is my duty to avoid an action if I can."

The crew at the boatswain's summons came tumbling up from below. All sail was immediately made, and the *Lily's* head directed to the north-west. She was seen, however, and quickly followed by the frigate, the freshening breeze giving an advantage to the larger vessel, which, having the weather-gauge, and sailing remarkably fast rapidly approached.

"We've caught a Tartar at last!" exclaimed Tom. "The sooner we go below and put on our best clothes he better; we shall be taken aboard her before the day's much older."

"How do you dare to say that!" cried Jack. "Look up there, you see our flag flying aloft, and I for one would sooner have our tight little craft sent to the bottom than be ordered to strike it. Our skipper hasn't given in yet, and if he falls our first lieutenant will fight the ship as long as he has a plank to stand on."

Some of the crew, however, appeared to side with Tom, and showed an inclination to desert their guns.

Rayner and Oliver went among them and cheered them up.

"Lads!" cried the commander, who had observed some of them wavering as they gazed with looks of alarm at their powerful enemy, "most of you have sailed in the *Lily* with me since she was first commissioned. You know that I have never exposed your lives unnecessarily, and that we have always succeeded in whatever we have undertaken. You have gained a name for yourselves and our ship, and I hope you will not sully that name by showing the white feather. Although yonder ship is twice as big as we are, still we must try to beat her off, and it will not be my fault if we don't."

The men cheered heartily, and went to their guns. Every preparation for battle being made—to the surprise of her own crew, and much more so to that of the Frenchman—the commandant ordered her to be hove-to.

"Don't fire a shot until I tell you, lads!" he cried out.

Many looked at the stranger with anxious eyes; the flag of France was flying from her peak. Eighteen guns grinned out from her ports on either side—twice the number of those carried by the *Lily*, and of a far heavier calibre. As she got within range she opened fire, her shot flying through the *Lily's* sails, cutting her rigging and injuring several of her spars, but her guns were so elevated that not a man was hit on deck.

"Steady, lads! We must wait until she gets near enough to make every one of our guns tell!" cried the commander.

Even when going into action a British seaman often indulges in jokes, but on this occasion every man maintained a grim silence.

"Now, lads!" shouted the commander, "give it them!"

At the short distance the enemy now was from them the broadside told with terrible effect, the shot crashing through her ports and sides, while the shrieks and groans of the wounded were clearly distinguished from the *Lily's* deck.

The British crew, working with redoubled energy, hauled their guns in and out, and fired with wonderful rapidity, truly tossing them about as if they had been playthings. The French also fired, but far more slowly, sending hardly one shot to the *Lily's* two. The officers went about the deck encouraging the men and laying hold of the tackles to assist them in their labours. At any moment a well-directed broadside from the frigate might leave the corvette a mere wreck on the ocean, or send her to the bottom. Every man on board knew this; but while their officers kept their flag flying at the peak, they were ready to work their guns and struggle to the last.

An hour and a half had passed since the French frigate had opened her fire, and still the little sloop held out. Commander Saltwell's great object was to avoid being run down or boarded. This he managed to do by skilful manoeuvring. At length Rayner, through his glass, observed the crew of the frigate running about her deck as if in considerable confusion. Once more the *Lily* fired, but what was the astonishment of the British seamen to see her haul her main-tack aboard and begin to make all sail, putting her head to the northward. To follow was impossible, as the *Lily* had every brace and bowline, all her after backstays, several of her lower shrouds, and other parts of her rigging, shot away.

Her sails were also torn, her mainmast and main-topsail yard and foreyard a good deal injured. Yet though she had received these serious damages aloft, strange to say one man alone of her crew had been slightly injured.

"We must repair damages, lads, and then go and look after the enemy," cried the commander.

The guns being run in and secured, every officer, man, and boy set to work, the commander with the rest. In a wonderfully short time the standing rigging was knotted or spliced, fresh running rigging rove, new sails bent, and the *Lily* was standing in the direction in which her late antagonist had some time before disappeared.

Not long after, however, the man at the mast-head discovered a large ship on the lee beam in the direction of Guadaloupe. The *Lily* at once steered towards the stranger, when in the afternoon she came up with a vessel under French colours, which endeavoured to escape. Several shots were fired. The stranger sailed on.

"She looks like an English ship," observed the commander. "It will never do to let her get away. See what you can do, Crofton."

Oliver went forward and trained the foremost gun. He fired, and down came the stranger's main-topsail yard. On this she hauled down her colours and hove-to.

She proved to be, as the commander had supposed, a large English merchantman, a prize to the French frigate. The prisoners were at once removed, and the second lieutenant sent with a prize crew on board, when the *Lily* took her in tow. The wind was light, but a heavy swell sent the prize several times almost aboard the corvette, which was at length compelled to cast her adrift.

The next morning the look-out from the mast-head of the *Lily* announced a sail on the lee bow. In a short time, daylight increasing, she was seen to be a frigate, and no doubt her late antagonist. Captain Saltwell at once bore down on her, making a signal to the prize to do so likewise, and at the same time running up several signals as if speaking another ship to windward.

On this the frigate, making all sail, stood away, and as she had the heels both of the *Lily* and her prize, was soon out of sight.

Captain Saltwell, satisfied, as he had every reason to be, with his achievement, ordered the course to be shared for Jamaica.

On his arrival he found his commission as post-captain waiting for him. He had won it by constant and hard service.

"As I cannot reward you for the gallant way in which you beat off the French frigate and recaptured the merchant ship worth several thousand pounds, I must see what can be done for your first lieutenant," said the admiral. "I will apply for his promotion, and in the meantime will give him an acting order to command the *Lily*, and to take her home."

Captain Saltwell, thanking the admiral, expressed his intention to take a passage in his old ship.

The news quickly spread fore and aft that the *Lily* was to be sent home. Loud cheers rose from many a stout throat, the invalids, of which there were not a few, joining in the chorus from below. One-third of those who had come out had either fallen fighting in the many actions in which she had been engaged, or, struck down by yellow fever, lay in the graveyard of Port Royal. No time was lost in getting fresh water and provisions on board.

Never did crew work with more good-will than they did on this occasion.

The *Lily* was soon ready for sea, and with a fair breeze ran out of Port Royal harbour. The war was still raging as furiously as ever, and the officers and crew well knew that before they could reach the shores of old England they might have another battle or two to fight. Perhaps, in their heart of hearts, they would have preferred, for once in a way, a peaceful voyage. A look-out, however, was kept, but the Atlantic was crossed, and the chops of the Channel reached, without meeting a foe. Here the *Lily* encountered a strong easterly gale, and in vain for many days endeavoured to beat up to her destination.

Having sighted Scilly, she was standing off the land, from which she was at a considerable distance under close-reefed topsails, when the wind suddenly dropped, and soon afterwards shifted to the southwards. The helm was put down, and the crew flew aloft to shake out the reefs.

They were thus engaged when a sail was seen to the south-east. The *Lily*, standing on the opposite tack, rapidly neared her. Every glass on board was directed towards the stranger. She was a ship apparently of much the same size as the *Lily*, but whether an English cruiser or an enemy it was difficult to determine.

The *Lily*, by keeping away, might have weathered the Lizard and avoided her. Such an idea did not enter the young commander's head. On the contrary, he kept the ship close to the wind, so that by again going about he might prevent the stranger from passing him.

His glass had never been off her. Suddenly he exclaimed, "Hurrah! she's French. I caught sight of her flag as she luffed up! Hands about ship! We'll fight her, Captain Saltwell?" he added, turning to his former commander.

"No doubt about it," said Captain Saltwell, "I should if I were in your place."

The drum beat to quarters, the crew hurried to their stations, and every preparation was made for the expected battle. The stranger, after standing on some way, hauled up, so as to keep the weather-gauge, and, at the same time; to draw the *Lily* farther away from the English coast.

Once more the latter tacked, and passing under the stranger's stern, poured in a raking broadside.

The stranger, coming about, returned the fire; but as the shot flew from her guns down came her mizenmast, and she fell off before the wind.

The crew of the *Lily* cheered, and running in their guns, quickly fired a third broadside.

The two ships now ran on side by side, Rayner having shortened sail so as to avoid shooting ahead of his antagonist. Notwithstanding the loss of their mizenmast, the Frenchmen fought with spirit for some time, but their fire at length began to slacken, while the British seamen continued to work their guns with the same energy as at first.

Rayner now ordered the mizen-topsail and spanker to be set, and directed the crews of the starboard guns to refrain from firing until he should give the word; then putting down the helm, he suddenly luffed up, and stood across the bows of his opponent.

"Fire!" he cried; and gun after gun was fired in succession, the shot telling with fearful effect as they swept the deck of the French ship. The latter put down her helm in a vain attempt to avoid being raked, but her bowsprit catching in the mizen rigging of the *Lily*, Oliver, calling to Jack and several other men, securely lashed it there, in spite of the fire which the marines from the enemy's forecastle opened on him and his companions.

The bullets from the Frenchmen's muskets came rattling sharply on board. Two of the seamen were hit, and just at the same moment their young commander was seen to fall. A midshipman and the purser, who were standing by his side, caught him in their arms.

Chapter Thirty Seven.

Conclusion.

"Keep at it, my lads, until she strikes!" cried the young commander, as he fell.

Captain Saltwell had meantime, seeing what would occur, ordered two guns to be run out at the after ports. Scarcely had they been fired when an officer, springing into the forecastle of the French ship, waved his hat and shouted that they had struck.

Oliver and Jack, on looking round for Rayner, and seeing him bleeding on the deck, forgetful of everything else, sprang aft to his side. At that moment the crew raised a cheer of victory; Rayner feebly attempted to join in it. He was carried below. With anxious hearts his officers and crew waited to hear the report of the surgeon.

It was Oliver's duty to go on board and take possession of the prize. Unwillingly he left his friend's side. Of the *Lily's* crew five had been killed, and many more beside her commander, wounded. But Oliver saw, as he stepped on board the prize, how much more severely she had suffered. Everywhere lay dead and dying men. How dread and terrible a fact is war! A lieutenant, coming forward, presented his sword.

"My captain lies there," he said, pointing to a form covered by a flag. "The second lieutenant is wounded below; three other officers are among the dead. We did not yield while we had a chance of victory."

"Yours is a brave nation, and I must compliment you on the gallant way in which you fought your ship," answered Oliver, in the best French he could command.

To lose no time, the prisoners were removed, the prize taken in tow, and all sail made for Plymouth.

At length the surgeon come on deck.

"The commander will do well, I trust," he said; "but I shall be glad to get him on shore as soon as possible. As soon as I had extracted the bullet, he sent me off to look after the other wounded men, saying that they wanted my care as well as he did."

The crew on this gave a suppressed cheer. It would have been louder and more prolonged, but they were afraid of disturbing the commander and the other wounded men.

All were proud of their achievement as they sailed up Plymouth Sound with their prize in tow, but no one felt prouder than Jack Peek.

"I knew Captain would do something as soon as he had the chance," he had remarked to Brown, who greatly shared his feelings.

Rayner was at once removed to the hospital. As he was unable to hold a pen, Captain Saltwell wrote the despatches, taking care to give due credit to the active commander of the corvette.

A short time afterwards Oliver carried to the hospital—to which he had never failed to pay a daily visit—an official-looking letter.

"Ah! that will do him more good than my doctoring," said the surgeon, to whom he showed it.

Oliver opened it at Rayner's request. It was from the Lords of the Admiralty, confirming him in his rank, and appointing him to command the *Urania* (the English name given to the prize), which, being a fine new corvette, a hundred tons larger than the *Lily*, had been bought into the service.

"It will take some time to refit her, and you will, I hope, be about again before she is ready for sea," said Oliver. "I have brought a message from my mother, who begs, as soon as you are ready to be removed, that you will come and stay at our house. She is a good nurse, and you will enjoy more country air than you can here."

Rayner very gladly accepted the invitation. Neither Oliver nor Mrs Crofton had thought about the result, but before many weeks were over Commander William Rayner was engaged to marry Mary Crofton, who had given him as loving and gentle a heart as ever beat in woman's bosom. He told her how often he had talked about her when away at sea, and how often he had thought of her, although he had scarcely dared to hope that she would marry one who had been a London street boy and powder monkey.

"I love you, my dear Bill, for what you are, for being noble, true, and brave, and such you were when you were a powder monkey, as you call it, although you might not have discovered those qualities in yourself."

He was now well able to marry, for his agents had in their hands several thousand pounds of prize-money, and he might reasonably hope to obtain much more before the war was over.

Our hero was well enough to assume the command of the *Urania* by the time she was ready for sea. Oliver, as his first lieutenant, had been busily engaged in obtaining hands, and had secured many of the *Lily's* former crew. The commander had some time before sent for Jack Peek, and urged him to prepare himself for obtaining a boatswain's warrant.

"Thank you, sir," said Jack; "but, you see, to get it I must read and write, and that's what I never could tackle. I have tried pothooks and hangers, but my fingers get all cramped up, and the pen splits open, and I have to let it drop, and make a great big splash of ink on the paper; and as for reading, I've tried that too. I know all the letters when I see them, but I can't manage to put them together in the right fashion, and never could get beyond a, b, ab, b, o, bo. I might in time, if I was to stick to it, I know, and I'll try when we are at sea if I can get a messmate to teach me. But while you're afloat I'd rather be your coxswain, if you'll give me that rating; then I can always be with you, and, mayhap, render you some service, which is just the thing I should be proud of doing. Now, sir, there's Tom Fletcher; he's got plenty of learning, and he ought to be a good seaman by this time. If you were to recommend him to be either a gunner or a boatswain, he'd pass fast enough."

Rayner shook his head. "I should be happy to serve Tom Fletcher for old acquaintance' sake, but I fear that although he may have the learning, as you say, he has not got the moral qualities necessary to make a good warrant officer. However, send him to me, and I'll have a talk with him on the subject."

Jack promised to look after Tom, whom he had not seen since the *Lily* was paid off. He returned in a few days, saying that he had long searched for him in vain, until at length he had found him in a low house in the lowest of the Plymouth slums, his prize-money, to the amount of nearly a hundred pounds, all gone, and he himself so drunk that he could not understand the message Jack brought him.

"I am truly sorry to hear it," said Rayner. "But you must watch him and try to get him on board. If he is cast adrift he must inevitably be lost, but we will try what we can do to reform him."

"I will gladly do my best, sir," answered Jack. When the *Urania* was nearly ready for sea, Jack did contrive to get Tom aboard of her, but the commander's good intentions were frustrated, for before the ship sailed he deserted with could not again be discovered.

Of this Rayner was thankful, as he must of necessity have done what would have gone greatly against his feelings—ordered Tom a flogging.

Honest Brown, however, who had gone to school as soon as the *Lily* was paid off; received what he well deserved, his warrant as boatswain of the corvette he had helped to win. He had shortly to go to sea in a dashing frigate, and from that he was transferred to a seventy-four, in which he was engaged in several of England's greatest battles.

Some years passed, when after paying off the *Urania*, as Rayner was passing along a street in Exeter, he heard a stentorian voice singing a verse of a sea ditty. The singer, dressed as a seaman, carried on his head the model of a full-rigged ship, which he rocked to and fro, keeping time to the tune. He had two wooden legs in the shape of mopsticks, and was supporting himself with a crutch, while with the hand at liberty he held out a battered hat to receive the contributions of his audience. Occasionally, when numbers gathered round to listen to him, he exchanged his song for a yarn. As Rayner approached he was saying, "This is the way our government treats our brave seamen. Here was I fighting nobly for my king and country, when a Frenchman's shot spoilt both my legs, and I was left to stump off as best I could on these here timber toes without a shiner in my pocket, robbed of all my hard-earned prize-money. But you good people will, I know, be kind to poor Jack, and fill this here hat of his with coppers to give him a crust of bread and a sup to comfort his old heart.

> "'Come all ye jolly sailors bold,
> Whose hearts are cast in honour's mould,
> While England's glory I unfold,
> Huzza to the *Arethusa*!'"

Suddenly he recognised Captain Rayner, who, from being dressed in plain clothes, he had not at first observed. He started, and then began, with an impudent leer, "Now, mates, I'll spin you another yarn about an English captain who now holds his head mighty high, and would not condescend to speak to poor Jack if he was to meet him. We was powder-monkeys together, that captain and I. But luck is everything. He went up, and I went down. That's the way at sea. If all men had their deserts I should be where he is, in command of a fine frigate, in a fair way of becoming an admiral. But it's no use complaining, and so I'll sing on—

> "'The famed *Belle Poule* straight ahead did lie,
> The *Arethusa* seemed to fly,
> Not a brace, or a tack, or a sheet did we slack
> On board of the *Arethusa*.'"

"No, no, mate, you was not aboard the *Arethusa*!" cried Jack Peek, who had followed his captain at a short distance, and looking Tom in the face. "You was not aboard the *Arethusa*. I'll tell you what kept you down. It was conceit, idleness, drink, and cowardice; and I'll tell you what gave our brave captain his first lift in the service. It was his truthfulness, his good sense, his obedience to the orders of his superiors. It was his soberness, his bravery; and if you, with your learning and advantages, had been like him, you too might have been in command of a dashing frigate, and not stumping about on one wooden leg, with the other tied up to deceive the people. It's hard things I'm saying, I know, but I cannot stand by and hear a fellow who ought to know better running monstrous falsehoods off his reel as you have been doing. You might have borne up for Greenwich, and been looked after by a grateful country; or you might have saved money enough to have kept yourself in comfort to the end of your days; but it all went in drink and debauchery, and now you abuse the government for not looking after you. Howsumdever, Tom Fletcher, I'm very sorry for you, and if you'll knock off this sort of vagabond life, which brings disgrace on the name of a British sailor, I'll answer for it our good captain will exert his influence and get you a berth in Greenwich or elsewhere, for he has often spoken about you, and wondered where you were a-serving."

Jack Peek had probably never made so long a speech in his life. It was perhaps too long, for it enabled the old sailor to recover his presence of mind, and looking at Jack with a brazen countenance, he declared that he had never seen him before, when off he went as fast as he could walk on his wooden stumps, and turning down a by-lane was lost to view.

Jack had to hurry on to overtake his captain. It was the last time he saw Tom Fletcher alive; but he afterwards heard that a man answering his description, who had been sent to prison as a rogue and a vagabond, had subsequently been killed in a drunken quarrel with another seaman of the same character.

Jack had followed his old friend and captain from ship to ship, and at length having overcome the difficulty not only of the alphabet, but of pothooks and hangers, he obtained his warrant, and for several years had charge of one of the ships in which he had fought and bled, now laid up in Portsmouth harbour.

In the course of years there was found in the list of English Admirals the names of Sir William Rayner, KCB, John Saltwell, and Oliver Crofton.

The End.